THE FACE OF THE ENEMY

I brought up the scanner and looked under the skin and muscle where the components were clustered, a network of nodes and hair-thin filaments where the spinal cord met the brain. An amber squiggle of light jumped across the scanner's display before snapping into a single waveform—the revivor's heart signature. I processed the signal and pulled the identification. The lot number wasn't on file, so it wasn't sold legitimately. Someone had this one made to order.

In the mirror, I could see its eyes staring downward. Its well-preserved porcelain skin made it look like a doll or wax figure. Whoever she had been, she didn't look like a local. A tourist maybe? Someone who wandered down the wrong street?

"Someone's probably still looking for you," I said. I said it to myself, but it answered.

"He is."

I had intended to use a small, directed electromagnetic pulse to short out the components and put it down before leaving the room, but I didn't. The girl kept looking up at me, still without expression. I hated revivors; I hated everything about them. I hated them for what they were and for what they had done to me, what they had taken away. When the time came to put it down, I had thought I would enjoy it.

"Stay here," I said instead. "Don't move, and don't say anything. Do you understand?"

It nodded.

STATE OF
DECAY

JAMES KNAPP

A ROC BOOK

ROC

Published by New American Library, a division of
Penguin Group (USA) Inc., 375 Hudson Street,
New York, New York 10014, USA
Penguin Group (Canada), 90 Eglinton Avenue East, Suite 700, Toronto,
Ontario M4P 2Y3, Canada (a division of Pearson Penguin Canada Inc.)
Penguin Books Ltd., 80 Strand, London WC2R 0RL, England
Penguin Ireland, 25 St. Stephen's Green, Dublin 2,
Ireland (a division of Penguin Books Ltd.)
Penguin Group (Australia), 250 Camberwell Road, Camberwell, Victoria 3124,
Australia (a division of Pearson Australia Group Pty. Ltd.)
Penguin Books India Pvt. Ltd., 11 Community Centre, Panchsheel Park,
New Delhi - 110 017, India
Penguin Group (NZ), 67 Apollo Drive, Rosedale, North Shore 0632,
New Zealand (a division of Pearson New Zealand Ltd.)
Penguin Books (South Africa) (Pty.) Ltd., 24 Sturdee Avenue,
Rosebank, Johannesburg 2196, South Africa

Penguin Books Ltd., Registered Offices:
80 Strand, London WC2R 0RL, England

First published by Roc, an imprint of New American Library,
a division of Penguin Group (USA) Inc.

First Printing, February 2010
10 9 8 7 6 5 4 3 2 1

PUBLISHER'S NOTE
This is a work of fiction. Names, characters, places, and incidents either are the
product of the author's imagination or are used fictitiously, and any resemblance
to actual persons, living or dead, business establishments, events, or locales is
entirely coincidental.
  The publisher does not have any control over and does not assume any responsibility for author or third-party Web sites or their content.

For Kim

ACKNOWLEDGMENTS

I would like to acknowledge:

Richard Tappan for fostering a love of writing.
Greg and Christine for showing me what was possible.
Mom and Dad for believing in me.
Jack and Jessica for rolling the dice on me.
Kim for being there, always.

1

Decay

Nico Wachalowski—Goicoechea Plaza

Everyone thinks they know what a revivor is, but the truth is the only ones who really know are the revivors themselves. The first time I ever saw one was during my initial tour in the grinder, where even at night it was like a furnace, and when a hot breeze blew through the brush, I could smell them. When that first one moved into the moonlight where I could see it, I was scared. I had never been as scared about anything else before. People argue about what goes on in their heads, but I couldn't tell what it was thinking, or whether it was thinking at all. All I can really say is that no one who has seen a revivor face-to-face would ever choose to become one. That was why I was in the elevator of that building the night that it all started.

Heading up to the eighty-second floor, I watched the numbers flip and tried to calm my heart. Assistant Director Noakes had put me on the case because of my prior experience with revivors, but I would have volunteered. Those things belong in the ground, but short of that, they belong on the other side of the world, not on mine.

The car ground to a stop and the doors opened into a barely lit corridor. I stepped out into the shadows and moved toward the door at the far end. Everything I saw was recorded and then transmitted to the men below through the implant wired near the base of my skull. They monitored the visual feed and even my vital signs as they waited for my signal. I opened the secure communications circuit and sent them confirmation.

I'm inside.

Roger that.

The words floated in front of me, then faded as I moved down the hall. Like a lot of properties in the area, most of the offices were empty; there were a few businesses scraping by, but past the sixtieth floor the place was vacant, except for one. The office I was visiting supposedly bought and sold small-scale third-party processing components, which was a nice touch. I had no doubt that front even made a little extra money on the side.

I made my way past the locked rooms and dark offices until I came to the one I was looking for. The door was closed and unmarked, with a black buzzer next to it. I pushed the button and waited.

They'd be watching me; I couldn't see it, but somewhere a camera was checking me out to make sure I was someone they were expecting. A few seconds later there was a heavy snap from inside the door. I opened it and went inside.

It was the first time I'd actually seen the place, and it was pretty much what I expected. The lobby was stripped bare, with nothing on the walls and no place to sit. What would have been the reception area was set up with a terminal and was being used as a workspace with wires trailing across the dusty floor. Tai and two of his men were waiting there for me.

"Right on time," Tai said. "I'm glad you decided to show."

Tai was a dark-skinned Asian with long hair and a long face. The two guys with him were tattooed, tough-looking types I didn't recognize.

"Check him out."

I raised my hands to shoulder height as the two men approached me. One of them swept an electronic wand up and down the front and back of me while the other took a more hands-on approach and patted me down. The one with the wand nodded at Tai, and he dismissed them.

"You ready?" Tai asked.

"Yeah."

"They're back there," he said, gesturing to a door behind him. "You were looking for ten?"

"Ten if I can use them," I said. "More if they work out."

Tai nodded.

"You can see them for yourself and decide," he said. "I've got one set up if you want to sample it. Last door on the left."

"Thanks."

"No rough stuff."

"How long do I have?" I asked.

"I'll give you five minutes to do whatever you're going to do," he said. "After that I'll show you the others, and we can talk about price."

"Assuming they're acceptable."

"They will be."

I headed through the door and it closed behind me. The hallway beyond was quiet except for the hum of

multiple terminals and a heating unit, with stacks of cardboard and some wooden pallets leaning against the
walls. Just above the white noise, I could make out the
sound of movement.

I blinked, activating the heads-up display that shone
back onto my retinas. The connection with the men waiting
downstairs was open, and everything was being recorded.
Using a backscatter filter, I could see tiny hidden cameras standing out in sharp relief just behind the drywall,
watching me as I made my way down. Cooling thermal
signatures across the floor indicated people had been
back there recently. I followed them to the last door on
the left.

I could feel my heart pounding as I pushed open the
door and the smell of urine drifted out. The door opened
into a restroom, where the stall doors hung open and
most of the toilets were covered with plastic wrap. The
floor had traces of half-wiped-away blood, and there was
some spattered across the wall where the sinks were.
Someone had met with bad news there, but my attention
was drawn to the middle of the room. There, standing
barefoot on the filthy tiles with its knees together and its
hands clutched by its sides, was the revivor.

The old fear took me a little by surprise. Despite the
fact that it was a female and practically a girl, I had to
force myself to move closer to it.

It stood maybe five foot six, a head or so shorter than
me, with thin arms and legs and long, straight black hair
that partly covered its face. From behind the strands two
large eyes looked out at me, the irises a pale silver color,
just barely illuminated with a glow that reminded me of
moonlight. They followed me as I approached.

It was an improvement over the ones I'd encountered during my tour. The skin was well preserved,

and its porcelain tone made the revivor look like a doll or wax figure. The synthetic blood they were using now made some of the veins stand out darkly, but some clientele actually liked that. The cosmetic surgeries had been well-done, too, with almost no scarring. The large, augmented breasts looked out of place on such a thin body, but otherwise might almost have been the originals. The small nipples pointed forward like bullets.

"Stand over there," I told it, pointing to one of the sinks that were covered in plastic.

It did, so it understood English. Its expression didn't change as its bare feet padded across the dirty floor and it stood in front of the sink, its back to the mirror.

"Turn around."

It did, gripping the sides of the sink through the plastic wrapping and bending over slightly in a movement that looked practiced. I focused on the back of its neck, just beneath the skull.

"Hold still."

I brought up the scanner and looked under the skin and muscle where the components were clustered, a network of nodes and hair-thin filaments around the spot where the spinal cord met the brain. An amber squiggle of light jumped across a circular screen, hovering to one side of the display before snapping into a single waveform—the revivor's heart signature. I processed the signal and pulled the identification. The lot number wasn't on file, so it wasn't sold legitimately. Someone had had this one made to order.

In the mirror, I could see its eyes staring downward as it waited to be violated. My investigations had suggested that Tai had the pleasure models smuggled from Korea, but whoever the woman had been, she didn't look like a Korean local. A tourist, maybe? Someone who wandered down the wrong street?

I focused on the revivor's face in the mirror as it stared through its dark hair, so that the men below could see it.

You getting this? I asked.

Confirmed.

I had three of Tai's five minutes left, assuming he stuck to his word.

"You can turn around now," I told it.

It turned, standing with its back toward the sink and staring up at me blankly.

"Someone's probably still looking for you," I said. I said it to myself, but it answered.

"He is."

I had intended to use a small, directed electromagnetic pulse to short out the components and put it down before leaving the room, but I didn't. It continued to stare into my eyes, expressionless.

Wachalowski, deactivate it.

I was well aware that everyone involved was watching this unfold in real time. Later, I would be questioned about why I did what I did. I had been picked for the operation on the assumption that I knew what a revivor was and wouldn't be prone to hesitation. If anything went wrong, I would be held accountable.

"What did you say?" I asked. Its eyes didn't betray any sadness, or any feeling at all as it answered.

"He'll never stop looking."

An uneasy feeling sank into my gut.

Wachalowski, deactivate it.

I hated revivors. I hated everything about them. They were the worst symptom of a sick arms race that had gotten out of control a long time ago. I'd shipped off for

my tour thinking I understood what they were. The day
I learned I was wrong came close to being my last day
on earth.

The girl looked up at me. When the time came to put
it down, I thought I would enjoy it

Instead I said, "Stay here. Don't move, and don't say
anything. Do you understand?"

It nodded.

"If things go bad, hide behind whatever you can, and
keep your head down."

I left the bathroom and moved down the corridor. A
door to the left was locked, but the next one on the right
opened, and I looked in to see a group of figures sitting
at desks arranged in rows. Each desk had a small light
that lit its surface in the otherwise dark room. Many
pairs of silvery eyes floated in the darkness, turning
toward me as the door opened. It looked like they were
assembling some kind of electronics.

Can you make them out? I asked.

Yes.

One of them spoke in an Asian dialect, turning its attention from the desk. The translator scrolled its words
across the bottom of my peripheral vision.

Who are you? What are you doing in here?

Something else had caught my attention, though. In
the back, behind the sweatshop laborers, a series of crates
were stacked. An automatic rifle was leaning against one
of them, and I switched filters to scan inside the crates to
see what else was in there.

Stop there. The words flashed at the bottom of my vision. I did.

Tai trafficked in black-market revivors; that I knew.
Some minor gunrunning or drug dealing wouldn't have
surprised me either, since he already had the smuggling

routes in place, but he dealt in revivors for the labor and sex trade. My investigation of him didn't prepare me to see anything like what I saw.

The crates contained mostly guns, but not the street variety. These were weapons designed to penetrate not just body armor, but tank armor. The varieties of assault rifle I could see included sophisticated targeting systems, multispectrum scopes, and heat-seeking ammo; it was all top-shelf stuff. These were weapons of war.

What are you doing in here? The revivor asked again.

I backed out and closed the door.

Move now, I told SWAT.

On our way.

"Hey," I heard Tai say in a low voice from down the hall. I turned and saw he had entered from the lobby. He wasn't smiling.

"Sorry," I said.

"I said the last door on your left," he said. "That's your right, and it's not the last door."

"I know. I just—"

"Never mind," he said. "Those aren't the ones you want. The ones you want are down here." He gestured down the hallway as he joined me, placing his left hand on my shoulder.

His fist hit my ribs like a stone, and the breath went out of me. I staggered and hit the wall, gasping. The door to the sweatshop opened a little and a female revivor's head peeked out.

"Get back in there," Tai said without looking at it. The head retreated and the door closed.

"Hold still," he said, fishing around in his inside jacket pocket.

"Tai, take it easy. . . ."

At the last minute, I saw the knife in his other hand. He shoved me back, smashing me into the wall with a forearm across my neck. I felt a hard blow to my groin as the knife's blade dug into the wall between my legs.

"Hold still," he said. He took his forearm off my neck and I saw it was a penlight he had taken out of his coat. He flicked it on and shined it in my left eye. I turned my head, but the hand with the knife exerted a little pressure.

"Look forward, and don't move."

If he got a clear look with the light, he'd see the iridescent reflection that would confirm I was implanted. The blade was an inch from my testicles, and the artery in either thigh.

"Tai, you're making a mistake," I said. "I just got turned around for—"

"Don't take this personally."

I blinked once, hard, shutting down the implant; it was the only thing that was going to buy me any more time. With the visual filters off-line, he wouldn't notice anything strange. I opened my eyes wide, and looked straight ahead before Tai could say anything else. He shined the light in my eye and leaned in close. He stared into it for a while, his breath on my face. After a few seconds, he snapped off the light.

I didn't say anything; I just kept holding my breath. The knife came out of the wall and moved out from between my legs.

He lunged, but I knew it was coming. I tried to move, but he kicked out my right leg and pushed me down against the wall. I fell into an awkward squat but managed to deflect his thrust, and the knife slammed into the wall just to the left of my throat.

I grabbed his leg and rammed my forearm into his

pelvis, knocking him back. He lost his balance and crashed back into the door behind him, the two of us spilling into the room where the revivors were working. It looked like he had lost the knife, but his hand was in his jacket. I grabbed his wrist and we struggled. I saw the gun coming out, and some of the revivors tried to pull me off of him.

I squeezed my eyes shut and reactivated the implant.

Jovanovic-Zaytsev Industries Cybernetic Implant model L65730001-M initializing . . .

The JZI came back online. Tai struggled to get the gun free as diagnostic information scrolled in front of me and the communications link began to reconnect. The translator module finished initializing, and as the revivors continued to chatter, words began streaming by.

Stop! What are you doing? Help!

I kept my weight on Tai, but he was stronger than he looked. I brought my fist back, my elbow crunching into the nose of one of the revivors who was trying to pull me away, then hit Tai with everything I had. His eyes swam, but he didn't go out. The revivor I'd creamed fell onto the floor next to us, clutching its face.

Before I could hit him again, a big hand grabbed my arm from behind, hauling me back like a rag doll. As I was pulled off of Tai, I kept a grip on his gun, and as my feet left the ground, I stomped my heel on his forehead.

That put him down. His hand went slack, and I grabbed the gun as a beefy arm came around the front of my neck and squeezed. The muscle felt like cold stone against my throat, and breath smelling of rot huffed down the back of my neck.

The fear was worse than I had remembered. My legs went weak and everything seemed to slow down. I put

the barrel of the gun against the thigh of the thing behind me and pulled the trigger. The blood that splashed
back was cold.

Tai's eyes fluttered open and he sat up, looking disoriented. He got to his feet and smoothed his clothes.

"Kill him," he said.

He took off, but I didn't see where he went. The
arm came off my neck and I pulled in a breath as I was
spun around, spots swimming in front of me. Something
crashed across my head, and my legs went out from under me. As I dangled by one wrist, the hand that gripped
it tried to shake the gun out of my hand. I looked up and
saw a big male revivor with cropped black hair standing
over me, its eyes ghostly white. Its mouth gaped open
and long strands of drool hung from its lower lip, all of
its crowded teeth on display.

This was the kind of revivor I knew. Low-end, made
for combat, with only one or two imperatives buzzing
around in its decaying brain. It might have come from
the same steamy hellhole where I saw my first one.

I hit it, but if the thing felt any pain at all it didn't
show it. It forced my gun hand around and I squeezed
off another shot, which grazed its ear. It pushed the gun
back, twisting it around toward me.

As the barrel began to move toward my face, I felt
the thing's thumb rooting around for the trigger. From
over the revivor's shoulder I saw the bathroom door
open, and the female revivor stepped out, staring at me
through its stringy hair. It held its hands up in front of it,
like a child who wasn't sure what to do.

There was a loud bang, and the female retreated back
into the bathroom. Shadows played on the wall as two
uniformed SWAT men barreled around the corner.

"Here!" the one taking point shouted. Without hesitation, he aimed and fired, causing the revivor's head to pitch to one side, spraying oily black fluid. The grip on my wrist released as it staggered away from me.

The SWAT officer fired again, and it dropped to one knee, then fell onto its back. The two men approached me as I rubbed my wrist. I moved over to where the revivor lay, trying to get back up as fluid pooled around its head. I aimed the gun and fired, putting a bullet between its eyes. I fired three more rounds and the top of its head broke open, spilling black guts out onto the floor.

"Whoa, whoa!" the officer said, holding up one hand. "You got him, chief."

"That is not a pleasure or a labor model," I said, pointing at it with the barrel of the gun.

Something was going on here. Tai was into something that went way beyond what I'd gone there to bust him for; something he'd managed to keep secret.

I turned and saw Tai being dragged into view down at the end of the hall. Two more officers forced him against the wall, and when he tried to turn around, one of them kicked out his leg and forced him onto his knees.

"Hands behind your head."

"Starting a war?" I asked him.

He grinned. "Keep your doors locked," he said in a low voice, glaring at me. He didn't look angry, just serious.

"Shut up," the SWAT guy said. I turned and started down the hallway.

"You hear me?" Tai called.

"Yeah."

I passed the wall where Tai had pinned me, and saw his knife lying a few feet away. I approached the squad leader.

"There are ten revivors out back," I said to him, "plus one in the bathroom."

"Looks like our guys picked up another ten," he said, "plus the rest of Tai's men. You all right?"

"Yeah. Process Tai and the others, then load them and the revivors into the truck."

"Roger."

"Were your techs able to get a connection into his computer system?"

"You should have access now."

I scanned and found the socket, then opened a connection to it and brought up the system in my field of view. I turned the antisecurity software on it and waited for it to drill down and disable his firewall. Tai's stuff was encrypted, but nothing fancy. I cycled through his files, which mostly consisted of inventory—the specs and identifications of revivors he had brought into the country, which ones had been moved already, and which ones were still on order. No pickup location was spelled out, but there was a series of docket numbers, and it didn't take long to match them to receiving ports at the Palm Harbor Shipyard. It looked as if they were being smuggled in among legitimate cargo from a bunch of different sources. I couldn't tell from where, but it was a good start.

I headed back to the reception area, where the SWAT team had gathered the revivors. They had been grouped in rows and were now kneeling, with their hands behind their heads. Most of them were female and had cookie-cutter versions of the same body modifications. They were all dressed in cheap paper hospital smocks.

As I headed out the door, I turned back and saw one of the men bring in the one from the bathroom, nudging it forward with the barrel of his rifle. It looked at me like it recognized me. The man forced it down onto the floor with the others, and I turned and headed back to the elevator, putting in a call to the assistant director.

Noakes.

This is Noakes.

Agent Wachalowski reporting. Four suspects appre-hended. Twenty-one revivors recovered. It looks like they've been bringing them in via Palm Harbor.

Where are the revivors now?

SWAT is loading them into the truck. We uncovered some pretty serious firepower here as well. Weapons, am-munition, and other military equipment. SWAT is cata-loging it; you'll have the list shortly.

What are we looking at?

Whoever wanted it knows his stuff. There's enough to arm a small militia.

Noakes didn't respond right away.

Get the seller down here. We need that information.

They're moving him and the revivors now. From Tai's records, it looks like something was just brought in to the shipyard. I'm on my way there. If we're lucky, no one has picked it up yet.

A team will meet you there. Find out where that stuff was going.

I will.

The doors opened, and I crossed into the lobby. Across the foyer, I could see someone standing in the shadows near the exit. He wasn't in uniform. I pinged the squad leader upstairs.

You guys have anyone in the lobby?

Negative. Two outside; the rest are up here.

The figure moved toward me, and when he stepped into the light I could see he was young, maybe college age. He had tangled brown hair and uneven stubble. He wore sneakers, running pants, and a gray hoodie. He wasn't carrying a weapon.

"What are you doing in here?" I asked him.

"Agent Wachalowski?"

"Who are you, and what are you doing here?"

I scanned into the soft tissue of his face and saw some bioelectronics fitted behind the eyes. He was here gathering footage. I was being recorded.

"I hear you've got some revivors upstairs," he said.

"Be careful what you admit to," I said, moving past him. "There's only one way you could have heard that."

As I pushed past, he followed, keeping pace with me.

"Come on, you can give me something, can't you?"

"Sorry, I can't," I said. "And listening in on even unsecured communications like that is a felony; you know that. The SWAT guys are on their way down, and if they find you here, you're going to be arrested."

There's a reporter down here looking for footage. Clear him out before you bring the revivors down.

Roger that.

"It's already out," he said. "You can't keep it a secret. Just give me fifteen seconds' worth."

"Technically, if you're not outside, you're supposed to inform anyone you talk to if you're going to record them," I said. "Like you're doing right now. If you want, I can slap an injunction on you, and the techs can take a crawl through everything you've got sitting in your buffers. How does that sound?"

That seemed to hit home, and he stayed behind as I headed across the parking lot toward my car. When I got in, I could see him still standing there like he wasn't sure whether or not he should chance going back. In the rearview mirror I saw him watching me, probably still recording as I pulled out and drove away.

With the scene behind me, I took a deep breath. I realized my heart was pounding and I tried to slow it down. I couldn't get the image of that girl revivor's face out of my head.

The first time I ever saw a revivor's face, it was dark out and hotter than hell. The revivor was a male, and when it came staggering up out of the wet grass, I knew for a fact that the man was dead because I was the one who had killed him.

The last time I'd seen one out in the grinder, I was being airlifted away in a helicopter, with a tube down my throat. It came lurching out of the brush, wet eyes staring right at me as we began to rise. Its teeth, stained bright red, were showing, and there was a terrible want on that waxy face that remained even as the gunner turned on it and made it dance.

Faye Dasalia—Shine Tower Apartments, Unit 901

"*Faye*," he'd whispered. I could almost still hear him as I roused from the dream, stirring in my cold bed.

"*You're a beautiful woman, Faye. . . .*" He'd breathed it into my ear, the stubble from his chin pricking the side of my neck. He had finally stopped, and was propped over me, smelling like sweat and that brand of deodorant he used. Even awake, I could almost still smell him. It was almost real.

"*You deserve better than this*," he'd said, as he said every time. "*The world should be yours.*"

Stretching under the covers, I tried to shake it off. I didn't want the world; all I wanted was to make it to first tier without getting shipped off to the grinder. I didn't want the things I dreamed, no matter how many times I dreamed them. Sometimes I thought they happened because he was the only man I knew, but I knew him only because I worked next to him every day. We never had so much as a drink together, and he had never even been inside my apartment the entire time I'd known him.

Besides, I didn't think of Doyle like that. It wasn't even a departmental or career thing; I just didn't think of him that way, and that made the whole thing all the more strange. Doyle Shanks was a friend and I liked him, but there was nothing else there. Not even the dreams could change that.

My phone was ringing. I cracked my eyes open and saw that neon was still seeping through the blinds, but otherwise the room was dark. It wasn't morning yet, then. I wasn't sure how long I had been asleep, but it hadn't been nearly long enough.

The room seemed to spin slightly as I oriented myself, finding the dresser where the indicator light on my cell made a mellow green strobe as it rang again. Cold air rushed under the blankets as I groped for it and brought it close to my face to check the number; it wasn't Shanks's cell, but I couldn't think of anyone else who'd be calling me.

They found another body. That was the first thought that came into my head. That would make a fourth. Four murders, all the same. I knew somehow that the case was going to go from bad to worse. I retreated back under the covers and flipped open the phone.

"Hello?"

"Ms. Dasalia?" a man asked. It wasn't Shanks; I didn't recognize the voice.

"Who is this?"

"Is this Detective Dasalia?"

"Yes. Who is this?"

"Detective, someone is walking in your shadow."

Terrific. A precious handful of hours of sleep, cut short for this.

"Look—"

"Stop following me, Detective."

That got my attention. I sat up in bed, pulling the covers around me. Fumbling with the phone, I began recording the call and started a trace. Had he actually decided to make contact after being virtually invisible for so long? Could I be that lucky?

"Who is this?" I asked.

"Did you hear me? I said stop following me."

"Am I following you?"

"Yes. You will find another one this morning. Your partner will find her first, but I want you to let it go."

"You want me to let you continue killing these people and do nothing?"

"Yes."

Glancing at the screen, I could see the trace was coming up empty. The 'bot was having trouble following the circuit connections back to the source, for some reason.

"Why should I do that?" I asked. "Why are you doing this? Help me understand it. Is it because they're all first tier?"

So far, that was the only thing any of the victims had in common; they all managed to make it to first tier without getting shipped off to serve. It was a category I hoped to fall into myself one day, but none of the victims so far looked like they had to work very hard for it.

"Your only way out of this is to wake up," he said, ignoring me.

The trace had failed. Whoever he was, he could be anywhere. He was quiet for a minute. I listened but I couldn't hear anything on his end. There was nothing to indicate where he might be. The line was eerily quiet, almost like a digital recording.

"What do you mean—"

"Try to wake up," he said, and the line cut out.

I stared at the LCD for a minute, trying to make sense of it as the screen flashed and the connection dropped.

The time said 3:13 a.m. I'd been in bed for a little more than four hours, and I had one more hour of sleep coming that I wasn't going to get. The cold was already invading my bed. It was time to get moving.

Stretching again, I felt aches in my lower back and other places that were harder to explain. One night I had watched people on TV debate the possibility that a dream could be so vivid, it could affect a person's physical body. At least one of them believed it was possible that dying in a dream that was vivid enough could result in a person's death. It made me wonder whether the same premise held true for an erotic dream, and if one were vivid enough, would it be the same as actually committing the acts? If it was, it was grossly unfair.

I got up, hating the way my joints cracked as I stood and stretched. Since the tenant below had moved out, the floor was always freezing and I had gooseflesh head to toe in seconds. I snapped on the carnival glass lamp next to the bed, found my slippers, and shrugged on my robe, pulling it tightly around me. The floor squeaked under my feet as I made my way in a haze into the kitchen.

I'd spent the previous night comparing everything I knew about the victims, trying to find some kind of thread that tied them together, but so far I had come up pretty much empty. The murders had a ritualistic quality that made me think the selection of the victims should be significant, but none of them appeared to have anything in common at all, except their first-tier status, which wasn't much to go on.

I poured a small glass of water from the filter and set it in the microwave, then took a single sugar cube from the little jar on the table. Using a dropper from the bottle next to it, I squeezed two amber drops onto the cube and watched the liquid bleed through the white granules. I was still staring at it when my phone rang again.

"Hello?"

"Dasalia, it's me."

"Shanks," I said. The microwave dinged, and I winced as I reached in and pulled out the steaming glass.

"What's wrong?" he asked.

"Nothing."

"They found another one," he said.

Your partner will find her first. . . .

"Female?" I asked.

"Yeah. How'd you know that?"

I plopped down at the kitchen table, put the sugar cube on my tongue, and tipped back the glass. The cube dissolved as the hot water scalded my mouth, and I swallowed the bittersweet liquid in one hard gulp.

"We're being watched," I told him, blowing out a hot sigh. "I just got a call announcing the new victim."

"The killer?"

"He implied he was. Have the officers look around; the call came literally less than five minutes ago. He could be watching you now."

"On it."

"Who's the lucky girl?"

"Her name was Mae Zhu," he said. "She was found in her car when they went to tow it. Same wound. Same chemical signature."

Those were the only two constants in each of the murders, and the only two links we had to the killer. One was the unique shape of the wound pattern, and the other was a faint chemical trace that indicated he either worked with explosives or carried them somewhere on him.

"Send me the address."

My phone beeped and I checked the incoming message; this murder had happened right in the middle of the shopping district.

"Any witnesses?" I asked.

"No one saw a thing."

"I'll see if any security cameras picked anything up," I said. "I'm leaving now; I'll meet you over there."

"Okay," he said. "Sorry to wake you."

"I was up."

"Your eval is today. Don't forget."

I sighed. I'd forgotten about the psych evaluation. I didn't have time for that. There wasn't enough time as it was.

"I'll meet you over there," I said.

I hung up and leaned back in the chair, feeling the warm, tingly feeling spread down my arms and legs as the stimulant kicked in. It was a sorry substitute for sleep, but it was better than nothing.

Try to wake up.

Pressing my palms over my eyelids, I felt my eyes aching behind them. That wasn't my problem; I spent my whole life awake, it seemed. If it wasn't for the sedatives, I'd never sleep at all.

My foot had started tapping as a surplus of energy surged through me, cutting through the fog and bringing me back to life. I had to get moving.

I'd showered the night before, so that was going to

have to do. I brushed my teeth, bundled up, and grabbed my maglev chit off the countertop. When I made my way outside, it was still dark and bitterly cold. Sometime during the four hours or so I'd been in bed, it had snowed, leaving a thin white blanket over everything.

I pulled my coat tighter around me and started making the arrangements to have the security footage piped over. I headed down the sidewalk to the subway station, hoping victim number five would tell me something the other four hadn't.

Calliope Flax—Arena Porco Rojo

"Calliope . . . Flax . . . is . . . *down*!"

A judge was screaming through the amp, but fuck if I could hear anything else with my ear in the canvas and the rest of my face full of sweat, muscle, and tit. No one ever called me pretty, but if that bitch wasn't XY, she was a freak. She was too thick and too hard, and to make weight she must have flushed out both ends for a week, because no way was she in my class. She was slow, though, and leaned too much on her size. I was seeing black, and all I knew was when I got loose, her size wouldn't save her.

I couldn't see her, but my palm was in her chin and I pushed until she had to move. When she went back and turned, I jammed my thumb deep under her jawbone so she couldn't back come down and pin me like she wanted. I grabbed her jaw and twisted, and she had to get off and deal with me or I'd break it. When she did, I let go and kicked back, but I cracked into the chain-link pole at the edge of the ring. She came right back, but I got a foot in before she bashed me in the face with her big man hand, pushing me into the chain so hard I felt the skin split above my eye and blood run down my face.

She leaned down on my foot, mouth hanging open and face red, as she tried to crush me. Sweat stung the corner of my eye as a string of spit blew around on the end of her fat bottom lip. Even with my leg there it was hard to keep her back, so when she went to change position, I locked my legs around her waist and tucked her in close. She saw where she was going but was too late to stop it, and I didn't give her a chance to tense up. I put the vise to her ribs full force and she screamed, face red and veins popping. For one split second, her brain was stuck on that and just that. I could see it.

A nose breaks easily, and hers broke flat when I fired my palm down on the bridge. Blood sprayed down her chin, and a lot of strength went out of her all at once. I let go of the scissor lock and brought one leg up on the back of her neck and locked that ankle under the opposite knee while I clamped down on her head and left arm.

By the time she saw what was up, it was too late and she knew it. That lock was death, and as I closed the triangle, cutting off her air, she knew it was done, but she kept at it. Even when I squeezed blood out of her nose and her face went dark, she tried to get up.

Tap, you bitch. . . .

The crowd went ape shit with cheers, boos, and feet stomping on the stands. A hand reached through the cage and grabbed my wrist. Where the hell was security? She bucked like a pig between my legs, and the hand that came through the cage didn't want to let go, so I twisted it around. The middle finger snapped as I wrenched it back, and someone screamed, then jerked it away.

As she pushed me back down to the canvas like a blind bull, I saw blood was running thick, some from my head and some from her nose, and there was a ton of it. The bitch should have just tapped; they'd have called it anyway. They should have called it.

She pushed, and her free hand grabbed a fistful of skin on my bare thigh. She twisted it and dug her thumb into my crotch.

I don't think she meant to. Later I thought that, at least. I didn't mean to do what I did either, but that's how it went down. The slow grind I had on the leg lock turned mean, and I pumped it closed all at once, just for a second, but that's all it took. Her whole body jerked, and the hand that had me let go.

"Match!" a judge screamed. I kicked her off of me and rolled away, the sight in my right eye going red as blood ran in it. From both sides I could hear feet pound the canvas as the refs charged out.

"Match!" someone in the ring yelled. The crowd sounded as if they would rip the place apart, cheering and cursing and shaking the chain link as though they were trying to tear it down. When I tried to get up, a heavy hand came down on my shoulder and pushed me back so I was kneeling.

"Wait," Eddie growled in my ear. I put my hands on my knees and tried to see as he pushed the blood clotter into the cut over my eye. Two guys from the other corner were with the man-girl as she wobbled on her hands and knees. She groped with one red hand as blood ran down her chin, trying to push at the guy who pinched her nose shut. Her eyes swam, and I thought maybe I broke her.

Refs and guys from both sides pointed and yelled at each other, trying to be heard over the crowd as the docs looked at her neck and talked in her ear. After almost a minute, she made a face, but she pushed them away. She needed a hand and she stood crooked, but she got up. Eddie clapped my shoulder.

"Up!"

"Winner!" the judge wailed on the amp. "Winner by submission: Calliope Flax!"

My face came up on the big board, and I saw that the whole right side was covered in blood with a big, open cut on a fat black-and-blue bulge over my eye.

My name is Cal, asshole. . . .

I hated my name. If I ever got out of third tier, I swore the first thing I'd do would be to change it. They made me put my full name, and Eddie said he liked it because of some sales shit. Ironic, he said. Asshole.

I faced the crowd and watched them freak, half of them wanting to shake my hand and the rest wanting to kill me. Some guy up front was going nuts, screaming something. He whipped a brown bottle at me and it smashed on the fence, spraying glass.

"Fuck you!" I screamed, sticking out my finger at him.

"Flax, you bitch!" he yelled, grabbing the fence and pulling on it. I kicked it, and he got his fingers out just in time.

One of the refs helped the girl limp to the center of the ring with me. She was hurting, and I could tell her neck was jacked up. She glared at me over the bridge of her broken nose and there were tears in her eyes.

"Shake hands," the ref said.

I held out my hand, and she took it, but her eyes showed how much she hated me. I pumped her hand twice, then looked at the crowd so I didn't have to look at her. All through the stands they were going nuts. The guy who threw the bottle now threw a folded chair at the fence, his face red. Another bottle hit the chain link and sprayed onto the ring.

"Come on!" Eddie shouted, calling me over to the corner where the exit was. A bunch of big dudes were pushing back the crowd on both sides as some of them tried to get to the spot I'd come out of, while other guys went after them from the stands. Eddie opened the door in the fence.

"Straight back to the lockers and don't stop!" he said as I went by.

I gave him the finger and hopped down in between the security guys, then stuck both fingers straight up in the air as I walked the line back to the lockers. Marko was up next and Jefe after him, so they were hanging near the door.

"You messed that bitch up," Marko said.

"Good."

I said it, but it still didn't sit right, the way she popped and went limp like that. The way she stared me down afterward wasn't like usual, and the look in her eyes was still on my mind.

"We're hitting the Bucket after the fights," Jefe said. "You in?"

"Yeah, I'm in."

So that was that. When the whole thing got going, that's where I was. Third tier, dirt-poor, beat to hell, and ready to drink. I didn't know shit about any of it or that half of it could even happen in this life, but that's that.

I guess you never know.

Zoe Ott—Pleasantview Apartments, Apartment 713

"Zoe?" a woman was asking. Through a window I could see the city was burning, the neon lights were dark, and cherry red cinders swirled in the cold night air.

"Yes?"

"Follow me."

"Why?"

"Because you are the last piece of the puzzle," she said, and she took my hand with her cold, dead one.

All I wanted, the only thing I wanted in the whole stupid world, was some peace. I would have been happy with a day, or even just one minute where someone or something wasn't in my face or buzzing in my head, but it was never going to happen, because even when I shut myself inside for days, they still managed to find me. They hounded me until I slept, and then they followed me into my dreams.

This time it was the dead woman with the short dirty blond hair. I wasn't sure who she was, but she had a look that made me think she'd been a professional of some kind. She wore a woman's suit, but it wasn't just that; it was her face, her hair, and the way she held herself. In the middle of her forehead, about the size of a quarter, the number 3 had been pressed into the skin with black ink.

She had been killed recently and looked a little disheveled, but even so, she managed to seem authoritative and sure. She had nice cheekbones, gorgeous eyes, and a strong jaw. She was a couple inches taller than me, with long legs and a good body. I hated her. I hated her for her looks, the way she dragged me around, and because she never left me alone.

"Why is the city burning?" I asked her, but she didn't answer me. Her hand was cold on my wrist as she pulled me along after her, away from the window and down a dark hallway.

"Where are we going?" I asked. She looked over her shoulder and caught me staring at her free hand,

which was covered in blood. It was clutched around
what looked like a human heart, a big gash cut into the
middle of it.

"It got split," she said, like that explained it.

"This is a dream," I told her.

She didn't respond to that. She dragged me after her
and pushed open a door that led into a green concrete
room.

"Not this again," I said. The room was rectangular,
about eight feet side to side, twelve feet front to back,
and eight feet again to the ceiling. The walls and floors
were smooth concrete painted dark green, and whatever
the place was for, it must have had some significance,
because it wasn't the first time I ended up there.

She let go of my wrist and grabbed the power switch
mounted on the wall, slamming it into the up position
and causing the overhead lights to flicker on with an angry electric buzzing noise. There were two people standing at the far end of the room, staring forward. One was
a man; the other I thought was a man at first, but it was
a very butch woman. There was a space between them
for a third person.

"Who are they?" I asked. A light came on over the
man, illuminating him, so I could see him clearly. I recognized him; I'd seen him on TV a couple times, on the
news.

"This one will need your help," she said, pointing.
"When he calls, go to him."

He was a tall, handsome man with very blue eyes
and short black hair. When I saw him on the news, I remembered he was wearing a suit. He carried a badge,
the kind you kept in a leather wallet. He was somebody
important, some kind of investigator or something. He
wasn't wearing his suit now, though; he was wearing a

white sleeveless undershirt. In the middle of his forehead, pressed in black ink, was the number 4.

"Where did the scar come from?" I asked. There was a big white scar that started up beneath his jawline and got thicker as it moved down his neck, then behind the undershirt. There was more scar tissue across his right shoulder. The woman didn't answer.

"Your chance of successfully navigating this relationship is fifty percent," she said instead.

"What relationship?" I asked, but she was on to the next one. The light came on over the woman, letting me see her clearly.

"This one will help you," she said, pointing. "When you call, she will go to you."

She was about six inches shorter than the man, and thinner, but even more muscular. She looked like she was all muscle and bone, with broad shoulders, narrow hips, and a mean face. Her lips were painted black and peeled back in a wide frown, and her nose had been broken at some point. Her hair was cropped almost to stubble, and her prominent chin jutted forward. I had never seen her before in my life.

Her left hand was a pale gray that went up to the middle of her forearm, and black veins stood out under the skin. The number 2 was stamped on her forehead.

"Your chance of successfully navigating this relationship is ninety percent."

"What about the middle spot?" I asked.

"That is where I stand," she said.

"So we're going to meet?"

"We will meet three times before this is all over."

"And what are my chances of success with you?"

"Respectively, in percentages," she said, "thirty, one hundred, and zero."

"Those aren't good odds."

"Only the first one will occur at this time."

She reached over and snapped the switch back down, cutting the lights. She looked down at her hand, still holding the wounded heart, and looked a little sad.

"Is it yours?" I asked. She ignored me.

The woman stepped back away from me, disappearing into the shadows, and then everything faded away. The green room dissolved around me, leaving nothing but blackness.

I opened my eyes. I was awake, or at least I thought I was. It seemed like I spent a lot of time wondering whether I was dreaming or not. I picked my head up off the couch and blinked until things stopped spinning, and strained to see out the window. It was still dark outside.

I felt a tickle on my neck and brushed at it. Something brown with feelers flicked onto the floor and scurried off. I turned my head and looked at the coffee table; the remote controls were spread out all over the place, along with some pens, a spiral notebook, an oil-stained paper plate, and a shot glass that was full to the brim. I sat up and looked at the TV, which was showing some cartoon with the sound down. I drank the shot, then grabbed the bottle of ouzo from the floor and refilled the glass as I burped up a pocket of air that tasted like cabbage, licorice, and soy sauce.

I poured more of the ouzo into the shot glass, which had kind of become a moving target, and spilled a little onto the floor. I wiped it up with the toe of my sock. I drank the shot and stared at the TV.

A green icon danced in the upper right-hand corner of the screen; the data miner was bouncing around, letting me know it had finished gathering information. I couldn't remember what I had been looking for.

Fumbling for the remote, I turned the sound back on and brought up the data miner. All the categories had hits. The timer showed the miner had been collecting information for almost two hours. . . . I must have dozed off for a while there. There were multiple hits on a bunch of topics: movie stars, TV stars, musicians. . . . One jumped out at me.

WACHALOWSKI.

The dancing icon bounced next to the name. It had eleven hits.

"Who the hell are you?" I asked.

I brought up his listings and had a look; they were all news channels, all short segments. I cycled through the stills. Three of them were the same shot of him standing in what looked like a dark building lobby, facing the person taking the footage.

It was the man from the green room, the one with the scar. He was with the FBI, it looked like. The scar I'd seen in my dream was there, going from beneath his jaw to down under his shirt collar.

I clicked the remote to play the first segment. Agent Wachalowski took out his badge and showed it to the person filming.

"Who are you?" he asked.

"Colin Patrick," a young man's voice, maybe dubbed in, said from offscreen, "freelance news. I received a tip that you uncovered a human-trafficking ring, right here in this office building. Can you tell me anything about what you found?"

"Sorry, I can't," Wachalowski said. The camera cut away to show the elevator door, where the numbers on the display indicated a car descending.

"I hear you've got some revivors upstairs," Colin said.

"Be careful," Wachalowski said, and the camera cut quickly a couple times as he pushed by, "the SWAT guys are on their way down."

The camera cut back to the newsroom, where two anchors were sitting.

"While there were no witnesses to the actual removal of the revivors," the woman anchor said, "a source at the FBI confirmed that a total of twenty-one revivors were recovered at the Goicoechea Building, which was, to all appearances, a hub for trafficking in bodies from outside the country, for distribution to the underground labor and sex trades."

I shuddered.

"Sources also report that at least one of the smuggler's clients was not apprehended," the male anchor said, "and that, based on the records recovered, there may be twenty or more revivors still unaccounted for inside the city."

The rest of the clip looked like the anchors going back and forth, so I flipped to the next one. Someone had managed to get some footage as the FBI came out of the building. One of them held a woman's arm as she walked, naked except for a blanket, through the snow. Her skin was grayish, and her white eyes looked like they were staring right at the camera. It was a revivor.

Weird. I took another shot, looking into those freaky eyes over the rim of the glass. You almost never saw video of them. It sent a shiver down my spine.

"This is just one more example of the sick, twisted, and ultimately debasing effect this whole endeavor is having on our people, our country, and our world," a man was saying. "Offering second-tier citizenship benefits to anyone volunteering for Posthumous Service is this administration's most appalling—"

"So serve," the woman countered. "Serve your country, is that so much to ask? Serve the obligatory two years and get first-tier benefits. Is that such a crime? Serve your country, and it will serve you."

"They don't even want that. They'd rather have a never-ending stream of cannon fodder they can buy on the cheap for second-tier benefits. The whole thing is—"

"Then don't serve," the woman snapped. "If you can't handle either form of service, then don't serve. No one is forced into it."

"No, they can settle for life below the poverty line. Less than one percent of third tiers ever make it to even lower-middle class. That's the life you can expect for—"

I flipped through the rest of the clips and found they were all just variations on the first footage I saw. There weren't any other revivor pictures, and there weren't any good pictures of Wachalowski.

I did a freeze-frame on the shot of him from the hotel lobby, and zoomed in on his face. He looked kind of mad, but maybe something else too. I couldn't read the expression in his eyes, but there was something about the set of them that seemed . . . distressed? Disturbed? They almost looked a little sad. He had really blue eyes. Light blue. I wondered where the scar came from.

What did you see in there? What did you see that made you look that way?

It didn't sound as though they were going to offer any more information. I took another drink and yawned, when I heard a medium-loud thump from the apartment below me. Just like clockwork.

The ticker under Wachalowski's picture said the office where the incident took place was right here in the city. He worked out of the local office. He was somewhere right in the city. Whatever was going on, it was happening out there, right now.

There was a loud crash from below. I heard glass break, and a man's angry voice. Couldn't they give it a rest for one night?

I stood up too quickly and stumbled into the couch a little before making my way to the front door. I shoved it open and knocked an old pizza box across the floor, then hurried down the hall, past the peeling wallpaper and the hole in the drywall to the stairwell. I pushed the heavy door open, then started down the stairs, holding on to the metal railing for support. The walls were covered in graffiti, and at the next landing something brown stained the grout between the grimy tiles. I pushed open the door and staggered out into the hallway.

The shouting was coming from down there, and I did a fast walk down that familiar path. I stopped at the door marked 613 and started knocking on it. I was still knocking on it when it opened suddenly.

My fist pounded the air and I stumbled forward before catching myself. He was standing there, holding it open, looking like he had opened the door and found dog crap. He was wearing a tank top and jeans, as usual. His hair was greasy, and he always looked kind of sweaty.

"What the hell do you want?"

I focused, staring at him until the room seemed to get brighter and the color kind of washed out of everything except the light that came into focus around his head. It glowed, like soft electric light . . . red, kind of like fire, and flaring up in little points and spikes. He was angry, as usual.

"What the fu—" he said, then fizzled in midsentence as I focused on that light.

"Calm down," I said, and the spikes began to settle.

The red shifted to violet, then blue. His stupid eyes changed, some of the meanness going out of them. He stood there like an ape until the light settled into a cool blue, like the sky on a sunny day.

His girlfriend or whoever she was peeked out from behind him, watching me from a few feet inside. She'd been crying, her shirt torn and her hair messed up.

"You should get some sleep," I told him.

He nodded, his eyes dull. I pulled my attention away from him. The light shifted back to normal, and the sharpness surged back into my surroundings. He rubbed at his face, then turned and waddled back inside. The woman met my eye for a second and gave me that look she sometimes did. That relieved, embarrassed, guilty look that was the closest she ever came to thanking me.

A chill ran up my legs and I realized for the first time that I was standing there in nothing but a nightshirt and underpants. I turned without saying anything, and went back upstairs.

When I got back inside, I closed the door behind me and locked it. I stood there for a second, leaning my back against it, and hoped she wouldn't follow me. She wouldn't, though; she never did. I hated going down there. Why did she stay with him?

The image of the FBI agent Wachalowski was still on the TV screen, like he was staring me down from across the room. There was something about his eyes, like he could see right through the screen and into my apartment and was wondering what he had just watched.

He wouldn't believe it if he knew. The woman downstairs had watched it enough times with her own two eyes and she didn't even believe it.

Sitting back down with the bottle, I tried to push the whole thing out of my head. I switched the channel be-

fore I had my next drink, because I didn't want him to
watch me do it. Later, when I got closer to the bottom,
I wouldn't care, but right then I didn't want anyone to
see. Tomorrow I'd stay sober. Maybe I'd take it easy for
a few nights, to detox myself and kind of clear my head.
I was too far gone tonight, but tomorrow definitely.

Using the tuner, I strayed out of the news bands and
into the movie area, where the search 'bot scanned hundreds of channels for things that interested me. It stayed
quiet downstairs for a while; then they had sex for a few
minutes; then it got quiet again. I wondered why the FBI
agent Wachalowski ended up in the green room, but not
for long before the booze started doing its job.

All I wanted was to be numb when the needle-head
finally did show up again. The rest would work itself
out.

Nico Wachalowski—Palm Harbor Shipyard

As I cruised down the interstate, I could still feel the
blood pulsing in my neck. Before I left, I'd signed out
a weapon. Having a gun strapped next to my ribs made
me breathe a little easier, but I could still feel the cold
meat of that dead arm around my neck.

Where had someone like Tai gotten a piece of meat
like that? Revivors like the females he kept were the only
kind most people outside of the military wanted to deal
in. They were weak and docile. They were predictable. The
one that attacked me in the hallway was old-school, third-
world military. I didn't think anyone made them like that
anymore. It drooled, so it was hungry. Revivors couldn't
process food; the newer ones had a shunt in the brain
that told them they were full. The old ones were always
hungry, with no way to make it stop. Back in the grinder,

sometimes they wired their jaws shut. Sometimes they just let them eat. No one stateside wanted units like that.

The kinds of people who might be interested in a revivor like that would also be interested in Tai's little arsenal. Someone on this side of the border wanted both those things and was willing to pay for them. Tai had at least one customer I hadn't known anything about. Whoever that was, he was into something worse than body-bag sex and slavery.

A horn blared, snapping my attention back to the road. A semi with a freezer car sporting a biohazard warning, probably filled with bodies and headed for the Heinlein labs, drifted into my lane.

A message came in from the Federal Building. I picked up.

Go ahead, Sean.

That kid from the lobby already has bites airing.

Great. How'd he edit?

Well. You two look like best friends. They want a statement tomorrow to defuse this.

I'll try to find something newsworthy.

Streetlights streaked by as I veered off the express lane and down toward the shipyard. A tight loop took me under a rusted bridge that was covered in graffiti and sent me toward a series of shadowed behemoths moored along the docks.

As I got closer, my long-range scanner picked up a revivor heart signature, although it was too far away to read. I brought up a map of the dock and laid the location of the signature over it, a soft orange flickering behind my eyes in the rearview mirror.

It's a revivor—I've got a signature. Where's the backup team?

On their way.

I homed in on the dock where the signature was emanating from and pulled over, stepping out of the car. It was windy, and the cold, damp breeze coming in off the water smelled like ocean and garbage. The dock planks and chain posts were covered in a thick layer of frost, jagged little icicles leaning into the wind. Beyond that, through fog and snow, the skyline rose up in a sea of neon and electric light.

I switched off the GPS and focused on the signal. It was coming from a stack of huge metal shipping containers that had been offloaded and were sitting in the fog. Were we going to get that lucky?

It looks like it's still with the offloaded cargo. I'm going to check it out.

The containers were stacked two stories high; mass vehicle transports, each capable of holding maybe twenty-four cars. I moved into the shadows between two rows of them, toward the signal.

How many?

Just one.

I found the container the signature was coming from and approached it. The front end of it had a huge set of doors to allow vehicles in and out, and it was barred and locked. To the side of the large doors was a small one to allow inspectors in and out. I scanned the scene and packaged the footage along with the rest of the case information, then sent out a warrant request.

Granted.

I approached the small door and put my thumb to the lock, issuing an override code. A few seconds later, the bolt opened with a loud snap. I pushed it open with a crunch that brought flakes of ice down over my head, and went inside.

Adjusting the night vision filter, I looked around. The crate was filled with tightly packed rows of electric cars sitting on metal skids, parked bumper to bumper and three rows high.

I scanned the inside of the container; the signal was coming from above me. After climbing up the scaffolding, I managed to follow it to a single car in the middle row. I peered in through the side window, trying not to fog it up.

There was a female revivor inside, lying on the backseat and wrapped in plastic. I opened the back door and leaned in for a closer look. The wrap was sealed, and the body wasn't moving.

Using my field knife, I slit the plastic down the middle and pulled it apart. I could tell right away it was a combat model; plain-looking with short hair, a scar on the forehead, and little in the way of curves. No fancy skin work or cosmetic augmentation had been done.

Leaning in close, I used the backscatter to get a look under the skin and saw some muscle work and joint augmentation. Resting in a chamber between the bones of the right forearm was what they called a revivor bayonet. For sure, it was a combat model, and not a hack job either. This one had rolled off some country's assembly line.

There was a low creak from below me as the door to the crate opened partway, and I froze. I backed slowly out of the car and drew my gun, peeking through the metal lattice where I saw a figure down below, moving through the doorway. I zoomed in on it.

"What are you doing here, kid?" I said, just loud enough to be heard. At the sound, he jumped. It was the same one from the lobby; he must have tailed me.

"Following the story."

"You pieced that footage together pretty quick," I said.

He shrugged. "Gotta move fast in this business," he said. "Did you find it?"

"Find what?"

"Oh, come on," he whispered. "What do you think? The reviv—"

A shot rang out before I could answer him, and the kid's head pitched to one side. His body bounced off the door and spilled out onto the dock.

I stayed crouched as the container door slowly ground to a stop with a metallic groan. I zoomed in on the kid; most of what had been inside his head was scattered over the planks, steam rising off it. Footsteps were approaching; someone heavy was running very fast across the dock toward the container. Given the weight and speed of the footfalls, whoever it was had to be augmented. I aimed toward the doorway as the footsteps thumped to an abrupt stop just outside.

I've got gunfire down here and one civilian dead. Where's backup?

A weapon was thrust through the doorway, and immediately automatic gunfire pounded through the inside of the container, sending sparks flying off the car I was crouched behind. One of the tires blew out and I was sprayed with bits of safety glass as bullets punched through the car. I fell back, slipped, and tumbled off the scaffolding down onto the floor. I pushed myself behind another car as the racket continued. A second later, the heart signature I was monitoring flatlined.

Damn it.

The backup team just entered the shipyard. Hang on.

Another burst of gunfire sounded, and as I moved

along the bottom row of cars, I caught sight of the shooter in the doorway. I fired at him three times, hitting him at least once before another volley ripped into the car in front of me.

He ducked back out and it got quiet. He wasn't visible through the exit where the kid's body was now holding the door open, so I listened for him, but my ears were ringing and I couldn't make anything out. He wasn't showing up on the thermal filter, but the door or the walls of the container might have been shielding him.

I moved to the far end of the container and followed the wall to the door. I still didn't see him, so I moved to the doorway and crouched down near the body. No one was on the left side of the exit, but the door was still hanging open to the right. I moved outside and spun around the door, but before I could bring my gun around, he grabbed my wrist and held it like a vise.

He was definitely augmented; he moved me easily, pulling me off balance and smashing my hand into the metal wall. My grip loosened, and he delivered a hard punch to my gut. The strength went out of my legs, and I felt the gun fall from my fingers.

He let go of me and I slipped on a patch of ice, coming down on my knees onto the dock. It hurt when I forced in a breath, and spots were swimming in front of my eyes. I felt like I'd just been hit by a train.

The guy was wearing a navy jumpsuit like one of the dockworkers might wear over a thermal body glove. He had dark skin and wavy black hair that stuck out from under a gray wool cap. He put the automatic weapon he'd been carrying down on the ground, the clip expended. He didn't bother to go for my gun, so he knew the grip was keyed to me.

"I'm a federal agent," I said, but he didn't show any

sign that he cared or that he even understood me. I went for my gun and he threw a kick, catching me in the chest and knocking me back.

I was lifted up by the lapels and felt my heels brush the ground for a moment before the back of my head crashed into the metal wall. Everything went white for a second, and his hand began to squeeze around my neck, crushing it.

I was going to black out. Warning lights were flashing red across my field of vision. I caught a brief glimpse of an override code flickering by as the world spun around me, and one of the internal stims popped and released into my bloodstream.

My adrenaline shot through the roof. About half the warning indicators blinked out and half stayed on as my EKG spiked and every muscle in my body jumped like I'd grabbed a live wire. I shot out my palm and his nose crunched underneath it, spattering us both with blood. I grabbed his head and jabbed my knee up into his jaw. The grip on my neck released.

I fell to the ground and tackled him, knocking us both onto the dock with me on top of him. I started hammering him in the face and neck with my fists, splitting his cheek open and shearing away his two front teeth before he could get his arms up between us.

The stim wasn't going to last forever; I put three right hooks into his ear as he got a hand on my chest and shoved me back. My last punch hit air as I floundered, and he kicked me square in the chest. I fell on my back and saw him getting up.

Blood was running out of his nose, dripping off his chin. His lips were red and his right earlobe was smashed. He grimaced, flicking a tooth out onto the ground with his tongue. A crimson strand of saliva from his busted lower lip waved in the cold wind as his breath plumed out of his mouth.

I tried to kick away and he grabbed me, pulling me up by my collar.

We've got him.

It took me a second to realize what the message meant; my backup was there, targeting him from somewhere nearby. The stim was wearing off, and I could feel the strength draining out of me.

Don't kill him.

Roger that.

He pitched back and dropped me just as I heard the shot ring out. I saw his leg collapse into a Z shape between the right knee and ankle as the flesh and bone were torn away and he fell to the ground. He rolled over on his side, staring bug-eyed at his leg.

Do I need to hit him again?

No.

I found my weapon and limped over to it. I knelt down and picked it up, then vomited.

You okay?

I watched the steam rising off it, waiting to see if there was any more coming.

Wachulowski, you okay?

I'm fine. Get a coroner down here.

After they were done scraping the kid off the dock, maybe we could pull something off him. The department would never foot the bill to buy up exclusive rights in order to sit on the footage. If it was bad enough, they could file an injunction and put a freeze on it, but not before it aired.

Two men were cuffing the shooter, while a third tended to his leg. Another man was approaching the body of the kid, not looking optimistic.

"You're a dead man," the shooter growled through his wrecked mouth, glaring up at me.

"I know."

"He knows who you are," he said. I was about to ask him what he meant by that when one of the men jammed a tranquilizer into his neck and he went limp.

"Have the medics pin his leg back together and make sure he doesn't bleed to death," I said. "Then I want him back at HQ and three keycards deep before anyone else sees him or talks to him."

"Got it."

I started making my way back to my car before the aftershock of the stims kicked in and knocked my body chemistry far enough out of whack that the ignition's safety catch would refuse to let it start. By the time I fell into the driver's seat, my stomach felt like a pound of ice was sitting in it and I was sweating despite the freezing cold. When I pressed my thumb to the ignition, the light flashed yellow, but it started.

Leaning back, I routed around my emergency systems and manually popped the last stim. A few seconds later, the aftershock backed off, but it threatened to come back, the worse for waiting.

Ice and grit crunched under the tires as I pulled out and aimed for the home office, which was the next best thing to home.

2

Fuse

Calliope Flax—Stark Street Police Station

". . . where it seems some number of revivors were impounded by the FBI," the guy on the TV said. I was squatting on the floor of the jail cell with my head back on the bricks and leaned against the bars that penned the boys from the girls. My face and head throbbed like hell.

I opened my eyes and looked up through the bars at the TV on the wall, which showed the front of some building. Blues flashed, and a crowd pushed at a line of cops to try to get pictures.

"No official statement has been made," the voice continued. "Witnesses, however, recorded the removal of several revivors. . . . No word on how many total were recovered, or what they were for, but this was clearly an organized raid on a major operation. Lead investigator Nicolai Wachalowski was not available for comment."

"On the subject of revivors," another guy said, "a bill that would allow corporations to utilize revivors to fill a portion of their manufacturing jobs, the so-called five-percent bill, was voted down yesterday by a fairly wide margin."

I shut my eyes again, wishing at least the hangover would let up. The last thing I remembered from the bar was that I'd shot some pool with the guys. A bunch of college snots showed up at some point, rich-bitch fight groupies and pretty-boy wannabes. One thing led to another, I guess, and here I was, waking up in the slammer.

"How about that shit?" a voice said near my ear. I rolled my head against the bars that one of the college boys had sat down on the other side of. Pretty boy had a dark shiner under one eye, but besides that he had skin like a baby. His hair and clothes said he wasn't from here and didn't belong here.

"How about what shit?" I asked. He pointed at the TV, where some old guy with white hair pissed on about something.

"This is a requirement moving forward in order to remain competitive in the global market," he said. "End of story. The bottom line is, the representatives are afraid of this bill because revivors don't earn wages, so they don't pay taxes, but what we are talking about here is a very small percentage of the overall workforce, even when compared to the percentage of overseas positions."

"Big-business interests," the news guy said, "including such corporate powerhouses as TeraSine and CyberTech, vow to continue pushing for what they are terming labor reform."

"It's bullshit," pretty boy said.

"What the hell do you care?"

He shrugged. "Could affect you."

"If those assholes give all the shit work to dead guys, I'll be screwed—that it?"

"Well, it didn't pass," he said.

"Score one for tier three."

I was hoping he'd beat it, but he didn't. Out of one eye, I could see him looking at me.

"You're Calliope Flax," he said.

"It's Cal, asshole."

"Right, Cal."

"What do you want, an autograph?"

"I've seen you fight."

"You watch the chick fights?"

"I've watched you fight."

"Most guys only tune in to silicone."

"Hey, there's nothing wrong with how you look," he said, and just like that, I'd had it with his smooth skin and his good looks. I clubbed the bars in front of his face and made him jump as everyone looked over.

"Settle down in there!" one of the guards yelled. The kid held up his hands.

"I didn't mean—"

"Shut up," I said. "Whatever you're selling, I don't want it."

My head hurt and I was in no mood. He seemed to get it and stopped talking, but he stayed put. I thought I would hit the bunk, but I was too whipped to want to get up. He took something out of his sock. A phone, I thought. He kept it near his crotch and punched in numbers with his thumbs.

"They'll take that," I said.

"I know."

He kept at it for a minute, then snapped it shut and stowed it back in his shoe.

"Call your mom?"

"Posted bail."

"Yeah, right."

"The code contacts a remote 'bot," he said. "I send the GPS coordinates so it knows who to contact, then it contacts their server, looks me up, queries how much the fine is, and posts it over the wire. It's instantaneous."

I put my head back on the cement.

"You royalty?"

"Second tier."

The way he talked, I had him pegged for tier one. Tier two meant he sold his ass to the man. His folks hadn't bought him up yet. There was no way his pretty face would ever see a real fistfight, never mind a firefight.

"Good for you."

"Luis Valle?" a guard called.

Still looking me in the eye, the college prick smiled. "That's me," he called back.

"You just got posted," the guard said. "Let's go."

He winked at me. God, I felt like hitting him.

"Your people will get you out of here, right?" he asked.

"I don't have people; I have Eddie," I said. "If I'm still in here when the next fight comes, he'll get me then, but I'll get docked."

"Valle, let's go!"

He got up and went with the guard. Marko shot him a look when he went by, and like a little bitch, he smiled and gave him a wave. Dipshit didn't even know where he was. He was a cat in the dog pound and so were his dumb friends, but at least they knew to sit still and shut up.

The cell door banged shut and it got quiet again, except for the TV. They were still going on about revivors; should they work, should they fight, and all that. It was the same shit as always. Who cared? At least so far, they couldn't take you without your signing up, so why bitch? Those bastards took your money and got to say how much you counted and what you could do. They took down all there was about you, from your ID to your DNA, and they never asked once and no one ever said shit. Now people cared? Stick me up the ass all you want while I'm here, just don't screw with me when I'm dead—what kind of sense did that make?

You didn't have to sign up. The way I saw, if it bugs you, don't sign. I hadn't.

The guys in the other cell were off in a bunch by then, laughing and talking shit like how hard and in what way they'd bang the newswoman who had come on if they had the chance, which they never would. It was stupid, but the bars made me mad, like even though we were all in jail I had to be in the girl cell. They were all in there, and I was stuck on my side with two high-class bitches who cried the whole time. The guys didn't want to look soft, so the only one who came over at all was the pretty boy who I didn't even know. Perfect.

My eyes drifted back to the TV. A reporter stood near a black car parked on a side street. The camera cut and showed some rich Asian woman dead behind the wheel, covered in blood. "The suspected serial killer has struck yet again," a voice on the TV was saying.

"Flax," a guard called, and I looked up through the bars. He was a big guy, on his way to fat.

"That's me."

"Let's go," he said. I looked at the guys in the next cell, but no one was calling them out and they looked as clueless as me.

"What for?" I asked.

"Today."

Things I might have done went through my mind as I got up and went to the guard, who slid open the door.

No way would Eddie come for me and not them. It must have been something I did, which was a lot of things.

"Out," he said. I went through the gate and he slammed it shut behind me. He didn't look at me twice, and just walked down the hall with me in back of him.

"Nice shiner," he said when we got out of holding.

"Thanks."

"You get that in the ring, or at the bar after?"

"The second one."

The night before was a blur, but it didn't happen at the fight. I got the cut over my right eye there, but not the shiner on my left. Someone caught me good at the bar.

"Well, Ms. Flax, it's your lucky day," he said.

"Yeah?"

"Yup. The guy you jumped dropped the charges, and in all the resulting bullshit of the little war you started, even the cameras couldn't pin anything too bad on you."

I shrugged at his back. That was pretty lucky, actually.

"Here we are," he said when we got to the main entryway.

"Huh?"

"You got posted," he said. "What'd you think, I was giving you a tour? You're free to go."

He handed me my leather jacket and I put it on.

"I left what I found in the pocket. Consider that a gift."

He held out a big yellow envelope like I should take it, so I did. I ripped it open and saw my cell phone and keys inside. When I looked back, he was pointing like I should get the hell out.

"A couple of your buddies dropped your bike off last night so it didn't get towed; it's in the lot out back."

"Who bailed me out?" I asked. He jerked his thumb toward the wall.

"Nice fight, by the way," he said. "The first one, not the second one."

When I looked at where he pointed, I saw pretty boy from inside the cell standing there, arms crossed and back against the wall like some kind of pimp. When I turned back, the guard was gone.

I looked back and pretty boy was still smiling that smug smile I was going to learn to hate in about five minutes. If he'd really bailed me out, I'd almost rather have gone back in, but not enough to actually have done it. When people did things for you, they wanted something back.

"You do this?" I asked.

"Yeah," he said, still smiling. He tailed me out. The sun was almost up.

"Why?"

"It wasn't a big deal."

Bail, even for a back-lot brawl, was a big deal, but maybe it wasn't a big deal for him. Maybe he was a fan, or maybe he did it just to pat himself on the back. Maybe it was to show off.

"What do I owe you?" I asked.

"I just—"

"Don't screw with me. What do I owe you?"

"How about a ride home?" he said.

I still didn't know what his game was, but a ride I could do. If that was all it was going to take, I could do that. A ride on the back of my bike in the cold might wipe that look of his face, even.

"A ride? Sure. Okay. You got it."

His shit was so slick, I even bought it a little. *Just a fan*, I said to myself, *or some punk with an itch to walk on the wild side.* If it got his rocks off to be nice to a three, why not take him up on it? It beat a week in jail, and he was nothing to be scared of. Tight, but slight, and never fought a day in his life. Harmless, right?

What a crock of shit.

Nico Wachalowski—FBI Home Office

Whenever I was put under for maintenance, my mind always went back to the same place.

I never found out what knocked me down back then. Later I was told it was probably a concussion grenade. The last thing I saw was Sean turning from the radio as if he'd heard something; then everything turned to white noise.

I could see before I could hear; when I opened my eyes I was on my back, being dragged by one foot through the brush. Wet grass and branches whipped across my face, and I could see the night sky above me. I lifted my head and saw a figure trudging forward, the hand that was gripping my boot trailing behind him. There were two others with him.

Screaming and the tearing of cloth cut through the ringing in my ears, then the crunching of metal and electronics. Someone was shouting into a radio, it sounded like, and gunfire was being exchanged.

I reached for my gun, but it wasn't there. My knife was gone too. I struggled, and three sets of dead, yellow eyes stared back at me from above. I tried to kick free, but one of them grabbed my other leg. They dragged me out of the brush and into damp, soft soil as I felt myself being pulled downward.

Dirt was forced up the back of my shirt, and ants and termites scattered as I was dragged underneath something. I craned my neck back to see the mouth of a tunnel getting smaller behind me, the earth swallowing the sounds of the screams and gunfire. . . .

"Nico?"

The memories scattered, and I opened my eyes. Sean's gaunt face looked down on me, his narrow eyes serious. His once-black hair had begun to turn gray, and he looked tired. After a moment, he smiled faintly.

Sean Pu and I had served together. He was a tech man now, running the soft side of many operations in the field. He specialized in bioaugmentations, and kept a section of the Agency field ready. Unofficially, he was still more like my wingman; my pair of eyes on the inside when I was out there. Un-unofficially, he was more like my personal guru.

"You know those stims are for emergencies only," he said.

"I know."

Everything felt more or less back to normal. I took a deep breath and felt pretty good.

"You threw everything out of balance back there," Sean said. "You shouldn't drive when you're like that."

"Am I okay?"

"Your blood levels are back to normal," he said. "I'm just finishing up replacing the stim packets."

"Thanks."

He continued working next to me. All I felt was a tugging at the back of my neck and an occasional tiny jolt down my spine.

"Why didn't you put down the revivor?" he asked.

"I did."

"The other one," he said. "The one in the restroom."

"Word travels fast."

"It does."

I sighed. The truth was, I'd had every intention of doing it; from the moment I walked into the building to the moment I walked into that bathroom, and even the moment I pulled the codes from it.

"Did they ask you about it?" I said.

"Yeah, they wanted to know if you've seemed unstable at all."

"What did you tell them?"

"That you're fine, which was a lie. Of course, if they listened to me, they wouldn't have sent you in the first place," he added.

"You recommended they didn't use me?"

"Yes."

"Why?"

"For the same reason they wanted to send you," he said. "Because you have experience with revivors. But unlike them, I know what some of those experiences were. I questioned how you might react, and I was right."

A strange sensation crept up my back and neck as he withdrew the thin series of tubes, the ends popping softly as they came free. He smoothed down the little dermal strip.

"Good as new."

I stretched, flexing my muscles and cracking my back. Everything felt like it was in order. When I ran the diagnostics on my heads-up display, everything came up green. I swiveled my legs around and hopped off the chair.

"It doesn't matter," I said. "All the revivors are going down after they're done with them anyway."

"You did everything right. No one's going to complain about the job you did, but why would you want to go back to that place? How often do that many revivors end up stateside?"

Sean had a way of echoing my own thoughts. The truth was, I could still feel that cold slab of meat crushing my neck, that saliva and breath that should have been warm but wasn't. I could still see those eyes, just barely glowing in the dark like they used to at night, and that damn girl, that walking sex doll and the way it spoke.

"It mixed me up," I said.

"Hmm?"

"The pleasure model they set up," I said. "I was just talking to myself, talking out loud. It looked like a snuff job to me. I said someone was probably still looking for her. You know, the girl."

"I get it."

"It said, 'He is.' It said, 'He'll never stop looking.' "

"I see."

I shook my head, remembering that wax doll's face looking up at me.

"It's crazy," I said, "but I was sure it meant her father."

Sean pressed his lips together.

"It got to you?"

"No. It wasn't that. It was the way it said it. It was like something else was in there looking out. . . . It was like it paged through the memories there, and dredged up a piece of information it didn't even understand."

Sean didn't say anything, and after a while, I thought maybe I should stop talking.

"I meant to do it," I said. "I'd have been doing it a favor."

He smiled a little, and clapped me on the shoulder.

"Nico, I won't bar you from the case, but as a friend,

my recommendation to you is to walk away from this one. It took you a long time to—"

"I know."

"You have never been quite the same."

"I know."

"When they ask me, and they will, all I have to tell them is your body is chemically stressed, and I recommend a short time to readjust. No one would blink at that. This case will move on, and the next one will move in."

My first reaction was to say no, but it didn't come out of my mouth. Instead I shook my head. I grabbed my coat and shrugged it on.

"Revivors are not human beings," he said.

People said that all the time. I'd said it too, early on. Revivors weren't living, but they weren't dead either. Their knowledge, their compulsions, were human. That I knew. I thought of the girl, her pale face and her dark hair. Her soft voice. She was not like the revivors in that hellhole, the revivors I had known. She was not like them, and she was like them.

I learned more about revivors than I'd ever wanted to when they dragged me into that hole. It made no difference what you were in life; strip away the brain chemistry, and you had a revivor. They were what lurked under the surface of all of us, even me.

"I don't know what they are," I said to Sean.

Sean watched from across the room, but he didn't say anything more as I left the lab and closed the door behind me.

Faye Dasalia—East Concord Yard

The sun came up shortly after we emerged from the tunnel. The lights from the previous night had flickered out, and the streets and sidewalks were thick with early-morning commuters. When the train joined the main railway, the concrete building facades flashed by, and in the distance, past the field of monorail tracks, the city sprawled for as far as the eye could see. Skyscrapers formed a mass of geometric shapes, dwindling to the horizon until they were lost in the haze of morning snow. Beyond that, the city proper's skyline rose like a huge monolith above the rest. I watched it for a while with a sleepy stare as droplets streaked across the window.

The car was clean but showing its age, with worn trim and fading LCDs that scrolled schedule information, advertisements, and public-service warnings. It was packed full but quiet, as passengers stared at their computer screens, keypads, and styluses, whispering just over the hum of the track. They had the heat on a little too high, and the air smelled like coffee and cologne. Despite the attacks and the general unrest on the streets these days, it was almost peaceful.

I had managed to pinpoint the security camera closest to the corner where the murder took place, and had them send me the contents of its recording buffer for the hours corresponding to the time of death. I watched it on my computer tablet as another train whipped by the window, heading in the opposite direction. I could make out the vehicle in the lower left-hand corner of the frame and was able to pick out the license plate number. The sidewalks were crowded with people on either side of the street, heading back and forth and ducking in and out of shops. Everyone was bundled up against the cold, making it hard to pick out facial details. After an hour or so it had begun to snow, further obscuring the image.

A message came in, flagged urgent. Someone was on

the line, waiting. Moving the footage off to one side, I brought up the image a second before I decided I should screen it. In a window I could see Serena's face, lips pressed together as she waited. A receipt had already been sent, so it was too late to try to duck her. The expression on her face said I'd already been doing that too long.

I opened the connection and typed.

Hello, Dr. Pyznar. I'm on the train. Nonverbal only, please.

She looked at me from the screen and frowned, but not in an angry way.

These psych exams are mandatory, Faye. For everyone in the department.

I know.

The results of your blood chemistry have come back.

And?

The bottom line is, it's obvious to anyone who looks that you take too many stims and too many tranquilizers. Knocking yourself out and then shocking yourself awake isn't the same as sleeping.

She didn't have to tell me that, but unfortunately, at the moment it was all I had. I was a second-tier citizen. I never served in the military, but I was wired for Posthumous Service. Making detective was the first step toward at least a first-tier retirement. My caseload would dictate the rest.

Are the levels within tolerance?

You mean, are they within the department's acceptable range? Yes, but—

So I'm okay?

She pursed her thin lips, fixing me with a frustrated look. *My recommendations hold some weight.*

My eyes drifted to the window containing the security footage. Scanning through, I watched the snow pile up in fast motion until it covered the windshield of the car. People continued to cross in front of it until a small figure broke off and approached the driver's-side door and got in. I stopped the image, backed it up, and let it play.

The figure was female: the victim. She approached the car, unlocked it using the remote, then opened the door. She didn't seem as though she heard or saw anything strange. She got in and shut the door behind her.

This shouldn't even count as the evaluation. Doing something else at the same time isn't helping.

Doctor, I'm in the middle of a murder investigation.

She sighed.

I know. Tell me, at least: Are you still having the dreams?

Yes. I had one last night.

How are they affecting you these days? How do they make you feel?

Sore.

If you're tense enough in sleep to wake up with muscle aches, that's not good.

Tell me about it.

What about the voice?

It's not a voice, it's my voice. . . . Talking to myself helps me think. That doesn't make me crazy, does it?

Not yet.

Can we call this done?

On the screen she frowned again, but again, not in an angry way. She wasn't mad; she was concerned, and I knew that, but there was just too much going on.

The next exam is in three months. You have to come in for that one. Physically come in.

I will. Thank you, Doctor.

There's no point in making first tier if you work yourself into an early grave. Slow down.

I will. Thank you.

Closing the window, I smiled, thinking that it had gone better than I expected. She was going to give me a pass for now; one more thing off the list. I turned my attention fully back to the security footage.

It had gotten dark out by that point in the feed, and the car was in shadow. Even after enhancing the image, all I could get from the driver's-side window was a reflection. The people on the sidewalk were passing right by the grille of the car, completely unaware that behind the blanket of snow on the windshield, Mae Zhu was being quietly murdered.

I watched closely, but there wasn't any observable movement to tell what was happening inside, and no one gave the car even a passing glance that might indicate they had heard anything strange. I followed the passersby while keeping track on the camera's timer; it took only fifteen seconds before anyone who had been close enough to see what happened had moved on, outside the line of sight. In that amount of time, not one of the hundreds of people on the street was even aware of the fact that anyone was inside the car. It would have been the same when he got in.

I started scanning through again and saw the back door open and a man get out. He shut the door behind him casually, and walked out of frame as if nothing was wrong.

I backed it up to try to get a better look at him, but he knew about the camera; he was wearing a long, dark coat that covered his body, with a hood that concealed his face, given the camera angle. More than that, though, when I tried to enhance the image, there was some kind of distortion, like something corrupted the signal. He must have been carrying a baffle screen in his pocket or on his belt. He obviously didn't mind being seen, but he didn't want to be recorded.

I scanned back, looking for the time when he actually entered the car, but he had been in there for a while; the security cameras began overwriting every twelve hours, and he had gotten in at some point before the beginning of the current buffer.

All those people around. That was bold.

I rubbed my eyes. He'd been sitting in that car as I was home in bed, finally managing to drift off to sleep.

"Holy shit," a young man said from toward the front of the car, his voice piercing the quiet. I looked up and saw the passengers in the seats ahead were focusing outside the window. I saw something flickering up ahead.

"Is that for real?" someone asked.

It took a few seconds to register—something up ahead was on fire. The train approached the source of the flames, and people began moving to my side of the car to get a better look.

When we got closer I saw what looked like an armored car was sitting in the middle of an empty parking lot where disused buildings towered on three sides. Fire poured out of the cab, and sent blue-black smoke upward in a thick column that rose high into the air. I could see a crowd of people had started to approach the vehicle before the train whipped by and passed out of sight. I called in to the station.

"Dasalia, what's up?"

"I'm on the L," I said, "just coming up on One Hundred Thirteenth at East Concord Yard, and I've got a burning vehicle here. Has anyone called it in?"

"First I've heard of it."

"Get someone down here," I said, "and coordinate with the fire department. I'm going to check it out."

The train slowed down as it approached the next stop. While the other people on the train were clustering around the windows I pushed my way into the aisle and headed for the nearest exit. As soon as the doors opened, I got off and started sprinting down the platform in the direction of the truck.

People were packing in tighter, looking over each other's shoulders as I forced my way through them toward the column of smoke. As I broke into the parking lot, I could already feel the heat from the fire. Bodies were crowded around the truck, phones and cameras thrust out, recording as the event unfolded on the tiny LCD screens.

I held up my badge, shoving my way closer. The truck was dark blue with some kind of emblem on the side. The paint was scorched, but I could make out part of it clearly. It wasn't an armored car; it was a police vehicle, used to transport prisoners. I could make out a charred figure still behind the wheel of the cab.

"Get a fire extinguisher!" someone screamed, and just then the doors to the back of the truck moved with a thud as something collided with them from inside. A set of keys that still dangled from the lock there jingled as it happened again.

The door was struck again from the inside, and everything kind of slowed down. The back doors were straining against the latch, being pushed from inside as the fire raged. The air rippled with heat, ashes fluttering upward into the smoke. I picked out faces in the crowd as they watched from every side, shouting all around me.

I ran to the truck, pulling my sleeves down over my hands. I grabbed the handle to the back door, turned it, and pulled. The doors immediately swung open and a wave of heat blew out over me, stinking of soot and cooking meat. The smoke stung my eyes, and I covered my face as I scrambled back. I fell facing the crowd and caught a brief look at that ring of cell phones, watching with their tiny cameras, and their owners, who had now looked up from the little screens and were staring behind me in horror. A woman covered her mouth, and someone screamed.

I turned back, following their eyes, and saw there were a bunch of bodies in the back of the truck. They were seated across from each other, facing in. Their heads were bowed and none of them were moving except one. One of them had somehow survived and was bent over in the doorway, struggling forward.

It was a young woman. She was completely nude and was burned all over her body. Her hair had been singed away, and her eyes looked haunted as they stared out of her blackened face.

She stepped forward and slipped, falling face-first onto the pavement. She managed to get back up, hands shaking, and took two more steps before falling down again.

I grabbed her wrists and dragged her back, away from the fire. The crowd parted around me as I pulled her until she slipped out of my grasp and I fell backward.

"Call an ambulance!" someone screamed. Everyone was screaming. I turned the woman over onto her back, cradling her head in my lap.

She looked up at me, and I saw her eyes were the strangest color. They were kind of a pale, silvery yellow, and the irises actually seemed to glow very softly. It took me a moment to realize what I was seeing.

"You're a revivor...."

I had never actually seen one before, not in person. It smelled terrible, like burnt hair, meat, and tar.

"Hide . . . behind . . . whatever you . . . can . . ." she whispered.

"Hold still. Help is coming."

"Keep . . . your . . . head . . . down . . ."

People had stopped watching the truck and stopped yelling, for the most part. They were gathering to try to get a glimpse of the revivor. The cameras had turned from the fire to the spot where I knelt. Some part of the body still sizzled quietly as I held it. Finally, a siren began to swell in the distance, getting closer.

A man moved next to me, trying to get a better view of the fire. I recognized him from the train; a middle-aged businessman with gray hair and a pink face. He had a smug sort of satisfied expression on his face. His eyes looked like they were seeing the rapture, and he was nodding very slightly to himself, arms crossed in front of him. He noticed me looking at him and looked down at me with contempt. When he saw my badge, some of the challenge went out of his expression, but not all of it. He sneered at me cradling the revivor like I was everything that was wrong with the world, then looked back to the burning bodies until his annoyance melted away, leaving only a sense of righteousness.

The revivor was trying to say something, forming words with its cracked lips. Its eyelids had drooped almost closed and the light behind them was flickering. I leaned forward, moving my face closer and turning my ear to its mouth.

"Zhang knew the truth," it gasped softly. "You have to wake up. . . ."

I shook my head, not knowing what it meant.

"I don't understand."

"Zhang knew the truth. . . ."

The revivor mouthed the words again, and not long after, its lips stopped moving. Its mechanical breathing hitched and stopped, then it sagged in my arms, this time gone from this world for good.

Back at the truck, nothing else was moving. The people around me got their fill and moved closer to the truck, trying to see inside and get shots of the bodies. The lettering on the side of the truck read FBI.

It's hard to say exactly what motivated me to make the call. Later I thought maybe it was something I could ask Dr. Pyznar about, if I actually made it over there for the next exam. On the surface of it, I was a law enforcement officer, calling a sister bureau with information. It was their truck; these were their prisoners. The trafficking of revivors fell into their jurisdiction; they would have to be called and told what had happened, if they didn't already know.

That call didn't need to be made by me, though, and the fact that the person I called was the one who wanted to know was just a coincidence. I called because he was the only person I knew who worked at the FBI, even though I hadn't spoken to him for years. Maybe that was why. Maybe I'd been waiting for a reason to break that silence.

My vision blurred as cold wind blasted me in the face, followed by a burst of hot, smoky air. I had to disengage myself from the defunct revivor and get moving. This wasn't my case. My case was still waiting for me. . . .

Blinking, I stared as, for just a second, it looked like someone was standing next to me. Not like a person; more like an outline. It was as if the smoke from the fire blew by, and for just a brief moment it revealed an invisible man standing there. He was looking down at me.

"Ma'am?" a voice in the phone said. Someone had picked up and was trying to get my name. The outline I had seen faded as soon as I saw it. I waved my hand across the spot, but there was nothing there.

"Ma'am?"

"Sorry," I said, still staring at the empty spot. "My name is Detective Faye Dasalia. I need to speak to Agent Wachalowski."

Zoe Ott—Pleasantview Apartments, Apartment 713

Someone was knocking. It must have been going on for a while if it brought me out of it. I opened my eyes partway and saw light around the edges of the shade, making my head hurt and my stomach turn over. Stretching out on the bed, I craned my neck back until it popped.

"What?" I mumbled, but whoever it was wouldn't be able to hear me.

My first thought, which was my first thought most every day, was that this better be real. It was kind of a hit-or-miss thing, that. One time I woke up because my phone was ringing, and talked for fifteen minutes before I realized there was no one on the other end. Another time I woke up and found a man standing in my bedroom, and was so convinced he was a dream that I just went back to sleep, only to find out later he was the landlord's brother checking to make sure I wasn't dead.

The knock came again and I decided one thing my dreams never did was knock. If someone was knocking at the door, they were probably real.

"Go away," I said.

My head was pounding now, and it looked like I wasn't going to get any peace until I took care of whatever it was. I crawled out of bed and looked in the mirror; my nightshirt was long enough to cover up everything that needed covering, which, admittedly, wasn't much. I plodded out into the living room and opened the front door a little bit.

"What?" I asked.

I guess I was expecting either one of the take-out guys or some kid selling something, because no one from the apartment complex ever knocked on my door. Once in a while I forgot that I ordered food and got surprised by the delivery guy, but even they knew to just leave it if I didn't answer.

It wasn't a delivery guy, though, and it wasn't a kid peddling something. It was the woman who lived in the apartment below me, standing there with a black eye and a cardboard box in her hands.

"Uh, hi," she said. "I'm—"

"Yeah," I said, "from downstairs. What do you want?"

"I'm Karen," she said. She was looking at me expectantly. My head really hurt, and I was dying of thirst. I couldn't figure out what she wanted.

"And you are?" she asked finally, extending her hand a little.

"Right," I said, "Zoe. I'm Zoe."

Her hand hovered between us uncertainly. I gave it a little shake.

"Look, no offense, but what do you want?"

"I just . . . wanted to . . ."

"Wanted to what?"

"Thank you," she said. "I just wanted to thank you. I've never thanked you."

"Oh."

"Here," she said, holding out the box, "I hope sugar cookies are okay. I would have made something better, but I didn't know if you had any allergies or anything."

I took the box.

"You made cookies for me?"

"Well, I bought them."

"Why?"

She gave me a frustrated look, and I could tell she was starting to get upset.

"I mean, thanks," I said. "Sorry, I don't know what to do in these situations."

"Usually you invite the other person in," she said.

"My place is kind of a mess. Like, really."

She smiled and nodded, but the smile didn't stay. She looked upset, and I felt bad. I actually thought about letting her in, but I couldn't. Even if I wanted to, I couldn't let anyone see my place the way it looked.

"It's okay," she said.

"No, really, maybe some other—"

"How do you do it?" she asked suddenly.

"Do what?"

"You know what I mean," she said. "Ted, when he gets like he does sometimes . . . like he was last night. You just tell him to calm down and he does. You just . . . switch him off. How do you—"

"Don't read too much into it."

One thing I learned a long time ago was not to talk about that. Bringing it up was a mistake.

"You shouldn't hide it," she said.

"I'm not hiding anything."

"You do something to him," she insisted. "I've watched it; it's like your face changes. Your eyes change. Something happens. It's like something passes between you, and he just stops being angry."

"Maybe it's my personality."

I had meant it as a joke, but she made this kind of "as if" expression when I said it. My face started getting hot.

"No offense, but it's not that," she said.

"Yeah, well, no offense, but go away."

"I don't know how you do it, but he's actually gotten better since you started coming down."

"I didn't do anything," I said. "If I could influence people, would I be living here, like this? Even if I could influence people, it doesn't mean I can change anything that's going to happen. I can't change anything that's going to happen; you should think about that."

I focused on her and the lights surged brighter, the colors draining away. She looked surprised for just a second.

"There," she said, pointing at my face. "That's . . ."

Her finger stopped, hanging there. The aura around her head was blue and red, licking out curiously. I pushed it back.

"I can't change what's going to happen to you," I told her. She didn't say anything; she just stood there, her eyelids drooping a bit. For a minute I thought about trying to give her the idea to dump the stupid ox, but there wasn't anything I could do. He had his hooks into her way deeper than I ever could, and nothing I did could change anything anyway.

He'd kill her eventually. It wasn't my fault.

"Thanks for the cookies," I said, "but I don't know what you're talking about. You have things to do. You should go do them."

"Yeah," she said slowly, and smiled. "I just wanted to swing by and say thanks. I'd better get going."

"Bye."

She turned and walked away, and I was just in the

process of snapping the door shut when someone spoke to my right.

"It's unfortunate."

When I looked over, an older guy with red hair and a red beard was standing in the doorway of the apartment next to mine.

"Unfortunate?"

"That girl."

Who was this guy? Why was he talking to me?

"Do you take care of the old woman?" I asked.

"The previous tenant passed away," the man said, smiling gently. "Over a month ago. I am your new neighbor."

Really?

"Oh. So, why is it unfortunate?"

"It's unfortunate you choose to waste your time on someone who doesn't want to be helped."

A few different responses came to mind, and later I thought up some better ones, but what came out was less biting than I'd hoped.

"Whatever, jerk."

He was talking, I think, when I shut the door and locked it. Who did he think he was anyway? My time was mine to waste on whatever I wanted.

I put the box on the counter and went back into the bedroom. Cookies. Why the hell did she go and do that? What was I supposed to say? Why did she even stay with him, and why did she have to just stand there looking like she did when I went down there?

I took the bottle off the nightstand, uncapped it, and took a swig. It burned going down and hit my stomach like a brick. I took two more swallows and put it back. Drinking when I first got up wasn't a good idea, but the whole thing had me totally on edge.

There was a glass on the floor next to the bed, half full of water. I picked it up and took a gulp; it was warm and it tasted terrible, but it soothed my throat a little. I put the glass on the nightstand next to the bottle. I really needed to brush my teeth.

She was just trying to be nice.

"I know," I said out loud.

The thing was, though, she was wrong. He hadn't gotten better since I started interfering; that was just wishful thinking. Sometimes I wondered if he had gotten worse. Maybe I could calm him down, but I couldn't change who he was and I could feel him getting worse, struggling to fill the gaps I'd created.

I made my way into the bathroom and grabbed my toothbrush out of the sink, dunking it in the mouthwash before scrubbing my teeth halfheartedly. That's when I noticed the needle-head.

She was sitting on the toilet with her elbows on her knees and her head bowed. As usual, the skin had been peeled away in two big flaps right down the back of her skull and neck, where the white dome of her skull poked out. A big hole had been cut through the bone and a bunch of long, thin probes were sticking out of her brain. She rolled one eye up at me, watching as I chewed on the toothbrush bristles. Under the eye were three little star tattoos.

"It's about time," she said. The needle-heads never responded, so I didn't say anything; I just kept brushing.

"He will lead you to us," she said, "and you . . . you will end my pain."

There was no way to know who they were, if they were even anyone at all, but one thing they all had in common was they always called for help. They never said where they might be. Maybe they didn't know. Maybe I was just crazy. I kind of hoped I was.

When I was done brushing my teeth, I spit in the sink and then left her in there.

"Go to him when he calls," she said, as I walked away and slammed the door on her. I plodded back into the bedroom and crawled under the covers.

The first time I saw something like that, I thought I'd gone nuts. It freaked me out so badly I didn't sleep for two whole days, and that just made it worse. When I got my first period, I thought it was a hallucination. When my father came to me one night in a dream and began to flatten to bloody pulp from his toes up, I told myself that's all it was . . . a dream.

I pulled the covers over my head, leaving just my nose sticking out so I could breathe. The problem was there was a lot of daylight left and nothing to do to fill it. I didn't want to see or hear anything anymore, I didn't want to talk to the woman from downstairs, and I wasn't tired enough to sleep. I just wanted to shut my mind off. Just for a few days, or even just a few hours.

When I got up to puke an hour later, the woman was gone from the toilet. I sat there, my forehead on the back of one hand and my face hanging over the cloudy water, and promised my reflection that I would go to him when he called, whoever he was, if they would leave me alone. If they would do that, then even if he was the devil himself, I would go to him.

Nico Wachalowski—East Concord Yard

The fire was out by the time I got there, and the local police had cordoned off the scene. Even so, the whole area was mobbed, with people pushing up against the perimeter and trying to get images. I had to flash my blues just to get them to grudgingly move out of the way enough for me to park on the sidewalk, but they crowded me on my way out. I held up my badge, pushing through.

"Federal agent; stand aside."

Bodies were clustered at the edge of the scene, shoulder to shoulder and leaning forward to get a better view. Handheld cameras, phone cameras, and tons of others fitted into palm tablets, pens, and anywhere else they could be squeezed stood out under the electronics scan. At least five people within spitting distance had them implanted behind the eyes, like the kid who got gunned down on the dock, and a helicopter was passing by overhead. Every move was being watched and recorded from every angle.

"Agent?"

One of the police officers was approaching from the direction of the burnt-out truck. He waved me over.

"Agent Wachalowski?"

I nodded.

"The fire's completely out and the remains of the vehicle have been screened for radiation and tox," he said. "It's safe to go inside, when you're ready."

"Thanks."

There was a body at my feet. Its pretty face was burnt and most of its hair had been singed away, but I could tell it was the revivor from the bathroom. Its bare legs were sprawled in the light dusting of snow, black toes pointed up at the sky. A trail, two heel marks, snaked from where the body lay back to the truck. It had been dragged there.

"Put a blanket on her," I said.

The officer nodded and hustled off.

Kneeling down for a closer look, I could see that whatever burnt her had come from in front of her; the left arm and shoulder got it the worst, along with the tops of the thighs. She had been partially behind something, or more likely someone, when the flames hit.

The left hand had been burnt down to the bone, the two smallest fingers gone completely. The body hadn't been on fire when it came out, and unlike the others, it was pulled away from the flames. This wasn't a bomb or a grenade, then. There were no shrapnel marks, and no sign of gelatinized gas or other propellant. It had been hit with a sustained blast of something hot enough to carbonize muscle and bone. A directed blast. Not the type of weapon you normally saw on the street.

The fire department had managed to put out the truck, and it sat in the middle of the parking lot, leaning to one side where the tires had blown out. The crowd had left behind chaotic trails of many footprints, but as I mapped them, one set in particular stood out; a pair of shoe prints that were near the body. Unlike the others, they didn't move much, and they'd gotten there early, because a lot of them had been walked over. The soles were large, definitely a man's. They stuck near the truck before moving closer to the body than any of the others. Whoever made them would have been standing very close to where Faye had knelt. He would have been right next to her.

A call forced its way in. It was Noakes.

Wachalowski.

I'm here.

Where are you?

You know where I am. I'm at the truck site.

Bringing up the various feeds that had made their way onto the wire, I filtered through them, watching Faye in a blur of overlapped images as she knelt by the revivor. In none of the shots was there anyone standing in the spot where the footprints were.

When I picked up the message, the last voice I ever expected to hear was hers. All I wanted to do was put the case behind me, but when I heard her voice . . . I don't know. I changed my mind.

I thought you were taking some downtime.

I didn't put in for any.

If you need to be off this case, then say it.

In a little window, framed in my field of vision next to the burned body, someone had zoomed right in on Faye's face. She wore no makeup and a masculine suit, but Faye Dasalia would never be mistaken for a man. I froze the image of her face, noting how her blond hair was shorter and her cheeks were more drawn, but how good it still was to see her. She looked tired, but her eyes were sharp. Her full lips were turned down at the corners, like they did when she was troubled.

I caught myself lingering, and closed the image. She had held the revivor in her arms like it was a human. She held it like a child. When she looked at it, there were almost tears in her eyes.

I think I need to be on this case.

It's your call.

I approached the vehicle, but it didn't look like there were any survivors. It was completely gutted, the back doors hanging open. I flashed my badge at the cops.

"Agent Wachalowski," I said. "Who's in charge?"

"Detective Hamilton," a man in a suit said, stepping forward and shaking my hand.

"What about Dasalia?"

"She's up to her neck in bullshit, chasing bodies," he said. "She tip you?"

"Yeah."

"I didn't know she had a contact at the bureau."

"Where is she now?"

"She got a fresh one just this morning. If I had to guess, she's at the scene."

"I'd like to speak with her; can you let me know how she can be reached?"

"Sure."

He peeled a card out of his wallet and jotted a number on the back.

"That's her," he said handing it to me.

"Thanks."

I looked at the back doors of the truck and saw a set of keys still dangling from the lock.

"Were those keys like that when the truck was found?" I asked.

"Yes."

The inside of the truck looked worse than the outside; blackened bodies sat opposite each other facing in, covered in soot. Their heads were bowed as if in prayer, and the parts of them that were exposed to the outside were burned down to the bone; skulls, arms, hands, rib cages, everything. I prodded one of the ones closest to the exit and its index finger crumbled and snapped away like charcoal.

The ones farther back fared a little better, but not much. They were all inanimate, there was no question. I did a head count, and including the one found outside the truck, they were all accounted for.

All the way in the back were the only fresh corpses in the bunch: Tai and his men. None of them looked like they struggled.

I ran the backscatter filter as I scanned the bodies, adjusting it until I could see behind the remaining flesh and bones. A handful of foreign objects stood out, but all I found were fillings and leftover surgical staples. The revivor components near the base of each skull were ruined; the heat had caused the fluid in them to expand and split them apart. Hopefully, the girl who made it out of the truck had fared better.

I crouched down, my knee grinding into the soot, and checked the floor. I didn't see any shell casings anywhere, so none of them had been shot. They were burned alive. In a sense anyway.

The only casings I could find were two on the pavement outside the cab. I didn't recognize the agents inside, but unlike the passengers, they'd been killed beforehand. Each had been shot in the head before the inside was burned out.

No one ever meant to spring Tai. They wanted him, his men, and his inventory destroyed. They wanted it badly enough to attack right in the open, and they managed it on short notice. Even the revivor from the dock had been targeted.

Noakes.

Go ahead, Agent.

This wasn't an associate trying to spring him or a rival trying to steal his inventory. This is someone who wanted to destroy every trace of his business with Tai.

You're sure?

Tai kept records of what was coming in where, and whom the product was lined up for. He did that for everything except for the weapons and the heavy revivors; there was no mention of any of that in the files we recovered.

He had a customer we didn't know about. The one he brought in the weapons and the military-grade revivors for. We may have uncovered a real rat's nest.

Any ideas as to who?

Not yet.

Keep me informed. By the way, you got a message last night.

A message?

An image file arrived, and I opened it. It showed what looked like a business card, with the front displayed on the left and the back on the right.

Someone left that for you last night. It was stuck to the front entrance this morning.

It was the size and shape of a business card, but the print wasn't quite straight. On the front was just a name: ZOE OTT. On the back was a messy handwritten scrawl that said AGENT WACHALOWSKI, I CAN HELP YOU, along with a number. In the bottom right corner was a doodle of a little waveform that looked exactly like a revivor heart signature. It had been traced over several times.

When was it left?

Camera twenty-three picked it up around three a.m.

I tapped into the security feed and brought up the image, relegating it to a window in my lower peripheral. The camera was pointed at the front doorway of the building. Scanning forward until shortly after three in the morning, I saw a figure step into frame. It was a small person, a woman or maybe even a kid; it was hard to tell because it was wearing a large overstuffed parka and a thick wool cap. The figure stopped with its back to the camera, swaying a bit as it watched the door. After a moment, the person stumbled forward on a pair of skinny legs and wobbled up to the door, clearly drunk.

I watched as a pair of gloved hands stuck the card to the window of the door; then the figure turned to look around, and I could see it was a young woman. She looked back at the card to make sure it was still there, then climbed back down the stairs and moved out of frame.

She come back?

No. Friend of yours?

Never seen her before. Who is she?

Some third. Father died in an industrial accident. She's living off the settlement, if you could call it that.

The smell near the truck was starting to get to me. I took a look at the revivor lying on the ground, now under a wool blanket. The components inside looked a little better than the others, but they didn't survive either.

Bring her in, Noakes said.

Sean got tasked with the autopsy of the dock revivor, but it had been a long time since he worked on one. Revivors were kept on ice when they were in the country, in case of public emergency, to round out National Guard numbers. They were only shipped out of the country, never in, except by black marketers like Tai. Finding useful information about them was going to mean going to the source: Heinlein Industries, the company that developed and built them. Since they were the country's largest government contractor and highly political, that was going to make a lot of people nervous, but it couldn't be helped. Smuggling a revivor into the country was not an easy thing to do, and someone who was able to manage it needed a lot of underworld contacts that put him at huge personal risk. That kind of service was expensive; no one spent that kind of money for nothing. Revivors and guns equaled one thing.

Someone out there meant to stir up some trouble.

3

Sub Rosa

Faye Dasalia — Shopping District

When I arrived at the scene, the car had been taped off
and the driver's-side door was hanging open. The sun
had started to melt some of the snow that was covering the windshield, and I could see the woman's stark
white face through the gap. Shanks was standing by
the car, holding two paper cups with steam coming off
them.

"You've got something on you," he said, pointing to
my sleeve. I looked down and saw a series of reddish-
black splotches smeared near my cuff; blood from the
revivor. It had taken some scrubbing to get it off my
hands, and I still couldn't get rid of that tar smell.

"Footage of the truck fire is streaming everywhere,"
he said, handing me one of the cups. "That was a hell of
a thing."

"Yeah."

"You actually touched one, huh?" he asked.

"What was left of it."

"What was it like?"

I wasn't sure how to answer that, mostly because I wasn't exactly sure how the whole thing had made me feel. I didn't want to think about the revivor. I didn't want to think about the fire or the call I made. Wachalowski hadn't been there. They said he was in the field and wouldn't forward the call. I had to settle for his office voice mail, leaving the information and asking him to call me. Now I wished I could take the last part back.

"Are you okay?" Shanks asked.

"It's not our problem," I said. "I called the FBI; they can handle it. I'll probably just have to make a statement."

"Lucky you."

FBI always meant first tier, and government-employed, first-tier citizens were pretty much golden boys. Wachalowski had served not just his minimum tour, but for years after that. When he'd left me behind, he'd done so in more ways than one.

"Yeah, lucky me."

I approached the vehicle and looked inside. It was the same as the other crime scenes; Mae Zhu had a single puncture wound to the chest that drove right into the heart. Death was almost instantaneous.

The woman had been in the car for hours and she was starting to freeze up, her white blouse stained almost completely red. She was a small woman, with pale skin and tiny hands. Her head lolled forward and her eyes were just barely open, still staring almost wistfully at the hole beneath her chin.

I crouched down, leaning in for a closer look. Her seat belt was unfastened. Her keys were lying on the floor near her feet, as if they had fallen there from her hand. Her purse sat on the divider between the driver's and passenger's seats, and an expensive leather wallet lay open on the dashboard. The driver's license was there, along with a few top-shelf credit cards.

"Mae Zhu," I said, reading off the license. "Do we know who she is?"

"First tier, but never served."

I nodded. So far, that was the one thing the victims all shared in common. None of them shipped off, and none of them were wired for reanimation, but they were all first tier. That didn't happen unless you had special skills or connections, but I hadn't been able to determine what either of those might be.

I looked down the street at the people moving past the barricade. They all wore expensive clothes. The cars on the street were all like Mae Zhu's vehicle: high-end, and built for luxury. The building faces were all glass and marble, towering to impressive heights. There were security cameras everywhere.

"A lot of people have money and connections," I said. "What's he going to do? Kill all of them?"

There was a faint depression in the leather of the backseat where someone heavy had sat for a significant period of time. The person sat in one spot and didn't move. He would have been visible in the rearview mirror when she got in, so he attacked right away. The mirror hadn't been flipped, so the victim arrived during the day and was killed before she adjusted it.

I looked at the wound. In all the cases so far, the wound to the chest was always the cause of death and it was always the same: a single penetration through the sternum and into the heart. The blade struck with enough force that it always went clean through on the first shot. It penetrated without fracturing, so it was also very sharp. The fact that there was never any bruising around the wound implied that the hilt never impacted, and so it was also fairly long. No metal traces were ever left in the wound, so it was most likely made of some kind of superhard plastic.

None of that narrowed it down much. A lot of blades fit that description, but the exact weapon was just another mystery in a case that was full of them. The dimensions of the wound didn't seem strange at first, but I had been so far unable to match them to anything, and that was unusual. The weapon was significant to the killer, most likely. Something he may have crafted himself, or that wasn't commonly available.

What now?

What Dr. Pyznar called my voice and what I called my intuition seemed to get more talkative the more tired I got. I still believed it was just that internal self we all spoke to at one time or another, that entity we consulted when we wondered if we were doing the right thing, or when we were alone and talked to ourselves. Mine was just louder than most.

Now we look for clues, I answered.

I looked at the rearview mirror; she would have seen him there after he grabbed her from behind. With her head pinned, she would have seen his face in that mirror as he leaned forward, bringing the knife around.

"CSI has to have picked up *something*," I muttered to the dead woman.

He doesn't leave hair, sweat, or skin flakes. Is that even possible?

Apparently.

Nothing obvious was missing from the wallet, and the glove box hadn't been tampered with. He never took anything, and he never left anything.

There's something unique about him, my inner voice

said. *He's not like other people. That's why you draw such a blank with him.*

That was true; a blank was exactly what I was drawing. It was truer than I would ever admit out loud, even to Shanks. Killers were usually passionate if nothing else, and the passion of their crimes, whatever they happened to be, were imprinted on their victims and their families forever. They left trails, even when they weren't physical ones. Even when they thought they planned well, they left trails, and every killer, no matter how far out there, had a reason for killing.

If I could just understand why, I thought, *that would connect them. It doesn't matter if the reason is typical or completely insane, but I can't figure it out.*

That scares you, doesn't it?

A little.

Let me do what I need to do, he had said. He had a reason.

You can understand why someone might want to kill a first tier, can't you? Especially one who never had to crawl through a trench to get it. You can feel that, can't you?

Yes.

People killed for jealousy all the time. They killed out of resentment, out of a sense of injustice, all the time. People who didn't have things resented people who did, even if it was only secretly. Sometimes they hated them. Sometimes it drove them to violence. Every one of the victims so far would most likely have looked down on me in life, so I could understand how the thing that seemed to connect them all might drive someone to kill.

I also knew that wasn't it.

It's because he's different, the voice said.

Well, if you know something, then clue me in.

Maybe I will, but not yet.

Backing out of the car suddenly, I had to grab the door to keep from slipping on the ice. The scene shifted in front of me like I was going to nod off right there, and I shook my head to clear it. Feeling a little dizzy, I took a deep breath and stood there for a moment, trying to focus.

"This is crazy," I said under my breath. Maybe Pyznar was right; maybe I was pushing it too hard. It was one thing to bounce ideas off yourself; it was another thing to suspect your inner voice of withholding information from you.

When I looked back at the crowd, no one seemed to have noticed, but everyone was filming. Every move from every angle was being streamed live and would replay on the news channels for the rest of the night or until something better came along. A crime scene was no place to start exhibiting strange behavior.

"You getting anything?" Shanks asked. He was hanging back by the curb, giving me room.

"There's a lot more to this story," I said.

"Drink it before it gets cold," he said, nodding at the paper cup. I took a gulp of the hot, bitter liquid.

"Something else is still bothering you," he added.

"That call this morning."

"He wants to rattle you."

Whoever it was, he was smart; the trace had failed to find the source of the call, and even the voice analysis had been a bust. He was using some kind of electronic filter that not only altered his voice to mask any accent or even any clue as to his age or ethnicity, but even canceled out all background noise. The techs couldn't get anything, not even traces of breathing or heartbeat. He was very careful before placing his call. He wanted to tell me something.

Shanks watched me, his eyes a little concerned.

"Never mind," I said. "It's just been a hell of a morning, you know?"

"I know."

I signaled to the coroner that it was okay to move the body.

What about Wachalowski? the voice wanted to know. *What are you going to say when you see him?*

I'm not sure.

What made you decide to call him? Who is he to you?

He can help.

How do you know?

I felt my head nod again and pinched the skin on my arm, twisting it until it hurt. I breathed in the cold air and focused, inwardly coaxing my body like it was an old car threatening to stall. On the one hand, I did wonder why I thought that, but on the other hand, I was sure that he could. I didn't even know how or why, but I felt sure of it.

That was going to have to be enough.

Zoe Ott—Pleasantview Apartments, Apartment 713

"It got split," the dead woman said, holding out the heart. I was back in the green concrete room, sitting at a folding table that was set near one end. She walked over to the switch on the wall and pushed it into the up position.

A single light snapped on at the far end of the room, shining down on a figure standing there. This time it was a man with leathery brown skin, dressed in an Army soldier's uniform. He looked part Asian, maybe in his thirties or so, but it was hard to tell. His hair and even his eyebrows had been shaved off, and his eyes were pale and silvery, glowing faintly in the dim light.

"A revivor?" I asked. The dead woman didn't answer; she just watched as I got up and moved closer to the figure under the light.

"Do you know who he is?" she asked.

"No."

His jaw looked like it had been wired shut, and even under his brown skin I could see black veins standing out. It was definitely a revivor. Leaning closer I looked at the name patch on his chest.

ZHANG

"He's dead," I said. "Who was he?"

"A piece of history few will ever know."

Looking away from the man, I turned my attention back to the dead woman to find her staring at him intensely.

"Why are you showing him to me?" I asked.

Just then a phone rang, startling me. The dead woman turned to the wall next to her and touched her fingers to a metal panel that I'd seen before but never paid any attention to. She pushed it and it swiveled outward, revealing a handset inside. The call light on the handset flickered as it rang again.

"Answer it," she said, and I woke up.

Cracking my eyes open, I found myself in stuffy darkness, and realized I was in my bed, under a pile of blankets. When I heard the ring, I thought it was a remnant from my dream.

A second later, I heard the ringing again. I thought it might actually be my cell phone.

Groping around under the covers, I felt it under there with me and rolled over, twisting myself into the blankets. In my hand the little call light flashed. Was this another dream?

Answer it, she had said. My hands trembled in front of my face like they did usually in the morning as the light kept flashing. I pried it open and answered it.

"Hello?"

There was a pause, and a man answered.

"Zoe Ott?"

"Yeah," I said. "Who is—"

Usually I forgot chunks of the previous night; that wasn't that strange. More often than not the memories never came back to me, and the only reason I knew they happened was because I'd left some kind of evidence behind. Sometimes, though, they'd come back to me in a flash.

"Shit."

"Excuse me?"

All at once I remembered the bitter cold, the monorail ride, and the snow banks bordering the sidewalk. The lights and the sounds all came rushing back to me.

I hadn't just left the apartment; I went all the way across town. I went all the way to . . .

"Is this Agent Wachalowski?" I asked weakly. I waited, hoping I was wrong.

"Yes, it is," the voice said. "How did you know?"

I had actually done it. I had actually gone and really done it. At some point during the night, after I thought I had safely passed out, I had gotten back up, found the FBI building, and left a note. No, not a note—a card. I left a little card.

My ears were burning. He must have thought I was a complete idiot.

"Ms. Ott?" he prompted.

"Yes?"

"I got your card. I'd like you to come in so I can talk with you. Is that okay?"

"You want me to come in?"

"Yes."

I needed a shower, and I couldn't remember the last time I shaved my legs or my pits. I hadn't done any laundry in as long as I could remember, and even washed I probably looked like a train wreck. My mouth tasted like sour puke, and when I held up my hand to check it, my fingers were shaking. I tried to concentrate on them, but I couldn't make them stop.

"Ms. Ott, is that okay?"

When he calls, go to him.

"When?"

"Can you come down now?" he asked. "I promise I won't keep you long."

"Am I in trouble?"

"No, ma'am, you're not in any trouble. I'd just like to speak with you."

"Why?"

"Because you indicated on your card that you could help me," he said, "and I'm hoping that's true."

My mind was racing and I felt like getting out of bed was going to be difficult, never mind getting across town. A million reasons why I shouldn't go came at me in a blur, and I answered before one of them could take root.

"Sure. I'll come."

"I appreciate that."

"Just give me an hour."

"I look forward to meeting you."

Folding the phone shut, I struggled out of the blankets and jumped onto the floor, which was freezing. I pulled off my nightshirt and threw it away in a pile, trying to get it together. On the bed next to the pile of blankets was an overturned glass in the middle of a big sticky stain, an open spiral notebook, a crumpled cardboard box, and a ton of sugar cookie crumbs. He couldn't see me like I was.

I took a shower so hot the bathroom filled with steam, then gargled and brushed the life out of my teeth. I washed my hair three times and started to shave my legs, but ended up nicking myself so many times I just gave up and put on pants instead.

I scrubbed my face, my hands, and combed my hair until it was completely straight, which it hadn't been in a long time. Pulling some clothes out of one of the unopened dry cleaning bags, I got dressed, drank a few shots until my hands stopped shaking, then gargled and brushed my teeth again.

A little over an hour later, I was standing on the sidewalk, facing the steps leading up to a big building and feeling self-conscious. I sort of remembered standing there the night before, but barely. The steps and the area extending out toward the sidewalk in front of them were polished marble, and the building itself looked big and imposing. The whole front of the place looked like black glass divided into panels, and in the center were two doors made of the same glass. It was pretty much the most unwelcoming building I had ever seen.

Taking a deep breath, I marched up the steps and right up to the doors. I grabbed the right one and pulled, but it didn't budge. I pulled again and it still didn't open, so I tried the other one, but it was stuck too.

"Name, please?" a woman's voice said, making me jump. It took me a second, but I realized it was coming from a speaker mounted in the glass. Someone was watching me from inside.

"Zoe," I said. "Zoe Ott."

There was a pause; then the woman spoke again.

"Identification?"

"Sure . . ."

I dug around inside my bag until I found the black laminated card with my picture and the worn gold emblem on it.

"It's kind of old—"

"Hold it up to the reader please," the voice snipped.

I found the scanner mounted near the speaker and held the card up to it. A little yellow light blinked on the front of the reader and began to flash.

"Ott, Zoe," the computer interrupted, loud enough to hear on the sidewalk. "Third class. Violations including public drunkenness place you as security risk: low."

"Thank you," the voice chimed back in. "You're expected. You may enter."

"Great."

I stuffed the card back into my purse and pulled the door handle again. It opened smoothly, and I stepped through into a small area where there were another set of doors leading in. I pushed those open and found myself in the lobby.

"Wow."

The lobby wasn't huge, but it looked impressive. The floors were polished marble inside too, with a big round seal etched into the center of it and ringed with brass. There were big potted plants and flags, and everything looked very clean and expensive. As soon as I stepped inside, there was a guard station with a metal detector, where a stern-looking bald man in uniform sat.

"Step through, please," he said.

I passed through and immediately a bell went off.

Everyone who was milling through the lobby turned to look as the guard stood up and stopped me.

"I'm sorry—"

"It's okay, ma'am."

He took my purse and jacket as I set it off two more times before I made it through. The guard scanned my things, the contents displayed on a screen as he passed his wand over them. He paused for a moment when he saw the flask, but he didn't say anything and he didn't hold me up any longer. Instead he picked up a phone and spoke into it.

"Sir? Yes, your visitor is here. I will, sir."

He hung up and handed me my things.

"Take that elevator," he said, pointing across the lobby. "Head on up to the fifth floor, then take a left. You want conference room B. Someone will be with you shortly."

"Thanks . . ."

I shrugged back into my coat and took my purse. The guard had already turned his attention to something else, so I walked away and headed to the elevator, pushed the button, and waited.

When the car came, I got in and stood between two tall men in suits who looked at me like I was a bag lady. The inside of the elevator was polished brass or something, and I could see my reflection in it as well as those of the two men. Neither of them said hello. The car moved so smoothly I didn't even notice it had started up at first, and it didn't make any of the noises the one at my apartment made. By the time we reached the fifth floor, I was so uncomfortable my heart was beating fast and my face was red and blotchy. Fortunately, neither of the men got off when I did, and I quickly left the car, turned left, and walked until I saw the room marked B.

I slipped in and leaned back against the big conference table inside, trying to get control. I took the resume I'd printed up out of my pocket and smoothed it out. I was still self-conscious about the wording, and I wasn't sure if "clairvoyant" was misspelled. I started to crumple it up, then smoothed it out again.

"Get a grip," I told myself, fanning my face with my shaking hands. What was I doing there? From the second I walked up to the place, it was obvious I didn't belong there. These people, in their suits and uniforms, thought I was a complete loser. Next to them, I looked ridiculous.

Before I let myself go any further down that road, I decided to risk using the flask. I took it out of my purse, uncapped it, and tipped it back, filling my mouth once, twice, then a third time before I heard someone in the hallway and almost dropped it. Clenching my mouth closed, I screwed the cap back on and stowed it back in my purse a second before he walked in.

"Ms. Ott?" he asked. It was him. I swallowed the fiery liquid down in one gulp, bringing tears to the corners of my eyes.

"Yes?"

He was going to smell it—there was no way he wasn't going to smell it—but it did make me feel better, calmer. I fumbled a stick of old gum out of the pack in my purse and stuck it in my mouth.

"You can take your coat off if you like," he said. "Just put it on the chair there."

I took the parka off and propped it on the chair. It was weird actually being in front of him. He seemed a lot bigger in real life, and having him looming over me was kind of intimidating. He wore a dark suit and white shirt and tie like the other men I'd seen, but his knuckles on both hands were covered with stick-on bandages, several of which had a dark spot seeping through. He had a cut on one cheek, and his face was bruised. He looked tired.

"I'm Nico Wachalowski. It's nice to meet you," he said, holding out his hand. I shook it, and he gestured for me to sit down, so I did. He sat down across from me.

"So," he said, "your card said you could help me. Help me how?"

The card. I tried to remember what was on it, but as far as I could remember it was just my name. It wasn't even a real business card; it was just some stupid thing I made. All I could think about was how I'd just seen him on the news, and how he must have been in the middle of something important. I was totally wasting his time.

"Why did you really call me down here?" I asked, and immediately kicked myself.

"Sorry?"

"It can't just be the card," I said, my mouth moving on its own. "You don't even know who I am. . . . Did it say anything else?"

As soon as I said that, I wished I hadn't. He raised his eyebrows a little.

"You wrote it," he said. "Didn't you?"

Booze or no booze, my face got hot again and I knew it was obvious. My mind went blank and I couldn't think of anything to say. The longer I went without saying anything, the worse it got, and I started feeling panicky. All of a sudden, I thought I was actually going to start crying.

Don't you dare . . . don't you dare . . .

"It was the doodle," he said. I looked back up at him and he was looking at me, but not like some of the others did. He wasn't looking at me like I was a piece of dirt, or like he was sorry for me or embarrassed for me; he was just smiling a little. His blue eyes were on me as I nodded, but I still wasn't sure what he meant.

He slid the card across the table with the back facing up, and tapped the corner where I had scribbled some kind of little pattern.

"Do you know what that is?" he asked.

"A doodle?"

"Well, if it is, it's a doodle of the waveform that's generated when a revivor's systems reanimate and come online. It's called a revivor heart signature. Does that sound familiar?"

I shook my head.

"What's really interesting," he continued, "is that your doodle is even more than that. Every signature is unique, and your doodle matches, for all intents and purposes, the signature I pulled off a revivor found at the Palm Harbor docks yesterday."

He was looking at me more intensely now, orange flickering in the pupils surrounded by that cold blue. The booze had finally started working its magic and was hitting me all at once, making it harder to concentrate. My anxiety was melting away, and I started to relax.

"Can you explain that?" he asked.

I couldn't explain it, because I had no idea what he was talking about. He was kind of cute in person, I decided. He was nice, too. He didn't treat me like a lot of the others.

His phone rang. He reached into his suit jacket and checked it, but didn't answer. It looked like maybe he was reading a text. When he put the phone away, I could tell something was bothering him.

"Who was that?" I asked. He raised his eyebrows.

"An old friend. She wants to meet for lunch."

"Are you going to?"

"Look, Ms. Ott—"

"I can help you," I said.

"How?" he asked. His attitude was different, and I thought I was losing him. I remembered the resume I held in my lap. It shook a little as I put it on the table and slid it across to him, just like he had done with the card.

He took the paper and looked at it. He read it for a couple seconds; then his face started to change.

"I'm serious," I told him.

"You know," he said, folding the paper and putting it on the table in front of him, "I can see that you are."

I had blown it. All at once, the anxiety was back and I sat up straight. Damn it, I knew the resume was a mistake; I shouldn't have given it to him.

"Wait," I said.

In a few seconds, he was going to send me home. I didn't know what else to do.

The room got brighter as I stared at him, until it was so bright that the only colors I could see were the ones that hung above his head. They were complicated, but shifting toward red. I pushed them back, soothing them until I saw his face relax.

"You need to give me a chance," I said. "If you could know one thing right now that you don't, what would it be?"

He paused for a couple seconds, considering.

"Did she love me?" he asked.

"Something to do with your case," I said.

"We have a suspect in custody. I need him to talk."

"Good," I said. That was perfect, actually. That was something I should be able to do. "I can make him do that. Don't think about it. Just trust your instincts and take me to him. When we get there, do what I say and I'll prove it to you. Do you understand?"

"Yes."

I let go of the patterns above him and let them resume their flow as the brightness subsided and they faded from view. The room returned to normal, leaving us sitting there facing each other. Agent Nico was looking at me now differently from before, but it was hard to say exactly what he was thinking. The seconds ticked by, but I didn't want to jinx it by saying anything.

"Follow me," he said finally.

"Really?"

"Really."

It had worked. He stood up and waited for me to come around the table; then he walked down the hall and I followed him to a door with a little glass window that was blocked from the other side. He opened the door, and I could see there was a man inside.

"Is that him?" I asked, trying to get a peek through the doorway. Nico seemed to be deliberately standing in front of me, trying to block my view.

"Yes," he said, "Ms. Ott—"

"I'm listening," I said. I caught a look at the man through the doorway; he was big like Nico, and dressed in an orange prison uniform. He was sitting in a wheelchair, and from the look of him, he'd been in some kind of accident. He was staring at the floor, and all around his eyes his face was swollen and bruised black and blue. He had cuts on his cheeks and a square piece of gauze was tented over his nose with a strip of adhesive tape. His lips were split, with a couple of stitches in the top one.

"No, you're not," Nico said, and stopped talking. I looked up to see him looking down at me, waiting.

"Not what?"

"You're not listening," he said. "Pay attention."

"Okay, okay."

"Stay on the other side of the table from him," he said. "He's in bad shape and he's restrained, but he's had extensive body modification, so he's tougher than he looks. He's on painkillers that will keep him calm and also keep his motor skills fuzzy, but play it safe."

"I will."

"What are you going to do?" he asked. "Do you need anything?"

"Just let me talk," I said, "and don't say anything."

He pushed the door open and went inside. He reached up over the door and did something, then motioned for me to follow. As we approached the guy in the wheel-chair, he was looking at his leg. I couldn't see it before behind the table, but one leg was held out straight in a metal brace. The pant leg was rolled up, and I could see two metal rings around his shin, one under the knee and one above the ankle. Metal pins were stuck into his skin and the whole middle portion was wrapped in gauze. His foot was swollen and black, the toes sticking out like fat little sausages.

I focused on him and saw a violet light prickling above his head, red spikes jumping out. Even with the painkillers, he was in pain, but he was also experiencing some turmoil. He didn't know what to do.

"Hey," Nico said to him. "You've got a visitor."

The man looked over at me like he hadn't noticed me before.

"No shit," the man said. He was hoarse and his nose was plugged up. His front teeth were missing so his t's came out like d's.

"Answer her questions."

Nico turned to me. I was on.

"Are you okay?" I asked. It was the first thing I could think to say, seeing him like that.

"I hope you're not my conjugal visit."

He smiled slightly and winced. His remaining teeth were bloody. I thought about the bandages on Nico's knuckles. Had he done this? I wasn't expecting the man to look like that. One part of me was saying that he must have done something to deserve what he got, but another part of me wasn't so sure.

"I'm helping Agent Wachalowski," I said weakly.

"You're wasting your time."

I was going to have to try it soon, before he got too riled up. I was hugely aware of Nico's eyes on me.

"Relax," I told him.

"Screw you, you ugly little bitch!" he yelled; then, before I could react, he leaned forward and spit at me. I saw a red glob shoot out of the gap in his front teeth and felt something wet land on my face, above my eye and down across the bridge of my nose to my cheek. I felt a big surge of anger from Nico, who stood up so fast he knocked his chair back. I held up one hand, easing him back.

"Calm down," I said. "Both of you, calm down."

The man in the wheelchair had been glaring at me with a kind of satisfaction, but now his face relaxed as I eased back the light around him, shifting the violets and reds to orange, then blue. Nico put his chair back and sat back down.

"Sleep," I said. The man's eyelids fluttered.

His eyes didn't close but they looked unfocused, staring into nothing. The pain was gone from his face.

I glanced over at Nico, who looked surprised. He handed me a paper towel.

"Is this for real?" he asked.

"Shh."

I took the paper towel and wiped my face, then folded it in half, covering the smeared blood. I looked back to the man.

"Can you hear me?" I asked.

"Yes."

Nico had pulled a pad of paper out of his jacket and was scribbling on it. He put it down on the table between us, facing me.

His name.

"What's your name?" I asked.

"Alek Katebi."

Nico pushed the pad toward me and tapped it with his pen.

Who is he working for?

"Who are you working for?" I asked.

"I don't know who he is."

"You don't even know who you are working for?"

"That's how it's supposed to be."

Nico turned the pad to me again.

What was the revivor for?

"What was the revivor for?"

"I don't know," he said. "All I did was pick them up when they came in, and drop them off. The buyer had a deal with some local trafficker to piggyback the units through his regular routes. I don't know who the trafficker is. The trafficker doesn't know who I am, or who I work for. I doubt he ever even saw the units himself."

Where did you drop off the revivors?

"Where did you drop them off once you had them?" I asked. "The revivors, I mean."

He paused, and the far-off look left his face. His sudden change worried me. Was he coming out of it? He turned and looked at Nico.

"He knows who you are," he said.

Nico didn't respond, and the man smiled, showing the gap in his teeth.

"He doesn't care that you know. You can't stop it now."

"Can't stop what?"

"Maybe before this is over," the man said, "we'll let them eat the rest of you."

Another surge of emotion came from Nico, but he clamped down on it, leaning across the table to face the man.

"Were you there to pick up the revivor? Or were you there to destroy it?"

"If—" the man said, but that's all that came out. He jerked in his wheelchair so violently that I jumped in surprise. His eyes bugged out, and I heard a muted popping sound as the mellow blue light around his head expanded into an orb and burst like a soap bubble. A spurt of blood shot out of one of his ears and spattered across the table, leaving red dots on Nico's pad; then the man's body went limp in the wheelchair.

"Shit!" I said. "Holy shit! What the hell was that?"

Nico didn't answer; he was already up and checking the guy. He put his fingers to the man's neck.

Shit. The light above him was gone. Blood was dripping steadily from his ear.

Nico took a step back; then, after a few seconds, he made a call on his cell phone.

"Get a medic up here," he said. "Interrogation room 5-C. I've got a suspect down; he's dead."

"It . . . wasn't my fault," I said. Nico hung up his phone, still looking at the body.

"I didn't do it," I repeated, standing up. My legs buckled a bit, and I was having trouble catching my breath. Blood was spreading all down the guy's neck, seeping into his shirt. Nico looked over at me.

"I need to get you out of here."

"I didn't do it," I said.

"I know, but you're not supposed to be in here."

"But I—"

"Now."

He turned me around gently and put his palm on my back, guiding me out of the room. I caught one last look at the body in the wheelchair as he closed the door behind us.

"I'm sorry."

"Don't be."

He took me back to the conference room and handed my coat to me.

"Go back through the lobby," he said. "You were never in that room, understand?"

"I blew it, didn't I?" I asked.

"Just the opposite," he said. "I'll be contacting you again. Soon, I hope. For now, though, it will be better if no one here knows about your involvement, understand?"

I couldn't believe it. I think maybe my mind was blown a little, and I couldn't interpret it all. Was it me? Had I somehow killed that man?

"Understand?"

"Yes."

He put his hand on my shoulder, and a shiver went up my spine.

"Go back out the way you came," he said. "I'll contact you again soon."

Before I could say anything else, he left, heading back to the room with the dead man. I noticed there was some blood on my shirt, so I zipped up my parka to cover it up. As I headed back toward the elevators, I passed a group of people moving quickly in the other direction, but they didn't pay me any attention. On the trip back down the elevator I kept waiting for an alarm to go off or something, but nothing happened.

I pushed open one of the front doors and went back out into the cold, leaving Nico and the dead man behind me.

Calliope Flax—Alto Do Mundo

As soon as I got close to his place, I knew I shouldn't be there. It was way the hell on the other side of town—that was the first thing. The twerp was way off his turf, hitting that bar and ending up in the tank with the rest of us. No wonder his friends were crying their eyes out; the dumb shits were probably scared stiff.

Not this one, though; I'd give him that. He'd had it all worked out and cut himself loose, no sweat. If he was scared, he fooled me.

He tapped the top of my helmet and pointed left when we got to a set of lights. A ways back, the streets got cleaner; then they got dug out; then they got plowed. Now there were even little green trees in a row right down the goddamned sidewalk. The road was smooth, as though it had been paved not too far back, and all four lanes were packed full of sports and luxury jobs full of uptight snobs. All down the walk, it was long coats, shiny shoes, and leather gloves. Every guy looked like he ran a bank, and every woman looked like she was on TV. All of them looked at me like I was the worst piece of shit they'd ever seen.

When I looked back at Luis, he was smiling. He was

getting a kick out of the whole thing, but I wasn't. At the light I thought about gunning the engine and giving those assholes something to get tweaked about, but I was tired. I just wanted to dump him, pee, and get the hell out of there.

"How much farther?" I yelled back at him. The light turned red, and I rolled to a stop.

"We're almost there!"

When I looked back at the walkway, a bunch of people looked away. Right then, I caught the blues in my rearview.

Great.

The light turned, but before I even got a chance to move, I got waved over by a cop on a bike as he cruised down the edge of the walk. When he was on top of us, he chirped the siren.

"It's us!" Luis yelled.

"No shit, asshole." I pulled off and he came up alongside me, while another one rode over to back him up. Just like that, there were two cops in my face.

"Sir, cut your engine!" the first one yelled. I cut it while the other one walked over, talking in his radio.

"Remove your helmet, please, sir," he said.

I pulled it off, then planted it in Luis's gut, and he grabbed it. The cop saw my face and frowned.

"Sorry, ma'am," he corrected. His eyes did a sweep up and down me, looking for metal. They stopped on my left tit.

"What's in your jacket?" he asked, still staring. He'd found the lined inside pocket, but he couldn't see in.

"Nothing," I said. "What's the problem?"

"What's in your jacket?"

"My ID."

"Your ID should be readable at all times," he said. "Remove it, please."

Keeping my hands where they could see them, I unzipped halfway and reached in slow, then pulled the ID from between my two pairs of brass knuckles. He watched closely while his buddy stood in back of him like he was his goon.

"What's the problem?" I asked, holding up the card. He stared at it for a second.

"You're from Bullrich Heights?"

"Is that a crime?"

"Ms. Flax, what is your business in this area?" he asked.

"Is it against the law for me to be here?"

"What is your business in this area?"

"Just visiting."

"Isn't it a little late in the season to be riding a motorcycle?"

"You're riding one."

His eyes started moving across the bike, then made their way back to my jacket pocket.

"Step off the bike, please."

"What, are you kidding me?"

"Step off—"

"Sir?" Luis piped up. They looked over at him.

"Sir, I'm Luis Valle."

"I got your information," he said. "Weren't you in jail not two hours ago?"

"Yes, sir," he said. "It was a misunderstanding and I was released. I couldn't get in touch with my parents, and I didn't have fare or a rail pass. This woman was nice enough to give me a lift, that's all. She's just helping me out."

The cop stared at me for a little longer, then back at him.

"Really," he said. "She's just taking me home, and that's it."

He sighed and waved to his goon, who turned and went back to his bike, talking into his radio.

"I'm not going to write you up for the ID violation or the helmet violation for your passenger," he said. "And I'm going to pretend I didn't see your trick pocket there, miss. From now on, keep your ID where it can be scanned, and if you're going to ride two to a bike, then both of you need helmets. Got it?"

"Yes, sir," Luis said.

"You take him straight home," the cop said. "Then you turn around and go back where you came from. Understand?"

"Yeah, I get it."

"Move along."

He and his goon got on their bikes and took off, and I grabbed back my helmet and put it on. They were two blocks off when I fired my engine back up and left a strip on their pretty goddamn road and a cloud of blue smoke in their pretty goddamn air.

"Sorry about—" Luis started to say.

"Shut the hell up," I shot back. "And keep your mouth shut the rest of the way!"

He had some sense, since that's what he did. He just tapped and pointed until we got to his street.

"Nice place," I said when we rolled up.

"Thanks."

He hopped off and jumped up and down to warm up.

"Can I use your john?"

"Huh?"

·

"I need to pee."

"Oh," he said, looking up at his building. "Um . . ."

"Jesus, never mind."

"No, it's okay," he said. "I just don't know if my mom—"

"You live with your parents?"

His face went red and he frowned.

"It's just for college. The rent—"

"Uh-huh."

"It doesn't make me a pussy."

"Look, can I pee here or not?"

"Fine."

I followed him up the steps to the front door, where he flashed his ID at the security eye. It blinked and flashed a white light at us.

"Hello, Luis Valle, second class," it said. "Who is your guest?"

"A friend."

"ID please."

I pulled out my ID and showed it.

"Hello, Calliope Flax, third class," it said. "Mr. Valle, due to multiple violations including assault, illegal possession of a weapon, public drunkenness, and speeding, your guest is considered a medium-high security risk and will require verbal authorization to enter. Do you authorize entry?"

"Yes."

"Thank you," the eye said. "Please proceed."

He opened the door and we went in.

"Shit."

The hall was wide, with some kind of flat red carpet and fancy lights down the walls. Big plants in big pots were in between the lights. The place looked like a straight-up palace.

"This way," he said.

He took us down the hall to an elevator, then up to the one hundred thirtieth floor, where he and his parents lived.

"What are you going to tell your mom?" I asked as he flashed his key at the door and opened it.

"That we're dating."

"In your dreams, asshole. Anyone else live here?"

"Just my sister."

It turned out it wasn't a problem, since no one was home. He hit the lights and dropped his keys on the counter, but no one showed up or said anything.

"Guys?" he called. The place was quiet. "Guess they're out," he said.

"Bathroom?"

"Down there," he said, pointing. "Go. Go pee."

My boots clomped on the wood floor as I went down the hall to their head. The door was dark wood and had a brass knob. I pushed it open.

"Shit."

"Put the seat down when you're done," he called.

"Funny."

His toilet was almost the size of my living room and ten times nicer. When I walked through the door, it smelled better too. There was a big white sink and a huge white tub with jets in it that was big enough to soak in. All the faucets were brass, like the doorknob, and everything was shiny and clean. It looked like a picture in a magazine.

The toilet looked as shiny as the rest of it. It seemed wrong to sit there, but I really had to go.

When I was done, I started to head out when I caught a look in the mirror over the sink, and for some reason it made me stop. The mirror was huge compared to mine, carved around the edges and framed with shiny brass. I saw myself standing there in the middle of it, and compared to everything else, I just looked dirty. Beat-up jacket, big black eye, and busted lip. The bandage over my other eye was the cleanest thing on me. My picture didn't belong there with the rest of it, and this was just their shitter.

When I looked down, I saw a bar of clear soap in a tray, and next to that were two more that were wrapped in colored paper.

Just like that, I didn't want to be there anymore. I didn't belong there. If his folks did come home and saw me, there would be a shit storm.

When I left the toilet, Luis almost plowed into me on his way back from wherever he went. He looked jumpy.

"What's your problem?" I said.

"Nothing," he said. He rubbed his face, and when he was done his grin was back, but not all the way.

"Trouble?"

"No."

"Thanks for the bailout, then. I'm out. Nice can."

"Wait."

I was at the front door, one hand on the knob. When he said it, I knew something was up. I knew that before I got out of there, there was going to be a catch. No one gives you shit for free; there's always a catch.

"What?"

"Actually, something kind of came up."

"While I was in the john?"

"I made a call."

"It must have been a quick one."

"It was," he said. "I can't stay here."

"So don't."

"I need another ride."

"Look." I sighed. "You're cute, and thanks for the help, but I'm not a taxi. Got it?"

"Just one more. I promise that will be it."

"Why can't you stay here?"

"It's complicated. Please?"

"Where?"

"Your place?"

There's always a catch. . . .

"I'm out of here."

"I'll pay you—"

"Pay me? For what?"

"Just to give me a place to crash for a few hours," he said, putting up his hands. "Just so I can make some calls, and then I'll be out of your hair. I'll even buy dinner. Please, I'm in a bind—"

"Jesus—"

"What if I said I could bump you up to a two?"

That stopped me. It had to be bullshit, but it did stop me.

"I'd say you must be in trouble."

"I am."

Right when he said that, I saw it was true. He was pretty much full of shit, but right then, he was for real.

"I'd say you're a liar too."

"Not this time," he said. "If you help me, I'll try."

I didn't see how he could pull that off, but then, who knew? He was some kind of tech geek, he had rich folks, first class . . . maybe he could rig it. What was there to lose?

"Why'd you bail me out?" I asked.

He shrugged.

"I gave you the shiner."

"Oh."

For the first time that day, I felt like I could laugh. It must have been a pretty good punch.

"Come on," I said, and the grin came back, but like before, not all the way. It never came back all the way again.

With what I know now, I guess I get that.

Nico Wachalowski—Restaurant District

The restaurant Faye had suggested in her text was a noodle house sandwiched between two buildings where the streets and sidewalks were so crowded, it was difficult to get through. Cars sat bumper to bumper just beyond banks of frozen snow, while people shouldered by each other on either side of the road so that all I saw in front of me was a carpet of hats and scarves. If I hadn't taken the subway, I'd have never made it.

The restaurant was bigger on the inside than it looked from the street, but the lobby was filled to capacity and probably beyond it. Brushing snow off my coat, I looked around to see if I could spot her.

I'd meant to break the date. I didn't have the time to spare, and I didn't know what I would say to her. We'd been close once. It was more than a friendship. I didn't have any excuse for disappearing like I did.

Then there'd been the interview with Zoe Ott.

I wasn't sure what I expected out of her, but it wasn't what I got. I figured in a best-case scenario she might have some kind of tip for me, and when she first came in I stopped hoping for even that. In person she seemed disturbed, and from the smell of it, she'd been drinking. My first reaction was to send her home.

She did something, though. Somehow that pint-sized

woman with the bony shoulders and shaky hands sat down across from an ex-military killer and started pulling information out of him that no one had been able to get him to give up. She'd managed that, as best I could tell, just by asking him. I couldn't shake the way that strange little woman had controlled that situation.

Then either the guy killed himself, or the person that hired him did it remotely. That left me sitting in an interrogation room with a corpse, a camera I had shut off, and a civilian who probably had a substance abuse problem. The inevitable question as to why I let her in there in the first place, I didn't have a good answer for. The meeting with Faye would make me scarce for an hour. That's what I told myself.

"Nico?"

I looked across the room and saw her standing by the far wall, waving. She smiled, but her eyes looked nervous. The lower lids were red and she had dark circles under both of them. She looked tired, maybe even sick, but I smiled too in spite of myself.

The last time I saw her, we argued. I told myself it wasn't as though I never expected to see her again, but when I saw her like that, I think I hadn't. In some ways, she looked exactly the same, but the picture of her in my mind looked much younger. Had it really been that long?

Making my way over to her, I could see she wasn't sure how this was going to play out. Neither was I, to be honest. When I got close enough, I offered my hand.

She shook it, her smile turning into a smirk that took me back. Gripping my hand, she pulled me closer, then got on her toes to hug me.

"I missed you," she said in my ear, but she didn't let the hug linger. I found myself a little disappointed when she pulled away. When she did, her eyes darted to the scar on the side of my neck. She didn't ask about it; she just made a note of it.

"Come on," she said. "I got us a table."

We sat down, wedged between the window and two businessmen who were talking animatedly. She reached across and switched on the noise screen, tuning it until the chatter of the businessmen faded into the general din.

She ordered hot noodles that came with an egg sitting in another bowl next to it. I got some kind of spring ramen.

"Since when are you a vegetarian?" she asked, peering down at my bowl.

"I'm not."

She picked up the egg and cracked it, dumping the contents raw onto the noodles. She stirred them with her chopsticks, letting the egg congeal as the steam rose in little clouds between us. When she looked back up at me, her eyes darted to the scar again.

"Ask," I said.

"What happened?"

"I was injured," I said. "It happened when I was in the service."

"How far down does it go?"

"Pretty far."

She looked back at my face.

"Were your eyes always that blue?"

"No. They're replacements."

"Oh."

"It's good to see you, Faye."

She smiled, but her eyes were sad. She looked like she wanted to say something but was having trouble with it. I'm not sure if I did it to spare her or to spare myself, but I spoke first.

"You saw the fire from the train?" I asked.

She nodded. This was familiar ground. This was something we could talk about.

"Yes. The fire was fairly close to the train stop, so I got off at the next platform and followed the smoke."

"It was hard to tell from the footage," I said. "Did you approach the truck because you heard something inside?"

"Yes."

"So the revivor was animate?"

"At first."

"What made you help it?"

"I didn't realize it was a revivor at first. I thought she was alive. Even so . . ."

She sighed, her eyes looking distant for a moment.

"I understand," I said.

"I've seen plenty of bodies, but I can't get her face out of my mind. She was burned so badly."

"They don't feel pain," I told her, but she didn't look so sure.

"They don't," I said.

"It just seemed like so many of those people there were glad to see her like that."

"It wasn't alive."

"She was once."

"Yes, but it was too late to do anything about that. What you saw in the truck, they weren't hostages. I didn't rescue them."

"What were they, then?"

"Evidence," I said, and I could see that it bothered her. This was one of the big reasons why the government didn't want the general public exposed to revivors if they could help it. When they had to deploy them locally, they used them sparingly. They kept them in full uniform, with their faces mostly covered. People weren't supposed to relate to them. They were supposed to fear them. It's what they were for.

"I heard what you did," she said. "You risked your life."

"Not for them. Those women didn't sign up or donate; they were kidnapped and murdered. All I could do with them was deactivate them, dissect them, and hope something in there would lead us to whoever did this to them. So we can stop them from doing it to anyone else."

She smiled, but looked down.

"You've changed."

"Sorry."

"No, I'm sorry; I'm running on fumes."

"Stim wearing off?"

"Yes."

"You want tea?"

"I want sleep."

She stared into her noodles, stirring them.

"The girl, the revivor, it spoke to me," she said. "Before it died, or deactivated, it was trying to tell me something."

"What did it say?"

"It said to hide behind whatever I could and keep my head down, but I think it was rambling at that point."

I recognized the words as the last thing I'd said to the revivor, but didn't point that out.

"Anything else?"

"Yes. It said, 'Zhang knew the truth.' "

"Zhang?"

"Yes. It said I had to wake up, and then it said it again: 'Zhang knew the truth.' "

Zhang. That name had not come up at any point in

our investigation. Not on the client list or Tai's contact list.

"Does that name mean anything to you?" I asked.

"No."

I sent a message via my implant.

Sean.

Yeah?

I'm interviewing the detective that responded to the truck fire—

You mean Faye.

She was with the only revivor that made it before it deanimated. It looks like it dropped a name: Zhang.

Is that a last name?

I think so. Sorry, but that's all we've got.

I'll see what I can find.

Thanks.

When I brought my attention back to her, Faye was looking into my eyes intently.

"You have a JZ implant," she said.

"Yes."

"Did you get that in the service?"

"After the standard tour, I specialized."

"I know."

A pause developed and started to get uncomfortable. Neither of us felt like eating, and there wasn't enough time to get into the things we needed to talk about. I felt like I should ask her if she had gotten wired up for PH service, but I knew she had, and she knew that I knew. I felt like I should tell her it wasn't too late to serve now. They wouldn't throw her on the front lines at her age; she wouldn't be exposed to the things I was. Her reasons for not wanting to go were probably the same as they had been, though, and the truth was I didn't know whether I could argue my original position with the same conviction I'd once had.

"You know, it was strange," she said suddenly. "Afterward, when I was waiting there, I decided to call you. I was still on the ground with the revivor, and I'd just gotten through. I swore I saw the strangest thing."

"What?"

"For just a second, I thought I saw someone standing next to me."

"What did he look like?"

"That's just it—I couldn't see him. Just his outline, like he was invisible. Just a hole in the snow and the smoke."

I remembered the footprints I had seen next to the spot where she'd knelt, and wondered. She laughed a little.

"Too many stims," she said.

"Maybe not."

She wouldn't have seen anything like that before, but I had. I wondered if the person responsible for the fire hadn't been still standing there when she arrived. Maybe he just couldn't be seen.

She frowned suddenly, and looked me in the eye.

"How could you come back and not even call me?" she asked. She watched me as I didn't answer.

Before either one of us could say anything else, her phone rang. She looked apologetic, but was still watching me when she answered.

"Shanks," she said. "What's up?"

Her face fell just a little as she listened, and I afforded her what privacy I could by turning my attention out the window. The stream of cars was inching forward on the other side of the snowbank, as somewhere down the street the signal changed. A white van in the midst of them began to slow down.

"Are you sure?" she asked. She listened again, then nodded.

The van slowed down some more, and the gap between it and the car in front of it got wider, prompting the traffic behind it to begin blaring their horns. People inside the restaurant and outside on the sidewalk began looking over to see what the problem was.

"I'm on my way," she said. She snapped the phone shut and looked out the window.

"What's the—" she began, but stopped in midsentence as the van skidded to a stop and a couple seconds later the back doors burst open. Immediately, we both knew something was wrong, but before anyone could do anything, another man jumped out of the back and into the middle of the street. He wasn't wearing a coat, and from where I sat, I could see the explosives strapped around his torso.

The guy in the car directly in front of him saw them too; he slammed it into reverse and immediately crashed into the vehicle behind him. People on the street started to scatter, streaming by the window as they abandoned their cars and ran. A woman was slammed into the glass near where we sat and went down onto the sidewalk as Faye and I both stood up.

"It's a bomb!" someone inside shouted. People began getting up uncertainly, some pushing their way out, while others clustered at the windows, holding out digital cameras.

This is Wachalowski.

Go ahead.

We've got a suicide bomber at my location.

The man outside turned toward the window and I got a good look at his face. The skin was ashen, and the

lips and eyelids were grayish-black. The eyes looked
bleached white in the daytime light.

*It's a revivor. There's a revivor armed with explosives
at my location.*

Roger that. Is it threatening to blow?

Someone sent it here. It will detonate.

"Nick!" Faye shouted.

I pushed my way through the crowd and out onto the
street, displaying my badge to try to keep the worst of
the foot traffic off me. A kid scooted by my legs, and
another man clipped me as he ran past.

The revivor had a communications system, so I started
flooding it with a connection request. The revivor began
to look around, trying to find the source.

"Nicky!"

It looked in my direction and I met its eye, holding up
my badge so it could see. It hadn't picked up yet, but it
stopped looking, keeping its dead eyes fixed on me.

Faye reached me through the crowd and grabbed me,
physically pulling me back. She was stronger than she
looked, one arm gripping me tightly around the waist as
she began to force me away.

Call connected.

The revivor accepted the connection. As soon as it
did, I tried a brute-force scan of its memory buffer, but
never got the chance. Still watching me, it raised the detonator in one hand.

Time to wake up, Agent Wachalowski. The words
blinked in front of my eyes for a brief second.

I turned and grabbed Faye, throwing my coat over
her as I pulled us down to the sidewalk behind a box
truck. There was a bright flash of light, and a beat later a
loud boom slammed through the air, shaking the pavement and rattling in my chest. A blast of air and dust

rushed by, and something struck the side of the truck as the windows of storefronts buckled and exploded. Through the ringing in my ears I heard dull thumps as debris rained down over the clogged street, bouncing off hoods, windshields, and rooftops.

The explosion thundered down the streets as people ran screaming. I looked back to see the mangled remains of the vehicles that were closest to the blast. The van the revivor had driven was twisted into shrapnel, burning in the middle of the street. The revivor was gone.

When I looked back at Faye, she was staring at the spot where the revivor had been.

"Are you okay?" I said, my voice sounding muted in my own ears. She nodded.

Panic had erupted on the streets. All around, throngs of bodies were pushing and shoving at each other, trying to move through a mob that was quickly getting out of control. Sirens began swelling in the distance, coming closer. My head was spinning.

Trying to get through the crowd was pointless. I could barely keep my position, and Faye wouldn't have a chance. Already people were shoving past with shoulders, hands, and elbows. Screams filled the air as I saw a woman slip and go down behind a parked car as people forced their way past. I couldn't even get to her.

"Come on!" I shouted, grabbing Faye. She gripped my arm and held on while we pushed our way back to the closest storefront. When we pushed through to the door, I saw faces staring out at us from behind the safety glass. A newspaper dispenser crashed off one of the windows, bouncing back onto the sidewalk and knocking someone over. A man on the other side of the door looked at me and shook his head.

I held out my badge, and that got him to back up. The

door opened enough to squeeze through, and I dragged Faye in along with me.

"Get back away from the door!" I shouted.

It's a madhouse down here. What's going on?

They're organizing a response; stay low until then.

We've got dead and wounded down here.

Get inside and stay put. You can't do anything out there. Help is coming.

A man who looked like he was missing a chunk of his shoulder stumbled against the window and left a streak of blood as he scrambled away. The crowd had become one giant organism, ready to consume anything that got too close.

With no way to stop it, we stood there and watched it happen.

4

I, Oneiros

Zoe Ott—Pleasantview Apartments, Apartment 713

I found myself becoming giddy as I headed down the hallway to my apartment, and by the time I got to my front door, I was smiling uncontrollably but I didn't feel happy. When I unzipped my purse, my hands were shaking and I had to fumble for my keys.

The door next to mine opened and the guy with the red hair stepped out, making me jump and drop my purse onto the floor.

"Good afternoon," he said.

"Yeah, hi."

I scooped up my purse and dug my keys out, trying to find the one to the door. The man stood there and watched me as I managed to find it, then tried to stab it into the lock, but I couldn't keep it steady. The tip of the key quivered as I tried to home in on the keyhole.

"You look like you've had some excitement," he said. "Where have you been?"

"What?"

He was watching me, his expression not changing. It

was weird enough that I was about to focus on him and make him go back inside, when my key found the lock and I pushed it in and turned it.

"I don't see you out much," the man said. He was still talking, I think, when I pushed the door open, then slammed it behind me and turned the bolt. Shrugging out of my coat, I dropped it on the floor and sat down on the sofa, crossing my arms over my stomach and leaning forward.

My visit didn't go anything like I thought it might. The place was uninviting and everyone looked at me funny, if they looked at me at all. I didn't think I'd talk face-to-face with a suspect, and I never expected to see anyone look like that. He was so beaten up, it made me feel sick.

The image of his face clenching up and the blood spraying out of his ear kept playing in my mind over and over again. The popping sound that came from inside his head was horrible. All I could think of was him lying there in that wheelchair with blood draining out of his ear, splattering all over the floor.

Why did I go there? What made me think I could go there and deal with something like that? Nico didn't even flinch when he examined the body. How could that not bother him?

It worked, though.

Yes, it had worked. For whatever it was worth, it had worked, and Nico Wachalowski was now very interested in me, I could tell.

I remembered his hand on my shoulder, and the electricity I felt when he touched me. I hadn't been touched in so long it made me ache a little, just in those seconds before he moved it away. I shook my head. There were tears in my eyes.

The room was dark, and behind the shade across the room the sky was gray. I needed a drink. I felt sick, but I needed a drink more.

Someone knocked on the door, breaking me out of my thoughts. I should have ignored it, but instead I opened it like a zombie. It was the woman from downstairs. She was standing there with her hands behind her back and smiling, but her face fell when she saw me.

"Hi," she said kind of uncertainly. I didn't say anything.

"Karen," she prompted.

"Hi, Karen. What do you want?"

"I was thinking about it," she said. "I think cookies were the wrong way to go."

"Cookies?"

"Yeah. I brought you something better."

"Better?"

She brought her hands out from behind her back and held out a bottle. It was clear, filled with amber liquid. I looked at the label; it was top-shelf stuff.

"Wow," I said. She pulled it back just a little as I reached for it.

"The only catch is, you have to share it," she said, "with me."

"Gifts aren't supposed to have catches."

"I know, but this one does."

I felt kind of embarrassed that she thought she could ply me with booze, and even more so that it was working.

"When?"

"Now?"

Maybe I was still just delirious from everything that had happened, but my mouth opened and the word came out.

"Okay," I said, and she smiled a great, big smile.

"My place is a dump," I told her.

"That's fine," she said.

"Seriously, it's bad. I don't want to hear anything about it."

"My lips are sealed."

This is a mistake. You know this is a huge mistake. . . .

"My life is a complete mess," I warned her.

"Birds of a feather."

She stood there smiling, and I wondered what it was that some people had inside of them that made them enjoy meeting strangers and interacting with them. I wondered how the prospect of coming up here and getting me to just let her in the front door could put a smile like that on her face.

Stepping back, I let the door swing open so she could come inside. She made a face when she first walked in, but true to her word, she didn't say anything.

"Still want to stay?"

"It could use a little light," she said.

"I had a lamp, but it broke," I said. "You can sit wherever. I'll get some glasses."

"What about the overhead lights?"

"They burned out."

There were no clean glasses, so I rinsed two of them out and dried them off with a paper towel.

"What's all this stuff?" she called. "The notebooks?"

"My notes," I said. "Don't read those."

"Can I move them?"

"Yeah, just put them anywhere."

"Notes for what?" she asked as I came in with the glasses.

My face got hot. I couldn't tell her they were full of dreams and visions and other stuff she wouldn't believe.

I couldn't tell her they were pages and pages, books and books full of a crazy person's rants. I didn't know what else to say, so I just stood there not saying anything until her face started to fall again.

"This is going well, huh?" I said.

She shrugged, trying to keep her smile going, but she was getting uncomfortable too. She looked like she was starting to think this was a bigger mistake than I did.

"Sorry," I told her. "I don't know what to say."

I thought she might leave, but instead she got a determined look on her face and the smile came back, at least a little. She patted the cushion of the chair across from her gently, inviting me to sit down, and when I did, she filled my glass about an inch's worth.

"Tell me about your day," she said.

I drained the glass, and it felt good. Whatever it was, it was sweet and fiery, and burned going down. Not too much and not too little, and as I felt that heat trickle down my throat and into my stomach, it filled my nose with the smell of spice.

"You'd never believe me."

She poured me another one, and one for herself. After that, it started flowing pretty freely.

"You don't want to tell me," she said.

I shrugged.

"Has it to do with your gift?" she asked.

"My gift?"

"That thing you do," she said. "The way you calm Ted down. How does it work?"

"I don't know," I said, and swallowed another glassful. With my nose in the glass, I breathed in, drawing in the fumes.

"Oh, come on."

"Really, I wish I did."

"Are you psychic?"

"I don't know what I am," I said, shaking my head. "For all I know, we're not even really having this conversation."

I didn't notice right away because I was starting to get drunk, but she was looking at me all seriously, and the smile was gone.

"You really see things?"

Instead of answering, I held out my glass again, and she poured some more in.

"Like ghosts?" she asked.

"No."

"Visions?"

"They're not hallucinations."

"I didn't say that."

"They're not. I wish they were."

"Why?"

Because they scare me. They scare me to my soul, and if they are real and I'm not crazy, then a lot of terrible things are going to happen. . . .

"Because it all burns," I said, looking into the glass. What little light there was looked red through the liquor, shimmering like little hot embers. When I looked back at her, her eyes had gotten wider.

"What does—"

"I don't want to talk about that, okay?"

Karen nodded.

"Why wouldn't you let me thank you before?" she asked.

I shrugged.

"You know he used to hit me all the time," she said, looking down into her glass.

"I know."

"But not anymore," she said, "and that's because of

you. I know this is a touchy subject for you, but just let me say it, okay? I don't know what it is you do or how you do it, but you've been a big help. Whether you meant to or not, you made a difference to me. I've always wanted to stop you, to talk to you. I've always wanted to thank you, but I was afraid."

As she spoke, I felt this sort of heaviness coming over me, like a fog or water. The light in the room seemed to dim.

"I need to be clear about something," I said, and I was suddenly very conscious that my words were slurring. "I can't change anyone or anything. Calming down a violent person doesn't make him not violent—you get it? If I know something that's going to happen, I can't make it not happen. I can't change anything."

"You might think that," she said, "but you're wrong. People change things all the time. Maybe they don't do it by reaching into people's heads, but they don't have to. They do it by reaching out to them, even if it's just something little. That's how you change things, and anyone can do it. Even you."

She looked up from her glass, and her eyes were a ghostly color. Like moonlight. They glowed softly, and in that instant before she looked down again, they watched me with a cold, dead indifference.

I felt like the floor dropped out from under me, and my face started to feel cold. From outside the window I heard what sounded like a transformer blowing or a loud firework going off from blocks away. I thought I was hearing things, but she heard it too. When she looked back from the window, her eyes were normal.

"What was that?" she asked.

"You need to leave," I said. Another sound, one she

didn't hear, was getting louder. It was a sound like voices all talking at once.

"I'm sorry—"

"You need to leave," I said again, getting up. I felt light-headed and stumbled, almost falling back onto the couch. "I didn't go down there to help you. I went down there because you were being too loud."

"I don't believe you."

The voices were getting louder, and I could hear they were panicked and screaming. The room was getting darker, and the floor felt like it was moving underneath me.

"Something happened," I said. "Something terrible happened."

"What—"

"Get out!" I shouted, and she jumped, almost dropping her glass. The heavy feeling was getting worse. Everything was slowing down. I heard a smash as the glass slipped out of my hands and hit the floor. I was hyperventilating and I couldn't stop.

"Hey, are you okay?" Karen asked, getting up and reaching toward me. I slapped her hands aside and she backed away. I didn't want her to see me like this. I didn't want what I was seeing to be true.

"It's not fair!" I screamed. She was looking at me like I'd gone nuts, but by then it was too late for me to even try to stop it.

I stepped back over a body lying on its back on the floor. Three other men with strange silvery eyes hunched over around him. One turned and raised his head, red, gristly meat clenched in his teeth as he tore away a long strip of rubbery skin.

This isn't real.

The room disappeared. The voices became a roar as a stampede of men, women, and children charged around me and drowned out everything else. Their faces were burned, their clothing charred off their bodies. Some were bleeding; some were missing arms or legs, stumps flailing as they clawed their way past; some were impaled with pieces of metal, with their skin, bones, and guts torn away. They were screaming as they ran, screaming with eyes wide and blind with fear.

This isn't real.

Pieces of glass and metal began raining down from the sky as they fought, pushing tighter and tighter against each other until they could no longer even punch or kick their way forward. They piled around me until there was nothing left but the stinking, shoving, and screaming, and I squeezed my eyes shut, clamping my hands over my ears.

"This isn't real!" I shrieked, but it was and I knew it. It was real, and everyone was going to die, and everything was going to burn. Karen and me and Wachalowski and the dead woman . . . none of it mattered because it was all going to burn.

Calliope Flax—Bullrich Heights

By the time we got close to my place, I was so goddamn cold, Luis must have been freezing his second-tier nuts off. The buildings were jammed close together down my way, and no one ever came to plow any road except the main one, so snow was piled up in the places where people bothered to dig out. Down most side streets, the cars were buried ass to nose on both sides, stuck in ice until spring.

I took a left down Iranistan and steered the bike

down the narrow path between the stuck cars. The building fronts were covered in graffiti, and half the windows were boarded up.

"How do they get to work?" Luis asked. I didn't answer.

Up ahead was the old gun shop, or what was left of it, and for the first time in months, there were some guys in front of it. The Turkish guy who ran the market next to it was there in his wool hat, talking to two patrol cops with rifles. A third cop shoved the gun shop's bent gate open and went in, while a black patrol car with tinted windows idled nearby. The shop used to deal stolen guns under the table and other shit too, but that was a long time ago. Since then it had been torched.

"Are there always so many patrols down here?" Luis asked.

"No."

The black car gunned its engine when we got closer, and moved into the road to block our path.

Son of a . . .

We were stuck, so I hit the brakes and we slid to a stop a foot away from the armored front door. One of the two guys with the Turk came up to us with his hand out.

"Hands up," he said as he came around the side of the car.

"What the hell?" I said. "What now? We're just—"

"Hands over your heads! Do it!"

Luis's went up the first time, I think, and I put mine up there too. This guy was tense, one hand on his gun when he came up. The other one was calling in.

"One vehicle, two passengers. Vehicle ID . . ."

The first one looked Luis over, then me.

"Where's your ID?"

"In my jacket—"

I went to reach for it, and as soon as I moved my hand the gun went right in my face.

"Hands over your head!"

"Alright! Jesus—"

"Quiet!"

He unzipped the front of my coat and stuck his hand in, right to the lined pocket. He fished in there and pulled out my ID and both sets of knuckles. He checked the ID and scanned it, then looked back at his partner and shook his head.

"Negative," the other guy said in the radio. "Both passengers were processed earlier today, and were stopped again across town less than an hour ago. . . ."

The goon held out my ID and both pairs of brass knuckles as the black car slammed into reverse and rolled back out of the way. It took a second for me to get that he was giving me my shit back, even the brass. I took it and stuck the lot back in my coat.

"Move along," he said. Just like that; no fine, no ticket, no speech, just beat it. He stepped back and I went through.

"What was that all about?" Luis asked when they were out of earshot.

"No idea."

"Something must have happened. They're looking for someone."

"Not us."

He shut up and didn't talk again until we got to my street. The buildings were mostly dark there, the concrete black from smog and the windows broken or boarded. Rusted chain link leaned around empty lots where new graffiti covered old graffiti. One titty bar–slash-whorehouse had some of the last lit neon, along with some shit-hole martial arts dojo to the left and up. I took us through the concrete pylons holding up the maglev rails that crossed between the housing units, then down between the huge piles of brown ice and snow, mixed with piles of trash bags and dead cars.

"This is where you live?"

"Down here."

I pulled into my unit and down the ramp to the under-ground parking area that held two cars that ran, one that didn't, and my bike. I cut the engine, kicked it, locked it, and armed it.

"Come on," I said, climbing off and heading up.

The kid looked like he changed his mind, but it was too late for that now. He held up okay in jail, but now he looked twitchy.

"Take it easy," I told him. "You're okay."

He didn't look sure, but he tagged along after me when I buzzed in the back door and turned the bolt. Another badge at my unit, two more bolts, then the security bar slammed down in its track behind the door and I shoved it open.

"Come on in."

He made a face when he went in, like he just saw a rat or worse. He stood right inside in front of the couch and stared.

"This is where you live?" he asked again.

"Yeah. Fuck you."

"No, I know. It's just—"

"Whatever," I said. "You want the tour? That's the kitchen, this is the TV room, the can is through there, and through there is where I sleep."

"It's so small," he said.

I thought of his bathroom and how huge it was. You could see my whole place from the front door. The kitchen had a half fridge, two burners, a sink, and that was it. The TV area had the couch, the TV, a weight bench, and a heavy bag in the corner. The can had a shitter, a shower with industrial plastic sheeting, and a sink with all plain metal and no colored soap.

"Can I use your TV?" he asked.

"Knock yourself out."

He turned it on and flipped. Not long after, he found what he was looking for.

". . . the site of what witnesses describe as a suicide bombing, in broad daylight, right in the center of one of the city's restaurant districts."

It was total mayhem. The camera looked over the crowd, where cops were pushing people back. People all up and down the street had blood on their heads and faces, and there was glass everywhere.

"That's why the patrols are out," he said. "Shit . . ."

"If a bomb went off there, why look here?"

"They must be following some kind of lead. Holy shit, look at that," he said, sitting down on the couch.

It was bad; I had to say that. The place got blown to shit. There were dead bodies all over.

". . . took authorities several hours to completely quell the ensuing riot, which resulted in many more injuries, deaths, and damage to local property and businesses. Initial estimates place the damage in the millions. Mayor Ohtomo and his administration have been quick to respond, with plans to deploy the National Guard to prevent looting and other crimes of opportunity until the area can be completely secured. Given the range and impact of this attack, that will be no easy task. . . ."

Luis turned down the sound and got on his phone. He tapped his foot like a junkie.

"Yeah," he said. "I'm trying to reach Dr. Edward Cross, please."

Someone babbled on the other end, but I couldn't make it out.

"I know," he said, "but it's important. Would it be possible to have someone get him, or patch me through to the lab? I understand. You're sure he's there, though? He signed in? You're sure he's there? Okay, thanks."

He hung up.

"Trying to reach your doctor?"

"He's not that kind of doctor," he said, eyes on the TV. "Anyway, he's my uncle. Hey, you mind if I use the data miner?"

"The TV miner? Knock yourself out." He typed away with his thumbs on the remote.

"You said you'd buy dinner," I said.

"Sure, whatever you want."

I watched him work the TV for a minute, until hits and lists popped up on the screen and he started typing in weird shit I'd never seen before and using stuff I didn't know was in there.

"Don't get me in trouble," I said.

"I won't."

Promises.

Nico Wachalowski—FBI Home Office

People edged quickly past my desk as I checked for messages, and the normally quiet halls were filled with rapid-fire chatter. There was no word from Faye, Zoe, or any contacts that might provide a lead, just a battery of alerts and notifications marked high priority. A sweep was being set up that covered voice, text, and anything else they could think of. Any circuit that could have a tap shunted in was being monitored as computers sifted through the data, looking for leads. The scope of the effort was huge. So huge that just to get enough bodies on the street, an unprecedented number of revivors had been deployed to supplement foot soldiers at key points through the city. Whoever initiated the attack, they'd stirred up a hornet's nest.

My ears were still ringing, and I could still smell the burned biochemical stink left behind by the revivor that had detonated the bomb. Nothing useful had survived, but pieces of it had been thrown as far as two blocks away. Fused components were being dug out of vehicles, concrete, and even victims caught in the blast. Initial reports indicated military-grade explosives in a configuration that maximized the blast radius, so whoever wired the revivor knew what he was doing. Despite the relatively small amount of charge, the force was devastating.

Getting out of the restaurant strip had been dicey. We were pinned down until riot control got there, and by then it was a war zone. The explosion had killed at least fifty-three people and wounded almost two hundred others; then another nine died in the riot that followed— five crushed or trampled, three from clashing with other citizens, and one choked with a police baton in the heat of the struggle. Even with escorts, getting Faye to the perimeter was a struggle.

The inventory had come in for the arsenal recovered from Tai's base of operations. It included explosives that easily could have caused the kind of damage that occurred downtown. The bomb that killed all those people had come through Tai; I was sure of it. Whoever killed him was behind it.

I sat at my desk and watched the footage I had recorded from the interrogation earlier, the window floating behind my closed eyelids. Off to one side I kept a smaller window tapped into a camera that watched from the wall behind me, in case anyone came by.

"*Answer her questions*," I heard myself say. Zoe was staring at the suspect, which I had pretty much expected. What color she had drained out of her face. If she was any paler, she could have been mistaken for a revivor.

Given the circumstances, I had switched off the camera in the interrogation room, and I didn't disclose the POV recording I'd made myself either, but I wanted a record of the interview for my own use. When I first found out why she had really left the note, I had almost turned it off and sent her home. I was glad I hadn't.

"*Are you okay?*" she asked in a small voice.

I remember taking a small amount of satisfaction in that. Honestly, I figured once she got a look at the guy, she'd turn around and that would be that. She did better than I expected, though.

"*Who are you?*" the guy asked.

I scanned forward, looking for the moment when she did whatever it was she did. When I saw her arms go down by her sides and her head start to drift forward, I stopped.

"*—lax.*"

"*Screw you, you ugly little bitch!*"

He spit and a glob of red squirted out at caught her right in the face. The camera rose as I knocked the chair back and moved toward him.

I wasn't looking at her when it happened; I was looking at him. He was glaring at me with a defiant smirk, when all of a sudden his face changed. The smirk disappeared and his eyelids drooped.

"*Sleep*," I heard her say, and his eyelids fluttered. They stayed open, but his eyes went out of focus. It was as if he suddenly had gone blind or something. I had scanned him, getting a bead on his vitals; his heartbeat had slowed, and he was totally relaxed. He seemed, in fact, to be very close to sleep.

The camera moved back to Zoe, my hand moving into frame with a paper towel. I froze the image.

She was staring at the guy, her pupils almost completely dilated, like she was loaded on amphetamines. Her face had changed dramatically. I remember thinking that at the time, too. When she first came in, she was nervous, shy almost to the point of paralysis, despite the fact that she had clearly been drinking. Her eyes were always cast downward at the floor, at her shoes, or at her hands. Now she was staring right at someone she knew to be a killer, looking him right in the eyes. It was like a pair of invisible beams connected her eyes to his and neither one could look away, but looking at her face again now, I could see who was in control. She could have looked away at any time, but he couldn't have. Not until she let him. It was like a completely different personality had emerged from inside her, and the expression in her eyes as she stared at him from over that beaky nose was something that didn't seem to belong there.

Was it real?

Having done some research on the type of device used to kill him, I found out that it typically monitored for two things: a loosening of the inhibitions caused by prolonged, extreme pain, and a brain-wave state indicative of drug-induced mind control or hypnosis.

He wasn't in any pain. After the beating he took and the surgery that followed, he was on enough painkillers

that he wasn't feeling much of anything. He wasn't coerced with drugs at any point.

"*Can you hear me?*" she asked, as I resumed the
recording.

"*Yes.*"

I wondered whether she had known him previously,
if somehow this whole meeting was a setup of some
kind. The image of the revivor heart signature she had
scrawled on the card she left wasn't just an uncanny
representation; when I compared it to the one I had recorded from the female I encountered in the bathroom
at Tai's place, it was an exact match. Every revivor's signature was unique. She had to have seen it somewhere.

"*What's your name?*" she asked.

I'd seen hypnosis before, but never anything like that.
I knew his type, and he was ex-military. He was trained
on how to behave if he was ever captured, and he could
endure a lot of pain and interrogation. It didn't make
sense that a ninety-pound woman could walk in and
make him give everything up in less than a minute, but
that's what it looked like he was about to do.

The kill switch implanted in his head seemed to believe so too.

The more I watched her, the more interesting the
strange woman became. I needed to get her back, but
I didn't know if after what happened, I wanted to risk
bringing her back in. Maybe I could set something up
off the premises....

Backing up the recording, I watched as the man re-
versed out of his stupefied state and the smirk returned.
The spit jumped in reverse through the space between
his teeth and Zoe backed away; then the camera did as
well as we both moved back down the hallway.

If I had known what was going to happen, I'd have

watched her more closely, but as it was, I was focused initially on the suspect and, I had to admit, the message from Faye I had gotten earlier. The only other time we were alone was when Zoe first came in and I met her in the conference room. That had been a short introduction, but it was better than nothing. I kept backing up, looking for the moment when I first walked in and saw her.

The camera turned as we backed into the conference room and then sat at the table. For a while I focused on her face as she spoke, glancing down self-consciously; then I saw her pupils dilate. They dilated completely, just as they had in the interrogation room.

I stopped rewinding and let the footage play.

"*. . . and take me to him. When we get there, do what I say and I'll prove it to you,*" she said.

My eyes had been fixed on hers, just staring, with her staring up at me.

"*Do you understand?*" she asked.

"*Yes,*" I heard myself say, and I froze the image.

As sure as I was of anything, that had not happened. I would have remembered it. Frantically, I searched my memory for any trace of that conversation, but it wasn't there.

Stunned, I scanned back until her pupils returned to normal a few seconds prior.

"*. . . can help you,*" she said.

"*How?*"

That I remembered. I watched as she pushed the paper, her skill list, across to me. I remembered the exasperation and annoyance I had felt when I first realized what I was looking at.

"*I'm serious.*"

"*You know, I can see that you are.*"

Her face changed, and then her eyes.

"*Wait*," she said.

"*Okay.*"

"*You need to give me a chance*," she said in a low voice. "*If you could know one thing right now that you don't, what would it be?*"

"*Did she love me?*" I heard myself ask. It was barely a whisper.

Zoe's eyes narrowed dangerously.

"*Something to do with your case*," she snipped.

"*We have a suspect in custody*," I told her. "*I need him to talk.*"

"*Good*," she said. "*I can make him do that. Don't think about it. Just trust your instincts and take me to him. When we get there, do what I say and I'll prove it to you. Do you understand?*"

"*Yes.*"

She stared at me as I paused the footage again. She looked at me exactly the way she had looked at the suspect. The nervousness, the shyness—they were gone, replaced by a confidence that seemed absolute. Was the awkwardness an act?

The JZI pinged. *Wachalowski, it's Noakes.*

Yeah.

There was nothing left. The blast destroyed everything. Serial numbers, lot codes—it's all slag.

What about organics?

A team is trying to track down a piece we can tie to the revivor, but the site is a mess.

I understand.

No radiation was detected, and no biological agents, but see Sean anyway and let him check you out.

I'm on my way down now. Sir, that bomb was strapped to a revivor, another combat model. It was fitted with a standard communications array. It was definitely military.

Did you make contact with it?

I had extended the connection roughly a minute before the bomb went off. It didn't think it was going to accept it, but with less than five seconds on the timer, it had. I wasn't facing it at that point; Faye had come out of the restaurant and I was moving her away when the revivor had suddenly picked up.

Time to wake up, Agent Wachalowski.

That was all it said. Before I could respond, it was gone.

Briefly. It knew who I was. It had to have come from Tai's unknown contacts. They know we're on to them.

What about the detective?

She gave me a name one of the revivors from the fire gave her. Also, she saw something I think might have been the attacker underneath an LW suit.

There was a pause before I got a response to that one.

Light-warping technology is top secret. Only a few countries even have access to it. Do you have any idea how expensive that would be?

Someone has money to burn.

What about the name?

A last name only: Zhang. No leads on it yet.

Could it be the name of one of Tai's customers?

Maybe. I'm following up on the dock revivor now. I'll let you know what I find.

I switched off the images and made my way to the subbasement, then into the dingy corridor that led to the morgue. The morgue was usually Judy's domain, and she wasn't used to sharing it. When the door opened,

Sean was leaning over a body that was facedown on the tray while she hovered nearby, her arms crossed in front of her. She glanced at me when I came in. As I approached them, I caught a faint, bitter-tar smell.

"How's it going?" I asked. The room was brightly lit, and Sean was still bent over the body, squinting into a magnifying lens that was strapped to his head.

"Getting there," he said. He was peering into a square hole he had cut in the back of the revivor's skull, teasing at something with his instruments. His white latex gloves were smeared with blackish blood.

"Find anything?"

"Your news jockey's eyes were mostly intact," he said, nodding toward a fluid-filled jar on the counter where they now stared out through the glass at me.

"They're slightly different colors," I observed.

"Only one is a fake; the other one's natural. I was able to pull a little bit out of the buffer of the camera eye. I flagged it for you."

I connected to the server and checked it out. The first clip was little more than a few frames strung together; it looked like the SWAT team escorting one of the revivors out of the building after the raid. The next was actually a shot of me, from when he had approached me in the lobby.

"They go backward," Sean said, "from the end of the buffer back toward the beginning. The last clip was actually recorded first."

The last clip was a little over four seconds long. From the looks of it, the kid was standing in someone's private office. Even though the quality wasn't good, everything in his field of vision still managed to scream wealth. The desk looked like real wood, and on top of it I could see a polished stone clock with what might have been a diamond at the twelve o'clock mark. A small figure sat behind the desk.

"Is that a kid?" I asked. It almost looked like a little boy at first, except the clothes were those of an adult and the earrings were definitely feminine.

"It's a woman," Sean said.

Once I got a better look, I could see it was definitely a female, maybe full-blooded Asian, maybe Chinese. She was definitely adult, but very small except for her head, which looked a little too big for her body. She wore a navy suit jacket and white blouse with a gold neck clasp. I could make out rings on both hands, gold earrings, a slim gold watch on her wrist, and cuff links with what might have been real diamonds on them. Her face was made up heavily but carefully, and she might have been pretty except her lips and eyes were vaguely fishlike.

". . . exclusivity?" the kid's voice asked.

"I don't care what you do with it after you bring it to me—" the woman said, then was cut off as the clip ended.

"Someone hired him," I said.

"Someone with money."

Someone with money, and someone, based on the little bit of footage there was, who seemed uninterested in the monetary value of the footage itself. Whoever it was knew what she was after and must have known where to send him, since there was very little time between their exchange and the images of the revivors. She didn't want to use or sell the footage if she was turning down exclusivity; she wanted information. She was using him for recon.

I looked back at the eyes floating in the jar. Someone had gotten the kid killed. Someone looking for information on Tai. Someone who wasn't us.

"Apparently, we aren't the only ones interested in what was going on over there," I said. "What about the unit we recovered at the dock?"

"Deanimation was straightforward," Sean said. "A bullet to the head. You say the other models you picked up there were sex models?"

"Pretty much."

"Not this one," he said. "Check out the caboose."

I took a look between the exposed, flat buttocks and saw that the vaginal opening had been sealed, along with the anus. They did that with legitimate revivors after bring-back in most countries; revivors didn't have sex urges, couldn't give birth, and didn't eat. Any unnecessary cavities were just places to invite infection; packing them with biogel and sealing the whole thing over with a skin graft eliminated the problem.

"Any other bullets hit it?" I asked him.

"No, why?"

"I'm wondering if that bullet was meant for it or for me."

"Was it destroyed intentionally? No way to know for sure, but if it was, your shooter didn't exactly succeed. Have a look."

I leaned in close as he reached into the hole with a pair of slim forceps and carefully began to pull something out. When the end of the tongs came out of the hole, I saw they were clamped around a small, rubbery object about four inches long. It made me think of a translucent, eyeless squid with tentacles coming out of both ends. Sean slowly eased the thing out until the last little tentacle dangled free, then placed it into a large beaker filled with clear liquid.

"That's the main node," he said. "If a revivor had a soul, that would be it."

I took a closer look. I was familiar with revivor technology, but I'd never actually seen one of those things outside the body. I'd imagined it looking metallic, but it almost looked organic. Millions of barely visible little threads ran through it.

"You can see the connections," I said. Up close it looked like some giant microbe.

"You guys are going to clean this up afterward, right?" Judy asked.

"Sure."

I looked through the glass at the strange amoeba, sitting at the bottom of the beaker surrounded by a little cloud of stringy goo.

"It hasn't gone inert," Sean said. "You might be able to scan it."

I zoomed in and ran the scan; sure enough, the wriggling amber line coalesced, snapping into the familiar waveform.

"Nice."

I was able to pull the lot number, serial number, model numbers, versions . . . everything. Unlike the one in the bathroom, this one was legit; it had a valid code, so it was wired as part of a national program, and it had a military assignment tag as well, meaning it had actually been deployed. Either it never got where it was going or it was AWOL.

Also, unlike the one in the bathroom, the revivor components weren't manufactured overseas; they rolled off the line at Heinlein Industries.

"Sean, could these parts have been reused?"

"You mean harvested out of an existing unit and put into this one? No. I mean, some of the nuts and bolts, sure, but not the important stuff."

"Then we may have another problem. Let me see if I can get into the memory buffer."

I opened a connection to the revivor's communication node, then sent a specialized virus over the channel. It chiseled through security, then implanted itself and began to map the revivor's systems. A few seconds later, it sent a bundle of information back over the circuit.

"I've got something."

I pulled the access codes out of the bundle and tapped into its memory core. From there I sifted through recent communication entries. Some of them were encrypted.

A series of text entries appeared before everything scrambled and feedback started coming across the connection. A second later, it dropped. Something made a popping sound from inside the body, followed by a high-pitched hissing.

"Step away from it!" I said. They didn't ask why; they just did it. The hole Sean had made in the back of the revivor's neck expanded as white smoke began to pour out.

All at once, the back of the head and neck collapsed, followed by the shoulders and back. A clear gelatin had formed inside.

"Jesus," Judy snapped, watching the body melt in front of her eyes. She had seen many strange things on her table, but never that. I had seen it, though, and so had Sean.

"You can't stop it," I said. "Let it go. It isn't toxic."

"What is it?" she asked.

"*Leichenesser*," Sean said.

The buttocks, the backs of the thighs, then the calves all melted down like wax within seconds. The gelatin dissolved everything, even the oily blood on the tray beneath it.

Leichenesser was another controlled technology used in combat. It could start as a small seed, but it fed on necrotized flesh. It was used by the field meds to clean out gangrene and other infections, but in combat, it was very useful against revivors. A lot of the newer ones were seeded with it, set to go off in case their memories were tampered with.

"It only consumes dead flesh," I told her. "That fuels its growth. When there's nothing left to eat, it dissipates."

The gelatin continued to dissolve the body, and then it began to boil away into mist. In less than a minute, a single blob of it sizzled around a pool of blood in the middle of the tray like water on a hot pan. Then it was gone.

The tray was empty except for a few surgical instruments, some lightweight shield plating from inside the body, and the long blade that had been concealed up inside the forearm. Sean used his forceps to pick up a cluster of nodules webbed together that had been the revivor components fixed beneath the skull and along the spine, but they were ruined.

"What caused that?" Judy asked, leaning back in.

"I think I did," I said. The text I'd managed to pull off before I'd triggered the gelatin's release still sat in a window in the corner of my vision. I brought it to the forefront for a closer look. It was a portion of a list of names.

5. Mae Zhu
6. Rebecca Valle
7. Harold Craig
8. Doyle Shanks

I didn't recognize any of them. There were four missing from the head of the list, and any number that might have followed.

"I'll catalogue what's left behind here and see what I can get off of it," Sean said.

"You do that," I said. "In the meantime, I think it's time I poked my head in over at Heinlein Industries."

"Yeah?"

"Their product is popping up where it doesn't belong."

I pushed through the doors to the lab, and Sean followed me out, glancing over his shoulder as Judy frowned at the cadaver tray.

"As a heads-up," he said, keeping his voice low, "I sat on my findings regarding your suspect's kill switch as long as I could, but Noakes knows. He's going to want to know what you did to set a device like that off while you were alone with that guy in the interrogation room."

"Okay, thanks."

"What are you going to tell him?"

"The truth."

Even as I said it, though, I was replaying the recording in my mind,

. . . *don't think about it. Just trust your instincts and take me to him. When we get there, do what I say . . .*

He'd been coerced, but not by me. Before I talked to anyone else on our side, I needed to track down that woman again, and try to find out what the truth was.

Faye Dasalia—Alto Do Mundo

"Green light," Shanks said from the passenger's seat. It was snowing again, but the streets were filled with people, and even this far from the restaurant district, the unease was palpable. News of the bombing had saturated every form of media before authorities could even lock down the site. Every time a new report came in, the death toll went up. The carnage had been horrible.

A horn honked behind us, snapping me out of it.

"Faye, it's green."

I gunned the engine and pulled out and veered down the next ramp on my right. At the bottom, I edged out onto the main street, nosing past the stream of foot traffic. When the GPS stopped blinking, I pulled off. Hitting the blues, I flashed them a few times and tapped the siren as I crunched over a snowdrift and partially up onto the sidewalk as pedestrians grudgingly moved out of the way to allow access to the parking ramp.

"Look, Faye—"

"I told you I'm fine."

I left the blues on steady, then sat there for a minute, watching the light flicker off the snow and concrete while the garage cameras scanned the car and people trudged past, rubbernecking as they went. They all wanted to know what was going on. Who had set off the bomb and why? Were more attacks coming?

I didn't know the answers to those questions.

"You don't look fine."

I felt Shanks move his hand over my own around the steering wheel. I glanced at him out of the corner of my eye. His hand was warm and dry.

"No one would think worse of you if you took five," he said.

Shanks was a good guy. A good partner, and a good guy. He knew me as well as anyone did, I guessed, and he knew me just well enough to know I was fraying at the edges. He understood it. I felt like I knew where I stood with him, and it was tempting to give in to the stress and the fatigue and rest, but I couldn't. If I did, I might never get back up.

He's right. You're not fine, but you can't stop, the voice in my head whispered.

The mayor has placed the city on high alert. Every cop in the city has been deployed. We just had a terrorist attack in a major population center, and we don't have any idea who was responsible. Shouldn't we—

It doesn't matter. The killer *won't stop.*

We've got bigger fish to fry right now. They'll pull me off this.

They won't.

He won't kill again while security is this high.

He will, and you're going to find him. Don't question the rest. Just shut up and do your job.

I shook my head. My heart skipped a beat.

"Faye?" Shanks prompted. He was starting to look at me like there might be something really wrong. I wondered if he wasn't far off.

"Let's just do this."

Shanks had called in the middle of lunch to let me know the killer had struck again, this time taking not one but three victims right inside their own apartment in Alto Do Mundo: first tier and very rich, with lots of security. He had walked in and walked out again, and somehow no one had seen him.

All those people, I thought. I'd never seen anything like what I saw outside the restaurant. There were bodies everywhere. I saw a man's head on the sidewalk.

There will be more, if you don't stop it.

Me? I—

My phone rang, and Shanks removed his hand as I reached to answer it. I thought it might be Nico. At least, I hoped it was.

"Hello?"

"Detective Dasalia, I thought I told you to stop following me."

Snapping my fingers, I signaled to Shanks to start scanning for the signal while I tried the trace again.

"You did."

"That man sitting next to you is not your friend," the killer said.

I scanned up and down the street, but didn't expect to see him. He was close, though. He had to be; he could see us.

"Why did you kill them? What did these people do?"

"If I tell you, you'll tell him," the voice said. "You'll tell him everything. You're going to have to figure it out yourself, but to do that, you'll have to wake up."

You have to wake up. . . . The revivor had also said that to me.

"What does that mean?"

"Have you imagined being with him?"

An uneasy feeling grew in my stomach. I looked over at Shanks and remembered my dreams. The dream I had been having just before the first call woke me up that morning.

"Have you imagined him touching you?"

"He's close," Shanks said.

"It's happening. Don't get in the way," the voice said, and the connection dropped. I looked to Shanks, but he shook his head.

"Close," he said. "That's the best I can do."

The arm barring the ramp rose and I squeezed the car through the gate, curving down the lit tunnel into the underground parking area. The complex was in a pretty good neighborhood, and there were a lot of nice cars down there. Shanks normally would have ogled them, but this time he didn't.

"What did he say?" he asked.

"He warned me off the case again."

"Anything else?"

His expression was one of concern.

"He's taunting me," I said. "I'll have them run it again and see if they can get anything else from it. In the meantime, our best lead is inside."

None of the doors were forced, so he either had duplicate keys or some kind of electronic lock pick. Security cameras were spaced regularly, and there were plenty more inside, but not one of them had recorded a thing as the killer walked right into the place and took three more victims not even six hours after taking the last.

I parked in the visitor's area and we headed inside, following the path the killer had taken. The door to the apartment hung open and was crossed with yellow tape. A police officer stood outside.

From the looks of it, the door had been forced in from the outside, leaving a clear shoe print next to the knob. On the floor outside the door were boot tracks, and maybe another set of footprints in sneakers. I ducked under the tape, and Shanks moved in behind me. There were three investigators left inside: one taking pictures down the hall, and the other two sweeping for forensics. Near the officers sat a man in a sweater who looked like a civilian. One of the investigators broke off and approached as we entered.

"Detective Dasalia?" he asked, looking from me to Shanks. I shook his hand.

"I'm Reece. Bodies are down here, off the living room...."

He led the way down the hall, which opened up into

a spacious living area with a massive sectional sofa on carved wooden claw feet, arranged so that it was facing a flat-screen television with what must have been a fifty-inch screen mounted on the wall. A home theater sound system was arranged around the room, and there was a fireplace with a brick hearth and bronze fixtures on the wall to the left of the sofa.

"Nice digs," Shanks said.

"They have any personal security?" I asked. Reece nodded.

"Yeah, but it was bypassed."

"How?"

"Not sure yet, but whoever did it has some know-how, because nothing got tripped. These people never saw it coming."

He led us to what looked like a playroom, where another television was mounted in front of a smaller sofa. Wires trailed to gaming devices and audio equipment. It was easy to imagine a group of younger kids in there, sitting on that sofa and playing, but instead something terrible had come to an end in that room.

"Who were they?" I asked.

"The Valles," the officer said. "The father, Miguel, the mother, Rebecca, and daughter, Kate."

Lying on the carpet in between the sofa and the television were the three bodies, a forensic examiner kneeling over them. Each was lying facedown, as if they had been on their knees and arranged in a circle like they had been facing one another. Their wrists and ankles were bound with plastic ties, and each of their faces lay in individual pools of blood that had joined in the middle. What looked like castoff and various arcs of arterial spurt had painted the carpet, the sofa, and even the walls. Whatever happened there had gone on for a while.

My eyes went to the young girl and stayed there. Anger and frustration welled up from out of the fog, and as I looked at her face, my throat burned.

"This is different," I said to the examiner. "He takes single victims."

"I understand," she said, "but we found traces of the chemical signature you keep finding, the one for the explosives. It matches the one you found in the vehicle earlier. The wounds are a match, too. They were made by your mystery weapon."

"Can they be moved?"

"Here," she said, grabbing the mother by the sleeve of her shirt and pulling her over onto her side. "This is different."

Rebecca Valle had been mutilated in a way that none of the previous bodies had been. There were cuts on her face, neck, and chest. Her sleeves had been rolled up and there were similar marks on her forearms, cut down to the bone in some places. Her belly had been slit open neatly, but not deeply. Just enough.

"He knew what he was doing," Shanks said in my ear, and I nodded. The mother hadn't just been killed; she was tortured extensively first.

"No one heard this?"

"Noise screen," the officer said. "Might be why he picked this room. You could throw a party in here and not hear it in the bedroom. They could scream all they wanted; no one would have heard them."

"I get it. Was the place searched?"

"Tossed," he said. "Yeah, especially the bedrooms."

"He was looking for something this time," I said to Shanks. That was different too; in fact, it was the closest thing to a motive I'd ever been able to attribute to him.

"The father and daughter didn't show the same signs of abuse," the forensics investigator said.

"What was the cause of death?" I asked. "For the other two, I mean."

"Actually," she said, "the mother's cause of death was a puncture wound to the heart via the sternum, made by your guy's weapon. The other two were killed with the same weapon, but they were struck at the base of the skull."

Why the mother? I thought. *Why not concentrate on the father, the one most likely to be a problem?*

Maybe it was to make him talk.

Then why not the kid?

Maybe he has half a heart.

No one with a functioning heart did this.

"So she was tortured; then all three were killed."

"Other way around," the investigator said. "Blood patterns indicate the father and daughter were killed first, and then he went to work on the mother."

She was the key, the voice nagged.

Whatever he was searching for, he thought she had it or knew where it was. He killed the others in front of her. When she still didn't talk, he tried to torture it out of her . . .

. . . but she didn't know.

"I saw footprints at the door," I said. The investigator nodded.

"Yes, but I'm not sure they belong to the killer."

"You matched them to the family?"

"No, but we were able to get an approximate shoe size from impressions in the carpet," she said. "The placement makes them the killer's. They don't match either of the sets of prints at the door, and neither do any of the victims."

"So someone else was in here?"

"Yes."

"Before or after the murders?"

"I can't say for sure, but I think after."

"Why?"

"The boot tracks left traces leading to and from the bathroom, and that's it. Whoever they belong to didn't go any farther into the apartment. The sneaker prints do, but only as far as this room. They were faint, but it looks like whoever they belong to came down the hall, through the living room to this room, stood in the doorway, then turned around and walked back the way he came."

"Then they should be on the building's security cameras."

"That's the other weird part," she said. "The logs on the cameras had been tampered with."

"Tampered with how?"

"The system was breached remotely. A section had been wiped out, but the strange thing is, I don't think it was the killer trying to cover his tracks. The time of death puts his arrival hours before the section that was missing."

"So what was he trying to cover up?"

"I'm not sure it was the killer at all."

"The two who came in after?" I asked, and she shrugged.

"It fits, time-wise."

Maybe for some reason the visitors who came after the murders—the pair of sneakers that found the bodies and the friend with the boots who used the john—didn't want anyone to know they had been there. Whoever they were, they didn't call the murders in.

"You said the killer didn't force his way in," I said. "Who kicked the door?"

"The tenant next door," Reece said, nodding toward the man in the sweater. "He said he got a call for help from the father, but it was over by the time he got in. He didn't see a thing."

"A phone call would have been a neat trick, tied up like that. Do you believe his account?"

"I think he believes it, but again, it doesn't fit. We pulled the call records, and the call he got came after the section of missing security tape was erased. We traced it to a public phone, paid for with a drugstore phone card."

"It was a tip," I said. Someone wanted the bodies found, without having to come forward.

A witness, the voice inside said. *That's promising.*

The witness didn't see anything.

He talked to whoever made that call. You should go talk to him. Have Shanks look around the apartment while you do it.

I sighed, my face suddenly flushed, and straightened my jacket. Maybe it did pay to listen to your gut, to trust your intuition. Things could hardly go much worse.

"Shanks, check around. I want to talk to him."

"Yes, ma'am."

The man in the sweater looked visibly disturbed when I approached him, although I didn't see any blood on him and there wasn't any sign he'd been attacked. I waved the officers away and knelt with him.

"What's your name?" I asked him. His eyes darted over to me.

"Roger. Roger Hammond."

"Bad night, huh?"

He nodded.

"Did you know the victims?"

"Yes. I mean, as neighbors."

"That's pretty brave, breaking in here like that."

He shrugged.

"Did you witness the attack?"

"No. They were already dead by the time I got inside."

"You said you got a call from the victim?"

He nodded.

"When he called, what did he say?"

"He was whispering. He said, 'It's Miguel Valle. Some-one's in the apartment . . . they killed them.' Then the line cut out."

"Why would he call you? Why not the police?"

He shook his head back and forth slightly, staring at the floor.

"It wasn't him. I know it wasn't him."

"Who do you think it was?" I asked.

"I don't know. Someone who wanted me to find them."

"You gonna be all right?"

"Yeah. Were all four of them dead?"

"Three."

"There's four," he said. "Miguel, Becca, Kate, and Luis."

"Luis?"

"His son."

"How old is he?"

"Luis? Maybe nineteen or twenty."

The second set of footprints. The son, and someone else . . . a friend? He was gone for whatever reason when the killer entered the apartment, and came back after the fact. He found the bodies, and he ran.

"Thanks, Mr. Hammond. That helps."

Shanks was heading back into the room from down the hall, and I rejoined him and Reece.

"Your guys searched the place room to room when you got here?" I asked Reece.

"Yeah," he said, making a face. "Whatever your guy was looking for, either he found it or it wasn't here."

"Fair enough. It looks like the Valles also had a son, Luis Valle, who may still be alive. We need an APB out on him immediately."

"I'm on it."

Reece stalked off to rejoin the others when I knelt down with Shanks.

"You think the kid had something to do with this?" Shanks asked.

"I don't know."

Maybe . . . maybe. The thought nagged at me. *But maybe he's what the killer was looking for. . . .*

"Maybe he's not running from us," I said.

We need him alive.

"We need him alive."

"If he's alive, they'll find him," he said.

"You dig anything else up?"

"Yeah. It looks like someone was on the computer when the attack occurred. You'll want to see this."

He led me down the main hallway to a room at the far end that was dark except for the illumination from the computer screen. The chair in front of it had been pushed back, leaving trails in the carpet.

"They didn't find any prints but the family's," Shanks said, "but look what I found on the system."

A little instant message window was sitting in the corner of the screen. There were entries still sitting on it.

"One of them was talking to someone," I said. One of the names read RVALLE0107. "Rebecca Valle. The mother."

"The killer must have shut it down, but didn't exit out completely. He probably thought he got rid of it."

Leaning closer, I read the tiny text on the screen.

CRAIGH01: Where is it now?
RVALLE0107: With him, I think.
CRAIGH01: Good.
RVALLE0107: Cross was detected, though.
CRAIGH01: Yes.
RVALLE0107: Hold on a minute.
CRAIGH01: What's the matter?
RVALLE0107: Hold on.
RVALLE0107: Sorry, we have a visitor. I'll get back to you.
CRAIGH01: Who is this?
CRAIGH01: Who is this?
RVALLE0107: I have to get back to you.
CRAIGH01: What have you done to them?
CRAIGH01: Why are you doing this?
CRAIGH01: Why are you doing this to us?
RVALLE0107: Because someone has to.

You know what that is, the voice said.

Yes. A connection.

These two knew each other.

But the other one isn't a victim.

Yet.

He said, "us." "Why are you doing this to us?" Who's "us"?

If I were you, the voice nagged, *I wouldn't inquire too deeply.*

Shaking my head, I stepped away from the screen.

"We need the rest of the conversation," I said. "Everything on this computer."

"It's gone," Shanks said.

"Gone?"

"Either the victim wiped it when she heard the intruder, or the killer did it. Maybe the techs can pull something off of it, but everything's gone. The message pane just happened to still be up. If you shut it off, you'll lose that too."

That's not the important thing, Faye.

Then what is?

The only living connection we have right now.

"Craigh," I said out loud. "Or Craig H? He knew. He knew what was happening over here."

I headed back out to the living room, Shanks in tow.

"Reece, did anyone else call this in?" I asked.

"Someone else?"

"Besides our witness, did you receive any other calls about a possible disturbance over here?"

"No."

I turned to Roger, the witness, who was still sitting with the officers.

"Does the name Craig mean anything to you?" I asked. "Craig H? Or H Craig?"

"Harold," he said. "He's a friend of Becca's. I've seen him around."

Harold Craig.

He's in trouble, the voice said. *You need to get over there.*

Why didn't he call it in?

I don't know, but there isn't time. Go.

"Shanks, we need an address for Harold Craig. . . ."

We'll get it on the way down. Go now.

"Are you okay?" Shanks asked in my ear.

"We've got to go," I said.

"Are you okay?"

"I'm so tired. . . ." I whispered.

You're almost there ... just keep going ...

"I know, Faye," he said. "We're going to get him. We'll do it together, got it?"

He put his hand on the small of my back, guiding me. It was the second time that day he had touched me like that. It felt firm and reassuring. Somehow, it made me feel like what he said was true, and that we would succeed, and that when we did, everything would be okay and I would finally get to sleep.

5

Voodoo Proper

**Nico Wachalowski — Heinlein Industries,
Industrial Park Drive**

Heinlein Industries was situated well outside the city limits, taking an hour even by bullet train to get there. It got dark early that time of year. The sky had turned gray already. As the rail approached, the complex was visible in the distance like a huge disc cut out of the suburbs that surrounded it. It was as if a comet had struck there, leaving nothing but black glass. Only when you got closer could you begin to make out the flat, rectangular structures there, but Heinlein was built largely down, not up. It kept low to the ground, hidden behind the security fence and guard posts that surrounded it.

I picked up a car and headed in through the maze of narrow streets. The structures there were tightly packed, built from sturdy concrete that was now weathered and defaced. Businesses tapered off as the main road crossed the perimeter and gave way to VP Industrial, which was Heinlein's main campus. VP stood for Verhoven-Pratsky, the names of the facilities' two primary donors, but everyone called it Voodoo Proper. I opened a channel back to headquarters.

I've arrived. I'm heading in now.

The whole first half mile was an open expanse that went around the entire park as far as I could see, and from the signals I was picking up, my vehicle was being tracked from several sources as I approached. Warning signs were posted along the way, threatening everything from prosecution to live fire as the inner fence loomed closer. The facility underground was deep enough to withstand a missile strike, and the airspace over the campus was a designated no-fly zone; I had no doubt the guards would shoot if provoked.

Heinlein is instituting a security lockdown, Noakes said.

Looks friendly enough to me.

It isn't funny, Wachalowski. So far they're being cooperative; don't do anything to make them nervous.

I'll tread lightly.

No communications in or out once you're inside. As far as both we and they are concerned, this visit isn't happening—got it? If the media gets even a whiff of this, it'll be a disaster.

Got it. Luckily, they had enough to distract them today.

The park had a guard station, which wasn't unusual, but unlike some places, this one had a fence and, from what I could see, it enclosed the whole park. I zoomed in on the warning sign bolted to the nearest pylon; it promised a lethal voltage.

As I approached, I felt my phone go off, but before I could see who it was, the signal cut and the phone went dead. A second later, a message appeared in front of my eyes as the JZI got an override communication.

You are entering a restricted area. No unauthorized communications are permitted in or out from this point forward. No unauthorized scans or visual, audio, or data recordings are permitted beyond this point. No unauthorized personnel or authorized personnel with a security clearance of less than three are permitted beyond this point, by order of the UAC Government. By continuing, you forfeit your right to refuse any and all searches, including your vehicle, its contents, and your person, up to and including full internal scanning. Any property including identification may be confiscated at the guard's discretion and held for an indeterminate period of time. Failure to comply with security will result in action up to and including lethal force.

"Welcome to Heinlein Industries," I said to myself as the words faded.

I pulled up to the guard and rolled down the window. He was a thick-necked man in uniform who wore a badge. He peered down at me over the bulletproof shield.

"Can I help you?" he asked. I didn't dare use the scanner, but I could see a faint bulge under his jacket. I could also see a shotgun racked against the wall next to him.

"Agent Nico Wachalowski," I said. "They should be expecting me."

The guard peered down at my breast pocket and scanned the badge through the material. After a couple seconds, he nodded.

"Yes, they are, sir," he said. "Go right on through. The layout of the place can be a little confusing, so I'll transmit a marker to your GPS. Just follow it down to the parking area and take the elevator up. A representative will be waiting for you."

"Thanks."

The guard arm rose, and I followed the marker toward the collection of squat, rectangular buildings. All things considered, I was glad for the guidance, because the park was huge and nothing was marked. I headed down into a short tunnel, which took me to a parking area.

From the garage, I took an elevator up. The doors opened and I stepped out into a dimly lit lobby that looked deserted. My footsteps echoed lightly as I made my way to a large, curved reception desk with an empty chair behind it.

"Hello?"

I saw several red points of light in the shadows near the ceiling. Cameras were watching me. There were two glass doors with badge readers that led inside, and a phone mounted on one wall.

I was beginning to wonder if I had the right place when a man in a suit appeared behind one of the glass doors. He was about my age, with wavy, graying hair, and dressed in an expensive suit. He noticed me as he held his badge up to the scanner.

"Agent Wachalowski?" he asked as he scooted through the door. He had an easy, salesman's charm, and when he smiled, crow's-feet formed at his eyes.

"Yes."

"Hi, I'm Bob MacReady. I am so sorry," he said, stepping forward and shaking my hand. "I thought I could beat you here. As you can see, we don't get casual visitors."

He held out a clip-on visitor's badge and I put it on, causing him to smile like I'd just performed a trick.

"Excellent," he said. "Come on, we can talk in my office."

He buzzed us in and led me at a brisk pace through a maze of cubicle areas and narrow corridors. Unlike the lobby, the inside was brightly lit with flat electric light. The area we passed through was huge but oddly quiet. Occasional voices rose over the hum of the climate-control system and the constant murmur of hundreds of fingers as they worked keypads. Along the far wall was a wide glass panel that looked in on some kind of laboratory. Men and women dressed in clean suits worked over racks of equipment that seemed to merge together into an organized mass of shiny silver tanks, tubes, and electronics. I didn't recognize any of it. One of the men inside noticed us, and watched me pass.

By the time we arrived at MacReady's office, I was thoroughly lost. He opened the door and I stepped into the small space, which was dominated by a wooden desk with a pair of computer monitors sitting on it. On the walls behind the desk hung diplomas and certificates, including one for a doctorate in applied cybernetics. Shelves ran along each wall, stacked tightly with technical specifications and texts. The air smelled like old coffee and body odor.

"Please sit down," he said, closing the door behind us. "Can I get you anything?"

"No, thanks."

He got behind his desk and casually switched on a noise filter. I sat down across from him.

"This is about the bombing, isn't it?" he asked.

"Not directly."

"News traveled quickly here, especially once it became known that a revivor had triggered the device. You do understand it wasn't one of ours?"

"Yes, but you know why I'm here, right?" I asked.

"I understand some of our components were recovered from a foreign combat revivor that had been smuggled into the country."

"Yes. Mr. MacReady, I'll be frank. I am only interested in tracking down the people who are bringing the revivors into the country. We don't believe Heinlein Industries is involved in anything illicit; we just want to know how the parts might have gotten there, to aid us in tracking the traffickers down."

"I understand," MacReady said. "We ran the numbers you sent along and were able to trace the components ourselves. The parts were surplus, unclassified and obsolete. They were sold at auction."

"Along with how much other product?"

"I've compiled the complete list and I'll make sure you leave with it," MacReady said.

"You understand this was a foreign combat model we pulled them out of?"

"Our current technology is so far advanced beyond those components as to make them irrelevant."

"I see."

"It's very complicated, Agent, and completely legal."

"I understand. In a nutshell, can you say what the specific components were for?"

"Different things," he said, "but mainly? Collective command."

"Which is?"

"Revivors are more sophisticated than they were back when you served, Agent. A collective-command structure allows revivors a common communications connection for sending and receiving information. That may sound like a simple thing, but it's fairly complicated. Think of it as a version of the Jovanovic-Zaytsev system you use to communicate with your teammates."

"So it allows revivors to communicate with each other?"

"Not exactly," he said. "It's a hub-and-spoke configuration; many to one, not many to many. It allows a single source to command many revivors."

"And by command, you mean . . . ?"

"Control. Usually they're given orders, but if the situation requires, the shunts are in place today to override and virtually control them from a remote location."

"Nice."

"The revivors also use the system to report back to that common source. Any modern revivor outfitted with one will automatically join a default command chain, if one is available."

"They can't talk to each other?"

"They can, just not directly," he said. He was quiet for a moment, then asked, "Have you recovered any others with the same components?"

"I can't comment on that."

"Well, if you have," he said, "or if you do, or suspect you might, then you would be dealing with someone who wanted to command a unified group."

"Hypothetically, how many nodes could be commanded in that way?"

"Typically, small groups—say, four to nine—but when commanding many such groups, it can add up. In the future, we hope to have a single command control hundreds of units."

"Hundreds?"

"The future of revivor technology is today, Agent. The M8 models we're currently creating far surpass what you would have encountered during your time in the service. Tomorrow will bring even greater advances."

"Field bring-back?" The ability to raise a revivor on

the battlefield, without requiring a trip back to Heinlein's labs, was something they'd been chasing for years without success. MacReady grinned and gave a shrug.

"Field administration too, perhaps," he said. "One day, being wired may be as simple as a shot in the arm."

That took me by surprise, and he seemed to enjoy that.

"You understand what I mean, then," he said, "when I tell you the components you recovered are no longer relevant."

"I see."

MacReady leaned back in his chair and sighed. He still held an easy smile, but his eyes looked grave.

"We are as concerned about this as you are, Agent," he said. "We want to help in any way we can."

"I appreciate that," I told him. "The most useful information for us right now is those auction records you've made available. For now, I think that's all I need."

"Very good."

"I did have one last question, though," I said. "Does the name Zhang mean anything to you?"

"You mean Zhang's Syndrome?"

I shrugged.

"That," MacReady said, "is a piece of Heinlein Industries lore, in a manner of speaking. The fathers of the modern revivor were two men named Isaac Ericsson and Olav Sodder, and while neither of them founded Heinlein Industries, they made it what it is today."

"How so?"

"The two men met during their tour in the service, where they were exposed to some of the earliest revivor technology," he said. "They were fascinated by it, especially Sodder, who studied the ones that came off the battlefield, looking for weaknesses to exploit, and then ultimately a way to re-create the revivor for our own use. He got pigeonholed as a tech specialist, while Ericsson, by all accounts, was more of a military man. Sodder saw the military benefit of a large, stable revivor force that could do more than blindly jump out of the bushes. When they got out of the service, the two pooled their resources and began development."

"They formed their own company?"

"Initially," he said. "In fact, Elise Jovanovic and Michael Zaytsev were part of that original endeavor, but Heinlein snapped the whole entity up very early on and then split it; Jovanovic and Zaytsev, whose names I'm sure you're at least familiar with, formed the team that perfected your JZ interface, while Sodder and Ericsson developed revivor technology. They all became very rich, and under the umbrella of Heinlein Industries, they were given all the resources they would ever need. Heinlein itself became even more profitable than it already was, and the marriage resulted in our obtaining one of the largest government contracts in history. In return, we provided the United American Coalition with the most powerful military force the world has ever seen."

"So what is Zhang's Syndrome?" I coaxed.

"It is the wedge that eventually came between Ericsson and Sodder," MacReady said. "Basically, it's a corruption of the memory pathways that occurs sometimes during reanimation, named after where the condition was finally isolated, Ning Zhang. It came up only in the later part of Sodder's life, because it wasn't until then that revivors became sophisticated enough to retain a significant part of their memories and cognitive abilities. It didn't affect memories that formed after reanimation, only preexisting ones."

"Affected them how?"

"Basically, a small percentage of those who were reanimated would describe a cognitive dissonance," he said. "Think of it like this: If a quantifiable memory event could be portrayed as an image, the same image would differ between the time of death and reanimation. They would be similar, but not equal."

"Give me an example."

"For example, a man comes to a fork in the road and goes right. Years later, upon reanimation, that man's revivor believes he went left."

"Maybe he just remembered it wrong."

"It's hard to say, but Sodder believed he had empirical evidence that this was not the case—and that was the crux of it. To someone like Ericsson it wasn't a problem, but to someone like Sodder it was a puzzle he felt compelled to solve. He felt such a discrepancy had to have an explanation."

"How did that drive a wedge between the two men?"

"Well, since only a small portion of the memories were affected and not all revivors exhibited the anomaly, Ericsson declared it a waste of resources to chase it," he said. "He was only interested in increasing the field capacity of the revivor itself; past memories were irrelevant to him. Sodder was the opposite; he was obsessed with the problem and with finding what caused it."

"So it was a professional disagreement, then?"

"It was more than that," MacReady said. "It came down to their beliefs. Ericsson didn't just think it was a waste of resources. He didn't think the memories should be preserved. If he had his way, I think he would have had all former life memory wiped out, but it wasn't practical. He viewed Sodder's work as attempting to blur the line between life and reanimation, to make reanimation an extension of life. He was offended by it, I believe. The two distanced themselves from one another."

"You said, 'in the last part of Sodder's life'," I said. "He's dead now?"

"Both men are dead now," he said, "but their legacies still live on, as do the two camps they established, which still lock horns over that same issue, though not so much these days."

"Why not?"

"Sodder had a protégé named Samuel Fawkes," he said, "who continued his work trying to pinpoint the cause of Zhang's Syndrome. Some years ago, he died as well, and since then it's almost completely lost steam. Samuel's primary partner in that endeavor was a man named Edward Cross, but honestly, when Samuel died, Edward moved on to other areas."

"How hard would it be to get what you have on Zhang's Syndrome to me?"

"Not hard at all. Blocks of the data are still classified, you understand, but I can give you plenty to chew on for now. I'll assemble them and then forward them to your office."

"Fair enough."

"Is there anything else I can help you with?" he asked. "I could arrange a tour of the facilities, if you like."

"No, thanks," I said. "I have all the information I need for now."

"Let me show you out, then."

I followed him back to the visitors' lobby, where we shook hands and he gave me his card before disappearing back behind the glass security door. I headed out to the parking garage, toward the car.

Zhang's Syndrome. Could that have been what the revivor was referring to?

Slowing down as I approached the car, I noticed something on the windshield. It looked like a business card had been slipped under the driver's-side windshield wiper.

No one else was around. I couldn't see any cameras but I was sure they were there, so I palmed the card and got into the car without turning it over. Once I was inside, I held it down out of sight and looked at it. The name and contact information had been scratched out.

Someone must have wanted to leave me a message without showing himself and without leaving any kind of electronic trail. Sometimes the low-tech approach was still the best way to go.

I flipped it over and looked at the back; there was a handwritten note there, printed in black ink.

SAMUEL NEVER LEFT

The card wasn't signed. There was no other information on it.

Someone else knew I was here, then. The reference had to be to the Samuel Fawkes that MacReady had mentioned to me, and that implied that someone else had managed to hear that conversation as well.

With the restrictions put down over VP Industrial, there was no way to check the information. I slipped the card in my pocket and headed back toward the railway.

Zoe Ott—Pleasantview Apartments, Apartment 713

When I first opened my eyes, I wasn't sure where I was. I was lying on something soft, but it wasn't my bed and it wasn't the couch. Also, I was covered with a thick blanket that wasn't mine. The lights were out and the room was lit by flickering candlelight.

I took a deep breath and smelled some kind of perfume smell, along with the smell of the bar soap I used. When I reached up to rub my face, it wasn't greasy, and the blanket was crisp and clean.

Pushing my face into it, I breathed in and it smelled good, but it wasn't mine. The oversized pink sweatshirt and sweatpants I was wearing weren't mine either. I heard slippers shuffle across the floor nearby.

"Oh, you're up," a woman said, looking down at me. It was Karen, my downstairs neighbor. I was on the floor, lying across sofa cushions that had been arranged there like a bed. I was still in my apartment.

"Your lights are out, so I brought up some candles. I hope you don't mind," she said, sitting down next to me. Near my head there was a large ceramic bowl filled with soapy water that had a facecloth draped over the lip. Three or four candles had been arranged around the room.

"What happened?" I asked.

"You flipped," she said, with a thin smile.

"Oh."

"You said something terrible happened," she said. "Then you started going on about dead people, and then needles in your head, and then I kind of lost track. Do you remember any of it?"

"No."

"It's just as well."

My body physically ached as I struggled into a sitting position. My head was throbbing.

"Why did you stay?"

"You needed help, and you helped me. It was the least I could do, right?"

The reality of what I was wearing and the way I smelled finally started sinking in, and immediately I felt myself getting anxious, the blood rushing to my face.

"Did you wash me?"

"I'm a nurse. It's okay; I do it all the time."

"You—"

"Look," she said. "You puked on yourself, and that's not even all, okay? I put up with a bucket full of abuse— I took it because I knew you weren't in your right mind, and I'm sorry if you're embarrassed, but I couldn't leave you lying in it like that. I just couldn't."

I didn't say anything, partly because I didn't know what to say and also because my mouth just wouldn't open. I felt like crying, but I was too exhausted.

"Besides," she said, leaning closer, "something terrible did happen. There was an explosion, a suicide bombing, just a few blocks away. Over fifty people died and hundreds more got injured."

"Someone blew himself up?"

"Right in the middle of the restaurant strip at lunchtime."

I did kind of remember that, once she said it. I saw a bunch of people running, bloody and burned and screaming.

"Bad things are coming," I said.

"That's what you said last night."

There was more—I knew there was more—but I couldn't remember it.

"There was a panic," she said. "A riot broke out. Everyone's freaking out. They're calling in the National Guard and there's going to be a curfew until they can get things under control. They say there are even going to be revivors patrolling."

"Revivors?"

"It's the only way they can cover such a big area. They say it's temporary."

"Oh."

"Will things get even worse?" she asked. Her eyes looked desperate in the firelight, like the next thing that came out of my mouth was going to be the most important thing she ever heard. She was looking at me like I had some kind of answer, but I didn't know. I couldn't remember.

"I think the best thing you could do right now is not get involved with me," I said. It was weird, but I kind of regretted that. Before she could say anything else, there was a knock on the door and she looked over at it.

"Are you expecting anyone?"

"I don't think so."

"Wait here."

She got up and went to answer it and I lay back down, hoping whoever it was, she would get rid of them. I heard her talking but I couldn't make out what was being said. She was talking to a man, it sounded like. After a minute she came back, looking nervous.

"It's the cops," she said.

"The cops?"

"An FBI Agent. He says his name is Wachalowski."

"What?"

"Wacha—"

"He's here? Right now?"

"Yeah, what—"

"It's okay," I said, before she got any more freaked out. "I'm not in trouble. He's a friend."

"A friend?"

"Yeah," I said. "He's, um, you know. Look, I don't want him to see me like this."

"Oh," she said, smirking a little. "Okay, I've got to go anyway."

"Wait—"

"Zoe, he flashed his badge. What was I going to say?

I told him you were here. Come on, you look fine, you look cute."

She started to move away and I scrambled to my feet. The sweatshirt and sweatpants must have been hers, but unlike her I couldn't even begin to fill them out. The shirt hung like a tent and the pants wanted to slide down over my nonexistent hips.

"Karen, wait!"

"Look," she said, "I'll come by later, but come on; I'm not getting in the middle of this one. Trust me, you look fine."

I tailed her to the door, but she slipped out before I could get there, smiling and waving to him and then me as I wedged myself in the crack of the door.

"Ms. Ott?"

"Hi."

He was wearing a suit and a long, dark jacket. He looked down at me with his amazingly blue eyes, and standing there in front of him in sweats, I felt even lamer than I even did before. Why did they have to be pink?

"I'd like to speak with you for a minute, if I could."

"Um, okay."

"May I come in?"

"No."

He raised his eyebrows, and just then my next-door neighbor's door opened and out he came. Things were getting better and better. The old man stood there, staring like some kind of weirdo at Nico.

"Can I help you, sir?" Nico asked.

"Who are you?" my neighbor asked back.

"I'm visiting my friend here. Is that okay?"

The old man peered over at me, then back at Nico.

"She doesn't have any friends."

That was it. I'd let it slide before, but now he was going

too far. While Nico was turned toward him, I focused on the old man until the light bloomed around me, causing me to feel a little sick to my stomach. The colors came into focus over his head, rippling there like smoke in the breeze.

There was something weird about him, though, something a little different. In addition to the patterns I was used to seeing, there was a thin, bright white arc that formed a kind of ring or halo, almost. It distracted me, and I was just wondering what might be causing it when he decided to forgo his usual nosiness and duck back inside. Nico looked back at me, and I let the lights fade back to normal.

"My place is a real mess," I said. "Please?"

"I have a car," he said. "Can we speak downstairs? I won't take much of your time."

"Yeah, okay. Just . . . hang on."

I went back inside long enough to slide on my boots, put on my parka, and then retie the waist on the sweatpants before the stupid things fell down. When I was zipped up, I slipped back out, then shut the door and locked it before he could see in.

We headed down to the building's entryway, then across the icy lot to his car, where he let me in, then climbed in himself, turning the heat on.

"That's a nice neighbor you have there," he said.

"He's a jerk."

"I meant your other neighbor, the woman who answered the door."

"Oh yeah. Karen."

"The man next door said you don't have any friends, but it doesn't look like that's true."

"Yeah," I said, embarrassed. "I have one."

"Well, now you have two."

He was smiling from across the car seat, and the way

he looked at me and the way he spoke to me made me feel good. It seemed impossible that we were sitting there together, alone in the front seat like that. I'd pulled some stunts in the past when I was drunk, but never anything that ended with me actually doing something useful or worthwhile. He looked at me like I really was somebody, not a joke, and when he watched me those pretty iridescent lights shone from behind his eyes like he was something out of one of my dreams.

"This is a lot," I said.

"I know."

"Half the time I'm not even sure how much of it's real."

"It's real," he said. "The information the suspect provided was accurate, and after going over everything, I believe it's real. I believe in you."

Before I could stop myself, I cried right in front of him. Not a lot, just for a second, but enough to make me have to wipe my eyes. He handed me a tissue from out of the glove box.

"I'm sorry," I said, pressing it to my eyes. On some level, I knew he was just being professional, just being polite. He had no idea how much what he was saying meant to me; he couldn't know. No one was ever nice to me. No one ever took me seriously, or talked to me like I was a real person.

"You're okay."

"No, I'm not," I said, laughing a little. I was getting punchy.

"Will you tell me more?"

"More about what?"

"About what you've seen. According to your resume, you've experienced a limited precognition?"

"You thought that was a joke."

"I'm not laughing now."

I wiped my nose on the tissue and thought about it. There was probably plenty I could tell him, but I didn't want him to think I was crazy.

"Some people are being held against their will," I said carefully. "Don't ask where or who because I don't know. They could be on Mars, for all I know. They have needles coming out of their heads."

"Needles?"

"Long ones, coming out of the backs of their heads. They're alive, but they can't move. One of them told me I would lead someone to them, and I think she meant you. She told me I would end her pain."

"You will lead me to them?"

"Then I will end her pain. That's what she said."

"Anything else?"

There's a dead woman with a split heart who shows me things, but she's keeping something from me."

"What does she show you?"

"You," I said, and his expression changed. When I probed him gently, I could see fear pricking up from the otherwise calm patterns that hung over him.

"Me?"

"You have a tattoo here," I said, pointing to his shoulder opposite the one with the scar, and the fear pricked up again.

"Why did she show me to you?"

"I don't know. She just said you would need my help."

"Do you know who she was?"

"I've never met her, but she says I will soon."

He paused, and looked down at the seat between us like he was lost in thought. The smile and the professional politeness were gone.

"I'd like to continue this," he said, "but right now I have an appointment. I stopped here on the way because this is off the record and I'd like to keep it that way."

"Okay."

"Can we meet again at some point?"

"I'd like that."

"Yes," he said, and the smile was back. The reassuring, professional warmth was back, like it had to be. "So would I."

He reached into his coat and pulled out a large office envelope, which he handed to me.

"In the meantime, would you mind looking at these?"

"What are they?"

"Some pictures and documents that are, for the moment, unclassified," he said. "But again, this is off the record."

I took the envelope and held it in my lap.

"They don't know you're here, do they?"

"No, and as I said, I'd like to keep it that way. Okay?"

"Okay."

"Thank you."

Not wanting to be dismissed, I decided to get out of there while things still seemed to be going well. I slid back across the seat and opened the car door.

"You're not going to lecture me?" I asked. I had meant to include the words "about the drinking," but I couldn't bring myself to say them. He seemed a little bit amused.

"Not yet."

"I'll look at them," I said, holding up the envelope as I slipped out the door. I was just about to close it when I remembered one other thing.

"Oh, and a revivor."

"What?"

"She showed me a revivor, an Asian-looking one with a foreign name. It started with a Z. His jaw was wired shut. Does that help?"

"Yes."

He was still smiling as I backed away and closed the door, but his fear spiked when I said it. He started the engine and pulled away, leaving me in the parking lot alone.

Calliope Flax—Bullrich Heights

My phone buzzed, and Luis shot me a look from over a slice of pizza. It was a text from Eddie.

You out? he wanted to know.

Yeah.

I got a slot open tonight. Can you fight?

What about the alert?

Screw the alert. I'll shut down when they shove an injunction up my ass. Can you fight or not?

Yes. Gotta go, I've got company.

No sex before a fight.

I shut the phone.

"Who was that?" Luis asked.

"None of your business."

We ate and drank some beer, and Luis made a shitload of calls on his phone. The more he talked, the less I liked him in my place. For one thing, he knew too many people and he called them all by fake screen names. For another thing, from the sound of it, he was into some shady shit. He didn't want me to hear a lot of what he was saying. He asked about shit like data and security and who knew what and how much. He was going to be a problem.

"So, what did you do?" I asked finally. He looked up from the TV.

"Nothing."

"No one hides their rich ass in this shit hole if they did nothing. What did you do?"

"I'm not rich."

"I was in your place, remember?"

"It's not my place."

"Whatever. Tell me what you did."

"Noth—"

"Tell me, or get the hell out now."

He thought about that, and I think it was a tough call for him. He sat there for a while; then he sighed.

"I broke in somewhere," he said.

"You robbed someplace?"

"Not that kind of break-in. I broke into someone's network."

"So?"

"Remember you asked me about Uncle Ed? Dr. Cross?"

"Yeah."

"Remember I said he works at Heinlein Industries? They're a government contractor. They make rev—"

"I know what Heinlein does, asshole."

"Well, he works for them," he said. "Totally brilliant. He worked right under Samuel Fawkes, the top guy in the field until he died. Anyway, not long ago, he got it into his head that someone was spying on them over there."

"Why'd he think that?"

"He wouldn't say, but I think someone put the idea in his head. He got obsessive about it."

"So call the fucking cops or something."

"He wouldn't; he was so nuts about it he wouldn't

even talk to anyone else there about it. It's like it was some kind of conspiracy or something, like he didn't think he could trust anyone."

"What does this have to do with you?"

"He asked me to break in and snoop around."

"Why?"

"Because he knew I could do it, and he trusts me. He got me some security codes, and I snuck in and set up a bunch of 'bots that watched everything, then reported back to a remote server. When I had enough data to go on, I downloaded it all and put it on a data spike so I could hand it off to him."

"Wait, that's why you're in trouble?"

"I think they realized I was in there while I was in jail—"

"This is all because you think you got pinched screwing around on someone's network?"

"It's more complicated than that," he said, pissed.

"What do you get for that, a fine? Have your top-tier mom and dad bail you out."

His face changed when I said that. It got all dark.

"I can't," he said.

"Yeah, right."

"You don't know what the fuck you're talking about."

"I know how things are."

"Money doesn't fix everything."

"It fixes most things."

"It wouldn't fix you."

"Yeah, well, fuck them and fuck you too."

"Even I had to take a PH tour," he said. "Drop the third-tier hero bullsh—"

"Don't compare us, asshole. People like you end up officers; people like me end up on the front lines. When they put me in a box, you'll still be drinking champagne in your high-rise, and we both know it. You live long enough, they won't even use you."

He didn't say anything. His face just got darker.

"You and your happy little fam—"

"Go to hell," he said, his voice low. "I'm leaving."

I don't know why, but I kind of felt bad right then. Something about his face, the way he looked. When I got pissed, I shot my mouth off. I didn't know what it was, but I thought I might have crossed a line, there.

"Hey, don't cry or any—"

"I'm not crying, bitch, and I don't need you," he said. "Take your bullshit and shove it back up your ass. It's not my fault your life is shit."

"My life ain't shit."

"Yes, it is."

His face was different. It was like he'd dropped an act, and I could see he wasn't as soft as I had thought he was. I don't know what it was, but I could tell he was on the edge. Whatever he was in, he was in deep, and there was fight in his eyes.

"Hey, look," I said. "I take it back, okay? Just forget it."

He just stood there and stared me down.

"If you won't take me, I'll get a cab."

"Cabs don't come out here, bro."

"Then I'll—"

"How's this?" I said. "Eddie wants me in the ring tonight, so unless the cops shut him down, I'm on. You hitch a ride with me there and get a cab at the arena. How's that?"

He still looked pissed, but I could see him take the bait.

"Fine. Can I use your shower?" he asked.

"Knock yourself out."

He got up and just walked into the bathroom and shut the door. A while after, the water came on and then I heard it splash off him, making him, I think, the only guy to ever take a shower just to hit Arena Porco Rojo. When he was good and wet, I grabbed his phone and ID.

On the card, his name said Luis Valle, and clipped to his keys was enough credit to buy the whole goddamn world. His phone showed a bunch of calls logged, but nothing that meant shit to me. He said something about putting the stuff he took from that company on a data-storage spike, but I didn't see one on his clip.

I put an ear to the door, and the water was still going strong. While he was tied up, I turned on the TV.

". . . where the bombing took place," a reporter was saying. "So far authorities have no leads on who perpetrated the bombing, and no one has taken responsibility. National Guard forces are moving into place in key areas of the city, while others will be patrolled by a backup revivor contingency."

"Key areas" meant "rich areas." Those would get guarded, and we'd get the backup, if that. That dick Ohtomo would send the zombies down to the slums to keep an eye on us and make sure we didn't start shit with the rest of his precious city while the real soldiers were tied up.

They cut to the mayor, a shitload of mikes jammed in his craw as he went to his car.

"Mayor Ohtomo, is it true a curfew will be imposed?" one asked.

"I will make an official statement on air in an hour," he said.

"Mayor what about the reports that this may be the first planned bombing of many?"

"I have not heard any report to that effect."

"What about the witnesses who survived the blast, and their statements that the suicide bomber was actually a revivor?"

"No comment."

The mayor could screw himself—what I really wanted was the miner. I had Luis's full name now. That was enough to find out if the cops were on him.

I fed in his name and the miner chewed on it for a second. Links started to pop up. The one with the most hits was on top.

Local Family Tortured, Killed.

It had a graphic-footage warning. I clicked on that one.

Sure as shit, the cameras were pointed inside his place. From the angle, they must have been right inside the front door. I had stood in that same spot.

". . . an anonymous tip alerted authorities to the murders," a voice said. "A search of the apartment revealed a grim discovery."

The camera moved past the bathroom I took my piss in and down the hall Luis came from when I walked back out. They turned the corner and went down a hall, where something was pooled on the floor. They moved through a door and focused on what was inside.

There were three bodies in the middle of the room, all lying on the white carpet with their hands bound by plastic ties behind their backs, facedown on the floor. The carpet around them was covered with blood.

One of the cops or someone else must have taken the video and sold it. It was bad, even for underground news. There was blood fucking everywhere.

They killed his family. While I was on the can, he went to look for them and found them back there. I was in that place with three dead bodies and I didn't even know it.

He knew. That's why he was so hot to get out of there. That's why he said what he did. He had no way to help me like he said he would; he just needed out of there and way the hell away.

". . . last remaining family member Luis Valle, whose whereabouts are currently unknown. Investigators are not commenting yet on whether or not he is a suspect in these murders, or another victim. If you have any information concerning Luis Valle, please . . ."

They flashed his mug shot and showed a number. I wrote it down and shoved it in my pocket.

The water stopped, and I shut off the TV.

He was trouble. He was big trouble. He was who the guys that murdered his family were looking for. They tossed his place looking for that storage-spike thing he talked about. Whoever he pissed off, they were hard-core, and they were still out there.

They were looking for him, and I let him right in my front door.

Faye Dasalia—Concrete Falls

"Any word?" Shanks asked. I snapped my phone shut.

"He's still not answering." No one had been able to reach Harold Craig. The local police had checked out his place, but at my request they kept it low-key; no one approached on foot. If the killer was going to make his move, I didn't want to spook him. His place was being watched while they waited for us, but so far no one had shown up.

"Body heat came up negative in his home. He's not there." Shanks said.

It had taken too long to get to the neighborhood where Harold Craig lived, and the sky was starting to get dark.

"That's what I'm afraid of."

The city had slowly begun to trade its superstructures for tight blocks of duplexes in what looked like a well-to-do area. Crowded brick houses stood tall and slim at the heads of short but individual driveways with individual mailboxes. A woman bundled up in a coat and walking a medium-sized black dog watched as we drove by. The dog strained against its leash and barked.

"This is Detective Shanks with Detective Dasalia," Shanks said into his radio. "Be advised we are approaching the residence."

"We see you," a voice crackled.

"Turn left up here; it should be down this street," Shanks said.

I turned onto the narrow street and followed the numbers down until I found it. A silhouette watched through a window from across the street as I pulled up to the house. There was a car in the driveway, so I parked on the street and cut the engine.

"Any movement?" Shanks asked into the radio.

"Negative. Nothing on infrared or thermal."

He looked over at me.

"Tell them we're going in," I said.

"Have your men stand by. We're going inside."

"Roger that."

We got out, and when I looked over, the figure watching from the window retreated.

"Maybe he's walking his dog."

"Maybe."

He followed me to the front door and I rang the bell, but no one answered. I tried the door; it was unlocked. I pushed it open and looked inside. The lights were off, but there was a soft glow coming from somewhere inside.

"Mr. Craig?" I called. No one answered.

"Mr. Craig, this is the police," I called. "We're coming in."

I glanced at Shanks, and he shrugged. I drew my gun and he followed suit as I pushed the door open the rest of the way and we crossed through.

The unit was quiet, although I could hear a television through the wall from the connected duplex. The front door opened into a good-sized living area and a pair of French doors leading into a study where the glow was coming from. Another doorway opened into a short hallway that looked like it led to a kitchen.

"Mr. Craig?"

Moving closer, I could see the glow from the study was coming from a computer monitor.

The study was small, crowded with expensive-looking wooden furniture and a single leather chair that was pushed away from the desk. This was where he had sat, conversing with Rebecca Valle over the message client. He had been talking to her when the intruder broke in at Alto Do Mundo and the Valles were killed.

The client was still on the screen, displaying the same snippet of conversation I had seen at the Valle place. In addition, Mr. Craig seemed to have a video display sitting above it that looked out from somewhere above Valle's monitor.

Don't touch it; leave it for the experts, my intuition warned.

"Valle had a cam set up," I said. "That would explain

how he knew the person who responded on the chat wasn't Rebecca."

Leave it for the experts.

On the camera display I could see one of the investigators cross by in the hallway on the other side of the room. They were still there, looking for clues.

"He probably looked right at the killer," I said, watching. "That camera probably recorded him."

"I'll have a look," Shanks said. He started to move toward the computer station when something inside the house made a thump and he froze. The sound came from the direction of the kitchen.

He looked back at me, and I nodded toward the doorway. He readied his gun and crept back out into the living area. I got ready to follow him, but first, there was one thing I wanted to do.

My intuition had told me not to mess with the information on the computer, but my intuition didn't seem to be as sharp as maybe it once was. There was a chance I might blow it, that I might be responsible for triggering something that would erase the data, like what had happened at the previous victim's place, but this one time I was going to go against what my intuition was telling me.

There was no time to look at it now, but I fished a data card out of my jacket pocket and slipped it into the first available bay. Working quickly, I dumped the entire contents of the client's buffers onto the card.

"Dasalia," Shanks hissed. I pulled the card and slipped it back into my pocket.

Following Shanks's flashlight beam, I looked into the kitchen and saw papers and envelopes scattered across the floor. A wicker basket lay overturned off to one side, and two kitchen knives lay on the floor beneath a butcher's block on the counter above. As we got closer, the air smelled like bleach.

The noise didn't recur, and it looked like it might have been the remainder of the stack of envelopes that had fallen from the counter. Listening carefully, there were no signs that we weren't alone; the house was completely silent.

The kitchen opened up into another short hallway where a door led into a half bath, and across from that was another door, which was closed. The bathroom was empty, but there were beads of water still in the sink.

The door across from it opened into a stairwell leading down to what looked like a small cellar or storage area. The smell of bleach was coming from somewhere down below.

I flipped the light switch and a light flickered on at the base of the stairs. The stairs creaked as we headed down and looked around. It was a small area, but it had been converted into some kind of hobbyist's machine shop. There was a workbench covered in tools and a bunch of small mechanical parts I couldn't identify. The walls were lined with shelves, which were stacked with uniform containers of screws, washers, nuts, and wire. The bleach fumes were strong enough to make me breathe through the fabric of my sleeve.

"Dasalia," Shanks said, nudging me. A foot wearing a slipper was sticking out from behind the bench. I holstered my gun and moved around to the other side of the work area, where a man's body lay sprawled on its back. He was an older man, dressed in casual clothes. It looked like there had been a struggle—the floor around him was scattered with tools, and a cardboard box had fallen down, partially covering his head.

The end result was the same, though; the killer had

overpowered him and landed his signature blow. A deep puncture wound gaped from the middle of his chest. Clear liquid had been splashed across the floor a few feet away over by the workbench, where a plastic jug of bleach lay open on its side.

"Damn it," I muttered. Shanks spoke into the radio.

"We're too late," he said. "Craig's here. He's already dead. Get CSI down here."

"On their way."

"How the hell did he beat them here?" I asked. It was impossible. We'd called the locals from the road. If he'd flown, he couldn't have beaten them.

"I don't know."

"He didn't surprise this one," I said. I moved the cardboard box aside and saw his eyes were wide open. The man's right forearm was bruised in a pattern that looked like it had been gripped tightly, and there was a gash on the wrist above it, in the center of a swollen knot. Shanks knelt down and fished out his ID.

"Harold Craig," he said. "It's our guy."

Looking around the room, I could see there was no other way out except the way we had come down.

"He had some idea about what was happening," I said. "On the messenger he asked, 'Why are you doing this to us?' Who's 'us'?"

"Are you asking me?"

"He seemed to think the killer knew something about him. He knew the killer knew that he'd seen him. Why didn't he call the police? If not for his friend, then why not for himself?"

"Maybe he figured he was safe way the hell out here."

"The chair upstairs was pushed away from the computer like he moved in a hurry, like he was surprised. The study door is between the front door and the kitchen, where the struggle took place. So the killer came in through the front and startled him, then chased him into the kitchen. After what he must have seen, he just sat there at the computer and waited?"

"Maybe he didn't," Shanks said. "Maybe it happened sooner."

"It would take forty minutes to get here."

You're assuming the killer worked alone, the voice said. *You're assuming there is only one killer. Maybe he made the same assumption.*

Could that be? Could the reason Harold Craig hadn't called the police after witnessing the crime at Valle's apartment be because he didn't have time? Because he was attacked shortly afterward himself?

The time of death will tell us that, I said to myself.

I'm just saying. With what we have so far, we can't definitively say others aren't involved. Right?

The fumes were making me light-headed. For all I knew, the bleach had combined with some other chemical down there and had created some kind of toxic gas. Why did he come down into the one place he had to have known there was no way out of?

They struggled in the kitchen, and he came down into the basement. The killer overtook him again at the workbench and they struggled. There was a wound on the side of Craig's wrist that looked like it was from an impact, like it had been smashed against something. . . .

"A gun," I said.

"What?"

"He kept a gun down here; that's why he came down here."

He managed to get it too. The killer closed the distance and grabbed him. He smashed his wrist against the workbench, forcing him to drop it. Had he gotten a shot off?

Yes. That's what the bleach was for. It hadn't just fallen over; the killer dumped it out. He did that to compromise any sample of his blood that might be collected.

"He shot him."

Using the ALS light, I adjusted the beam's spectrum and scanned the area around the body, then over near the workbench. There was nothing on the walls or ceiling, and nothing on the surface of the bench. The bullet, if there was one, must have gotten lodged inside its target.

"Come on," Shanks said. "Let's get forensics in here."

"Hold on."

Kneeling down and shining the light up under the bench, I could see a spatter there. He had been hit. I scraped off a small sample.

"Come on, before we both pass out."

If he had any kind of record, it would identify him. Even if he didn't, we'd have his entire genome. After six crime scenes and not one hair, not one speck of saliva or sweat, not one thing that could be used as a reliable identification, he left behind the most damning thing he possibly could have.

The room spun for a second, and I grabbed the leg of the workbench until it passed.

"Faye, CSI will take care of this. Come on."

"I'm fine."

"No, you're not," he said, shaking his head. "You're not. Call it in."

You've done what you came to do. Do you still want to know why he's different?

Was my inner voice taunting me now?

Yes, why is he different?
The answer is in the sample you just took.
I know.
No, you don't, but you will soon.
How? I asked, but the voice wouldn't say. It didn't pipe up again.

I called it in.

6

Syndrome

Nico Wachalowski—FBI Home Office

Wachalowski, this is Noakes. What have you got for me?

Heinlein's rep came through with the data they promised.

Any lead on the parts we dug out of the dock revivor?

It was all legit. The information on the Zhang lead will take a little longer to sort through.

What about the other lead you were following?

I still hadn't told him specifically about Zoe, and he was getting impatient. It had been hours since I'd dropped the evidence off with her, and I hadn't heard back yet.

Nothing yet.

Things were tense out there and getting worse. Rumors of more terrorist attacks were flooding the airwaves, and the FBI circuits were jammed with false tips, confessions, and more bomb threats. The police and the Guard had their hands full trying to keep order and enforce the curfew. The first revivor soldiers were due to hit the streets in the next few hours.

It's a mistake, deploying those revivors, I told Noakes. *Find out who did this before they strike again and maybe it won't be necessary. Let me know when you can pin that name on anyone.*

Understood.

After sifting through Heinlein's data on Zhang's Syndrome, I was able to come to two conclusions. The first was that the condition was not as much of a footnote as MacReady indicated it was. The second was that although Olav Sodder may have been the one who first became aware of it with Samuel Fawkes as his protégé, it was Fawkes who had the obsession with it, far more so than his mentor ever had. Most of the data I'd received had been gathered by Fawkes.

With pages of information scattered in the background, I watched one of hundreds of archived sessions Fawkes conducted with the revivor for whom the condition was named, Ning Zhang. Zhang, in life, had been a second-tier citizen who worked in sanitation, specializing in substructure plumbing. Zhang had also been a convicted criminal.

He was a short male revivor, lean but stocky, with Asian features. His eyes were flat white and his skin, even after reanimation, leaned toward dark. In the footage he was seated at a table with a series of what looked like index cards in neat stacks in front of him. His face had no expression as Samuel Fawkes approached him.

In contrast to Zhang, Fawkes was thin and very pale. There was dense stubble on his face, and he wore his thick black hair fairly long. He'd removed his tie and rolled up his sleeves. He looked tired, but his eyes were sharp as he regarded the revivor.

"Stack zero," he said. Zhang looked to the leftmost

stack of cards. He reached over and slid them closer with one hand.

"Event series N through R," Fawkes continued. "Each card relates information regarding documented events. Some of the events are compiled from information on record, cited by you, prior to reanimation. Some of the events are compiled from information obtained from interviews after reanimation."

"Why?" Zhang asked, still looking down at the stack of cards.

"Each event is reduced to the salient, documented facts. Review each event and—"

"We did this."

Fawkes ran one hand over his face, then rubbed the bridge of his prominent nose.

"Are you refusing to cooperate?"

"No. I will do whatever I'm told."

"And if your first commander removes your ghrelin inhibitor and commands you to eat human flesh?"

"Then I will."

"Would you have done so in life?"

"No."

"Would you have found it repulsive?"

"I believe so."

"The event on the card in your hand, is it accurate?"

"No. Are you trying to trick me?"

"We know the event is accurate. You were convicted of murdering that woman—this is a verifiable event. You're claiming now that your confession was a lie?"

"I was not lying."

"So you did, in fact, stab Noelle Hyde with a kitchen knife?"

"I did not."

"You confessed. All the polygraph sensors and computer models validated your confession."

"I was not lying."

"Then you're lying now."

"No."

"They can't both be the truth. The event occurred once, in one way. Not two."

"In both cases, I was asked to tell the truth. In both cases, I related the information without alteration."

"So you feel now the information you believed in life was false?"

"I don't know. I gain nothing by denying it now."

"You either did or did not commit that crime. Events happen only in one way," Fawkes insisted.

"Are you sure?"

"Yes," he snapped. "Reanimation doesn't open the mind to parallel experiences and somehow replace perceptions of events with alternate possibilities."

"Are you sure?"

"You killed her. Something corrupted those memories."

"If it did," Zhang said with the certainty of one who didn't care one way or the other, "then I will never have any way of knowing which ones. By extension, neither will you."

"Don't be so sure."

I paused the footage and dug up what information there was on the Zhang trial. It looked cut-and-dried. For whatever reasons, Ning Zhang had followed Noelle Hyde one night, pulled her into an alley, and stabbed her repeatedly. Her body was never found, but Zhang's prints were on the knife, and traces of her blood were found on his clothes. Witnesses were produced who saw him approach her that night. Eventually he confessed.

Less than a month later, he was killed in a prison altercation and picked up by Heinlein. Even as a revivor, though, he could not or would not say where the body ended up.

I gain nothing by denying it now.

That was true on one level, but people often had strange reasons for lying, especially to themselves. Had his mind somehow purged the information? Had he convinced himself, somehow, of his own innocence at the end, and carried it with him into death?

The problem probably existed long before, but in the early days, revivor brains were so simplistic that no one had noticed. The problem surfaced more as time went by and the records contained the same kind of experiments for almost fifty other revivors, but his obsession had started with Zhang.

It could have been a scientist's curiosity or even an obsession, but having sat through and conducted as many interrogations as I had, it looked to me like Fawkes was digging for something. The isolation, the repetition, and just the way he held himself, the way he kept at it—it was standard stuff whether Fawkes even knew it or not. He was trying to extract information. He was pretty good at it too.

Regardless, he never figured it out. The experiment eventually ended. The revivor was shipped off across the ocean, where its ghrelin inhibitor was eventually removed, despite being in violation of international law. In the resulting state of perpetual hunger, Zhang most likely committed atrocities far worse than he ever had in life.

A red warning light flashed at the apex of my line of sight. I snapped open my eyes.

Wachalowski.

I'm here. What is it?

Security camera twenty-three. We have a vehicle approaching with a driver who says he's looking for you. He looks like he's being pursued.

On my way.

I sprinted to the stairwell and down to the ground floor, heading for the lobby. On the security feed, I could see the car as it tore around the corner, tires smoking. It fishtailed and then began picking up momentum, heading right for the front doors. Was he planning on ramming the place?

We got a partial message from him before he cut out, the guard says. He says he's got information, and he needs protection.

Weaving through the suits in the main corridor, I picked up speed, moving toward the guard station.

Who is he?

Checking . . .

"Out of the way!" I shouted, drawing my gun as I hurried toward the entryway. I was about a hundred yards down the hall when through the glass doors I saw people on the sidewalk scatter as the car screeched to a halt, bucking up over the curb.

"Out of the way!"

He identified himself as Edward Cross. We're still referencing.

Cross. MacReady had dropped that name back at Heinlein.

Outside, the car door opened and a middle-aged man lurched out, his face red and his eyes wild. He tripped on the curb and went facedown on the sidewalk just as the rear window of the car exploded and a loud report boomed down the street.

We have gunfire.

People on the street outside began fleeing from the car as two more shots went off and one of the tires blew out. The man picked himself up off the ground and looked around.

Stay down. . . .

On the security feed, I looked but I couldn't see which vehicle, if any, had been following him.

"Stay down!" I shouted, waving the man down as I approached the doors, but he had already committed to making a run for it. He got as far as the steps when he was struck in the side and went down on the concrete.

Two armored guards appeared and barreled through the door just ahead of me, each carrying an assault rifle. They immediately took aim down the street, but didn't fire, as if they were trying to get a bead on the shooter.

Another shot went off and struck the man in the shoulder blade as he lay on the steps. The two guards began firing controlled bursts.

Suppressing fire. They still don't see the shooter.

I pushed through the doors and grabbed the wounded man, dragging him back by his suit jacket. Another bullet slammed off the bulletproof glass as I got him through the doors.

We need a medic down here now.

"Help him . . ." the man muttered. He was alive anyway.

"Take it easy, sir," I told him. "Help is coming, understand?"

"Help him. . . ."

The guards outside were scanning the street again, but the gunfire had stopped. I abandoned the man for a moment, pushing the glass door open and using it as a shield so I could see out onto the street with my own eyes.

"You see anything?" one guard asked the other.

"Negative."

The street was clogged with cars that had either been abandoned or had passengers cowering inside. Several windshields were pocked with gunshots, and the blacktop was littered with glass. Smoke drifted from beneath the hood of one of the vehicles.

"Hold your fire," I said, looking down the street.

Where had the shooter come from? He might have been pursuing in any one of the abandoned cars, but those shots had come from street level.

Several car doors still hung open. I could hear some people sobbing faintly, and far-off traffic, but that was all. Where had he . . . ?

There. The smoke from one of the cars parted suddenly as it drifted across the street. It was subtle, but I saw it. For just a second, there was the outline of an arm and a leg in the smoke; then it flickered and moved away.

He was there. He was right there. Whoever it was really did have an LW suit. I hadn't seen one of those since my tour.

"Is he out there?" one of the guards asked. I didn't answer. I didn't want to spook the shooter.

Switching filters, I managed to at least get a fix on him. It was definitely a male, carrying a rifle of some kind. I couldn't make out any features, just an enhanced silhouette, but I could see him. He stood in the middle of the street, between two cars, looking toward the steps, which were still covered in the man's blood. The shooter lingered, like he was debating whether or not to press the attack.

He opted not to. He took two steps back, then turned.

I moved out from behind the door, took aim, and fired three times. I hit him twice for sure, but it didn't stop him. He crouched down and darted down a side street.

"Sir?" one of the guards said.

"Let him go."

We could get a team together with the right hardware to track him, but not before he was long gone. For now I had gotten at least a recording of him, proof that he existed. Faye wasn't seeing things; someone or something had been under an LW field at the truck fire as well.

Stepping over the slick of blood on the stairs, I followed the trail back inside. The medics had arrived and were treating the man, but he was hemorrhaging badly. I knelt over him, and his although he looked very weak, his eyes found mine immediately and fixed on me. He spoke, struggling to get the words out.

"His name is Luis Valle. . . ."

"Luis Valle."

"Luis . . . they're looking for him. Help him . . ." he whispered, groping with one hand.

"I will," I said. "They told me you asked for me by name. Is that true?"

"Yes."

"Why me?"

"You were there. . . ."

His face tightened and his eyes went wide; then everything relaxed. His eyes began to swim out of focus.

"Where?" I asked.

"Heinlein . . . Samuel never left. . . ."

"You left that message for me?"

He nodded.

"Samuel Fawkes?"

"Yes," he whispered. He could barely speak. "He found me out. . . . I had to run. . . ."

"Samuel Fawkes is dead. Isn't he?"

"I suspected . . . he was in the system. Luis found something . . . for me. He's in danger. . . ."

"What does that mean? What did he find?"

His eyes met mine one last time, tears brimming.

"Help Luis. . . ."

He flatlined. The medic closest to me gave me a look.

"That's it."

I stood up. The knees of my pants were wet with blood. I called back to security.

What did he say when he contacted you?

Just that he was coming in fast, and he needed to see you. His records show he had a doctorate in applied cybernetics. Full citizen with a high security clearance.

No doubt. Bob MacReady, the representative from Heinlein who met with me, had mentioned his name, in passing anyway. He had worked at one time for Samuel Fawkes, up until the time of Samuel's death. The two had worked on Zhang's Syndrome.

He worked at Heinlein Industries, I said.

He was a key player there. How did you know?

MacReady dropped his name. What about the name Luis Valle? Any relation?

Hang on.

Heinlein Industries, and the name Zhang in particular, had a way of cropping up during the course of all this.

I've got a Luis Valle, age twenty, son of Tara Valle, maiden name Tara Cross. It's his nephew. Looks like he's got a record; all computer crimes.

One of the names on the list we recovered from the dock revivor was Rebecca Valle.

Hang on.

Rebecca Valle's name was right after that of Mae Zhu, who had been murdered in her car the night before. None of the others on the list were reachable, and none had responded to repeated messages. That last name could not be a coincidence.

Got it, the security agent said. *Rebecca Valle is the second wife of Luis Valle's father, Miguel, and get this— Rebecca, the husband, and their daughter were all found dead in their home earlier today.*

The medics hoisted the body onto a gurney, leaving behind nothing but a mess on the tiled floor. Whatever else he was, Cross wasn't the kind of man who dealt with men like Tai. It sounded as though he found something at Heinlein, something that made him enlist the help of his computer-savvy nephew. Rebecca Valle's name on that list of targets tied them together, though, somehow. Did she prompt Cross to get involved in whatever he had gotten involved in?

"Hold on," I said, stopping the medics before they wheeled the body away. I found a cell phone in his pocket. Sure enough, Luis Valle was on his list of contacts. I punched the number in and the phone started to ring.

Someone was looking for that boy. By now, he most likely knew he was in trouble and was on the run.

He's not answering his phone, I said, snapping it shut. *Coordinate with local police and find that kid. Offer a reward—whatever it takes. I think we don't have much time.*

I'm on it.

Dig up some information on a Samuel Fawkes, too.

According to Heinlein, he's deceased, but find out if he was candidate for reanimation, and if so, where he ended up.

Will do. Can I ask why?

The coroner zipped Cross into a bag. I wasn't sure why, but he took a bullet in the back because he wanted me to know that Samuel never left, whatever that meant.

Because something is going on at Heinlein that someone is trying to hide.

The kid, Luis Valle, might be the only one left who knew what.

Zoe Ott—Pleasantview Apartments, Apartment 713

When Wachalowski first left the envelope full of evidence with me, I was so excited that I didn't think that much about what exactly he expected me to do with it, or how I was going to be able to give him any information he didn't already know. It had been a while since he left, and although I had been looking at some of the stuff he gave me, I was mostly just a lot drunker.

Gray light peeked in from behind the shade, but the bedroom was lit by a couple of the scented candles Karen had left behind. Usually I didn't use them, because candles and me didn't mix, but the overhead was out. The light flickered over the walls where I had tacked up about half the stuff from the envelope so far.

Mostly it was a bunch of documents, but I wasn't about to read through all that. Mixed in were copies of ID cards, what looked like schematics of some kind, and some other things I didn't recognize. There were also ten printouts of waveforms like the kind I doodled on the card I'd left for him that night. They were all labeled RHS, along with a number code in the lower right-hand corner. Those squiggles meant a lot to him, but I didn't even remember drawing the one on the card and I had no idea what I was supposed to be able to tell from them.

I'd been staring at them tacked up on the wall and letting my mind drift, but like I said, I was pretty much only getting drunker. I held the empty shot glass against my lower lip, smelling the fumes and waiting for inspiration to come.

Someone knocked on the front door, snapping me out of it. I sighed into the glass, fogging it up. Considering that up until a few days ago I hadn't had any visitors for years, now it seemed like I never stopped getting them.

Putting down the glass and the bottle, I crawled off the bed and made my way to the door, thinking it was probably Karen and that maybe she wanted her clothes back. Nico had said he had someplace he had to go, so it probably wasn't him. At least I hoped not, because I didn't have anything to tell him.

Usually I used the peephole, but this time I didn't. I should have, because it wasn't Karen and it wasn't Nico; it was my asshole next-door neighbor.

"God, what do you want?" I asked. He stood there watching me in that weird way he had.

"You get a lot of visitors lately," he said.

He was too much. I'd had it with him. How did I end up with this spaz living next to me? The old woman had never done anything but smile at me in the hall every once in a while, which was almost never, because she came out of her apartment even less than I did. What was wrong with this guy? Was this just his weird way of trying to make conversation, or was he some kind of nut job?

Either way, I didn't care anymore. Without bothering to answer, I focused on him until the color drained away from everything and the lights swelled.

The colors that drifted above him came into view, and so did that strange, thin white halo I noticed before. In fact, since I was concentrating harder this time, it was much brighter. It was brighter than anything else, and got even more intense until it threatened to wash out everything.

Right then, I started to feel funny, and instead of his curiosity or whatever it was disappearing, it was my anger and frustration that just melted away. This total relaxation kind of came over me that was even better than drinking.

The lights dimmed back to normal around me and his colors faded until they were gone, along with the odd halo. He was looking directly into my eyes and smiling faintly.

"How do you feel?" he asked.

"Pretty good," I said.

"Your new friend is a federal investigator," he said, still smiling.

"Yeah."

"What did he want?"

"I'm helping him on a case he's working on."

"Oh?"

"Yeah," I said, feeling a little proud of that fact. "He left me some stuff, some evidence to look at."

"Really?"

"Yeah."

"I would like very much to see that."

"You want to see?"

"If it's appropriate," he said, still staring into my eyes.

"Well, he said none of it was classified. . . ."

I opened the door wide enough for him to enter, pushing over a stack of notebooks as I did. His face changed for a second, showing what might have been disgust or contempt, but it was gone as fast as it came. Stepping back to let him through, I gestured to my bedroom door.

"Through here," I said. "Follow me."

He came inside, one of his shoes knocking into something that skittered across the floor before he closed the door behind him. His footsteps sounded behind me as I headed back into my room, where the contents of the envelope were tacked up.

As I looked over the array of things hanging on the walls, I felt him also looking behind me.

"Your friend works with revivors," he said.

"Yeah, it's something about the case he's working on."

He moved closer to the printouts with the heart squiggles on them and studied them. His eyes moved across the walls, looking at the other documents, IDs, and whatnot before they landed on the evidence envelope sitting open on my bed.

"May I?" he asked.

"Sure."

He picked up the envelope and looked inside before shaking out what was left out onto my bed. Among the other papers were a stack of photographs that he spread out over the mattress.

One was a dark-skinned Asian man with a long face and long black hair. He was creepy-looking, and I knew right away I'd never seen him before. Another one looked like a video still of a girl revivor. She was standing completely naked in what looked like a public bathroom, with those electric eyes staring out from behind strands of straight black hair. I recognized that one; I'd seen her on the news in one of the clips the data miner had picked out when I was filtering on Wachalowski's name.

He pushed the photographs around for a moment so that he could see them all. He didn't show any particular interest in the naked ones, but he did linger on one in particular.

"Do you know who that is?" I asked. The picture looked like a still taken from somebody's point of view as they were standing inside an office or something. Sitting on a desk was a polished stone clock with what looked like a diamond above the twelve. A little Asian woman with a big head was sitting behind the desk. She had an overbite and weird lips, and her eyes reminded me of a fish's, for some reason.

"Do you?" he asked back.

"No."

He looked at the picture a little longer, then looked back at me.

"How is it that you are helping your friend, the federal investigator, on his case?"

"I have special talents," I said.

"But why you?"

"I'm the only one that can do what I do."

He nodded like he wasn't even listening. He didn't ask me to clarify what I had just said.

"I see," he said, stepping back from the photographs. He took one more look along the walls at the other things tacked there, then moved to the bedroom doorway.

"Thank you for showing me this," he said. "It was very interesting. Good luck helping your friend. I hope you are successful."

"Thanks."

"If there's one thing this world does not need, it's more revivors."

On that note, he moved back to the front door and opened it, giving my apartment one last look before that expression of contempt came back for a second.

"You should tend to this," he said. "Human beings shouldn't live in filth like you do."

All at once, the sort of lighthearted feeling left me and I remembered why I couldn't stand that guy. My face got hot all the way to my earlobes.

"I should have known better," I said. "I knew you were a jerk."

He shrugged as he turned to leave.

"Get out!" I snapped at his back, then slammed the door behind him.

I was so angry. Who did he think he was, asking to come in and then insulting me to my face?

Turning the lock, I stormed back into the bedroom and grabbed the bottle. It took five shots to calm me down again; then I took a deep breath and sat down on the bed next to the photographs.

I meant to look at the one with the big-headed woman again, but I didn't see it on top of the stack. Pushing the photographs off to the side to spread them out, I saw one underneath that I hadn't looked at before, and stopped short.

The image looked like a video still of a woman. In the picture she was kneeling down in the snow, holding what looked like a body in her lap while a truck burned a little ways away from her. She had short dirty blond hair, nice cheekbones, and a strong jaw. I recognized her immediately.

I picked up the photo to get a better look. It was the

woman from the green concrete room, the woman who carried the split heart. It was the dead woman.

The picture started to shake in my hand. Why did he have a picture of her? What did she have to do with anything?

"It's how I was," a woman's voice said from behind me. I jumped, dropping the picture, and turned to see that she was actually standing there. The woman from the photo, the dead woman from the green room, was standing three feet away. She wasn't dead this time, though. Her skin and her eyes were normal. She looked sad.

"You know Nico?" I asked. She didn't answer. She just turned suddenly, her eyes opening wide like she was startled by something only she could hear.

"He's here—" she started to say, then clutched her chest with one hand.

I waited to see if she would continue, but her eyes just bugged out and her mouth opened and closed.

"What's wrong?" I asked.

A second later, blood began to run between her fingers as she held it to her breastbone.

"Hey!"

Jumping off the bed, I stood in front of her, but there was nothing I could do. She wasn't even really there. She looked down, her face terrified as blood pumped out of the hole that had appeared in her chest. As it did, a black spot grew on her forehead and I watched it form the number 3.

"Help me," she whispered.

"I can't," I said.

"Help me," she whispered again; then her eyes went out of focus. She began to fall; then she was gone.

Standing there in the candlelight, I waited to see if

she would come back, but she didn't. After a couple minutes, I realized she wasn't going to. Had whatever happened to her already happened, or was it going to happen? Was it happening right at that moment?

Scrambling, I began searching for my phone so I could call Nico. I couldn't help her, but if he knew who she was, then maybe he could.

7

Friendly Fire

Calliope Flax—Bullrich Heights

Not long after I saw the bloodbath on TV, I knew what I was going to do. It took a couple beers and some sweet talk, but Luis dropped the attitude. The fact was he was screwed, and I think he knew it. He decided to stick around until I at least got him out of no-man's-land, which was what I wanted.

Luis was the kind of guy you didn't want to take your eye off of. He was a sneak, and was too good at palming shit not to be a thief. Not that I had anything to steal, but any guy that could walk in and find his family dead on the floor, then look in your face and act like nothing was wrong could probably do a lot of things. I had to change, so there was a door between us for two minutes, but that was as much time as he got out of my sight.

When I came out, he was still in the can, getting pretty. He messed with his hair in the mirror.

"You all set?" I asked.

"All set."

"Go warm up the seat. I'll be right down."

He put up his hands, but he went. When he was out the door, I threw on my jacket and zipped up. I checked the pockets, but it was all there: the ID, the knuckles, the keys, my phone, and my black lipstick.

The door downstairs slammed shut and I saw him step out and hang near the building. I stepped back and punched up the number from the TV bulletin that came on right after they showed the bodies.

The phone rang twice, then picked up.

"Federal Bur—"

"I can deliver Luis Valle to you," I said. The voice on the other end stopped for a second, and the line clicked but didn't go dead.

"Do you still want him or not?" I asked.

"Hold on just one moment, please," the guy said. The line went quiet.

Through the window, I saw Luis put his hands in his pockets and pace, shoulders hunched.

The line picked back up.

"This is Agent Wachalowski," a new guy said. "You have information regarding Luis Valle?"

"I can give him to you."

"Give him to me how?"

"There's a reward for this, right?"

"Is he alive?"

"He's alive."

"Where is he now?"

"I'm not saying where he is right now, but I can tell you where he's going to be. Am I getting paid for this?"

"Yes. Where is he going to be?"

"You know where the Arena Porco Rojo is?"

"I'll find it."

"That's where he'll be."

"Where in the arena?"

"In the audience. I don't know."

"When?"

"In a half hour."

"I'm on my way."

"Wait, don't you need my name?"

"I have your information, Ms. Flax," he said. "Keep your phone on. I'll find you."

The line cut.

I headed out and locked the door. It was best anyway. Luis was in deep shit whether he knew it or not, and the Feds might pinch him, but at least they'd let him live. He'd live to fight another day, and that was the best he'd get at this point. Fuck him. He got himself into this mess. He put me in it too. Fuck him.

When we got to the fights, he called his cab, then sat in the bleachers to wait. With luck, he'd get grabbed before I even got in the ring.

By the time I put my gear on and got back out there, I'd lost track of him. In the octagon, Eddie waited in my corner while the other bitch tried to stare me down.

"You seen her before?" Eddie asked.

"No."

The canvas had blood on it, but she just sat like she didn't see it or didn't care. She was skinny and tall, with skin black as night.

"She wants you," he said. "Because of the last fight. Watch out for her."

Yeah.

When I climbed up, there were cheers, but more boos. A lot of them hoped I'd get stomped after last time. I'd knocked that bitch off the roster for the rest of the season.

"You ready?" Eddie asked. I rolled my shoulders.

"Yeah, I'm ready."

The bitch looked up then. She looked like she could stick a knife in my neck and twist it.

"In the left corner," the judge barked into the amp, "weighing in at one hundred forty-two pounds, a newcomer to the arena . . ."

The crowd started stomping the bleachers and I wondered where Luis was.

". . . here to replace the injured Brick-House Bonnie Bast . . ."

That kicked things up. The canvas shook with all the stomps and screams. They were geared to rush the fence already.

"Skinny . . . Minnie . . . Botma!"

Minnie? The bitch's name was Minnie?

"And in the right corner," the judge said, "weighing in at one hundred fifty-one pounds, undefeated this season in her class . . ."

More boos. More stomping. I stuck up both middle fingers.

"The Bitch from Bullrich . . . Calliope Flax!"

We met in the middle of the ring, and the more she stared me down, the more I could not wait to force those big teeth of hers straight down her bitch throat.

"Shake hands," the ref said, and we did.

"Guard up!"

We put them up, and waited for the buzzer.

The second it went off, she threw a hard punch at my throat and almost caught me. If I was a hair slower, she'd have put me out. As it stood, she just clipped my neck on the left side. She was quick too, and blocked me when I whipped an elbow at her face. For two beats, we both backed off.

She had a long reach, so I came in like I meant to throw a punch but threw a heel right at her ear at the last second, and I almost had her. It would have dropped her too, but that bitch was quick. She went down flat and scooped my other leg out from under me with an ankle sweep.

My back slammed down on the canvas, and as soon as I looked up, I saw her big black foot coming down on me. I rolled, and it stomped down right where my head had been with a loud boom.

"Point!"

I got up quick, but she didn't try to pounce when I was down. She didn't want it to go on the ground, so first chance that's where I'd take it.

To do that, I had to get in close, past that reach. I lunged in at her, throwing a flurry of punches and getting my knee up in her gut. She got some in too, but by then we were face-to-face. She tried to pull back and I grabbed on, trying to get hold of a leg while pushing her back. I thought she was off balance, and steered her away from the fence. . . .

Right then, a face jumped out at me from the crowd. Luis was there, cheering and waving his fists. A row back, a big guy in a dark coat was going for him.

I saw the fist just before it connected, dead on my right cheek. Sweat and blood sprayed in a burst of white light, and all at once I was falling.

"Ten points!" the judge screamed. "Minnie Botma! Ten points!"

The lights spun in front of me. I was going down.

"Calliope Flax is down!"

I hit the canvas on my back as that big foot came down again.

"Flax is d —"

There was no time to think. I rolled back and got the balls of my feet on the ground as her heel left a dent in front of me.

I sprung from a squat and blasted my elbow out like a jackhammer. It dug deep in her solar plexus and she choked. She had one arm out and I grabbed it, clamping down on her wrist. Blood poured out of my nose. I was in a rage, and she was going to get it.

When I rolled her arm, I put my full weight on and it came out at the shoulder. I heard it. She showed me her ribs, so I fired a side kick and broke those too.

Her eyed bugged out and her jaw dropped. Her legs gave out, and when I let her go, she dropped like a stone.

"Ten points! Calliope Flax!" the judge screamed.

The ref came out into the ring and ran over to her, but she wasn't getting back up. He looked up at the booth and made an X with his forearms.

"That . . . is . . . the . . . fight! Winner, Calliope Flax! She takes it again!"

The ref had a needle and stuck her with painkillers so she could breathe. Two other medics came on to take her out back so they could put her shoulder back in. She stood—I'll give her that—but she didn't stare at me anymore. She didn't even look my way.

"In round one, Minnie Botma is out of the fight!"

The crowd screamed so loud it hurt my ears. They spit and threw trash, stomping on the sides of the cage. I felt something cold on my back and something brown and sticky splashed down my leg as a paper cup hit the fence. Chew spit, by the look of it. A bottle skipped across the top of the cage; then another one smashed on the corner.

"Okay, settle down, people!"

It was a mob scene. I tried to see if Luis was getting picked up, but I couldn't see shit. Something was wrong; I knew when I saw the guy going for him. That guy didn't look right.

"Flax! Flax is number one!"

"Flax, you bitch, rot in hell!"

I was getting dizzy. Christ, that bitch rattled my cage. . . .

There was blood all down the front of my tank top, and when I grabbed a towel and wiped my face, there was a lot of red. One of my front teeth was gone. I grabbed my water bottle and poured it over my face, letting it run down my neck and chest.

I had to get the hell out of there. Maybe Luis would try to meet up with me. He might try the locker room or the lobby. I climbed out of the ring and shoved past Eddie.

"Hey!" he yelled. "Where the hell do you think you're—"

I pushed through the crowd, heading for the lockers. My hands were shaking as I got my padlock open and took my jeans and sweatshirt out, pulling them on over my fight clothes. I threw on my boots and jacket and made a run for the lobby. That's when I heard the scream.

It was a guy, and it was loud, but it came from outside. I slammed through the doors and out to the sidewalk. No one was there. The fights were still on, and most everybody was still inside. I looked left and right; then I heard the scream again, real low, like it was from the gut. It gurgled and stopped.

I stood there, listening. My breath came out like smoke in the cold, and every time I sucked in air, it stabbed my broken tooth. A second later I heard another grunt.

The bathroom. There was a public can that filled up after the fights, but now there was no one hanging around them. I moved to the door and looked, but it opened so you couldn't see in from outside.

"Hello?" I called. No one said anything.

I reached into my jacket and pulled out the brass knuckles, just in case. Blood still dribbled down my lip as I squeezed one set into each fist.

"I'm coming in!"

I gave it another second, then marched down and turned into the men's room.

It took a second for it to sink in. A guy was in there, wearing a dark coat with the hood up. He stared at me when I walked through the door. On the floor in front of him was Luis, or what was left of him.

"It's you," the man said.

I didn't see a knife, but Luis was cut up bad. One arm was hacked off at the elbow and was on the floor next to a toilet. His other hand was short a thumb, and the other fingers just dangled there. His guts were in a pile under him where he lay facedown, with his ass still in the air like he was trying to get up. The floor was wet with blood. It was fucking everywhere.

"That was quick," the man said, stepping toward me. He had a weird look on his face, like he was zoning in front of the TV. An orange light was lit up in his eyes.

"What was?"

"Your fight."

"Look, I don't want any trouble," I said. I took a step back, but he pulled out a gun and pointed it in my chest.

"Quickly," he said. "I monitored the call you made to the FBI. I know he was with you, and I know the FBI is on their way to pick him up."

"What the hell do you want?"

"The data spike," he said. "I know you have it."

"I don't have it," I said. "He told me about it, but that's it—"

"He told me you have it."

He was stepping in on me. I tried to fade back again, but he stuck the gun right in my chest. The look on his face never changed. The barrel was aimed dead center, right at my heart.

"This is your last chance," he said. I smashed the wrist of his gun hand. The gun went off, but the bullet slammed into the tile next to me and I punched him in the side of the head. I gave him everything I had, and I had plenty. Something crunched under my fist. Even without the brass knuckles, it should have dropped him, but it didn't.

When he came back around, still holding the gun, I bashed him with the other fist too. He fell back and I grabbed his gun arm, then rolled him, slamming him face-first into the wall.

I broke his wrist on the urinal, but he wouldn't drop the piece, so I smashed the side of his face with my elbow a few times, then blasted a knee into his ribs. He went down, cracking his head on one of the sinks and rolling onto his back.

Black shit was coming out of his mouth. With the light on his face, I saw it was white as a sheet. The veins underneath looked black.

He was getting back up. I stomped down right on his face and he fell back. More of that black stuff was coming out of a cut on his forehead and his nose. One of his eyes had turned light gray or silver.

He hooked the butt of the gun on the urinal pipe to pull himself back up, so I stomped his elbow on the side and broke his arm in half. His coat fell open, and I saw the bricks underneath, each one with a thick wire coming out of it. Some kind of timer display was counting down on his chest. The guy had a bomb strapped to his chest.

I don't know how his hand still worked, but he still had the gun, even though it just hung there. Something made a loud snap, and just like that there was a big knife in his other hand. It came out of nowhere.

He was still coming, and I would have hit him again, except for the bomb. The bomb changed everything.

The tip of the knife scraped the tiles behind me as I turned and ran like hell.

Nico Wachalowski—Arena Porco Rojo

Two blocks from the arena, the signal from Calliope's cell started moving. Without the exact layout of the place, it was impossible to tell exactly where in the area she was, but from the basic blueprint, it looked like she was leaving the premises. She left the building, lingered near the outside, then went on the move again in the parking area.

Wachalowski, this is Sean. We just got wind of a disturbance down at the arena; we've got shots fired, one dead, and one missing.

Who was killed?

No name yet, but a young male. It could be our guy.

They beat us to him. They got to him and she got too close; that's why her signal was moving. She was running.

Try to get the cops to hang back. I'm almost there.

By the time I got to the arena, blue and red lights flickered over the faces of patrons who had streamed out to see what the commotion was about, and the cops had their hands full keeping them back. Inside the lobby, faces were pressed against the glass, looking out. I pulled over near the blockade and got out of the car, holding up my badge. A handful of the arena-goers hooted when they saw me, but the officers looked less impressed.

"Who's in charge?" I asked.

One of the men held up his hand, looking at me under the brim of his cap.

"You," he said. "I got the call to hang back until you got here."

"I appreciate it. Can we get these lights off?"

He nodded to one of the officers, who ducked away, and a few seconds later the flashing lights went dark one set at a time. I switched to a thermal filter, but there was still too much interference; too many people had been through to pick out any one signature.

"There's a woman down there somewhere," I said. "Has anyone seen her?"

"Not since the attack. Word is she took off down toward the lower levels, and the guy went after her."

"Who was the victim?"

"Name was Luis Valle."

"Where'd it start?"

"Men's room," he said, pointing. "One of the fighters came out and heard something, then went to check it out and got into it with the shooter. There was an altercation that spilled out into the garage; then Sawed-off Sam over there comes out and starts shooting."

He gestured to a stocky, balding man with a thick neck who was standing cuffed next to a pair of officers. Following the path he traced, I saw one of the cars nearby had sustained several shotgun blasts at medium range. Glass and spent shells littered the pavement.

Wachalowski, this is Noakes. Secure that body immediately.

If he had what they were after, he doesn't have it now.

I'm not asking you.

"I need the crime scene locked down," I told the officer. "No one in or out."

"Already done," he said evenly.

The attacker might still be here, and I've got a civilian in trouble. I'm going to try to bring him in.

Without the kid, the information he was holding is the first priority.

I get it.

"The fighter was female?"

"Yeah."

On my map, I was still reading the signal from her phone. The blip was stationary, so the phone was still in one piece, even if she wasn't.

"Start getting these people out of here," I said.

He shook his head, but he got moving. I dropped the thermal filter to 20 percent transparency and bumped the light up a little as I headed down the ramp through the rows of cars. At the same time, I started scanning the JZI communications bands, pulling out the police chatter until it got quiet. If the attacker tried to communicate with anyone else, I wanted to pick it up.

Crouching next to one of the vehicles, I scanned the area, but again, there were too many signatures. I listened, but I didn't hear anyone nearby. The blip was brighter, though. It was close.

Staying low, I adjusted my visual filters until I found recent thermal prints that probably belonged to Flax. With the concrete to my back, I scanned the area in front of me, but the garage was quiet.

"Calliope Flax," I said, "this is Agent Wachalowski with the FBI. If you can hear me, don't speak out. Stay where you are."

Her signal was maybe five spaces away to my left, keeping perfectly still. I put one hand on the cold pavement and leaned down to look under the vehicle I was using as cover. Beneath the undercarriages of the other cars, I saw a tiny light move somewhere in the distance near the ground.

I zoomed in toward the movement. It was the LED on her phone. She had spotted me and was waving it to get my attention. Her chin rested on the pavement as she lay flat under the axle of a truck, her face flecked with blood and her eyes wide.

I wasn't sure how well she could see me, but I held out one palm to indicate she should stay put. That was when my phone rang.

It was a rookie mistake, and it was almost a fatal one. The shooter had a pretty good bead on me already, and that cinched it; the garage erupted with gunfire, and bullets punched into the vehicle I was crouched behind. The windows sprayed out, and several shots sparked off the ground less than a foot away from me, one of them puncturing the rear tire.

Stupid . . .

I grabbed the phone as air hissed out of the hole, struts groaning as the vehicle leaned onto the rim. The display on the phone flashed the name ZOE OTT as I shut it off.

The shots stopped for a minute, and I could hear him reloading. Staying low, I changed positions, moving several cars down before scanning in the direction the shots had come from. No thermal signature that I could see was there, but when I flipped through the other filters, I finally got an outline. He was hiding under another LW suit about three cars away, but based on the body structure, it didn't look like the same guy I'd shot at outside the FBI building.

I've got him.

I raised my weapon and turned up the intensity on the filter until his outline stood out sharply and I could target the shoulder joint of his gun arm.

A three-round burst caught him and he pitched back. His gun fell out from under the LW drape and clattered to the ground.

"Freeze!"

He moved like he was going to go for the gun, but his arm wouldn't cooperate. He stood up.

"Kick it over!"

He did, and the weapon skittered to a stop in front of me. I picked it up and slipped it under my belt, keeping my gun trained on him. He kept the LW suit active, still appearing as nothing but a silhouette in front of me.

"Ma'am," I said, "come on out. Stay on the other side of the car."

I heard her come out from under the car, and moved to join her. She was kneeling on the ground, and I reached out to help her to her feet, but she batted my hand away. She stood up, glaring at me.

"Nice ringtone."

"Go back to the barricade and stay with the cops," I told her.

"Who the hell are you looking at? There's no one over there."

"Just do it."

The shooter moved, his outline shimmering as he started closing the distance between us.

"Stop right there," I yelled, even though I knew it wouldn't work.

He kept coming and I fired three bursts, nine shots in all. On the third burst, the air in front of us rippled as the LW suit shorted out and the guy came into view.

"Holy shit!" Calliope yelled.

"Go back to the others!"

As the LW field flickered away, he opened the defunct suit to reveal a device strapped around his middle. He raised a detonator in his good hand.

I fired one last burst, tearing through his throat. I didn't look to see what happened; I grabbed the girl and carried us both behind a concrete divider.

"What the he—"

The bomb went off, and for a second the inside of the garage lit up. I clamped my hands over her ears as the explosion pounded through the air. Everything went white as glass, metal and concrete sprayed across the divider, scattering tiles. It was over in a second, a cloud of flame huffing back up the ramp as the twisted remains of a vehicle rolled off another one, crunching onto the blacktop. I grabbed her hand, and this time she held on. I pulled her to her feet and half dragged her back up toward the barricade.

Through the muted ringing, I could already hear footsteps approaching as the cops came storming down. I stopped, holding her back by her wrist, and pushed her to the wall.

She was maybe five-eight, with short hair that was cropped on the sides and back. She was all muscle, solid and scrappy. One of her front teeth had been knocked out very recently, and her lips were painted with black lipstick. She glared up at me, a pixie-haired prizefighter.

"Did he give you anything?" I asked into her ear.

"What?"

"Luis! Did he give you anything? Anything to hold on to? Anything like that?"

"No!"

"Hold still!"

Taking a step back, I peered through the fabric of her

clothes, starting at the top and working my way down. The pocket over her left breast was shielded with something and I couldn't see in, but in her right-side pocket I could see a set of keys, a tampon, and what looked like a tube of lipstick. I focused on it, turning up the intensity of the scan, and she frowned.

"What are you looking at?"

There was something inside of the tube. Something besides the lipstick itself.

"Give me the lipstick," I said.

"What?"

"Now! Just give it to me!"

She continued to glare at me as she reached in and pulled out the tube.

"I don't think it's your color," she said, tossing it over.

I uncapped it and turned the stick out all the way, pulling it free. When I shook the tube, a data spike fell from the hollow base into my palm.

"What the hell is that?" she asked. I held it up so she could see.

"That," I said, "is the thing five people have already died for today. You were almost number six."

She looked at it, and her thin lips, lacquered with that same black lipstick, curled into a sneer.

"He put that in there."

"I know."

She didn't look scared anymore; she looked angry. She never even looked back at the carnage behind her.

"You owe me a lipstick," she said.

"Yes, I do."

"And a reward."

The police were heading down the ramp, and in the distance I could hear sirens approaching. Somehow I knew better than to touch the girl in front of me again, so instead I gestured toward the uniformed officers.

"You'll get both," I told her.

"Your goddamn phone almost got us killed," she muttered.

"Quiet."

I fished it back out and turned it on. Zoe had called twice; the first was a hang-up, and in the second she left a four-second message with a picture attachment.

When I opened it, the picture expanded to show a photograph of Faye kneeling in front of the burning prison transport, the revivor in her lap.

I listened to the message. Her voice was heavily slurred.

"She's in trouble," she said. "She's going to die."

Faye Dasalia—Shine Tower Apartments, Unit 901

By the time the blood sample had been dropped at the lab, it was dark, and I was grateful when Shanks offered to swing me by my place and deal with signing the car back in himself. As he cut the engine on the dark street in front of my apartment, wind buffeted the vehicle, peppering the windows with snow and grit.

"You going to be all right?" he asked.

"Yeah."

"Come on, I'll walk you up."

Shanks had never seen the inside of my apartment before, but he had seen the street I lived on, and it looked a lot worse from the outside than it did from the inside. For a moment, the whole thing felt a little awkward, and all of a sudden the dream came back to me. When he looked across at me, I remembered the feel of his hands on my hips, how rough he was.

It was just a dream; don't be ridiculous. He's a good man and he's doing you a favor; be nice to him.

The irony was that Shanks was far too polite to ever even suggest something like that. He was the kind of guy who would wait forever to be asked. He'd wait until the moment had long passed. As he looked at me, what I saw was the look he seemed to always have these days when he saw me, and that was concern. It was unnecessary, but I found myself being grateful for it. Even though we'd never have a romantic relationship, he was one person who would care if one day I ended up in that cold box or in the ground.

"I'm sorry," he said. "You don't need me to—"

"No, come on up."

"Yeah?"

"Yeah, have a cup of coffee before you drive all the way back."

"Thanks."

Outside on the steps I flashed my ID at the security camera, and it made Shanks show his too before it would open the door. We didn't speak as the elevator made its way up, and he didn't say anything until we actually got inside.

"Nice place," he said.

Dropping my satchel next to the door, I made my way into the living room and hung my coat on the rack. Scanning the room quickly, I saw it was reasonably clean, which wasn't surprising, since it seemed like I barely set foot inside my apartment myself these days.

"Take off your coat. Make yourself at home," I said, gesturing at the sofa.

He hung his coat next to mine and sat back on the couch, looking around.

"Looks like you've got a message," he said, pointing

at the computer terminal set up at the edge of the living area. A green light flashed on the printer, where a couple of pages were sitting in the bay. I grabbed them on my way to the kitchen.

"You want coffee or a drink?" I asked. "I'm having a drink."

"Make it two, then."

"Wine okay?"

"Sure."

I probably didn't need the alcohol, but I definitely didn't need any more stimulants, and there wasn't much time available to wind down. Uncorking a bottle of red wine on the kitchen counter, I poured out two glasses before shaking out a blue capsule and dropping it in mine. I drank the first sip, making sure to get the floating pill, and swallowed it as I looked at the papers from the printer. It was a copy of the lab report.

"That was fast," I said, bringing the other glass to Shanks.

"What?"

"It's the results of the blood sample we just dropped off. How can they be done already?"

The header on the top sheet read ERRSAMP. That was the code for "Erroneous Sample," which was shorthand for a field slipup. They had decided it was an innocuous substance. No wonder it came back so fast.

"Son of a bitch. They're saying the sample was a mistake."

Double-checking the sample code and identification number, it looked like they had processed the right sample. I read farther down to see what the determination was.

SAMPLE TYPE: BLOOD.

DETERMINED: INORGANIC OR INERT.

That couldn't be right. The sample was organic; it had showed up as organic under the ALS light; that's why I had taken it. The pattern was consistent with the spatter from a gunshot wound. It had to be blood.

"I must be losing it," I said, skipping to the end.

SUBSTANCE: UNKNOWN.

"The report says it's not organic, that it's some kind of silicate or something."

"It's an error at the lab," Shanks said. "Let it go for now, and forensics will find something."

I put the wineglass down and crossed over to the computer terminal. Originally, I had planned to wait until I was alone to look at the contents of the data card that I copied from the Craig house, but suddenly I didn't want to wait anymore. I wanted to see who I was dealing with; I wanted to see his face.

"Faye—"

"This will only take a minute."

The footage came up and I saw Rebecca Valle, still alive and sitting facing the camera as, presumably, she typed on the keyboard, which was out of frame.

"What's that?" Shanks asked, leaning forward.

"I grabbed it from the computer at Craig's place."

On the screen, Rebecca's face looked pale in the glow of the monitor. She glanced at the camera every so often, sometimes smiling, sometimes frowning. There was no sound to go along with it.

"Score one for me," I said, "and zero for the voice in my head."

"Huh?"

"You say I'm not losing it, Shanks, but I don't know. I think I am."

"You're not, Faye. It's not your fault."

There was something strange about the way he said

that, but I didn't pick up on it right away. I was too busy watching the woman on the video screen as she wiled away the last moments of her life. It was so mundane, almost like watching someone watch television, that it was eerie in a way. She had no idea that her life was about to end. She had no idea that this was how she would live the last sane moments of her life, sitting in front of a computer screen.

"I got a pass on my last psych evaluation," I said, "but I'm coming apart, Doyle. You see it. You pretend you don't, but I know you do. I'm on too many chemicals and my body is getting too old for this. My mind is getting too old for it. I want to slow down just a little bit, but I can't."

The footage continued to stream by as I watched, and Shanks had gotten quiet. I wasn't looking at him, but I guessed he was probably trying to figure out the shortest path to the front door. When I agreed to have him come up, I was pretty sure I had no intention of dumping all this on him, and I wanted to stop—I knew I should stop—but the relaxant I had taken along with the wine had loosened my tongue.

"There really is a voice in my head. I'm not even kidding about that, and the worst thing about it is that this voice, this inner me or intuition or whatever it is, makes half of my decisions for me, it feels like."

Shanks sighed, and I thought he might leave. Instead he spoke again in that odd tone of voice.

"It's not your fault, Faye," he said. "This hasn't been fair to you. I haven't been fair to you."

"What?"

He was quiet for a minute, and I could see he was struggling with something.

"You don't know how important you are," he said

finally. "What you do, I could never do. I realized that after I got assigned to you and I'd worked with you for a while."

"Shanks, that's not—"

"Sometimes I think we forget that. Sometimes I think we forget that people like us will always need people like you."

Slowly, my mind was refocusing. I realized that Shanks was behaving more strangely than I had ever seen him before. Something about his tone of voice had become very disconcerting.

"What do you mean, 'people like you'?" I asked.

He looked me in the eye then, and for a minute I thought there might be tears forming in them.

"I'm really sorry, Faye."

"Shanks, what—"

"You deserve to know."

"Know what?"

"The truth."

On the screen, Rebecca Valle turned as she heard the sound that lured her to her death. She got up and left the room.

"Wait," I said, watching. The image stayed static for several seconds.

Shanks stood up and moved next to me, but I couldn't look away from the screen. As I watched, the killer walked into the computer room. There was a little blood on his right hand, but he wasn't carrying a weapon. He sat down in front of the camera, not realizing it was there, and I looked right in his face.

"Oh," I whispered.

His skin was pale and waxy. He had a heavy brow and a wide face, with some kind of scar in the middle of his throat. He was wearing a dark coat with the hood up over his head, which appeared to be bald. At the bottom of the frame, around chest level, I could see what appeared to be explosives strapped around his torso, but that wasn't even the strangest thing.

His eyes, looking down at the screen as he typed, had irises that were pale and silver, like moonlight. In the darkness of the room, they emanated a soft glow. I realized then that the scar on his neck came from the entry wound of a bullet. It was a revivor.

"We suspected," Shanks said.

The blood that showed up under the ALS but wasn't human blood, the complete absence of trace hair, skin, sweat, or saliva at the crime scenes, the lack of any detectable breath or heartbeat on the phone recordings; it all made sense. The killer wasn't human at all. These people had been killed by a revivor.

"Doyle, no offense, but what are you talking about? Who the hell is—"

On the screen, the revivor turned and looked over its shoulder, as if something startled it. It started to get up, and disappeared.

I rubbed my eyes and checked the video, backing it up. When I replayed it, I got the same thing: the revivor turned, started to get up; then the area around it flickered and faded away until it was gone. It was as if it had turned invisible. For just a second, there was a distortion in the shape of a man in the air, then nothing.

Sometimes a single detail caused a series of others to suddenly fall into place, and what I saw on the footage was like that. The killer was wearing some kind of suit that cloaked him or camouflaged him. At the truck fire, I wasn't seeing things. The human outline in the smoke that I thought was my imagination was real. The revivor that killed the Valles had been there; it stood right there in front of me. What was it doing there? Was it following me?

Standing up quickly, I felt the blood rush from my head and I stumbled back into the chair. Shanks started to catch me, but I had righted myself. What had he been talking about?

"Doyle, what did you mean, 'we suspected'?"

The killer couldn't have followed me to the truck; even if it was unable to be seen, it was far too big and the train was too crowded for it to go unnoticed. There was no way it could have been waiting there for me, because I didn't know I'd be there myself.

The only explanation was that it was already there for reasons that had nothing to do with me. It was responsible for the attack on the truck. It was up to something bigger than a string of simple murders.

Shanks held out his hand like he was going to touch my arm, and when I pulled away, he looked hurt. The way he was looking at me made me very uneasy, like he had dropped some kind of facade. The things he was saying and the way he was acting seemed out of character. Had he been working for some other department this whole time? Had they had him watching me for some reason?

I thought of what the revivor had said on the phone. *The man sitting next to you is not your friend. . . .*

My phone vibrated in my pocket. I glanced at the display. It was Nico.

"Faye, please," Shanks said.

"Shut up."

"I—"

"Doyle, shut up."

I flipped open my phone and started talking.

"Nico, I know who the killer is. These murders and what happened that morning are related, I—"

My voice trailed off as I noticed the spots on the floor, like blood but darker. As I watched, several more appeared, dripping down from out of nowhere. I followed the drops upward, and the source should have been right in front of me.

"Faye, you're in danger," I heard him say. "Where are you?"

The air rippled, and all at once the revivor appeared. It was standing right there in front of me. It must have already been in the apartment when we came in. It had been watching us the whole time.

I was still staring when it lashed out and I caught a metallic flash under the light. Something warm spattered the side of my face and neck. Shanks collapsed onto his knees, then forward onto the floor, his gun falling free from his hand.

"Faye!" Nico's voice barked from the phone.

It turned to me. The moonlit eyes glared down at me, orange light flickering behind the pupils.

"It's here—" I said into the phone, as the revivor reached forward and took it, snapping it closed before placing it on the end table.

There was no way it was going to leave me alive. I went for my gun, but before it was fully clear of the holster, the revivor's right hand and forearm split apart to reveal a dark gap inside where something metallic caught the light.

It struck me in the chest with its palm, hard enough to knock the wind out of me, and at that same instant, I heard what sounded like a burst of air followed by an awful crunch.

"What a waste," the revivor said.

All the strength went out of me, and my fingers slipped off its wrist. Looking down, I saw that some kind of blade had actually thrust out of a chamber inside its forearm, impaling me through the middle of the chest. With a loud snap, the blade pulled free and disappeared back into its arm, which closed over the seam, and the gun slipped from my fingers and onto the floor as I began to fall.

Don't leave me like this, I wanted to say, but my lips wouldn't move. *Don't let them bring me back....*

At the last second, terror welled up inside me. It came on like a light from inside, and everything seemed crystal clear. There were no flashes or memories from my life, just that terror, pure and solitary, for just an instant.

The fear subsided, and I was floating weightless, drifting backward into the darkness and a long, long overdue sleep.

8

Coil

Nico Wachalowski — Shine Tower Apartments, Unit 901

The city was crawling with police and soldiers. After the second bomb went off, Ohtomo had begun deploying the revivor soldiers. They'd all be animate and on the ground by nightfall. Checkpoints were being set up at the bridges. Overhead, a military helicopter passed between two buildings as I turned, numb, onto Faye's street.

At the end, where her apartment sat, trash bags and snow bordered the road. There was no place to pull over, so I nosed into the no-parking zone in front of her building and cut the engine. Sitting there, feeling the heat leech out of the cab, I tried to take some solace from the fact that the girl, Flax, would most likely be dead if I hadn't been there, but it didn't provide much.

She's in trouble. She's going to die.

Zoe's warning had come too late. I called Faye immediately, but the call was cut off. Before I'd gotten to the main drag, I got word from the local police. I was too late. Noakes had ordered me back to the arena, where I dealt with the fallout for half the night. Part of me was glad.

Wind blew over the car as a jeep slowed down at the intersection ahead and the soldier riding shotgun peered in at me from behind his visor. I held up my badge and pressed it against the inside of the windshield. After a few seconds, the jeep continued on.

When I shouldered open the car door, it crunched into a bank of snow, and a blast of cold, damp air blew into the car. The sky was overcast, a sliver of gray trailing through the building tops. Even though it was barely afternoon, it looked almost dark. Somehow it seemed fitting.

I pulled myself out of the car and pushed the salt-covered door closed with my foot. Looking around, I saw dirty slush and snow that had refrozen so many times it formed a slick, gray-black trench that bordered the narrow street. Cars were jammed in tight, some covered up to their windshields. Garbage bags stood in piles, waiting to be picked up, stinking faintly even in the cold.

This was where she lived? Sometimes I forgot what a difference full citizenship could mean, even for a public servant. I remembered how tired she'd looked at the restaurant, and how the stress had worked its way into her eyes. She was jacked up on stims and strung out. I'd known something was wrong, but when she smiled I looked past it. When she smiled, it took me back those ten years to before we'd made our choices, back to when she looked happy, and when, if the right song came on, she would dance.

It's here—

It wasn't like I never expected to see her again. On some level, I think I hoped our paths might cross someday, but when I extended my tour, the months turned into years, and before I knew it a decade had passed. When I heard her voice out of the blue, I wasn't sure how it made me feel. But when I saw her in the restaurant, I knew I'd made a mistake back then. Things should have been different.

How could you come back and not even call me?

I didn't have a good answer for that. Something stopped me. It had been a mistake. Now, after all those years, we reconnected just long enough for me to listen to her last words over a cell phone, unable to lift a finger to help her.

The face of the apartment building looked old and weathered. The front doors were double locked with bulletproof glass. I held my badge up to the scanner, which made a ticking sound.

"Unauthorized for access," a voice said. "If you are visiting a tenant, you may—"

"I'm a federal agent," I said, still holding up the badge. The scanner ticked again, reading the badge number then running it.

"Go right in, Agent."

The doors snapped and I pushed them open. A bank of mail slots were arranged on the wall to my right in ten-by-ten grids. Scanning them, I found hers was empty. At the end of the empty entryway was a single elevator door. I took it up to the ninth floor.

The hallway was quiet as I made my way down toward the yellow tape that had been crossed over the door at the far end. Most of the commotion seemed to be over.

"Hello?" I called. Someone stirred inside, and a moment later a man with graying hair approached the door. His eyes narrowed when he saw me.

"Who the hell are you?" he asked me from the other side of the tape.

I showed him my badge. "Sorry to barge in."

His expression stayed fixed for a few more seconds; then he sighed and took a step back.

"Sorry," he said. "We've had to chase camera eyes off all day. Name's Bill Turner."

"I understand. I'm Nico Wachalowski."

I ducked under the tape and moved inside. It looked like everyone else had gone, leaving the place eerily quiet.

Her apartment was small but clean, and had a warm, cozy kind of look, in contrast to the exterior of the place. She had a decorator's sense I didn't have. The furniture looked secondhand but mostly real wood, and the prints hanging on the walls were picked carefully. It had warmth to it, a haven from the outside world.

"You were her partner?" I asked.

"No," he said. "That was Doyle Shanks."

As soon as he said it, the name began to eat at me. I knew that name.

"Was?"

"He got it too," he said, pointing down at the floor in front of the sofa. The outline of a human body had been drawn there, arms and legs sprawled. A large bloodstain had formed there, trickling across the slightly uneven surface. Traced over the sofa around a swath of blood was a second outline: all that remained of Faye Dasalia.

"What did you say her partner's name was?" I asked.

"Shanks," he said. "Doyle Shanks."

Doyle Shanks.

The dock revivor; it was carrying a partial list of names in its memory. I brought up the list.

5. Mae Zhu
6. Rebecca Valle
7. Harold Craig
8. Doyle Shanks

"Who was the last victim before him?" I asked.

"Guy named Harold Craig," he said. "He was killed shortly after victim number six, Rebecca Valle. Before that was—"

"Mae Zhu."

He looked at me, his eyes sharp.

"That's right."

My gut felt hollow. I never even asked her partner's name. We were sitting face-to-face; all it would have taken was one question. All it would have taken was just one piece of small talk, as I struggled to think of what I was going to say to her next. I would have known her partner was a marked man, and the danger that put her in.

"I'd like a full list of the victims' names."

"You got it."

"He was here, then?" I asked. "Her partner?"

"Probably dropping her off," he said.

Zoe knew. She tried to warn me. She knew this was going to happen.

"What is your interest in this case?" Turner asked. "If you don't mind my asking?"

"Detective Dasalia was a witness in an ongoing investigation," I said. "I'm sorry, but I can't tell you any more than that right now."

Nothing appeared to have been disturbed. Her coat still hung on a coat rack near the wall, and a remote rested on the sofa next to the dark stain that had seeped into the cushion. The white outline in the shape of her body was seated upright. Based on the position, it looked like she had fallen there from a standing position. I'd seen tracings like that plenty of times before, but this one hit home. It was like she was suddenly erased from existence, leaving behind only an outline to indicate the space she had once occupied.

"Forensics been through already?"

"Yes."

"So they've been taken to the morgue, then?"

"Shanks was."

When I looked back at him, he was frowning.

"Heinlein's got Dasalia. She signed up for it," he said.

Right. "She signed up for it," I said. I kept my voice stony.

"That all you've got to say?" he asked.

"I wish she hadn't. I was told she was returning home from the last crime scene."

"They dropped off a sample at the lab, then came back here. He must have already been inside."

"Security pick anything up?"

"Nothing, but that's this guy's MO; he uses a baffle screen, stays off the cameras. Seems to trick the motion sensors, thermal sensors, even a heartbeat monitor, and just slips in and out. The cameras didn't pick up anything. I'm not sure how he got in."

"What kind of sample did she drop off?"

"Substance found at the crime scene," he said. "She thought it was blood, but I called the lab and it came up false positive. Some kind of silicate."

"Does that sound like the kind of mistake she'd be likely to make?"

"No."

I wondered. I could think of a substance that resembled blood even at the molecular level but contained silicates. After reanimation, marrow stopped producing red blood cells, which had limited the life span of early revivors. They'd eventually switched to a synthetic.

Flipping through a series of filters, I brought up a custom set I'd created back during combat duty in order to zero in on revivor activity: their heart signatures, their unique heat signatures, and their blood. I hadn't used it in years, but it still worked like a charm. Everything went flat, almost monochrome, and a series of dots stood out, bright white, each about two feet apart. They traveled from the front door to the center of the living area, where they stopped. It looked like that spot had been cleaned. No one would have picked it up unless they were looking for it. A revivor had been here. One that had been injured.

"What are you looking at?" Turner asked.

Based on the position of the body outlines and where the revivor must have stood, it was impossible that they wouldn't have seen it. It was standing right there in the same room with them, not six feet away.

Except they don't need to breathe, I thought. They don't even have heartbeats, not in the traditional sense. When they need to, they can be very quiet and very still for long periods of time. They could fool thermal sensors and duck heartbeat monitors. I thought about the outline Faye said she saw, the one that had seemed to stand nearby in the parking lot where the prison truck burned. It wasn't an illusion; someone was there, wearing a light-warping suit. The suspect in the garage too had worn one, and so had the shooter outside the FBI building. It was very unlikely that this was unrelated to the high-grade military contraband uncovered at Tai's operation.

"I'm going to have a look around," I told Turner. "Are you finished here?"

"For now," he said. "It's been a long day. I'll leave you to it."

He walked away, stopping when he reached the tape crossed over the door to ask, "Do you know why she died?"

"I don't. I'm sorry," I said.

He looked at me warily, then ducked under the tape and started down the hall. I watched him on the other side of the wall through the backscatter filter as he paused, looking back. He stood there for several seconds before turning and continuing on, out of sight.

I moved back to the sofa and stood in front of it, looking down at the outline of her body. Keeping it in view, I tapped into the police network and accessed the photographs taken by the Heinlein technicians, then relegated them to a window in the left side of my field of vision. Cycling through them, I compared each to the scene as it was now. Nothing had been moved.

Before transporting her, they photographed her body extensively. In the pictures, she sat there with her arms by her sides and her head tilted forward. Her eyes were open, staring down at the puncture wound in the middle of her chest.

I'd seen many bodies in my life, but I couldn't look at that one. I closed the file, feeling dizzy and sick. I'd seen what I needed to see.

I knew that wound. More than a few soldiers got surprised in a foxhole or tunnel or at the edge of the bush and had taken a hit like that. They zeroed the blade in on the closest major organ, and sometimes that was a kidney or the liver, but the target of choice was the heart.

If there had been any doubt before, there wasn't any

longer; the police records indicated no murder weapon was ever found, and that wasn't surprising. The wound was made by a revivor's bayonet. These people were all killed by a revivor.

A call came in through the JZI. It was Sean.

Nico.

Yeah, Sean?

How are you holding up?

I'm holding up.

I've pulled the preliminary information from the data spike you recovered at the arena. You ready for the results?

What did you find?

Looks like the kid planted a virus right in the middle of the high-security systems of everyone's favorite contractor.

Heinlein Industries.

Yes.

For what reason?

The virus was looking for something. It monitored the network and logged every transfer, every port that was opened or closed, everything that went on. It bounced between systems, gathering samples for months, then compiled them all together.

Did it find what it was looking for?

Yes. That information was pulled out and set aside from the background noise. It paints a clear picture; someone from the outside is using Heinlein's systems.

What do you mean, using Heinlein's systems?

Someone is using a back door that was set up from the inside to access all of their computer systems. Whoever it is has been making use of their data regularly, and also stealing CPU cycles from just about every available system.

Boil that down for me.

Someone on the outside is basically using Heinlein's systems, not just for horsepower but also for their simulators and archives of data.

Why?

Whoever's doing it is very interested in brain function specifically. The most commonly referenced information all involves the bridge between the revivor components and the brain, as well as higher brain functions including memory, with an emphasis on—

Zhang's Syndrome.

You got it.

How could Heinlein not know this?

The back door was set up by someone inside, someone trusted. It allows access under the radar, and since the usage is taking place in nanoseconds across thousands of systems, you'd have to be looking to see it.

I thought about the message, the one Cross left for me, and then repeated as he died in the Federal Building lobby. *Samuel never left.*

Did you get the information on Samuel Fawkes? I asked.

Yes. He's dead, just like they said.

How did he die?

Mugging gone bad. He was stabbed and died in the hospital.

Who killed him?

Some junkie. She died some years back.

Was he reanimated?

Yes, but according to the records, he's not on active duty.

Where is he?

I wasn't able to track him down, but he's in cold storage somewhere.

That I didn't like. Tracking down a single unit might be difficult even if it was where it was supposed to be. Until it could be traced, it left a lot of possibilities open. Cross had said twice that Samuel never left; was he even dead? Revivors didn't get funeral services, and no one except the technicians at the Heinlein laboratories ever laid eyes on them again after pickup. Was all this just a way of disappearing that wouldn't be questioned?

Do you have any idea what the intruders were using Heinlein's systems for specifically?

You've got me there, but the amount of number crunching all those CPU slices add up to is enormous. They're doing something specific; some long-term analysis and modeling, all to do with highly classified information that only Heinlein would have. Like I said, it's something to do with human brain function. I'll know more when I've had more time to look at it.

Thanks, Sean.

No problem. Where are you now?

Following a lead. Do they have any more information about the bombings?

Nothing to trace them to anyone. It's a madhouse back here. The governor and Mayor Ohtomo are organizing a secondary deployment of troops and using revivor fodder for the meat of riot control.

That should go over well. I'll talk to you later.

Later. I'm really sorry about what happened.

Me too.

Heinlein, Zhang . . . something happened over there. Something Cross became aware of and tried to bring to light. Faye had thought our cases were connected. Maybe she'd been right.

You were about to tell me something . . . something important.

Looking at the spot where Faye had sat, I remembered her face as she'd sat across the table from me. Revivors could kill; there was no question about that. In a lot of ways, it was their primary function. There had been a handful of times where I had to fight for my life, and at least half of them had involved some kind of revivor. They were different from people or even animals in that regard, because unlike people, they felt no anger, hatred, or fear, or so I'd always been told.

Revivors didn't conjure up their own motivations.

Or they never used to. Times changed. I flipped open my cell and made a call to an old friend from back in the grind. We hadn't spoken since then, but I'd kept tabs on him. He had an in at Heinlein. "Nicky," he answered, like no time had passed. "What's up?"

"I need a favor."

It was a debt I'd never intended to collect, but he didn't hesitate before he answered.

"What do you need?"

"A body."

"Any body in particular?"

"Yes," I said. "Once Heinlein does a collection, where does the body go from there?"

"After being refitted, they're put into stasis for long-term storage," he said. "They're packaged and stored right there until a specific order is filled; then they're shipped out."

"They just made a collection. I need it back."

"You need to talk to Heinlein about that. Maybe they'll set up—"

"They won't."

"You're a civilian now, Nico. They don't ship revivors internally except to bases."

"In my official capacity as an FBI agent investigating a possible domestic terrorism case," I said, "I need to question that revivor. I'm asking you: with your help, can I push this through?"

There was a pause on the other end of the line.

"Send me the information," he said.

I streamed over her name.

"I'll call you back," he said, and cut the line.

Walking through the apartment, I found her bedroom. I opened the closet and grabbed a pair of slacks and a shirt, then threw them onto the bed. I pulled open the dresser drawers one at a time; the top drawer contained stockings arranged on the left side, and underwear on the right. I grabbed one of each, a bra, and threw them down with the rest. I folded everything up and stacked them together, then stood in the dark and waited for the phone to ring.

Eventually it did. I picked up.

"I can make it happen," he said.

"Thank you."

"Don't thank me, because you never had this idea and I never helped you."

"Got it."

"You don't know how you ended up with it, and you're never going to."

"I understand."

"You won't listen," he said, "but I'll say it: this isn't a good idea."

"She . . ." I began. I stopped, and started again. "It knows something."

"Revivors aren't people," he said. "Remember that."

"I've heard that before."

He hung up. I grabbed the clothes off the bed and made one more phone call. There was another person I could think of who could help me with this who would also be off everyone's radar. The phone rang several times before it bounced to voice mail.

"Zoe, this is Agent Wachalowski," I said. "Call me when you get this; I need your help."

Calliope Flax—Guardian Metro Storage Facility

An hour went by, and my ears still rang. My face still hurt, and the stub where my tooth broke off throbbed like hell. All the way back home on the bike, I had to breathe through my nose, and every block my nose got plugged with blood. My knuckles were raw, my fists felt like I'd been punching bricks, and they dicked me on the reward since Luis got killed. The docs made sure I was in one piece, then slapped a bandage on my face and gave me the boot. The cops never even said thanks, and the fed bolted right after he got that call he picked up in the garage.

So I got my face mashed up, got shot at, got dicked on the reward, and Luis bought it anyway. Eddie got booked for taking potshots at the psycho with a shotgun, then sent word from the tank that I was off roll for a month. Great fucking night.

I parked the bike and kicked the front door open. Someone bitched when I stomped up the stairs, but I didn't care. I shoved the door open and whipped my helmet into the kitchen right through a stack of plates in the sink. Glass pinged off the wall as they smashed and slid in pieces onto the floor with a huge crash.

"Shut the hell up!" a voice yelled from under the floor, banging it with a fist.

"Fuck you!" I yelled back, stomping the floor with my boot.

I was so pissed, I was glad when I heard the door slam

down the stairs. Heavy footsteps thumped down the hall, and the door down there crashed open.

"You got a problem?" I heard him yell.

Kicking my door back open, I hit the stairs before he got halfway up. He was some big, fat piece of shit with a sweat-stained shirt and tattoos on his shoulders. Beer foam or snot was stuck to his little bushy moustache. He had a wooden bat in one hand.

From the stairs up over him, I stomped my boot down on his chest and he went down like a big sack of garbage. A floorboard cracked when he hit the landing, face red and bloodshot eyes bugged out.

"Get up and get out," I told him, "or I'll jam that stick up your ass!"

"I'll shoot you through the floor, you ugly bitch!" he spat, grunting as he rolled onto his hands and knees.

"You better not miss, asshole!"

I stormed back through the door and slammed it, so mad I was seeing red. I felt like I had to tear something apart or I'd lose my mind. People were banging and yelling on the walls and floors, and with each thump my blood got hotter and hotter. It would have felt so good to just trash the place, to break every last thing inside it to pieces. To take what I started with the dishes and not stop until it was all gone. To—

Over the racket, my cell went off and I flipped it open.

"What?" I snapped.

"Ms. Flax?" a voice asked. It was the G-man, Nico.

"It's Cal. Not Calliope, not Ms. Flax, and not ma'am. Cal."

"Cal," he said. "I need some help."

"Help? You guys screwed me—"

"I said you'd get paid for the tip on Valle," he said.

"You will. I'll take care of it. You help me out, and there's a little more in it for you."

My heart was still thumping, and I could still hear people yelling in the units around mine. I sucked air through my nose.

"Why me?" I asked.

"Because I don't want anyone else involved."

"You mean you don't want to tell anyone."

"Yes."

His voice sounded rough. It was different from before.

"Illegal?"

"No. Just a favor."

"Why should I?"

"Because I think you're worth more than the cage at the arena," he said, "and I think you do too. Besides, you could use a favor in return."

There was something about the way he said it that made me think twice. Usually guys like him didn't ask; they took. With the back of my hand, I rubbed my eyes and wiped the blood out from under my nose.

"I'm listening."

"I need some things dropped off somewhere," he said. "I won't have time to get them myself."

"That's it? Drop some shit off?"

"Drop it off, wait, and then go back."

"Why?"

"In case I don't come out on my own."

I thought about it a minute. He saved my life. I guessed I owed him something.

"What am I picking up and where am I taking it?"

He gave me the list. Loading up the bike was a trick, but it didn't have to get far. I strapped on a pack, threw a bag over the gas tank, and stuffed the rest in my coat.

He gave me the credit to get it all, and said I could keep what was left.

The drop point was some piece-of-shit storage hole that I didn't like the looks of, and I'd seen some shit holes. It looked like no one had been there in years, like the people who kept their stuff there died and the guys that ran it skipped town. Who knew what was left down there, but I hoped not a bunch of junkies and hobos.

The lock was still there, so with any luck it was empty. He had given me the code to get in, and it worked, so I rolled the bike down to the freight elevator and rode it right in and cut the engine. With the tip of my boot, I kicked the button marked 8; bottom floor.

The underground part was as nasty as the part up top, and it looked like no one had been down there for years either, except for a set of wheel tracks that looked like they came from a hand truck, and some footprints following them. Another set followed them down and to the right.

Walking the bike, I followed the tracks, and sure enough, they went right where I was going: a green metal door marked C. The tracks went through the door, but when I pushed it, there was no give. I tried the handle and it was locked, so I banged on the door. No one answered. I was alone down there.

It didn't matter. Wachalowski said just bring the stuff, leave it, and don't ask questions. After I dropped it off, there was a bar nearby where I could knock back a few and watch some TV, then go back and check on him. I could do that.

I dropped the stuff next to the door in a pile, as he said: four gallons of water in two plastic containers, one bundle of plastic ties, a sharp knife, a first-aid kit, a battery-powered lamp, a length of chain, a padlock, and three clean towels. I wondered what it was for.

If he was still alive when I came back, maybe I'd ask.

Nico Wachalowski—Guardian Metro Storage Facility

Getting the box turned out to be the easy part. I never found out how it was managed; I just told them where to send it. I picked an old unit in an underground storage facility that I'd rented back when I left the country. When I came back, I never reclaimed anything in it; in fact, I never set eyes on it again until that night. I hadn't been down there in many years, and from the looks of it, neither had anyone else. When I arrived, a fresh set of dolly tracks stood out in the crud slicked over the metal floor, and there it was, left next to the rusted door to my locker.

Noakes pinged me over the JZI. *Wachalowski, where are you?*

Following a lead.

In Dandridge?

If you know where I am, then why do you ask?

You—

I cut the connection.

Getting the box was easy. Opening it was another thing altogether. On the floor of the mostly empty storage cell, under a ton of street and subway with the steel shutters pulled and only the light of a flashlight to see by, I sat and stared at that box for an hour.

Back in the grinder, when those things pulled me down into that tunnel, something happened to me. A piece of that memory never returned, and I was glad for that, but I remembered the pain and the horror as they began to tear me apart. When my last tour ended, they honored me, gave me a medal, and recommended I go home. Now, more than any other time since, I felt like I was being dragged down through that tunnel again.

Incoming message.

A drop of brown water dripped from above, and landed with a solid pat on the surface of the box. I should have faced Faye long ago. I'd owed it to her.

Now I had to face her as a revivor.

The words "incoming message" floated across my vision again.

I closed my eyes, shutting out the silver box.

This is Wachalowski.

Agent Wachalowski, this is Bob MacReady from Heinlein Industries.

If you're contacting me like this, can I assume my request for a follow-up interview is being denied?

You can.

I'll get a court order.

No, you won't.

He was probably right about that. Heinlein had powerful allies in all kinds of high places, and they had decided to take the safe path. Getting a judge to issue a grant like that and having it stick would probably be beyond my means alone.

Do your superiors know you're talking to me? I asked him.

Yes.

What is it that they want you to tell me?

That Heinlein is not behind this.

I never said I thought you were.

I've done some digging, Agent. Our name has come up in conjunction with your investigation too many times to be dismissed as coincidence. You must at least suspect it.

If he knew that, Heinlein had some pretty deep contacts. I opened my eyes and went back to staring at the box on the other side of the room.

Why are you telling me this?

Because despite how it may look, Heinlein is not involved. No one here knows why Cross was killed. Heinlein Industries, understandably, doesn't want their shell peeled back too far, but Cross was a good man. He was respected here.

Sometimes circumstances make for hard choices.

Agreed, but that isn't what happened here. I can't make you believe that, but it's true.

Cross stumbled on something; that I was sure of. That it was something sanctioned by Heinlein Industries and that they were behind his death I found unlikely, because I couldn't make a huge entity like Heinlein and a relatively small-time criminal like Tai fit together. It was related to Heinlein, though. Whatever Cross had found, it got him killed, along with the others.

Another drop of water drummed onto the top of the box, then trickled down one side.

Just answer me one thing, I said.

If I can.

How much of a person really makes the transition, after reanimation?

I think there's only one way to truly know, Agent.

I thought of the young girl's body I found in that bathroom, back when the whole thing started. I didn't get it then, but it was the first time I'd thought of a revivor as something human, and I wondered whether I was unraveling. Part of me only wanted to see the case through to the end no matter what the cost, but another part, a simpler, selfish part, had lost something and wanted it back. I wanted the lost years back. I wanted to forget what happened when those things pulled me underground.

I wanted Faye back.

But Faye was gone. I told myself that the thing in the box was not her. It was dangerous to believe otherwise.

Thanks, MacReady.

Thank you for listening, Agent.

Is there anything else?

Yes.

And that is?

Don't open the box.

The connection terminated.

I stood up then and crossed the room. I lit the lamp and put it down in the middle of the floor as I went. The locker became illuminated in flickering light, causing roaches to scatter.

It's now or never.

I pulled the box open. There was a high-pitched hiss as the cover came free, and a cold white mist puffed out through the seam. I lifted the top away and put it on the floor. A thin sheet of black plastic was stretched across the inside, and sitting on that was a small index card. I picked it up and flipped it over to find a handwritten note.

Deanimation in twenty-four hours. Leichenesser will take care of the rest. Get what you need before then. Good luck.

Twenty-four hours. I hadn't even thought about what would happen after the fact.

There was nothing I could do about it now. Maybe it was better that way. She hadn't wanted this; I knew that.

I took a deep breath and pulled the black plastic apart to reveal what lay underneath. The inside of the locker was filled with a transparent rubber blister, filled with clear fluid so that its skin was taut. Through the plastic I could see the shape of a bare human figure cocooned inside. It was her.

Her eyes were closed and her hair had been completely removed, but the face was hers. A thick tube extended down her throat, her lips forming a seal around it. Dozens of small electrodes covered her body, trailing threads that hung suspended in the liquid surrounding her. Her skin was ashen, and the veins underneath had turned black from the synthetic blood they contained.

There was a drain fixed to the middle of the storage-unit floor where I could send the stasis fluid. Gritting my teeth, I nestled my hand between the skin of the blister and the inside of the storage container. I felt beneath it; it didn't seem to be attached anywhere, so I lifted the sac and it came free with a sticky peeling sound.

The whole thing was hard to get a grip on, and it was heavy. I managed to pull it up over the edge of the container, when the whole thing oozed over the side of the crate before I could stop it. The rubber skin got snagged on one of the latches as it went, tearing it open top to bottom and spilling its contents out onto the floor.

I swore as cold liquid poured over my lap and gushed down into my shoes. I stumbled back and fell as her body slipped out and slid across the floor, bumping to a stop against me.

I pulled myself up, trailing strings of sticky fluid as I scrambled back. Her body lay on its back on the wet floor. As I watched, her nipples hardened in the cold, pointing straight up at the ceiling from either side of a wrinkled, oval skin graft.

Faye is dead. This thing is not her. Wake it up and do what you need to do.

I grabbed her wrists and dragged her off the plastic. The electrode filaments stretched and snapped as I pulled her over to the drain and let the fluid ooze through the grate. I grabbed the plastic tube that snaked down her throat and dragged it up out of her stomach until the end popped out of her mouth.

I grabbed one of the plastic water jugs and peeled the top off, then dumped it over her body. Once the stasis fluid was rinsed away, an internal electric jolt would trigger reanimation.

I looked down at the body. The vitals monitor was still showing a flatline. I knelt down next to her and peeled one of the electrodes free from her shoulder. Her face was slack and lifeless. My throat began to burn.

"I'm sorry, Faye."

I heard a dull thud from inside her chest, and her whole body went rigid. Her eyes snapped wide open and she convulsed, leaning forward. The cords in her neck stood out and her face contorted; then her head fell back onto the concrete as she pulled in a long breath.

I stared as the monitor picked up signs of life; to all appearances, she seemed alive. Her eyes turned to me, bugging out of her head and reflecting the light from the lamp. She began hitching in breaths, forcing out words one at a time as ropes of fluid sprayed from her blue-black lips.

"What . . . happened . . . ?"

Faye was staring up at me. For just that second, I swore I saw recognition.

"What . . . happened . . . to . . . me?"

I saw it at the last minute. I was looking right in her eyes, and I saw fear. Her stare looked through me into something else, something I couldn't see. She saw something that terrified her.

"Don't . . ." she whispered.

The muscles in her face relaxed. The terror went out of her, and a soft glow flickered on behind her eyes. The monitor wavered, then snapped into the waveform of the revivor heart signature.

I had no conscious memory of moving, but suddenly I was kneeling over her in the muck, one hand held out in front of me and the other raised near my head. An old dresser had crashed over, and a can rolled across the concrete and rattled to a stop among pieces of broken glass. Blood trickled out of a cut on my forearm.

I realized I was holding a pair of rusted scissors in my hand, grabbed from the dresser. The tips were pointed down at that oval-shaped scar.

Glass crunched under my heel as I started to stand and half fell, half sat on the wet floor. I threw the scissors away and heard them clatter across the concrete. After the initial jolt, a revivor might not move for as long as an hour.

Before I could change my mind, I gathered the chain and the lock.

9

Wake

Faye Dasalia — Guardian Metro Storage Facility

There was no sound, no sensation, and no light. I did not know what I was or where I was, only that I existed. Enough of me survived to at least know that.

When the darkness came, it had been absolute. There were no dreams, and I sensed no passing time; only a black, empty void. There was nothing and no one, not even me. I was lost in darkness until the warmth came.

Primary systems initializing.

The words hung there in the dark and then faded. Warmth gathered in my chest, then bled down my spine and trickled through my body. It wormed through each limb to find fingers and toes. It found the nape of my neck and gathered there.

Secondary systems initializing.

Cold pinprick light flickered to become a strobe. A connection inside my head seemed to spark and sent a pulse through my brain. I began to sense different parts of myself, like lights turned on through rooms of an empty home. My mind willed it, and my fingers and toes flexed.

I opened my eyes, and light poured through each lens. Images began to form.

I was lying on my back, staring upward. Above me were pipes and water-stained concrete, lit by flat electric light. I did not recognize the things around me.

I breathed in and sensed particles in the air. They were smells: decay and mildew. Beneath them were sweat and men's deodorant. The smells opened up pathways inside my mind. Connections opened to dark and disused cells. My memories began to reawaken. I sensed them, endless points of light in a void. The sum of them, taken as a whole, was me.

Tertiary systems initializing.

A drop of liquid splashed in a shallow pool. The air was cold, and goose bumps rose on my skin. Somehow, somewhere, I was alive.

I sat up, naked in the cold, damp shadows. I sat on a bedroll on a concrete floor, surrounded by old boxes. I saw furniture, some covered and some not.

"Hello?" I called out, but no one answered me. I stretched, and tiny jolts twitched through my muscles. Vibrations hummed inside my chest. Energy flowed through me and urged me to move. Behind me, a drip of water splashed again.

I stood up and wobbled there in the dim light. Tiny jolts sparked through the muscles of my legs, making minute corrections.

Calibrating . . .

I noticed the heavy chain for the first time. It was wrapped tightly around my left ankle and fastened with a padlock. It snaked across the concrete six feet or so, where the other end was locked to a floor drain.

"Hello?"

The room was dimly lit, but I could still see. I saw

boxes and furniture and old crates. These things triggered memories. From that sea of tiny lights within the void, certain points rose to the surface and I saw that the things around me were things I once knew.

Past a stack of crates, I saw electric light. I stepped toward it, dragging the chain behind me. It was a lamp on a box. It sat next to an old water-stained sofa. Lying on top of the sofa was a man.

A memory, brighter than the rest, swam up. I knew that man, and when I saw him, I froze. When I saw him, it hit me.

I am Faye Dasalia.

That was my name; I was Faye Dasalia. The vibrations in my chest seemed to grow. Who was this man, and why was he here with me?

His face was handsome, but it had been beaten. His Roman nose had been broken at least once, and his face was freshly bruised. He wore slacks and a sleeveless white undershirt. A scar stood out on the left side of his neck. I followed it to the meat of his shoulder, which was pocked with thick white scars.

I stepped closer, and glass crunched under my foot. A jar had broken, littering the concrete. I saw coins and a toothbrush. Off to one side was a pair of sharp scissors. I skirted the glass and took another step. The chain pulled taut as I knelt down beside him.

Who are you?

As his chest rose and fell, I felt warmth from him. As I watched, hot orange light pulsed at his neck, a thick branch on either side. I could see them, coursing there under his skin. They came from his chest, where a fiery coal pulsed.

His heart.

As I watched it slowly beat, more words appeared.

Primary systems active.
Secondary systems active.
Tertiary systems active.

More messages scrolled by, but they were too fast. After a few seconds, they stopped and vanished. A new message appeared there.

(1)Communication(s) pending.
Displaying.
Database synchronization pending.
Updating . . .
Header mismatch: Valle, Rebecca. Murder.
Header mismatch: Craig, Harold. Murder.
Header mismatch: Shanks, Doyle. Murder.
Removing . . .
Removing . . .
Removing . . .
Header mismatch: Ott, Zoe. Experimentation.
Adding . . .
Database synchronization complete.
(0)Communication(s) pending.

The words faded as I watched the sleeping man. Those thick scars covered his neck, shoulder, and chest. There was a pattern to them. I leaned over him, moving my face closer. My breath made the hairs on his chest stand on end. Up close, I could see what it was that caused the scars. They were teeth marks, many sets of human teeth marks.

Something cold and hard pressed underneath my jaw. I heard a metallic click, and knew that sound; it was a pistol's hammer. I raised my hands, my face still near his chest.

"Back away," he told me. His eyes had opened. I

hadn't seen the gun or noticed him move. I moved back from him slowly. He forced my chin toward the ceiling with the gun. I sat back on my heels while he held me there and sat up on the sofa.

"You don't have to be afraid," I said.

"I'm not afraid," he said, but the pulsing in his chest said otherwise.

"I'm sorry," I said. "I don't know where I am."

I looked at his face, and thought he would shoot me. His eyelids drooped, but there was fear in his eyes, like he had lost his senses.

A memory swam up from the sea of lights; it opened like a portal to show the inside, where this man knelt over me. Blood dripped from his hand as he held something sharp. A pair of scissors was pointed at my chest. The portal went dark, and shrank to a point of light that flew back to join the rest.

"I wasn't doing anything," I told him.

He stared at me until his eyes seemed to clear. He eased the pistol's hammer back with his thumb and then moved the gun away.

"What are you going to do with me?" I asked. He didn't respond to that.

"Do you remember me, Faye?"

Points of light sparkled through the memory field. I'd known him for a long time, and very well, though he seemed like a stranger. One light displayed our fingers, laced together. I remembered the warmth of his palm in mine.

"Yes, I know you. You're Nico."

His heart sped up and he said, "Do you remember what happened?"

I scanned the sea of lights, but I wasn't sure. It was difficult to make sense of them all. He watched me, waiting.

"I don't know how I got here."

"It's okay," he told me after a while. "Someone is coming to help you retrieve them."

"What do you mean? Retrieve what?"

"Your memories. You learned something . . . just before. You were in your apartment. You thought our cases were related . . . do you remember that?"

I did remember. Spots had formed on the floor, like blood but darker. They dripped down from the thin air. The air rippled, and a dark figure appeared. It had been right there, watching us the whole time. It raised the pistol it held in its right hand . . .

"It killed him first," I whispered.

"You weren't the target. It was your partner. You just got in the way."

Doyle had been about to tell me something. . . . What was he going to say?

"How can you be sure that's true?"

"We recovered a partial list of names from an illegally trafficked revivor. The list contained four names: the victims of the last three murders, and that of your partner, Doyle Shanks. I'm sorry, Faye. I didn't know who he was."

"But why was he on the list?"

"I was hoping you could tell me. What do you remember about him? Who was he?"

Again, light sparkled through the field of memories. I had known Doyle Shanks for a long, long time. I worked with him every day. We tracked the killer who finally killed us both. He was with me the night before Mae Zhu's death, and dropped me off at my place. The next morning he'd called to—

The associated memory had come forth. It hung suspended over the rest of them, opened up like a portal. The images from that night were beyond it. He dropped me off; then I saw a distortion, like a glitch left by a splice. I slept, then was awakened by the strange call.

"What's the matter?" Nico asked.

"The memory," I said. "It's wrong."

"Wrong?"

I focused on the memory distortion. The glitch tied the two memories together, concealing a missing piece. I concentrated, peering through the strange gap. I saw Shanks drop me off at my place, and then . . .

Faye, I wish it didn't have to be like this.

Shanks sat on the edge of my bed, getting dressed. I lay on my stomach, nude and still sweaty.

Me too.

When I said it, I was upset. I felt sick. He was rough and left me feeling sore and used. He smiled, though, like I had just agreed with him.

I do care for you, he said. He brushed my hair behind my ear with one hand. Why had I agreed to this?

This was a mistake, I said.

No, it wasn't.

It was.

His eyes narrowed, and he leaned in very close. The warm brown of both his eyes was blotted out as his pupils dilated.

No, it wasn't, he growled.

The anxiety left me, bleeding away. In its place, I felt relaxed. Happy, even.

This never happened, he said, no longer looking at me. *I left you at the door and I never came inside. I have never been inside your apartment.*

He got up and left me lying there in bed. He never looked back at me.

"I remembered it wrong," I said to Nico. His heart went even faster.

"Zhang's Syndrome," he said to himself.

Through the memory's portal, I studied the gap. What I saw there wasn't real. It was a dream I'd had a long time ago. My brain's decay had overlapped the memories. I couldn't tell a dream from reality.

The portal closed and shrank to a point of light. I noticed then that it stood out from the rest. It appeared different somehow. It was dimmer than the rest. When it rejoined the rest in the field of lights, I saw more that were like it.

I drew one closer and peered inside of it. The memory itself was inconsequential, but the same strange glitch was there.

They've all been corrupted. . . . None of them are real. . . .

I gazed down on the sea of information. When I did, I picked out more tainted memories, more than I could imagine. They were spread through the others like a cancer.

How many of them weren't real? I saw ten, then twenty, then one hundred. . . . There were more than I could count.

"I remembered it wrong," I whispered again, while the man named Nico just stood there and stared.

The life that I'd known was gone.

Zoe Ott—Unknown

"Zoe, wake up," a woman's voice said.

I opened my eyes and found myself slouched in a folding chair behind a metal table. The walls were concrete, painted green, and at the far end, the overhead light was on but there was no one there. Before I could stop my-self, I began to cry. I didn't want to be there anymore.

"He needs you. Wake up," the voice said. It was the dead woman, the one who got stabbed. She moved into the light where I could see her.

"Go away."

"He called you, remember? You need to go to him."

Tears were blurring my vision, but I could see something shifting at the far end of the room, under the overhead light. It was like a heat ripple or something, a distortion.

"You need to wake up right now!"

When I squinted, the ripples in the air took the shape of a person, like the outline of a big man. Before I could get a better look, they disappeared again.

"Zoe!"

The images faded as I snapped out of it, gasping in air. Over the years, I had gotten used to waking up and not knowing exactly where I was, but this time something was wrong.

When I gasped, something that was touching me pulled away all of a sudden. Someone had a hand on one of my legs and was dragging me. I was lying on what might have been a chair or a sofa, but it wasn't mine. A breeze cut through the stuffy, warm air and blew over my face; it was outside air.

I opened my eyes and saw it was dark, but I could see the city lights through a window above me and I heard one of the monorails clacking by over the howl of the wind.

Startled, I tried to sit up, and my arms and legs hit something as I flailed. I was in an enclosed space, and there was someone leaning over me. Someone big, with sour, smelly breath.

Kicking with one leg, I scooted up until my back was

to the window behind me, and I realized I was in the backseat of a car. I was bundled up for going outside, but my parka was unzipped and my purse was lying open on the seat beside me.

When I jumped, the man in the backseat with me recoiled but he didn't leave. He was holding my ID card in one hand and looking down at me uncertainly. He was bundled up in dirty clothes and a thick, dirty jacket. He had a thick black beard, and a cap pulled down over his hair.

"What are you doing?" I slurred.

With my ID still in his hand, he hooked my purse on his thumb and used his other hand to grab my ankle. He gripped it hard, and I felt myself being pulled from the car.

There wasn't any time to think about it; I stared at him, and the city lights all bled together as the backseat got as bright as daylight. As the colors leeched out of everything, the lights above the man's head became visible, prickling oranges and greens and reds. Anger, fear, guilt, and greed all mixed together.

Reaching out, I changed them, and the grip on my ankle relaxed.

"Stop," I told him, and he did.

Still sitting half in and half out of the backseat of the car, I looked around for the first time and saw the car was parked under one of the monorail junctions where several tracks merged and then branched back out, forming a concrete canopy above. Everything was covered in graffiti, and the ground was littered with trash and pieces of brown ice that formed on the rails, then crumbled off whenever one of the trains passed. There was traffic in the distance, but we were parked away from the well-used streets and sidewalks.

"Let go of me," I said, pulling my leg until he dropped it. I zipped up my coat and scooted across the seat, out the door so that I was standing in front of him.

"Put my ID and anything else you took back in my purse."

He did as he was told.

"Now give it back."

He held it out and I snatched it out of his hand. Once I was outside, I could see the car was actually a taxicab. I got a better look at the guy and saw that he also had a laminated badge clipped to his jacket, displaying his license information. He must have been the driver.

"How did I get here?" I asked him.

"You hailed my cab," he said. "You told me to bring you here."

"I told you to bring me out here?"

"Well, not here exactly. You had the directions on a phone message. You played it for me and told me to bring you there."

"So, what were you doing?"

"You stopped moving. I thought you passed out."

"And you decided to rob me?"

"You wouldn't move. I thought maybe you were dead."

He was going to dump me. He was going to take my things and dump me under a monorail platform.

"Stand there," I said, "and don't move."

My phone wasn't in my purse or in my pocket, but I saw its green signal light glowing softly from the floor of the cab's backseat. I leaned in and picked it up.

Pulling one glove off with my teeth, I managed to get it open and punch in the voice-mail code, despite the fact that my finger was shaking like crazy. Putting it to my ear, I clamped my other hand down over the one holding the phone to keep it still.

"Zoe, this is Agent Wachalowski . . ."

I smiled and felt little pricks of pain as my chapped lips cracked. That was right: he called. As I listened, he gave me an address where to meet him.

". . . I'm sorry to call you out here, especially at night. If you're not comfortable, call me back and I'll come get you. . . ."

I climbed back outside where the cabbie was still standing, breath streaming out of his nostrils. I held up the phone so he could hear.

"Is that where I asked you to take me?"

"Yeah."

"How long was I out?"

"Maybe five minutes."

Nico might still be there, although why he was there and why he wanted me to meet him in the middle of nowhere was beyond me. Why I had decided to even go was beyond me right at that moment too, but for whatever reason, I had gone that far.

"Get back in the cab," I told the man, "and bring me to the address."

"You're here."

"This is the middle of nowhere."

"Down there," he said, pointing. There was a chain-link fence hanging open down at the bottom of a concrete slope under the monorail. A rusted sign hung from it.

GUARDIAN METRO STORAGE
SEGURO. SECURE. BLOQUE.

"It's for storage."

"That's the address you told me to bring you," he said. "What do you want?"

I glanced back at the fence. It looked like it led to a ramp that went underground.

"Just get back in the cab and leave."

"What about my fare?"

"Go!" I snapped as the lights surged for a second. He didn't say anything else; he just lumbered back around the car.

As the engine started up and he pulled away, I made my way down to the fence. It looked like normally it was locked, but now it was hanging open. Beyond it, a concrete ramp led down under the pavement, the way dimly lit by a single remaining light. I followed it down to a heavy-looking metal door with a keypad mounted next to it, and a glass window to the right that was dark. A strip of printed tape stuck over the keypad said AFTER HOURS ENTER CODE.

The message had given the address and then "8C 1101," which I thought was an apartment unit or something, but maybe it was the pass code to get in?

I punched in the combination and sure enough, there was a beeping sound and the door thumped and then squealed open with a sound that put my teeth on edge. Behind the door was a dingy, rickety-looking elevator car. I climbed in and the door slid shut.

The numbers started at 0 and went down to 8. I pushed the button for 8, causing it to light up halfheartedly, then flicker on and off as the car made its way down. As the metal walls of the elevator rattled and groaned, I could almost feel the surface getting farther and farther away. What was he doing down in a place like this, and why did he want me there?

The doors opened and I stepped out. After they

closed again, it got very quiet. I stood there and listened for a minute, but all I could hear was the occasional drip of water. The musty corridor met a junction about ten feet in front of me, lit by fluorescent bulbs behind corroding metal cages.

"Hello?" I called. My voice echoed once, but no one answered.

A sign at the junction said A-I with an arrow pointing right, and J-R with an arrow pointing left. I took the right, and found the door labeled C.

Looking back the way I came, I began to wonder what the hell I was doing there, and reached into my purse for the flask. It was still half full, so I finished it off and put it back. When it hit my stomach, my forehead beaded up with cold sweat and I felt as though I might have to sit down, but after a minute it passed. This had to be the place. Whatever he wanted, I was supposed to go to him. I was supposed to help him.

I put my hand on the door and leaned against the frozen metal as my mind opened and what little light there was brightened. After a few seconds, I saw it; somewhere behind the door was a presence, a single consciousness. He was there, after all, and he was alone.

Before I could knock on the door, it opened, and he was standing there in the doorway. He was wearing his suit pants and shoes, but he had taken off his shirt and was wearing just a sleeveless undershirt. He must have had some kind of heater working inside, because hot air was drifting out from behind him. He looked down at me with his eyelids drooping. He looked out of it.

"You came," he said.

That outfit he had on, it was the one from the green concrete room when the dead woman first showed him to me. I could see the scar branching out over his right shoulder.

"Yeah."

He stared at me a minute longer, then took a step back, giving me room to get by. He looked drunk or drugged.

"Does anyone know you're here?" he asked.

"Just the cab driver," I said, slipping through the door. It was nothing but a big concrete box, filled with old junk. As I looked around, I saw furniture underneath plastic tarps, stacks of boxes, and other stuff filling up most of the available space.

"Why are we here?" I asked.

"I had to," he said.

"Had to?"

As messed up as I was, I could see something was really weird about him. I hadn't been around him that much, but he was acting totally different from before, like he was a totally different person. His eyes looked dull and his expression didn't change when he talked.

"What happened?" I asked. When his aura phased into view, there was a thin membrane of light rippling under everything else, like a torn parachute falling from the sky. There was a bright cord tethering the membrane to someplace deep inside of him. I recognized that.

"Why are you so scared?"

He started to protest, but I soothed the membrane back, calming it.

"Don't—"

I'm not sure what made me do it, but I put my hand on his.

"Shhh."

The billowing light faded a little more but wouldn't quite go away. Even as his expression and his breathing relaxed, the tension wouldn't completely go away, and my heart kind of went out to him. Underneath his fear were other things: guilt, uncertainty, sadness, loneliness, and all the other things I knew so well. In him they were more structured than usual, but in some ways that seemed to make them all the more intense, like the colors were reined in but more concentrated and brighter.

"Stop doing that," he said, but there wasn't much conviction in his voice.

"Why?"

There was no one there to see. I put my other hand on his stomach, right under where the gun was strapped. It felt flat and firm under his shirt. Right away, I could tell from the way his patterns shifted that he hadn't been touched in a long time. I knew how that felt too.

Maybe it was the alcohol, or just the total weirdness of the whole thing, but all I could think about right then was the way he felt under my hand. Without thinking, I ran my palm up and down his belly, feeling the ridges of muscle underneath his cotton undershirt.

"I know you miss it," I said. "I know you know how I feel."

He didn't say anything, but he didn't pull away either. He put a hand on my shoulder like he might push me away, but he just left it there as the colors shifted in front of my eyes. His eyes drooped further as I moved closer, my forehead almost touching his chest.

"I wanted to thank you," I said into his shirt.

"For what?"

"For caring about me, even a little bit."

Something flashed from the darkness behind him just then. When I looked over, I saw a pair of eyes glowing softly back in the corner.

Not now . . .

There was no one else there; I had checked before I went inside, so I had to be seeing things again. But then the eyes moved. Something got knocked over, and the eyes began to move closer.

"You . . ."

Breaking out of the trance, Nico jumped, looking disoriented. I pulled my hands back in surprise as a figure stepped out of the shadows, moving toward me. It was her, the dead woman from my dreams, naked except for a button-up shirt that was open at the top. She stepped forward again, then stopped short with the jingle of metal as she reached the end of the chain that was padlocked to her ankle.

"You can't be here," I said, as Nico turned to look and saw her too. She was really there. For some reason, her hair was gone, even her eyebrows, but there was no mistaking her. She even had a thick, puckered pink gash closed up in the middle of her chest.

She stood there, following my eyes down to the wound.

"It got split," she said.

"What are you doing here?" I said, taking a step back. Nico looked from her to me.

"Zoe, calm down."

"Why is she here?"

"I need to know what she knows," he said, gripping me by the shoulders. He held me hard enough so that it hurt a little.

"What?"

"She might be the only one that can tell me," he said. "I need you to help me."

It was a trick. He didn't call me to him because he needed me; it was because he needed her. All he wanted me for was to do something for him. He wanted me to make his woman friend talk.

"Help you do what?" I asked, but he didn't answer. His patterns were so chaotic right then that I doubt he even knew himself.

"Please," he said.

"You want to know what's in her head," I said. "Fine."

So I pushed, and I pushed hard. Maybe because I was drunk or maybe just because I was angry; it wasn't fair that another woman was there, and it wasn't fair that even though she was dead, he could only think about her and not me. It wasn't fair that he only called me to do a trick for him. None of it was fair. Right at that moment I wanted to control her, to make her leave or back off, or maybe even hurt her if I could.

So, I was drunk, and I was mad, and I pushed hard. I pushed real hard.

The room got very bright, and everything went almost gray. I focused on the woman in front of me with more intensity than I think I'd ever turned on anyone. I reached out to the place where the light would bloom.

"Zoe?"

They didn't appear. No lights, no colors . . . nothing. When I stared into her eyes, they didn't change, they didn't get dull and stupid. They just stared back.

My heart started beating faster. This had never happened before, not ever. Out of the corner of my eye, I could see the patterns rippling around Nico's head. It was working, just not on her.

I pushed harder, concentrating until the light got so bright she was all I could see; her face, her eyes, and the empty space where it should have been. Her thoughts, her consciousness, her self, her soul . . . whatever it was, it wasn't there. The light blotted out everything else until the only thing that was dark was that empty spot, that empty hole where she should have been. It was like looking into an abyss or a black hole. When I pushed against it . . .

"Zoe!"

All at once, the lights dimmed back to normal. He was shaking my shoulder. The dead girl was still standing there, looking at me. I wiped my nose and there was blood.

"What happened? What did you see?"

She was just standing there, staring at me the way she did in my dreams. Those electric eyes watched me lifelessly as I backed away. I had to get out of there.

Nico reached out to me and I shrugged his hand off my shoulder. What was I doing there? What in the world ever compelled me to get involved in this whole thing? All I wanted was to get back to my apartment, lock the door, and forget about the whole thing—him, her . . . everything. It was a mistake. The whole thing was a mistake.

I stumbled to the door, and he followed me. I pushed on him again, making him stop before he could reach me.

"Your friend is gone," I told him, and left. He didn't come after me.

He didn't even come after me.

Nico Wachalowski—Guardian Metro Storage Facility

After Zoe ran, I wasn't sure what I should do. Faye had sat back down on the bedroll and hadn't spoken in minutes.

"Who was that?" she asked finally.

"No one."

I hadn't wanted to risk poking around in her systems, because I knew she was seeded with Leichenesser, and the memory of the dock revivor melting away on that autopsy table was too fresh in my mind. That had been triggered when I started rifling through sections of memory I wasn't supposed to be in.

"Where am I?" she asked.

As I looked down on her, she just stared up at me, her brown eyes replaced by moonlight silver. It was amazing how dehumanizing that one change alone was, but it was more than that. This was the first time I had ever seen a revivor that I had previously known so closely, and the change was subtle but startling at the same time. More than just the color of her eyes or her skin, it was her body language, her expression, the way she held herself; everything was different. It was as if her body had been inhabited by some completely different entity.

I sat down on the bedroll in front of her so that we were facing. Immediately, she reached out and took my hands in hers.

"Why did you do that?" I asked. Her palms and fingers were cold, with no pulse.

"I don't know."

"Hold still," I said, "and stay quiet. I need to concentrate."

Closing my eyes, I scanned the communications band until I found her signal. She was on an encrypted broadcast band.

"I can't force my way in," I told her. "I'm extending a connection; can you see it?"

She didn't respond at first. I opened my eyes and saw her staring into space, slightly out of focus.

"Yes," she said.

"Can you accept the con—"

Call connected.

Are you picking me up?

In front of me, her lips curled very slightly, forming the ghost of a smile. Or was that wishful thinking?

"Yes," she said.

Answer back over the connection.

Yes. I'm picking you up.

Good. There should be a copy of any communications you've received in your memory buffer.

This feels strange.

I'm going to try to retrieve it.

Okay.

Her hands were like ice, but my palms were sweating.

The last time I tried this, I accidentally triggered a device designed to prevent anyone getting in.

Okay.

The revivor was destroyed.

Okay.

I moved more carefully this time around, sending a data miner across to feel out any security instead of brute-forcing it. Her systems were protected, but since she hadn't been deployed, there were no modifications, and the miner managed to clear the way in.

What are you looking for?

Having only been reanimated for a short time, there wasn't much in there. The bulk of it was a dynamic database. It looked like a full copy of the list I'd pulled off of the dock revivor.

I've got it.

I compared the list fragment I'd pulled from the dock revivor to the database of names I'd just recovered. There were no matches.

As I watched, it changed size in front of me. A couple seconds later, it did it again. It was getting smaller.

Do you know what this is? I asked Faye.

No. Do you?

A list of names, but the ones I was looking for aren't there.

It keeps changing.

What?

It keeps getting updated.

How often?

It varies.

How do these updates occur?

A connection opens and they arrive, Faye said. *First the list came; then, after that, the updates.*

The list was keeping track of the names dynamically. That was it; the names were no longer on the list because the people they represented were dead. The database had been updated, and the names removed. If it was a synchronized database, then the updates were coming from somewhere. As the Heinlein rep had pointed out, revivors communicated in a hub-and-spoke fashion, not directly to one another but through a common point. That common point, that hub, must be where these people were based. If I could locate that . . .

The last change in the list size was already complete. I set up a monitor to watch all incoming ports to trace the next one when it came in, then went back to the list.

What do these names have in common? I asked her.

I don't know.

Was your name on the list?

No.

I'm going to try to view the history. Hold on.

There were backups going back several iterations in case of corruption. Fishing through them, I found the names from my list fragment. They had been removed eight iterations ago:

Database synchronization pending.
Updating . . .
Header mismatch: Zhu, Mae. Murder.
Removing.
Header mismatch: Valle, Rebecca. Murder.
Removing.
Header mismatch: Craig, Harold. Murder.
Removing.
Header mismatch: Shanks, Doyle. Murder.
Removing.

There were several iterations preceding that one.
There were a lot of names in there. At least twenty had
already been removed, and there were hundreds more.

*I'm going to need a copy of those names. I'll be
careful.*

Okay.

Rather than try to mirror the entire database, I decided it would be safer to go through and just scan the
names one at a time and copy them manually. As I got
closer to the most recent version, I noticed one of the
iterations actually increased the overall size by a small
fraction instead of decreasing it.

Hold on.

Shuffling ahead to that entry, I brought it up to view
it.

Database synchronization pending.
Updating . . .
Header mismatch: Ott, Zoe. Experimentation.
Adding.

I jerked my hands back, but those cold fingers locked
around my wrists.

Who's Zoe?

Let go.

Who's Zoe?

Twisting my wrists, I knocked her hands away. I put a call in to Sean.

Sean, the revivors are communicating with a base of operations somewhere. That partial list we recovered from the dock revivor is part of a much larger one, and they're making their way through it.

Why? Who are they?

I don't know why, but do some digging. I'm sending the names to you now.

Roger that.

The entries have been getting crossed off more and more frequently. It looks like it started to ratchet up maybe six iterations ago. . . .

That was around the time Ohtomo dispatched the National Guard. There was a string of removals prior to that, in between.

Faye, these early names are all your victims. The ones you were investigating.

I noticed that too.

It looked like in addition to that, the suicide bombing was referenced as well:

Database synchronization pending.
Updating . . .
Header mismatch: Strike 0. Terror.
Removing.

The equipment, bodies, and weapons Tai was bringing in, the victims of Faye's killer, the recent bomb attacks; all of it was planned in advance.

Sean, I need to know who these people are. They have

*something in common. Someone out there wants them
dead, and they've gone to a lot of trouble and expense to
make it happen.*

If there's a connection, I'll find it.

*In the meantime, I'm monitoring the channel so the
next time a communication comes through I should be
able to trace it back—*

Faye twitched in front of me, her eyes widening. All
at once her body tensed up, cords standing out in her
neck.

Shit.

I backed off, recalling the miner and retreating from
the memory I had accessed. Her fingers curled and I
could see warnings spilling past. Was I too late? Had I
already triggered it?

"Faye?" I asked out loud. She didn't respond. Her
eyes didn't turn toward me.

Agent Wachalowski.

I turned my attention back to the connection between
us. The message hadn't originated from her. It came over
another connection to her that had just been opened.

Who is this?

*Agent Wachalowski, this is Samuel Fawkes. Why are
you playing with one of my revivors?*

Samuel never left.

It's not your revivor.

It is now.

An override code was running; he'd taken remote control of Faye's systems. Her command center
switched over. If he wanted to, he could shut her down
completely.

Wait. How do you know who I am?

Because I've been watching you.

Why?

Because you have been sticking your nose in my business for longer than you realize.

Why are you killing these people? What did they do? Who are they to you?

You wouldn't believe me. Not for long anyway.

What does that mean?

They've already gotten to you, Agent.

The warnings stopped streaming by. Faye's body relaxed.

What do you mean 'they'? I found footage in a reporter's memory of someone sending him to Tai's place before I arrived. Is that who you mean? Are these the people who are on your list?

You'll never know, Agent. I was going to wake you up, but now it's too late.

Why are you killing them?

"Nico?"

It was Faye. She looked up at me with eyes that were wide and innocent in their lack of understanding. I remembered back to the female revivor at Tai's place, the way when she spoke it had seemed like some alien intelligence had spoken through her, referencing memories it had never experienced. It didn't feel that way when Faye said my name. She said it the way she used to say it. She remembered me. Maybe her memories were corrupted during the transition, and maybe some were even false, but she remembered me.

"Nico, help me—"

By the time I heard the sound, it was too late. The sound of sliding metal ended with an abrupt crunch as something pounded into my chest, sending burning pain up my neck and down both arms, all the way to my palms. My reaction was too late, and by then I couldn't move, not even to take a breath.

She was still staring up at me, those electric eyes looking faintly distressed. Her fingers touched my chest gently as beneath them a blade extended from the base of her palm to the center of my rib cage, the point buried somewhere inside. Neither of us could speak as the hydraulics hissed, unable to push any farther. With a snap the blade retracted, tugging free from me and disappearing back into her arm. She reeled above me as I fell back, my vision swimming with black blotches that turned everything dark.

"Nico?"

I couldn't move. Even with my systems firing off, trying to right me, I couldn't move a muscle. I sensed her there, still looking down on me as warm blood seeped through my shirt. Had she finally remembered me? Would she help me, or leave me?

I wondered that as the stream of warnings ceased and went out.

Zoe Ott—Pleasantview Apartments, Apartment 713

At my front door, I fumbled for the key. My hands were shaking badly, and all I wanted to do was to find it and get inside before the jerk next door came out, because I really didn't think I could handle him right then. Whatever had made me get involved in this whole mess in the first place was a drunken mistake in judgment. I wasn't cut out for any of it. I just wasn't the kind of person who got involved in whatever it was I had gotten involved in.

I found the key and started to put it in the lock, but I couldn't keep it steady. The tip of the key scratched around the keyhole as I moved closer to the knob. I wanted to forget any of it ever happened. I didn't want to see Nico or the woman or any of them ever again. All I wanted was to get warm and watch TV, and drink until I stopped feeling like I did.

The tip of the key found the slot and I jammed it in, turned it, then pushed the door open and went inside, letting it swing shut and slam behind me. I turned the bolt, wishing there were three more of them.

After having not been in my apartment for a little while, I couldn't help but notice it had an off smell. I needed to clean the place up. I threw my keys on the coffee table and shrugged out of my coat, hanging it on the rack. I felt dizzy. Why did he show that revivor to me? Why was he with that woman? Why was she chained, and what was he doing with her down there?

Shivering, I went into the kitchen and poured a drink, drained it, then poured another one. The heat moved down my throat into my belly, but when I wiped my face, my hand was still shaking and the sweat there was cold. That had been the woman from my dream. It was definitely her. Three more drinks, and the shaking still wouldn't stop.

I hated the thing that Karen called my gift. From the bottom of my soul, I hated it all the way back to when I dreamed of my father's mangled body, and every second since. I hated everything about it, but I learned something back in that storage room, and that was that hate it or no, I relied on it. I never realized until that moment how much I relied on it.

When I pushed on that revivor, I felt something I'd never felt before in my life. When I focused on her and nothing happened, it felt like I had gone blind. None of the colors appeared and I couldn't sense any of her thoughts or her feelings or even her mood. Until she stepped out where I could see her, I hadn't even known she was standing a few feet away from me. It was terrifying.

There was no way to make her go away, or make her go to sleep, or decide to leave me alone, or tell me who she was, how she got there, how she knew him . . . nothing. She could do whatever she wanted, and there was nothing I could do about it.

I couldn't stop replaying that moment. There was just a gap, like a dark pit. Looking into it was like stepping through a door and finding no floor. It felt like if I pushed into that void, I would fall inside with no way of knowing what was down there or if it even had an end.

I drained the glass and poured out another one, and that's when the ripples appeared in the air in front of me, right between where I was standing and the fridge. The distortion took the shape of a man, and then just like that there was someone standing there, as if he'd appeared from out of nowhere. The glass slipped out of my hand and smashed on the floor between us.

"Damn it!" I hissed.

He was a big man dressed in a jacket and coat, with some kind of cloak or poncho draped over that. The coat's hood was up over his head. It struck me that it might have been the first time I actually saw a vision appear while I was watching.

"You guys need to start wearing bells," I said. "Look at this."

He stood there, not moving, as I grabbed a paper towel and sopped up the booze, pushing the broken glass away against the bottom of the counter. I grabbed a new glass and filled it.

"Look," I said, feeling tears forming, "I don't think I have anything left today, okay? How about you all leave me alone and let me just pass out tonight?"

He didn't say anything; he just kept watching me.

"Please—"

He reached out and grabbed my shoulder. His hand was real. He wasn't a dream or a hallucination; he was real.

He squeezed, and it hurt. I panicked, hitting at his arm, but he didn't even seem to notice.

"Help!" I screamed.

I tried to focus on him and nothing happened. Just like earlier, I couldn't see him or feel him. It was just like it had been with the dead woman in the storage unit: nothing but an empty, dark hole.

"You're—"

He shook me hard and bashed me into the counter. Everything went white for a second when my head bounced off the wall; then he pulled me back toward him. No one had ever moved me like that; it was like I weighed nothing to him at all. Before I could do anything, I was dragged backward, out of the kitchen, and thrown down onto the sofa.

He was dead, just like the woman. It was a revivor, and I had no way to control it.

When I looked up, he was coming right toward me. I glanced to the front door and saw my next-door neighbor standing there. He was looking in, his eyes wide, but he wasn't doing anything.

"Help!"

The dead man turned and saw him. For just a second, the old ginger man looked calm, almost confident, but as the revivor closed the distance, his eyes went wide and he just stared, like he was frozen.

With a loud snap, the revivor's palm split apart and a big, sharp blade shot out of it. It arced over his head with a whistling sound, and the next thing I knew Red was gasping as blood began to gush out of his neck. The blade whipped around again and he grabbed his belly as a squiggly red mess spilled out into his bloody hands.

The big guy pulled me away, and I heard my neighbor's body fall wetly onto the floor. He reached into his pocket with his free hand and pulled something out, yanking the cap off of it with his mouth and spitting it onto the floor. It was a needle.

I struggled, but he was too strong. I felt a prick as the needle stuck into the side of my neck.

. . . but this isn't how it happens, I thought. *I'm supposed to meet her three times. . . .*

He pulled the syringe away, and all of a sudden he convulsed. His eyes bugged out and his whole body started to shake as the fistful of my shirt slipped from his hand and I fell back onto the floor. When I looked up, Karen was there, standing behind him. She had something black in her hand with two prongs sticking out of it. She had stuck them right in the guy's side, and I heard an electric popping sound.

She pulled the prongs away and the popping stopped. I tried to get up, but my legs wouldn't move and I fell over onto my side.

The guy turned around toward Karen. She tried to stick him again with the stun gun and he hit her hard, causing her to stumble, waving the stunner blindly. He batted her arm away and shoved her down onto the floor.

"Karen?" I mumbled, trying to focus. Blood was coming out of her nostrils and she was trying to get up as his foot stomped down and kicked the stunner away. I looked up in time to see the blade pulling back.

"Wait!" I screamed, holding up my hands. I tried to

scramble back, putting myself between them as he got ready to cut her. "Wait! Don't!"

He paused for just a second and looked from me to her, then back to me. I saw an orange light flicker behind his pale yellow eyes, and for a second it looked like he was reading something only he could see.

"I can fix it!" I said. Karen was shaking her head, and her eyes were starting to clear.

"Zoe, don't. . . ."

With some effort, I managed to get back up on my feet. He watched me as I staggered a few steps closer to him.

"I can fix it," I told him. The orange light continued to flicker in his eyes, and the blade was still poised like it was ready to strike.

"I can make her forget," I said.

"I know you can," he said.

The orange light went out, and with a loud snap, the blade disappeared. His hand went back together and he relaxed his fingers.

Before he could change his mind, I went over to Karen and dropped onto my knees next to her. With my remaining energy, I concentrated until the brightness came.

"What are you —"

"Sleep."

Her eyelids got heavy, and she started to sink back down onto the floor.

"Zoe, no. . . ."

"Sleep."

She rolled onto her back and went limp, her breathing becoming slow and easy.

"You didn't hear anything tonight," I told her. "I was

never in trouble and you didn't come up here to help me. You didn't see anyone else here tonight."

"Okay . . ."

"As far as you will remember, no one was here."

She nodded and I wiped my eyes, then leaned in closer so I could whisper in her ear.

"If I don't see you again," I said, "thank you, Karen."

She murmured something in her dreamlike state, but I didn't hear what it was as the big, cold hand came down and grabbed me by the back of my shirt. I was lifted up off the ground as everything went black, and all I could do was hope that whoever he was and whatever he wanted, he would just take me and go, because if he decided to kill her, there wasn't anyone left who could stop him.

10

Rise

Nico Wachalowski—Guardian Metro Storage Facility

I woke up to the sound of something sputtering softly, then a single drop echoing as it splashed into a puddle somewhere below me. It was somewhere dark and cold.

"Hey."

The voice came from out of the darkness. It was deep, but female.

Drip.

There was a tingling in my face and my neck that ran all the way down my arms and legs to my hands, fingers, and toes. My head was resting on something hard, and my back hurt. Everything hurt.

"Hey."

Something nudged me in the ribs. Something hard. Messages scrolled by behind my eyelids, and I cracked them open. The room was mostly dark, but the walls were flickering with a dim light. Turning my head slightly, I saw a young woman was standing over me. She wore black leather boots and skintight jeans. She looked down

at me, muscular arms hanging by her sides. It was the girl,
Calliope.

"Are you dead?" she asked.

"No."

"You want me to call somebody?"

"No."

My whole body felt like it had taken a beating, but
everything still seemed to work. A deep pain dug into
my chest when I tried to sit up, forcing me to roll over
onto my hands and knees.

Revivor bayonet. Faye stabbed me.

Not Faye, Fawkes . . . he was controlling her.

The box that had contained Faye's body lay open,
and the empty sac of fluid from inside was plastered to
the floor like a giant piece of skin. I scanned around, but
she was gone. All that was left was the padlock key from
my pocket lying next to the discarded chain. I tried to
check the chronometer to see how long I'd been out, but
it looked like every system had reinitialized. I checked
my cell phone instead. An hour had passed.

"Was anyone else here when you got here?"

"No, just you."

"Did you pass anyone on the way in?"

"No."

Great.

Wachalowski. It was Noakes.

Yeah?

Where is the revivor?

The words hovered there. I tried to think of a good
response, but I was still reeling. A dark spot swam in
front of my eyes that wouldn't go away.

Never mind how I know, Wachalowski. Where is it?

Squatting back on my heels, I ran a regimen of stims,
painkillers, and anti-inflammatory serum, but the stims

got overruled by the system because of drug conflict detection. Running down the list, it looked as though the emergency systems had delivered a massive dose of clotting agent to the wound site, along with a bunch of other stuff. No wonder I was dizzy.

I don't know where it is.

You don't know.

No, but I think I know where it's going.

What do you mean?

The revivor was a police detective involved in a series of murders that turned out to be directly related to my investigation. I had reason to believe it had information about the man responsible for the prison-truck hijack and also the shooting outside headquarters.

Go on.

The killer is one of the revivors Tai smuggled in for his special client, the one we're looking for. However many revivors this person has gotten his hands on, he's commanding them remotely over their communications system. A list of names has been distributed to them, and they're eliminating the people on that list. The revivor that was with me ended up receiving a copy of that database when it came online.

There was a pause on the other end of the line.

Why are the people on the list being targeted?

I don't know yet.

Who is commanding the revivors?

I believe it's a former Heinlein employee named Samuel Fawkes. Look, someone who is helping me with the case appeared on that list. I'm heading there now, but I need some units over at her place right away. I gave him Zoe's name and address.

Done. What about you?

I'm fine.

Your heart stopped. Your vitals were flat long enough for the implant to report you KIA.

Peeling my shirt back, I could see there had been a lot of blood, at least initially. A dark crevice sat in the middle of my chest, hardened over with black.

I'll live.

Even as I said it, though, that dark blotch still floated there in front of my eyes. It was like a blind spot that even the implant couldn't write to. If the implant sent a KIA beacon, then I was technically dead for at least ninety seconds.

Looking around, everything around the dark patch had a sharpness to it that seemed strange. Everything felt very clear and focused, but almost to the point where it felt like a drug trip. Was it a side effect of all the chemicals, or was it something worse?

Wachalowski?

I said, I'll make it.

The drugs coursed through my system, and the pain and stiffness retreated. Joints cracking, I managed to get to my feet and take a look around. The corner of the bedroll was stained through with blood where a pool of it had formed, and three footsteps in that same blood led from the spot toward the exit. It looked like she had stood up and immediately left, like she was moving with a purpose.

You shouldn't be out there alone in your condition.

I'm not alone.

Fine. Go. Someone is going to answer for that revivor, though, Agent.

Understood.

That's going to be you. Find it.

The connection closed. Calliope continued to watch me.

"What?"

"There's this orange light," she said, "behind your eyes."

"It's reflection from the internal display."

"It's cool."

"Thanks."

The results of my decisions were less cool. Faye was gone, Zoe was in trouble, and I was in it up to my neck. The only thing that might pull it out was the connection I monitored right before the remote override code came in. A quick check of my internal buffer showed the link was still there.

Sean?

Yeah.

I need you to run a trace on this connection.

You got it.

I need to know where it originated from, the physical location. Is there enough?

I think so. Give me some time.

Let me know as soon as you have it.

"How are you still standing?" Calliope asked.

"There's a piece of armor plating behind my breast-bone."

"What the hell for?"

"In case something like this ever happened. I had it installed during my tour. The blade went through the bone but never reached my heart."

That didn't stop it from impacting it, though. The plate itself got pushed back and shocked my heart so hard it had stopped. If the emergency system hadn't jolted it, it would have stopped for good.

"Come on," I said. "I have to move. Someone's in trouble."

Her eyes narrowed.

"I'll take you there."

"I've got a vehicle."

"I've got a bike," she said, "and I know how to ride it. How fast you want to get there?"

My chest was still aching despite the drugs. Dragging her into this would probably be a mistake, but the streets would be jammed with patrols and people trying to beat the curfew; a motorcycle would skirt around a lot of it. Zoe needed help now, not later. I could commandeer the bike, but honestly, with the wound in my chest, I didn't think I'd be able to control it.

I checked for my gun and found that Faye had left it behind. Breaking out the magazine, I saw it was still fully loaded. I never even got off a shot.

Header mismatch: Ott, Zoe. Experimentation.

Experimentation . . . Whatever that meant, I didn't like the sound of it. I was the one who brought her into the whole mess. There wasn't time to argue.

"Alright," I said. "Let's go."

Zoe Ott—The Holding Pens

"Can you hear me?"

A voice was whispering loudly somewhere nearby, but I could barely hear it over the constant hum that filled the air. I was lying on my back on the floor. Was I still in my apartment?

"Hello? Can you hear me?"

I opened my eyes and looked around. It was dark, but I could see a little bit. Wherever I was, it wasn't my apartment; there was metal scaffolding somewhere off in front of me, and I could see a ton of spastic little blinking lights.

"Hello?" It sounded like a woman's voice.

"I can hear you," I said.

"Get up. You're in trouble," she hissed.

My body was so stiff I could barely move. I rolled over and got up on one elbow, just managing to raise my forehead a few inches off the ground. My body was shaking all over.

"You'll be all right," the woman said. My hair trailed on the floor as I lifted my head and let it bob there, looking for her. There was some kind of glass wall or window in front of me. I reached out and touched it, streaking fingerprints. It was hard plastic that looked clear, but there was cardboard taped to the outside so I couldn't see through.

It started to sink in that I was in a box, a clear plastic box. It was no bigger than my bathroom. I went to brush my hair out of my face and felt some threads there, a whole bunch of them, but when I pulled at one, it tugged at my forehead like it was stuck there.

"Here."

A fingernail tapped on the plastic nearby and I looked over where a piece of the cardboard was torn. A pair of eyes looked at me through the little gap.

"Where am I?" I asked.

"Look here," the woman said, and moved her face away from the gap. I crawled across the floor and put my forehead to the wall so I could see through.

Through the hole I could see another plastic box that looked just like the one I was in. They were right next to each other with the cardboard in between them. Sitting in the middle of the floor was a black woman wearing a plain white shirt and pants, and she looked even sicker than I usually did. Her hair had grown into a thicket of kinks that hung around her face, and underneath I saw a bunch of electrodes stuck to her forehead that trailed thin white wires.

Pulling some of the threads out of my hair, I held them up to my face. They were the same thin white wires. My heart was beating faster. Was this another dream? I hoped it was another dream.

"Calm down," the woman said. "Don't try to pull off the electrodes; you'll get shocked if you do."

"Who are you?" I asked. Skin was flaking off her lips, and her eye sockets were dark and hollow.

"Anna," she said. "What's your name?"

"Zoe."

"Do you know where we are?"

"No, where?" I said, and she looked like she might cry.

"I was asking you."

I rubbed my eyes and found that my face was all sweaty and my hands were shaking really badly. The side of my neck itched, and as I scratched at it, I remembered the needle poking me there.

"Are you sick?" she asked.

I hated that question. Even in the situation I was in, I hated it. People always looked at me like I was a hobo or a cancer patient or something, always with this look like they were either grossed out by me or felt sorry for me. Asking someone who wasn't sick if they were sick was such an insult.

"Zoe?"

When I tried to swallow, though, my throat was totally dry and my stomach turned over. Maybe this time I really was.

Either way, I needed time to think. Peeking through the hole in the cardboard, I focused on the woman in the cage next to mine until the lights got bright and the glow appeared around her head. After a second I could see it rippling with deep shades of blue, with small flares of red licking out. The patterns were all of sadness and depression and despair, worse than I'd ever seen before. I meant to push and try to make her feel a little better, when I noticed something else: a thin white band, like a little halo circling her head.

"Hey, my next-door neighbor had one of those," I said without thinking. It was faint, like the ring of a planet, and when I concentrated on it, I felt a kind of resistance. It pushed me back gently, not allowing me to get any closer and not letting me change the other colors.

The woman wiped her eyes.

"You shouldn't do that," she said.

"Do what?" I asked, guilty.

"What you just did. They're watching."

"Watching?"

She pointed to the electrodes stuck to her head. My brain was moving in slow motion, but I was starting to understand her.

"Wait, you felt that?" I asked.

"I can do it too, Zoe," she said. "It's why I'm here. It's why we're all here."

"Other people can do it?"

She gave me a pitying look then, and it was a look I knew well. "Yes," she said.

"Then my next-door neighbor could do it too the whole time?" I asked myself out loud. "Why was he—"

"Maybe they were getting ready to contact you," she said, looking away. "Maybe they just wanted to keep an eye on you."

"Who's 'they'?"

"Coming in," a man's voice said from somewhere nearby. The woman's eyelids drooped.

"Don't fight them," she said.

"Turning on the light," the voice said, and there was a loud snap that made me jump as a bright light flooded the room from above. Everything went white and hurt my eyes, making my stomach flip.

"When they start," she said, holding up the thin white electrode wires while still staring into space, "the person on the other end of these wires is going to try to take control of you."

"What? Why?"

"Because they're like us," she said. "Because they can. Because they're in even deeper trouble than we are, and they need help. They're desperate."

"What?"

Heavy footsteps came closer until a shadow fell over me and I saw two men standing in front of my cell.

"Try to remember that," Anna said.

"You're awake," one of them said. I didn't recognize either of them, but I could tell right away that they were both revivors, just like the woman Nico brought me to see. They were like dead men or robots or something, with no thoughts to read or influence.

"We're ready to begin," one said to the other.

"Begin? Begin what?" I asked. What the hell was going on? What was I doing there?

Please let this be another dream. Please, please let this be another dream. . . .

"The new Patient Nine is awake. Has the template been arranged?" the other one said into a walkie-talkie. It let out a pop of static, and another voice came out of it.

"The probes are in place," it said. "We're recording."

"Open the gate," the one with the radio said.

"Get ready," Anna muttered from behind the plastic.

"Get ready for wh—"
The words stuck in my mouth, and I found out.

Faye Dasalia—Factory Entrance

A GPS appeared in front of my eyes. The floating image jittered at the edges, and a point began to flash. Impulses cracked down the length of my spine. A low electric hum rattled through my brain. It urged me to move toward the point on the map. I'd managed my way back up to street level, where I walked forward blindly.

Is Nico alive? I asked.

I had felt Nico's presence inside my head. He'd dug down in my mind, deeper and deeper, when something else intruded. The other presence reached in and took control.

Answer me, I urged.

The other presence was still there—I sensed it, though it hadn't responded. It had referred to itself as Samuel Fawkes. Samuel Fawkes had forced me to kill Nico.

I could still feel Nico's chest beneath my palm. His skin had been so warm and so full of life. I never meant to do it. Something triggered the blade, and the warmth seeped out. It gushed through my fingers and over my hand. He fell back, spilling onto the concrete floor. Blood bloomed through his white shirt until it turned red. The vibration in my chest grew more urgent. I wanted to go to him. Instead I rifled through each of his pockets. I found the keys that would free me from the chain. With the padlocks undone, I stood and left him.

Please tell me, is he alive? I asked again, but the presence was silent.

The snow had gotten heavy. Flakes sprayed over my face and my mostly bare body. I was still wearing only a button-up shirt that reached the tops of my thighs, but I didn't feel cold. A man stared as I trudged barefoot down the street, a passenger inside my own body.

This was a mistake, I said. Shanks looked down and shook his head.

No, it wasn't.

It was.

His eyes narrowed, and he leaned in very close. The warm brown of both his eyes was blotted out as his pupils dilated.

No, it wasn't, he growled.

The anxiety left me, bleeding away. In its place, I felt relaxed. Happy, even.

This never happened, he said, no longer looking at me. *I left you at the door and I never came inside. I have never been inside your apartment.*

Those memories weren't real, I was certain of it. Other memories referenced them as just a dream. I'd shared those dreams with the department psych rep. I was sure that they weren't real. When Shanks came up to my apartment that night, it had been for the first time.

That man sitting next to you is not your friend. . . .

I shook my head, scattering cold drops and snow. More people were watching me, pointing at me. . . . I began to walk faster, and then I ran. I darted down a side street. One foot plunged into a puddle of water, splashing slush and flakes of ice. I ran through the dark maze of streets and alleys.

As I ran, I tore frantically through my thoughts, through the gaps in my corrupted memories. Inside so many of them was Doyle Shanks, saying and doing things he had never done.

I should have been terrified. What happened when
that blade went into my chest? Between the time my
life slipped away from me and the time the warmth first
came, what was it, exactly, that I had become? Though I
knew my identity was the same, something had changed
when I fell into that darkness. I should have felt something, anything, but I did not.

Snow covered everything now. People and cars fell
off; then I was alone. I didn't know where I was. I'd
come out in a wide, open drift of snow. Dark structures
loomed through the haze in the distance. The GPS point
was somewhere up ahead.

I saw a squat, blocky shape some ways away. It poked
up from out of the expanse of white. I moved toward it,
dragging my feet through the snow. It was a small guard
station. The door lay open, and the glass was all smashed.
An old, rusted breaker box had been torn down. A shopping cart lay on its side next to it. Just beyond, a ramp
descended underground.

Squinting through the snow, I made out a figure.
There was a man at the ramp. He wore a long, dark coat,
with the hood up over his head.

You . . .

A thrumming began to swell in the distance. It came
from up above me. I turned and shielded my eyes against
the snow. There were several black shapes hanging in
the air. As they came closer, the thrumming grew louder.
It was a formation of helicopters.

Quickly. The message floated there in the stark, gray
air.

I turned back to the man who stood at the ramp. He
gestured for me to come.

They've found us. Come quickly.

I recognized the man's face. He was the one who had

pushed the blade through me. It was the killer I had chased for so long. Somehow he was there, waiting.

Don't you mean that they've found you?

There is no difference between us now. Not as far as they're concerned. They won't rescue you; they'll shoot you on sight.

The group of helicopters drew closer. As they did, they spread into formation.

Come on, he said. *They'll fire on you from the air. Come with me. I will explain.*

The vibration filled my head, urging me on. As the helicopters closed in behind me, I staggered through the last length of snow to him. He held a blanket and wrapped it around me.

"You killed my friend," I told him, "and you killed me."

He wrapped the blanket tight around my shoulders. His cold, electric eyes stared and met my own.

"I killed your shadow," he said, "and I didn't kill you. I freed you."

Nico Wachalowski—New Amsterdam, Warehouse District

She wasn't much on social graces, but I admit I had taken an immediate liking to Calliope Flax, despite her foul mouth and the frank hatred of authority that included my own. It wasn't just that she came back to check on me, which she didn't have to do. Most people would have called us even by that point, but she was still taking point for a ride that could put her closer to trouble instead of the other way around. She had guts.

When we got back up to street level, the snow was coming down hard. We got on the bike and headed for Zoe's apartment, but we didn't get two blocks before I spotted the first military patrol. The armored vehicle was moving slowly down the main street, a soldier sweeping a spotlight across the building fronts and down the side roads. Another soldier on the back of the truck held an automatic rifle, keeping watch with an infrared scope. Further on I could see another beam scanning the street while a group of three uniformed revivors marched down the sidewalk, rifles slung over their shoulders as they crunched through the snow. It seemed like whole sections of the city had come under occupation.

Sean, talk to me. What's going on?

Your civilian is gone, Nico.

What do you mean "gone"?

The units that showed up at her place found one dead, one injured, and no sign of Zoe Ott.

Show me.

Images from Zoe's apartment appeared in my field of view. The feed from the officer scanned the inside of the place, shining a flashlight through the dark. The place was filthy, spiral-bound notebooks arranged in skewed stacks along the walls and leaning against the furniture. Trash, dust, and grime seemed to cover everything.

Do the officers have a lead on her?

Not yet, but they're saying abduction, not murder, at least for now. Any idea why they'd take her?

No.

A struggle took place in there; that was clear. Some of the many empty liquor bottles had been toppled and smashed, and notebooks, papers, and pieces of glass were scattered across the floor.

Near the front door was a man's body, lying in a wide pool of blood with what looked like his guts spilled out in front of him.

Who's the victim?

Next-door neighbor.

The older man, the one she didn't get along with. Maybe he tried to help her out and got more than he bargained for.

What about the survivor?

Downstairs neighbor.

Karen. Did she see anything?

According to her, she missed the whole thing. Zoe was gone when she got there.

She missed the whole thing?

That's what she says.

Sean, how did she step over a dead man and get hit by the attacker if she missed the whole thing?

I'm just telling you what she said.

They'd dose her to be sure, but I had a feeling it wasn't going to matter. I had a feeling she didn't miss the whole thing, but Zoe had influenced her otherwise.

She doesn't know anything, Sean said.

You don't think she's lying?

I think she believes what she's saying.

A shot rang out off to my left up ahead, and I saw a muzzle flash light up the concrete wall of the building. I felt Calliope jump in the seat in front of me, but she kept us steady. As we passed, I looked between the buildings and saw a luxury vehicle idling there on the side street, one wheel up on the curb of the walk. The driver's-side door hung open and two revivor soldiers stood there, one holding its rifle with the barrel still drifting smoke. It moved to one side to let the other one in as it pointed a short weapon with a large, tubelike barrel into the vehicle. A gas-powered thud came from the street behind us as we passed.

"Cal, stop the bike!" I yelled, but she kept going.

"Calliope, stop the bike!"

"Fuck you. I'm not going near those things!"

The bike veered, fishtailing for a second on a patch of ice as Calliope took us down a side street to avoid a patrol up ahead where flames were shooting out of a storefront. Garbage and debris littered the sidewalks and the intersection where the soldiers were standing.

Sean, what's going on out here?

They authorized a troop increase to help keep order.

Because of the explosion at the arena?

Where have you been? After the garage bomb, two more went off, one in a mall and one in a nightclub.

Calliope took the bike into an alley, then scooted by a Dumpster through a narrow passageway. The vibrations from the engine were making my chest throb from the inside out and I was freezing, but I had to admit we would never have gotten as far as we even had if I'd tried to take the car. Whole blocks were closed to traffic and there were checkpoints everywhere. Every face we passed looked terrified; the presence of the revivors on the street had stirred up a primal fear in people. Bombs or no, it was a mistake to deploy them.

Sean, what's the protocol on the PH soldiers? What are their orders?

Containment and suppression only. Why?

Nothing lethal? For any circumstances?

Sean paused for a moment.

No. Did you see something?

I'm not sure. I think so. Does any of the deployment include the use of Leichenesser canisters?

Why would a revivor be issued Leichenesser?

Sean, yes or no?

No.

The substance was used primarily for medical reasons and to destroy revivors, but it would consume any dead flesh. It was also handy for cleaning up messes. For making things disappear. Where had they gotten it?

Look, there's something else you should know, Sean said.

What do you mean?

There's another problem. Some of the revivors, the ones deployed with the troops, they stopped checking in.

What does that mean, "they stopped checking in"?

Isolated pockets of them broke off from their assigned groups. Some turned up not long after and acted like it was a malfunction in the command network. Some are still unaccounted for.

Another update came over the connection I was monitoring.

```
Database synchronization pending.
Updating . . .
Header mismatch: Mullvue, Horace. Murder.
Header mismatch: Vesco, William. Murder.
Header mismatch: Hibiki, Fran. Murder.
Header mismatch: Phang, Shin. Murder.
Removing . . .
Removing . . .
Removing . . .
Removing . . .
```

The names continued to peel off. This was a much larger change than the ones I had witnessed before; at least fifteen names were removed.

What do you mean "some are still unaccounted for"? How many?

Seventy-two and counting.

Fawkes was behind this. He had to be. He knew revi-

vor technology intimately; he would know how to infect
the command matrix. Whatever he was up to, this was
part of it.

That connection trace—

*One step ahead of you. I followed it back to a site
called Fioplex right here in the city. It's an underground
factory that used to produce optical cable, but it's been
shut down now for almost a decade.*

You're sure?

*Yes. Once we pinpointed the site, we did a satellite scan
and detected electrical activity down there, way too much
to be noise. Someone's using a lot of juice. You think
whoever's been bringing in the illegal revivors and tapping into Heinlein's system is also directing the rogue PH
soldiers?*

He's not doing it on his own.

The question remained, though: why? Samuel Fawkes
might have the knowledge to take control of a large
group of revivors—he'd already demonstrated he could
take control of one—but he wouldn't do it for nothing.
If that was his intent all along and he just needed more
revivors than he could bring in illegally, then the purpose of the attacks leading up to this point might have
been to pressure the authorities into doing exactly what
they did: deploy the National Guard with a compliment
of PH soldiers. It would be one of the only set of circumstances under which anyone would ever see so many revivors out of stasis on American soil. Was this what he
wanted all along?

There's something else down there too, Sean said.
Thermal signatures, a bunch of them.

Living people?

Quite a few of them.

Thanks, Sean. Keep me informed.

Will do.

I tapped Calliope's helmet.

"What?" she yelled over the engine.

"Forget the apartment. Head toward the industrial sector!"

"What about your friend?"

"Change of plan!"

11

Strike

Zoe Ott—The Green Room

I remembered falling, and my head hurt like it had hit the floor, but when I opened my eyes I was sitting down in a folding chair. The white light was gone, and it had gotten very quiet.

Looking around, I saw I was back in the green concrete room, a single fluorescent light flickering above my head. The table was in front of me, and down at the far end were three figures, the first two kind of hanging limp in the dark and the last one standing with a light shining down on her from the ceiling.

This isn't real. I'm not really here. I'm back in the cell. . . .

The green room wasn't real. Whatever happened back in the real world, it zapped me into a vision.

We're recording. Open the gate.

That's what the guy said right before it happened. . . . Another consciousness rushed into my head all at once, filling my brain with her thoughts. She pounced like she'd been struggling to reach someone for a long time and finally got the chance.

Whoever she was, she was in pain and she was desperate. When her mind flooded mine, I had the feeling she couldn't see me and didn't know who or where I was. It didn't matter that it was me; it didn't matter who I was. I was someone—anyone—who might be able to help her.

She wasn't just calling out for help; she was trying to dominate me. She was using the same abilities I used on others all the time. When she tried to take control, I reflexively threw a wall up between us. The next thing I knew, I was sitting in the chair.

The chair legs scraped across the floor as I pushed it back and stood up. When I looked around, I saw the metal door that led out of the room was hanging open. A woman was standing in the doorway, but she was pushed up against the empty space like there was an invisible wall. She had really hollow cheekbones and sunken eyes. Her hair was ratty, and her forehead was pressed to the invisible wall like it was too heavy for her to hold up straight. I could see two big flaps of skin draping down over either side of her neck, and the whole back of her skull and top of her spine were exposed. A square hole had been sawed in the bone, and a bunch of long needles stuck up out of the hole like she was a human pincushion.

I made myself step closer. There were three star tattoos near one of her eyes.

I know that face. She'd appeared to me before.

"Who are you?" I asked.

She was saying something, over and over. I couldn't hear her, but I could make it out when I watched her lips.

Help me, please help me. Get me out of here. . . .

When I looked close, I could see very faint, very thin

threads of light trailing from my head and stretching out between us. I followed them to the ends of the needles.

We're recording. Open the gate.

"I know you," I said.

She was the one that showed up in my bathroom, back before I met Nico. She told me that I'd end her pain. She was like me. The ones who took me, they did this. They connected us together. They wired us up so they could watch this happen.

"Why are they doing this?" I asked out loud, but she looked as though she couldn't hear me.

"Your place is with us," a voice said from behind me. I turned around and saw what I thought at first was a little boy, but it turned out to be a very small Asian woman with a short haircut. She was standing off to the side where the dead woman with the split heart usually stood, and was dressed in a smart little navy skirt and suit coat with a white blouse. Her shoes and clothes all looked very expensive, and if the diamonds in her jewelry were real, then they must have cost a fortune. Her tiny nails were manicured and painted, and her makeup was carefully applied so that she almost looked pretty, but her lips and eyes were a little fishlike and her head was too big for her body.

"You were in the picture," I said. She was in one of the photos Nico had left with me, the one my neighbor was interested in. She looked around the room, her eyes settling on the figures against the far wall.

"I'm not really here," she said. "Neither of us is; this is a construct of your mind. You are alone, and you are in great danger. Do you understand?"

I nodded.

"The people who have taken you set up this facility in order to learn how our minds work. No one here will survive what is to come except for you, but only if you do what I say. Do you understand?"

There was something about her stare. I found myself nodding again.

"Yes."

"Your life doesn't have to be as pathetic as it is," she said offhandedly. "People with less have achieved more."

She gestured for me to follow as she moved toward the three figures. I moved around the other side of the table to join her.

The first two figures were Nico and the woman, the dead one with the broken heart that he had with him in the storage room. They both looked limp, like they were hanging from hooks. Her eyes were closed, but his were just a little bit open, orange light flickering behind them as they watched me.

"Why are they in the dark?" I asked.

"You failed them."

"No—"

"You failed them."

My face burned as I looked at Nico peering down at me. It wasn't true. Maybe I failed the woman, but not him.

My eyes blurred and I felt tears run down my cheeks. The little woman didn't seem to notice or care; she just turned to the last one, the one that was still lit. It was that ugly, muscular woman, the mean-looking one with the short hair. The light over her got a little brighter.

"I didn't fail him," I said, but the woman ignored me.

"It's time to call her," she said.

"Why her?"

"Some are more open than others, and like it or not, there is a connection between you. Reach out to her now."

I was going to ask how I was supposed to do that when I didn't know where she was and I didn't even know where I was, but the woman just kept staring into my eyes, and after a couple seconds an image started to form in my head.

"Focus."

The image took shape and I saw the mean-looking woman on a motorcycle, snow spitting past her as the collar of her leather coat ruffled in the wind. I thought I saw someone riding in back of her—a man—but it wasn't clear.

"Focus."

I tried to focus on her, but the woman with the needles kept pushing at the invisible barrier across the doorway. The thin threads of light that connected us pulsed, getting brighter and then fading as her thoughts washed over me.

Help me, please help me. Get me out of here. They're hurting me. . . .

A sound like electricity crackling came from her direction, and the lights flickered as her face clenched up. The thoughts got even more urgent, making the picture of the woman on the motorcycle fade in and out.

"Your life can be much more than it is," I heard the Asian woman say, "but only if you succeed here."

I tried to concentrate. If this woman knew where I was, then why didn't she send someone to help me?

"I have sent someone," she said, like I had spoken out loud, "but that facility must be destroyed. Nothing can survive. If you cannot do this, then I cannot use you, and you will not survive either."

The electrical cracking filled the hallway beyond the door again, and the woman with the needles seized up like all of her muscles had contracted at once. Another wave from her hit me.

"Focus!" the woman snapped. "If you fail here, it's over!"

I wasn't going to be able to hold the image of the motorcycle if the signals from the other woman kept coming at me so strong. If I was going to do anything at all, I had to get her to stop.

Usually I would concentrate on a person and I'd see colors, but this time it was like I had a direct connection right into her head. I reached out and pushed through the current toward her.

When I found her, the colors finally appeared, only instead of being fuzzy patterns, they formed a crisp map where the different colors and shades were all distinct. I reached past the blues, the reds, the yellows, past the fear and the anger and the desperation and doubt. I reached past the thin halo, as deep as I could go until I saw a single hot, white band that was more concentrated than anything I'd ever seen in anyone before. It was as if all things were connected to it. This was the source of her energy, the source of her terror.

With less effort than I expected, I concentrated on it, and like a valve, I turned it off. The flow of light through the band stopped and it went dark. All the colors followed immediately afterward, blinking out until everything was dark. The flow of thoughts stopped, leaving complete silence.

"There," I said. I looked over at the Asian woman and she was staring at me, this time with a different expression, her mouth parted a little bit like she was stunned. When I looked back to the doorway to see what the needlehead was doing, she had fallen to the floor and wasn't moving. Any trace of light around her was gone.

There wasn't any time to think about it. I got the image of the woman on the motorcycle back. Sweat beaded up on my forehead. I saw the colors begin to appear.

The colors formed patterns, and all at once I could read them. I reached out and with all the strength I could muster, I grabbed hold of her.

Nico Wachalowski — New Amsterdam, Warehouse District

Calliope had been reckless on the bike all along, but all of a sudden I felt a lurch as she throttled the engine and picked up speed. The road cleared as we raced beneath a monorail platform, and while the back tire kicked sand off the pavement, the front wheel almost came up off the ground.

"Cal, take it easy!"

We'd left the residential and business districts behind us, along with most of the patrols, a while back. The road ahead merged into a clover, which led into a series of open industrial-park areas, none of which looked like they'd seen much recent activity. Through the snow I could make out warehouses and cargo lanes, but they were all covered over now. We lost traction for a second as she hit the clover way too fast and veered down one of the off-ramps.

"Cal!"

There was a chain-link fence up ahead with a gate that hung open partway. She sped toward it, banking at the last second, and the bike tilted wildly. I gripped her waist in a death lock as slush sprayed up over me, and I heard the heel of her boot doing a high-speed scrape across the pavement. Somehow she righted the bike, and I pulled my knees in tight as we flew through the narrow opening in the fence. The blacktop disappeared under the snow again as she took us onto one of the lots.

"Damn it, it's too deep—stop the bike!"

What was the matter with her? She couldn't have any idea where she was going, not when I hadn't even zeroed in on the exact GPS location yet. Over her shoulder, I saw that other vehicles had been here before us, and that she was taking us down a narrow trench formed by their treads. Every few seconds the bike fishtailed and she managed to right it. My chest throbbed and my stomach began to knot.

I got a bead on the location and brought up the map. Somehow she was taking us in the right direction. There was a guard station in the distance, and a ramp leading down.

You should be picking up a radio beacon about now, Sean said. I tuned to the frequency he indicated, and sure enough, it was there.

Got it.

Follow it.

Up ahead, several large, dark objects were called out on the display.

"Calliope, stop the bike. This is close enough!" I shouted. Things were going to start getting dangerous, and she had already gotten closer than I wanted her to. The dark objects were getting larger as we got closer, taking shape through the snow. They were definitely vehicles of some kind.

I zoomed in on them, bringing them into focus; they were helicopters. Three of them, military choppers used for troop deployment.

Sean, what's going on over here? I've got three military helicopters. Who sent them?

Hold on.

He went idle for a minute, then dropped off completely. A second later, a new ID came in. It was Assistant Director Noakes.

Wachalowski, where are you?

I'm at the site, but I don't see SWAT. I see some military helicopters here.

I know.

What do you mean, you know?

I could see three revivor soldiers standing in front of the remains of an old guard tower. They had spotted us, and one of them was waving us down.

When did they get involved in this?

I'm doing what I was instructed to do. The word came down that this little rat's nest you've uncovered is to be shut down immediately and completely. Stay out of their way and let them handle it.

How can you say that? We've lost—

This comes from high up. It's not our place to second-guess them, Wachalowski. You've helped stop a significant terrorist threat. Just stay out of their way.

"Son of a bitch!" Cal snapped. I looked up and saw the soldiers ahead raising their rifles.

"Cal, stop!"

Are you receiving me, Wachalowski? Why are you still approaching the site?

Behind the revivors, I could see the remains of a thick metal curtain that had blocked an entrance ramp that led down underground. It looked like explosives had been used to blow the gate, and dozens of boot tracks headed past the guard station and down into the factory entrance.

A shot rang out and snow sprayed off to my right. Calliope veered, plowing through the snow and coming out in a second set of tire tracks. Two more shots boomed through the air.

Wachalowski—

Tell them to hold their fire.

Tell them how? I'm not—

We were getting close now, way too close. We passed the helicopters and started coming up fast on the soldiers. They weren't going to let us get much farther, and Calliope, for whatever reason, was not slowing down.

One of them fired again, and this time it hit the bike an inch from my thigh, throwing sparks. It stared down the barrel, trying to get a shot.

There was no more time. They weren't people; they were just revivors. I held on to Calliope with my left arm and drew my gun. I fired two three-shot bursts and the revivor spun, then fell onto the snow. A second one tried to grab me as we passed, and I fired a shot that sprayed black fluid out of the back of its skull.

"Cal! What are you doing? Slow down."

I could see muzzle flashes coming from somewhere down the ramp. She braked, and tipped the bike so that it began sliding sideways toward the entrance, colliding with the last soldier and dragging it. We bucked over the edge of the ramp and through the entrance, into the dark and out of the snow. The bike slid, pinning the soldier and throwing sparks as the exhaust pipes met the concrete.

I lost my grip and fell off the bike, rolling across the ramp as the bike crunched into a parked car a few meters away. When I righted myself, I looked down to see a series of vehicles had been arranged to form a makeshift barricade in front of the entranceway into the factory. A group of revivors were pinned down behind the cars, firing at the soldiers who had taken cover behind the concrete pylons and were shooting back.

I looked over to the bike and saw smoke trailing from it. It looked like the pinned soldier took the brunt of the slide. Calliope was moving again. She pulled herself out from underneath the wreck.

"Cal, stay down!" I yelled, but she didn't stop.

Bullets were spraying the barricade and return fire was punching divots into the pylons, scattering tiles and concrete dust. Stray shots buzzed through the air, glancing off the ramp behind us.

A roar filled the underground garage and the whole area lit up as I scrambled across the ramp toward her. Down where the fighting was taking place, one of the soldiers had stepped out from behind the pylon and turned a flamethrower on the barricade. Superhot plasma sprayed out in a directed cone and washed over the vehicles, peeling away the paint and causing the windows to blow apart. The upholstery ignited as the flames spilled over onto the revivors who were taking cover there.

As the underground was lit by the fire, I saw that all soldiers were armed with flamethrowers. They were dressed in protective gear that included a black rubber hood with shielded goggles and long aprons to protect them from the flames. While another jet of plasma washed over the barricade, I reached Calliope and pulled her closer to the side of the car. Who the hell were these guys?

"Get off me!" she grunted, pushing me away. There was a strange look in her eyes, almost like she was delirious.

"Calliope, listen to me," I said, trying to get her to meet my eye. "What's the matter? What's wrong with you?"

Below, someone screamed, and when I turned I saw a figure engulfed in flames run out from behind the burning vehicles. Its flickering eyes stared out of a blackened face as it pulled off its long, burning coat and tossed it to one side. Several bullets punched through its torso as it ran for the pylons, and I could just make out the electronics and wires strapped around its chest before it met the group of soldiers.

"Get down!" I shouted, pushing Calliope onto her back and covering her head as the bomb went off. The sound was deafening as everything was lost in a bright white flash. Through the spots I caught a glimpse of debris, blood, and body parts shooting through the air as at least two soldiers were caught directly in the blast. Shrapnel rained across the side of our cover, and I saw an arm attached to what looked like part of a rib cage glance off the divider and tumble into the shadows.

"Cease fire!" an amplified voice shouted as the boom faded. "Stop! Cease fire!"

Chancing a look, I saw that the order was being given because there was nothing left to shoot at. The barricade was still in flames, but there was no further movement behind it. The soldier who had given the cease-fire looked over his men, taking stock. It looked like half of them were down, maybe more.

"File in," he said, gesturing to the factory entrance. "We continue down."

Stepping over the bodies, they quickly reorganized, ducked through the flames, and headed through the door.

"Let me up," Calliope said, pushing me. I gave her some room and offered her my hand, but she batted it away.

"You have to get out of here," I told her. She stood up, still a little shaky, and stumbled out from behind the car. The carnage was sinking in. Her eyes were wide.

She looked over the damage in front of her like she

was taking the whole situation in for the first time. She took two steps, then got down on one knee.

By the time I realized what she was up to, it was too late. She picked up the gun she had found and was back on her feet.

"Hey!"

She looked at me for just a second, and her eyes looked scared, but at the same time there was commitment there. Whatever she intended to do, and for whatever reason, she meant to do it.

Without checking to see if the gun was even loaded, she sprinted down the ramp toward the factory entrance. I took off after her as she ducked past the flames and out the other side through the doorway.

The vehicles that had formed the barrier had been forced back by the blast, one of them tipped on its nose and leaning against the wall, and the other on its back. In the burning carnage, I could make out a boot and what looked like an arm with a long blade sticking out, but nothing else was recognizable. Between the blast and the flamethrowers, the heat was incredible. Holding my jacket up to shield my face, I ran past and made it through the entranceway.

Sean, are you there?

I'm here, but it won't be private.

Who the hell are these guys?

Special Forces. Someone internal had them standing by.

Standing by for what?

Someone wants that place buried, Nico. Get out of there.

Inside, the corridor went left and right. The soldiers were down the right passage, filing onto an electric lift that led down to the lower levels. A metal door a few paces to the left was just latching shut when I entered.

That had to be her. As the lift carrying the soldiers started down, I pushed open the metal door into a stairwell.

I've got a civilian down here and I've got to get her out.

Nico, you've got Special Forces in front and another wave coming in behind you.

How long?

Minutes. They're at radio silence, and they don't know anyone else is there. I don't know all the details, but the word is that they're to erase any trace of that place. That's going to include your civilian and you if you get in the way.

As the door shut behind me, I caught a glimpse of Cal one flight down, boots clomping as she barreled down the steps.

I know.

My chest burning, I followed her down.

Faye Dasalia—Factory Clean Room

Draped in the blanket, I followed my killer down into the underground facility, while behind us the sounds of destruction raged. He didn't look back as he led me deeper, into near-total darkness. An icon flashed at the corner of my eye.

Adjusting light levels . . .

We were walking through an office corridor. The walls and doors were covered in graffiti, and the whole area was littered with trash. Material for bedding was strewn about. People had taken shelter there at one time, but they had all been cleared out.

What is this place? I asked as I followed him. He led me through a large, rusted metal door, into the darkness beyond. The doors slammed shut behind us with a loud thud, and we moved down the dark hall. Farther on, we descended an old stairwell.

It used to be a factory.

Used to be?

No one has come here in a very long time. That's why Samuel picked it.

You said his name before. Who is Samuel? I asked.

Samuel Fawkes. He organized all of this. He was the one who first realized what was happening, and he knew he would need someplace like this. Someplace no one would look.

Who is he?

He was an important figure at Heinlein Industries. He was the one who figured out Zhang's Syndrome.

Zhang.

My memories sparked, and a point of light rose. It opened to reveal the face of a burned woman, a revivor. It moved its mouth, whispering that name to me.

Who is Zhang? I asked him. *What does the name mean?*

We didn't realize the trafficker's pleasure models were outfitted with surplus communications nodes, he said. *They joined our network. It's why they had to be destroyed before they could be questioned. You set a lot of things into motion when you passed that name on to the FBI.*

From somewhere up above came muted gunfire. A few shots turned quickly to sustained fire, echoing down the hallway.

What is that? I asked.

The military has arrived to destroy this place.

So you've failed? I asked, but his face didn't change.
They'll never find Fawkes, he said.

A boom shook the floor and rumbled through the air.
Grit sifted down on my head from the ceiling.

Come on, he said. *Your partner was one of them. You
were his puppet. You've been a puppet your whole life. I
freed you.*

He took me down into the lower levels, where huge
cables ran down narrow corridors. They hung from the
walls and tracks on the ceiling. The spaces were tight
and cramped. There were few lights, just pinpricks in
the distance, but he seemed to know the way, and I
followed.

You were your partner's puppet.

I remembered standing in the Valle home, looking
down on the bodies of the family. Investigator Reece
was talking to me.

*A phone call would have been a neat trick, tied up like
that. Do you believe his account?*

Then I saw that small trace of interference; right
around that time frame, something had been changed.
Shanks leaned in, giving me an intense look. Then his
eyes changed, the pupils growing wider.

A witness, he said. *That's promising.*

The witness didn't see anything.

*Go and talk to him, and I will look around the apart-
ment*, he whispered, leaning closer. *Do not disturb me
for the next several minutes. Justify it any way you need
to.*

Got it.

*You will remember this only as a product of your own
intuition.*

Right.

Someone is targeting us, Shanks said to himself. He

looked worried. *I'm sorry, but I'm on that disc. No one else can know about this. Not even you. I'm sorry.*

He glanced past me then, and his eyes flashed hunger. He made sure none of the others could see us; then he slipped one of his hands into my coat. I felt the warmth of his palm on my left breast. He squeezed it, and rubbed the nipple with his thumb.

"You're a beautiful woman," he said, removing his hand. He stepped back, away from me. The memory resumed from the point of the splice. I straightened out my jacket. My face was flushed.

Shanks, check around. I want to talk to him, I said.

Yes ma'am.

I knew the memory was wrong. I used to talk to myself, that much was true, but Doyle Shanks never whispered in my ear. He never touched me; I would have remembered.

This way, the revivor said.

He pushed aside a large sheet of thick plastic, then passed through it to where the air was warmer. I could see rows of large, metal cylinders, stacked sixty feet to a rusted iron grid. Above it was a huge mechanical arm, where a length of thick, black cable still hung. He led me past, through another plastic sheet. Through a doorway, I spotted rows of people; they were all sitting in chairs. All of them were bent over. I made out IV racks and surgical tubes. We passed them and came to a flight of stairs. They led up to a small door.

Through here.

He opened it and pulled me along after him. Unlike the rest of the factory I'd seen, it was clean and brightly lit. Air whistled between my toes as I stepped through. It was some kind of clean room.

It was filled with lots of high-tech equipment. Screens

displayed different parts of the factory. In some I could see different people's faces, trailing electrodes. One showed the concrete ramp where I first entered. The vehicles there were twisted and burned black. A fire raged out of range of the camera. I stared at it while words formed in from of my eyes.

```
Database Synchronization Pending . . .
Header mismatch: Auerbach, Lillian. Murder.
Header mismatch: Fifield, David. Murder.
Header mismatch: Tang, Hsu. Murder.
Header mismatch: Ury, Kate. Murder.
Header mismatch: Ng, Gilllan. Murder.
Header mismatch: Rios, Carlos. Murder.
Removing . . .
Removing . . .
Removing . . .
Removing . . .
Removing . . .
Removing . . .
```

More names streamed by, filling my field of vision. I counted dozens, then hundreds of them. They were all being removed.

"What is this?" I asked out loud. "What's happening?"

"They're too late," the revivor said. "It's already begun."

12

Descent

Nico Wachalowski—The Lab/Factory Clean Room

Despite the beating she took, Calliope was still going full tilt. That was pretty good considering she didn't have the benefit of any augmentation. As I eased adrenaline into my bloodstream, I wondered how much longer my body would hold out, but it was the only way to keep up with her. By the time she hit the last landing, I was a half flight behind her, my vision starting to tunnel around that dark spot that floated in front of my eyes. She shoved open the door at the base of the stairs and barreled through.

I ducked through after her, and the cold in the stairwell gave way to air that was warmer and damper. There were some lights mounted farther down the corridor, but not many. I bumped up my visual filters to allow more light in. How could she even see where she was going?

A sheet of clear plastic hung across a doorway ahead, cut down the middle, and Calliope swiped it to either side as she punched through. I got past it in time to see her darting through another sheet across the room, but before I could close the distance, my foot collided with something and I fell forward, crashing down onto the concrete floor.

"Cal!" I shouted. Somewhere not too far away I heard the buzzing and squealing of the electric lift coming to a stop and the gate rising open. Radio chatter began to echo down the dark corridors.

Damn it . . .

Bleeding again, I got back onto my feet and looked behind me to see that I had tripped over a body. There were a pile of them stacked along one wall, arms and legs sprawled. They were all nude, facedown, and arranged in rows. Some of them had the flesh cut away from the backs of their necks and heads. A woman's body had slid off one of the stacks and was lying faceup, tangled black hair plastered to the floor and a series of electrodes stuck to her forehead.

Sean, are you getting this?

I'm reading you, but they're blocking the visual feed. What do you see?

I'm not sure. There are a lot of bodies down here.

Leaning in to one of the bodies that had the skin stripped away from the back of its head, I zoomed in on a square hole that had been sawed through the skull to expose a section of glistening brain matter. Scanning the tissue, I saw several thin objects, like tiny rods or tubes, embedded inside. I looked back to the corpse's face; it was a young man, his blue eyes clouded over.

These aren't revivors; they were human beings.

I jumped as a few bursts of gunfire went off not far from where I was. Several more single shots followed.

"Hold!" a voice barked over an amplifier.

"There!" another voice shouted. It was the Special Forces team. They were getting closer.

I pushed the plastic aside and ran down the hallway, where a series of thick cables snaked along the floor and walls. Through another sheet up ahead I saw a cloud of flame shoot through the air, accompanied by a high-pitched hiss. I heard the roar and crackle of fire as hot air began to blow through the seam and down the corridor.

When I pushed through the last sheet of plastic, I immediately smelled burning flesh. The air was heavy with a stinking mixture of charred hair and meat. Ahead I could see stacks of huge, rust-corroded cylinders that were used to store long-distance cable. They towered up into the darkness where I could just make out a giant mechanical arm reaching across them, sixty feet overhead.

A doorway to my right led into a large open area where I could still register a bunch of human thermal signatures, in spite of the rising heat. As I watched, another jet of flame arced through the room and lit up rows of figures strapped down into chairs before fading again. Just past the doorway against the wall, I could see a stairway leading up to some kind of control room. I ducked through into the room and hugged the wall on the other side as the smell of blood, urine, and antiseptic hit me.

Shit . . .

The room was filled with dozens of people, all sitting in chairs and each with a small table in front of him or her. They were all bent over, foreheads touching the tabletops where their heads and shoulders were strapped with bands of packing tape. Each of them had a surgical opening cut along the back of the head and neck that exposed the muscle and bone underneath, and the back of the skull was cut away in a neat square to expose the brain tissue inside, like the bodies I had seen piled in the back room. It looked like each hole contained a bundle of neuron probes that were inserted into the brain.

The people were arranged in rows that stretched off into the shadows. In the far corner, a fire was beginning to rage.

Sean, I found the bodies you picked up on the satellite scan.

Are they still alive?

I think so.

Each body had an IV rack next to it, the tubes trailing down under the hospital robes they wore. At each station, a wire connected a high-voltage battery cell to a thick needle embedded into the occupant's chest. A throw switch allowed them to be jolted on cue. Beneath each chair was a plastic bucket stained with human waste. The bottom of each chair had been bored through so they could eliminate without being moved.

This is bad, Sean.

One of the victims, a young woman with a cluster of star tattoos near one eye, was dead. Her vitals monitor showed a flatline, but the others were alive. Crouching next to the man sitting closest to me, I pulled the packing tape away from his face so I could see one of his eyes. When I shined a light in it, the pupil contracted. His limbs were atrophied and pocked with bedsores.

I don't know if these people can be saved.

A high-pitched hiss screamed through the air again as another jet of flame lit up the room and washed over the bodies in the rows. In the swell of light, I saw skin wrinkle and blacken before being peeled away, IVs bursting open in the heat. None of them moved as their flesh was seared away.

"There and there!" a voice boomed, as two rows of

the hooded Special Forces soldiers began filing in from across the room, each taking one side. More flames shot through the air, and heat singed my nostrils.

There was no way to stop it from happening. If I gave my position away, they'd turn on me as well, and there was nowhere to take cover from the flames. The smoke was getting thick; it wasn't safe to stay down there without protection. I had to find Calliope and get her back up to the surface.

My knees buckled under me without warning and my stomach twisted. For a second my vision blurred around that blind spot, and I felt sweat trickle down my back.

Sean, the Special Forces soldiers are here. They're burning everything—

Get out of there, Nico.

Keeping low, I scanned the room for an exit. There were three options; back the way I came, up the stairs to the control room, or another door on the far wall where a series of wires trailed from the direction of the burning bodies.

The backscatter showed more people through that doorway, along with rows of what might be computer equipment. The bodies were seated, except for one that might have been Calliope.

Looking to the top of the stairwell, I could clearly make out two figures through the wall, both of them revivors. I picked out their signatures; one of them wasn't on file, but the other one I knew.

It was Faye's.

"Hit each one!" the radio voice barked. Over the racket, a gunshot boomed and I saw the commanding soldier stride down a row of captives. Smoke drifted from the barrel of his gun as he placed it to the temple of the next one in line, even as her flesh burned. He fired, blowing out the opposite side of her face.

"Nothing left behind, people! That means nothing!"

Faye was there. When Samuel took control of her, he brought her to this place, for whatever reason.

Wachalowski, get out of—

I cut off the communication feed. The fire was consuming half of the bodies by then, and the air in front of me was rippling crazily in the heat. The cacophony of voices, gunfire, and roaring flames began to sound as if it was underwater, punctuated by the high-pitched screams of the flamethrowers.

A warning message appeared in front of me, then another. Warning me about the temperature, warning me about my wounds and the chemical imbalances inside of me that were beginning to hit critical. A choice had to be made. I had to go one way or the other.

My legs felt like lead as I moved up the stairs, wondering whether I would be shot or burned before I ever got to the top. I didn't turn around to see what was happening behind me; I just moved forward until my palm touched the door and I pushed it open. Everything seemed to slow down as a blast of cool air blew over me, condensing the sweat covering my face and neck into cold, hard drops. Inside, everything was white and clean and crisp.

Faye was there, sitting in a chair and looking up at me, while a large figure stood behind her. The warm hazel of her eyes had been replaced with that cold synthetic light, but it was close enough. Even without her hair, and the dark veins that branched beneath her skin, at that moment, I felt as if it was close enough.

Faye was dead. I walked away from her a long time ago, and by the time I regretted it, she was gone for good. She was dead; I had seen it with my own eyes, but the figure sitting in that chair and that face looking up at me were hers. That voice and the memories in that cold brain were hers. It was close enough.

Wasn't it?

I fired, the muzzle flash lighting up the right side of her face for an instant before the figure behind her jerked and began to fall.

Her face was specked with black, and an oily drop began to roll down her cheek like a tear.

Stop, Agent Wachalowski.

The warning messages filled my entire line of sight, scrolling by until everything else was blocked out and I felt myself falling. The warnings flickered and snapped off just before everything in front of me went white except that one black blind spot. After a moment, that dissolved too, and I felt my head hit the floor.

Who is this?

Faintly, I heard what sounded like my gun landing nearby.

This is Samuel, Agent.

Nothing hurt anymore. I was disoriented, but I thought that I had finally pushed it too far. I had finally gone as far as I could go, and my body failed me.

His words floated in front of me: *This is where it ends.*

Calliope Flax—The Holding Pens

I followed a bunch of wires away from the strapped-down bodies and through a metal door that led into another big room, and that's when I stopped. I was where I needed to be.

Across the room, the back wall was stacked top to bottom with big, clear plastic boxes, all with a door on the front. There were people in the cages, some up against the glass and some on their sides. Wires were spread out over the floor and up the sides of the plastic boxes, where they dropped through to connect to the heads of the people inside.

A loud screech came from behind the door in back of me, then another. I heard flames pop and burn. The goons were right behind me.

The room spun, like I got a head rush, and I heard screaming. It hit like a wave. It felt like the noise came from the people in the cages, but they weren't moving. Their mouths were shut. There were no screams, not really, but the one who called me was there.

Eyes watched through the plastic as I went to the cage on the far bottom left and looked in. There was a girl in it, some scrawny little bitch I'd never seen before. She looked like she weighed ninety pounds, if that, with long, greasy red hair and a big beak nose. She sat on the floor and looked out at me.

"Who are you?" I asked. She just stared over that beak. Her hands were shaking in her lap, and she was sweating like a pig. Blood had come out of her right nostril in a big fat drop on her sweaty top lip.

Somewhere nearby a gun went off, and snapped me out of it.

"Hey!" I said thumping the glass with the gun I forgot I had. "Who are you?"

She put her face to the glass, and all of a sudden her eyes went freaky. The black part twitched, getting bigger and smaller. The blood drop got fatter and ran down her chin. With one bony finger she tapped the glass next to the lock, and I knew what to do. I pointed the gun at the bolt housing and pulled the trigger.

The plastic was tougher than it looked; I had to shoot it three times. I pulled open the door and went to grab her when she flinched, and all of a sudden I felt like a hand pushed me back. I stood there with my hand out.

"Who the hell are you?" I asked.

"Zoe," she said, and right then the goons came piling in. Our own guys . . . they just came in, guns out, and started shooting.

Bullets punched through the cages in front of me and I saw blood spatter inside. A woman's head blew apart as specks of shattered plastic came falling down over us.

I grabbed the redhead's wrist and dragged her out of the cage. Her knees hit the floor; then she got her legs back and hid behind me with two fistfuls of my jacket.

"Get off!"

Something hit the glass nearby and I saw some kind of brick with a flashing light on it stuck to the middle cage. I shoved her back, and the bitch pulled me down on top of her behind a rack of equipment. When I looked up, it was just in time to see the thing go off. The floor shook as the boom pounded my ears and a blast of heat hit me full-on. The glass blew into dust in a circle around it, until the whole thing was gone.

Through the ringing in my ears, I could hear her screaming behind me. I turned around to shut her up and saw two of the soldiers standing over us just a few feet away.

The girl was standing between us, hands clamped on her ears, toe-to-toe with the goons. She stood there staring at them, and they had us in their sights, but they stopped.

Then, just like that, one of the soldiers pointed his gun at the one next to him and put a slug right in his ear. No reason; he just blew his fucking head right off. His buddies got splattered, and turned on him like he'd gone nuts. The one that got shot was still falling when the guy that did it dropped his rifle and turned the flamethrower on the rest.

"Come on!" she yelled, pointing at the door that led back out the way I came. She didn't have to say it twice.

We barreled through the door, gunshots booming over the shriek of the flamethrower.

Nico Wachalowski — Factory Clean Room

I opened my eyes and saw a blue sky above me. It was a cool blue, with just a few white clouds, and even though I was shivering a little, it made me think of summer. The sound of wind and surf filled my ears, and just under that, faintly, were the sounds of others nearby as they talked and laughed and played.

Was I dreaming? Had I lost consciousness at the last moment in the factory, and was I imagining this place? Maybe I blacked out and the revivor finally killed me. Maybe it was all some kind of euphoria caused when my brain sensed the shock to my body was too much and released a flood of dopamine to ease my slipping away. Maybe I was finally going to die.

Agent Wachalowski.

That was no dream. The words hung there against the blue sky, then faded. I recognized the communications signature from when Fawkes broke in and hijacked Faye back in the storage unit. For better or worse, he was keeping me alive. I accessed my JZI and found a security lockdown had been initiated. He'd hacked into it, then, and been detected.

Where am I? I asked.

You haven't moved. Your friend Ms. Dasalia is still

near you. She is kneeling directly next to you. I know that matters to you. I found the way you looked at her when you stormed in a little touching.

What did you do to me?

Your cerebral implant was also developed at Heinlein Industries, Agent. You might be surprised how similar some of the technology is to the implants used in revivors.

No, I wouldn't. What did you do?

I used a back door to communicate with your implant, briefly. I convinced it that fatal toxin levels were detected in your bloodstream. It put you in deep sedation to stop the spread until it could neutralize them.

I tried to move, but my body wouldn't respond. Even when I rolled my eyes to look around, my view didn't change, which meant the images were being fed to my brain directly and that my eyes, in reality, were still closed.

Warning messages began to flash over the image of the blue sky. He was hacking through the security locks to get access to the JZI's main command functions. The only way to stop him would be to shut down the implant, but the emergency protocol was still in effect. It wouldn't accept the shutdown code until it determined it was safe to do so.

Why not just kill me?

The systems you're outfitted with are impressive. I could use a revivor like you in my ranks.

I'm not wired for reanimation.

Not yet.

I'd faced revivors in the field back in the service and again at home. In all that time, I'd never had one try to hack into my systems before; I didn't think they were capable of it. I'd broken into the control center of many revivors before, though. I understood them. I knew how they functioned.

Before Fawkes could break through, I shunted a virus over the connection back toward the source. There was a noticeable lag before it dropped into his memory and executed.

I realized he wasn't in the factory. Wherever he was, he was far away. Really far.

His next communication was garbled. The virus mapped his systems, then took control of them. When it was finished, it sent a full report, which included access codes to all of his systems.

His assault stopped. Before he could give the command to the revivor in the room with me, I severed his command spokes. Every revivor in the facility was cut off from him.

Agent, wait.

I sifted through the access codes and found the trigger to the small capsule of Leichenesser that Heinlein implanted in the skull of every revivor.

Agent, I have placed a lock on the necrotizing capsule contained inside Faye Dasalia. If you kill me and that connection times out, she'll die too.

You're already dead, Fawkes, and so is she.

You understand what I mean. Destroying me will be a mistake, Agent. There's more going on here than you realize.

I connected to his system and tried to trace his location. Wherever he was, it was outside the country. He'd set up some elaborate chain of reroutes on the circuit.

Where the hell are you? I asked.

I'm right where I'm supposed to be, suspended in stasis fluid, in a plastic blister, in a metal box buried under a warehouse of other identical metal boxes. The only differ-

*ence between me and the rest of the PH soldiers awaiting
deployment is that I arranged to be outfitted with capabil-
ities they don't have. They keep me conscious and allow
me to still act, even though I can't move.*

I wondered if that could be true, or if it was meant to
keep me off his trail. If he had developed some means to
do what he said, it was possible he was on a base somewhere in the world, still awaiting deployment. A PH soldier might sit in a storage depot for years before it was
needed. If he had contact with the outside world and
enough resources, he might have been able to orches-
trate everything remotely.

This was planned a long time ago, he said. *If you're
going to destroy me, at least take the information I have.
If you don't, it was all for nothing.*

What information? What are you talking about?

It all goes back to Ning Zhang.

What does that mean? I asked. *What does Zhang have
to do with this?*

*What Olav Sodder first discovered wasn't what he
thought it was. I realized after studying the revivor Zhang
that his memories weren't corrupted at all, as everyone
had believed. When I studied him long enough, I found
that it was actually just the opposite; as a revivor, he had
an almost total command over his memories, so much so
that he could pick them out and access them almost like
pages of computer memory. I can definitively say now
that this analogy is not far from the truth.*

*You said yourself in one of the interviews with Zhang
that events happen one way, not two,* I said.

*Yes, but the assumption was always that the revivor's
memory was corrupted somehow during reanimation
and that one memory was the original true one, and the
other was the corrupted false one. I compared the brains*

and the components of many different subjects, and there was no physical or chemical difference between those that were affected and those that weren't. Whatever happened, it wasn't a corruption that happened during death or during reanimation. There could only be one other explanation: the corruption occurred before death. Zhang's reanimation didn't cause the memory corruption, Agent, it removed it. The original memory, the living memory, was the false one. Not the other way around.

At that moment, I finally understood him. He was talking about Zoe. Not her specifically, but the phenomena she could create.

Are you saying someone altered Zhang's memory when he was alive?

Yes.

And he remembered the truth, the way things really happened, after he was dead?

Zhang never committed the crime he was accused of; someone convinced him that he did.

Who? Why?

The ones who actually did it, I imagine. As for why, who knows? It served someone's purpose.

Eyewitnesses came forward in the Zhang trial.

I was able to interview one such witness after reanimation. The memory of witnessing that event was a lie as well.

The memory was implanted? Is that what you're saying?

I know you have some idea of what I'm talking about, Agent. Memory is a tricky thing. It plays tricks on us all the time. In the hands of a master, it can be manipulated, I promise you. You yourself were a victim before I had Zoe Ott removed.

She's just one—

She's just one of many, Agent. Your friend isn't unique; she's one of thousands, and they have been using you to get to me. When I started analyzing the new revivors we brought online, I began uncovering more and more instances of what we called Zhang's Syndrome. As reanimation technology got more sophisticated, the memories became more specific. I catalogued them, trying to create a bigger picture, and eventually one formed. I began to see an order to the thousands of alterations, and an organization took shape. As I studied the recovered memories, I began to see themes, policies, agendas, and, eventually, names.

The list. A fragment of that list had been pulled from one of Samuel's illegal imports; the rest later from Faye.

If these people really exist and they're so powerful, then how did you manage to kill them so easily?

Because they have an Achilles' heel. One that your friend may have noticed. They can't read revivors.

I remembered Zoe's reaction when I put her in front of Faye back in the storage unit, the surprise on her face and the fear in her eyes when she backed away. It sobered her, as much as anything could have. At the time, I thought it was a reaction to seeing the body walking and talking again. Some people could handle it and some couldn't. Now I thought I understood.

They can't read them, they can't control them, and now they understand; we know too much.

My mind struggled with what he was saying. I couldn't deny the reality of Zoe's power. If she had it, others like her could too. Could there be any truth to what he was saying?

It doesn't matter, Fawkes.

You don't believe that.

You can't justify those bombs going off downtown.

I knew how to take control of as many revivors as I needed; the only trick was getting them out of storage so I could do it. I used the ones I smuggled to strike the key players who might get in the way, then caused enough chaos to threaten the security of the city. When the troops were finally deployed, I used them to eliminate the rest.

All of them?

Enough to hurt them. Enough to set them back decades.

The blue sky warped, then flickered in front of me for a second. The sound of the voices and the surf skipped, and there was a pop of static.

Have you seen the prisoners they keep down here and the experiments they're conducting on them?

To defeat an enemy, you have to understand them, Agent. I designed those experiments. It's one thing to know people can influence the minds of others; it's another thing to understand how it's done and if anything can be done to stop it. Those experiments are the result of years of brain-pathway data amassed at Heinlein Industries. If the experiments hadn't been necessary, I wouldn't have to take the risk of breaching Heinlein's system.

Or killing Cross.

These people knew someone was on to them and they were starting to figure it out, with the help of the likes of you and your friend Dasalia. They traced it to Heinlein, and one of them, Rebecca Valle, decided to influence Cross and her own son. They dragged them into this, not me.

But you had them killed.

We have to win at any cost. I know you understand that.

The floor shook underneath me again, making my

teeth rattle. Whatever was happening, it was getting worse.

It's time for you to wake up, Agent.

I went to trigger the Leichenesser capsule—even if it meant losing what was left of Faye—but before I could, the connection dropped. The blue sky went dark. Somehow he'd managed to isolate the virus and get control back.

His command functions all dropped off and my JZI reset, then began to reinitialize. As soon as the system came back online, I fired a stim into my bloodstream.

My eyes snapped open. The big revivor was kneeling over me, its shirt sticky with black blood. For the first time, I noticed the explosives strapped underneath its coat, the blue light of the timer counting down slowly. Its right forearm was splayed apart down the middle and the tip of the blade inside was inches from my neck. It was waiting on the order from Fawkes, but the command spoke was still cut.

Faye was next to it. She was looking down at me with what I wanted to believe was concern or compassion, but the truth was I couldn't be sure.

"Nico—"

My gun was gone. I swatted the revivor's arm away, and the point of the blade slammed into the floor next to my ear. I grabbed its coat and reached behind my back for the field knife tucked in my belt. Pain bored into my chest as I pulled myself up and planted my shoulder in its gut, pushing it back. When it braced one foot, I dug the knife in behind its Achilles' tendon and sliced through it.

Off balance, the revivor began to fall. I followed it down, then straddled it as it hit the floor. It bucked underneath me as I put one knee on the side of its face and jammed the knife in the back of its neck. With a violent jerk, I severed the spine.

"Nico!"

According to the counter, Faye had only minutes left before the Leichenesser capsule triggered. The Special Forces team was close. It was only a matter of time before they found the clean room. I opened the revivor's coat and saw the LCD ticking down in the mass of wires. There was no way I could defuse it, but it had a reset mechanism . . . a dead-man's switch in case the revivor was taken down. The revivor watched, unable to move as I pushed the button and the timer reset.

"Faye, come here," I said, pushing a chair toward her. "Sit there. Hurry."

She did as I said, then turned suddenly as something crashed behind us. I saw her hands go up as the door flew open and Calliope stormed in with a gun in her hand.

"Don't shoot!" I yelled, holding out one hand. Zoe was with her, blood smeared under her nose as she lingered by the doorway.

"We've got to get out of here," Cal barked, and there was fear in her voice but not panic.

"Hold on," I said.

"Now!"

I spun the chair around and used my knife to cut through the skin at the base of Faye's skull. As I scanned through the muscle and bone, I could see the revivor components clustered there. I had to go deep, but not too deep. The tip of the blade shook and I grabbed my wrist with my free hand to try to stop the tremors caused by the stim.

"What the hell are you doing? Let's go!" Cal snapped behind me.

Faye, hold still. This won't take long.

Okay.

If it doesn't work, I'm sorry.

I dug the tip of the knife through to the casing where the Leichenesser capsule was housed. The black fluid was greasy under my fingertips as I coaxed it back.

Using the edge of the blade, I pried the casing free and pulled, breaking the connections. It slid out of its chamber and I pulled it away. The unit popped in my hand and white smoke began to pour off my fingers as it consumed the revivor's blood.

"Faye?"

Black fluid leaked from the hole, branching down the back of her neck, but the Leichenesser hadn't touched her. She turned back and looked at me from the corner of one eye. Cal was still sticking the gun out, not sure what to do. I waved the remaining smoke from my hand.

"Faye, you're okay," I said. "You're okay; I'm going to take you out of here."

"What happened to Fawkes?"

"He's shut off from the rest of the revivors, but it won't last. We have to get out of here."

Footsteps were clambering up the steps toward the clean room. Two figures barreled through, and I caught the glow from their eyes before one turned to shut the door behind them. They were both armed with automatic rifles.

"This way," Faye said, pushing a narrow panel open. Her voice was swallowed by a high-pitched shriek from the stairs. Flames poured through the space in the doorway, crawling across the ceiling, before one of the two new revivors managed to push it shut and cut off the flow in a puff of blue. Its palm sizzled as it held the door shut and then locked it.

"Cal, Zoe, this way!" I shouted. Cal was one step ahead of me, and Zoe followed her. I pushed them through the narrow opening.

"Where does it lead?" I asked Faye.

"I don't know. He said away from here."

Something hit the door to the clean room hard, and charred paint chips scattered to the floor. The two revivors ignored us and took up positions at the corners of the room. Each took aim at the entrance, waiting for the Special Forces team to come.

I took Faye by the wrist.

"Faye, come with me," I said. She didn't move. Cal grabbed my arm and pushed a gun into my hand.

"Faye, come on," I said. "Come with me. I'll take you out of here."

She just put her hand on mine, though, and pushed it away. She gave it a gentle squeeze, her palm and fingers cool and dry.

"Faye—"

She put one hand in the middle of my wounded chest and shoved me back.

That was the last time I saw her.

Cal pulled me the rest of the way as the panel slammed shut.

Go, Faye said; then the link cut out.

When I looked back at them, Calliope was shouting something and Zoe was just staring up at me like she was seeing me for the first time. Even for her, there was something strange about her expression. It was like she had forgotten who I was.

On the other side of the panel, I heard gunfire and the shriek of a flamethrower. I felt the heat on my face as it radiated from the panel in front of me.

I checked the magazine of the gun Cal had handed me. Half the rounds were left.

"Stick close," I told them. The heat was starting to get intense, and at this depth, between the fire and the smoke, the air would get used up fast.

We didn't encounter any soldiers on the way back. We ran through the passageway until we came out near the elevator, which was shut down, so I followed the route Cal had taken us when we came in. We headed back up the stairs, back out through the bombed factory entrance and into the underground parking garage, where the shells of the cars were still burning.

As we moved up the ramp, the hot air below became a warm breeze, rushing over us from behind and smelling like smoke. We stepped out into the night and the crisp, cold air. Snow began to fall on my face. It felt good.

The helicopters had been joined by three more, sitting there quietly in the dark. There were no soldiers around, so they had to still be down there. Did they follow the revivors as they tried to get out, or did the whole lot of them burn?

I tried to open a connection to Faye. She didn't respond.

"What do we do now?" Cal asked.

Sean.

Yeah?

I need an EMT at my location.

You got it. Good to hear from you, Nico.

You too.

I knelt down in the snow next to them, the last reserves of my energy trickling away. Zoe stood near me, shivering in the snow as the wind whipped through her thin white linens. I took my coat off and pulled her down to me, placing it around her shoulders.

"It's okay," I said. "Come here."

I guided her into my lap to keep her bare feet out of the snow, and held her as she shook.

She's just one of many, Agent. Your friend isn't unique; she's one of thousands. . . .

Fawkes believed it. He'd provoked the deployment of the National Guard so he could take control of its revivor ranks, then used them to kill the people on his list. He thought he was bringing down a massive conspiracy. He'd been torturing those people in that underground facility to try to learn how they did what they did and how to stop them.

Zoe shivered in my arms. Was Fawkes insane? Or could there be some truth to what he said?

Nico, what happened down there? Sean asked.

If my memories had been altered, I wouldn't know it. Zoe proved that the day I first met her.

. . . she's one of thousands, and they have been using you to get to me. . . .

The kind of destruction going on below us wasn't sanctioned by the FBI. Whoever was behind the operation, it wasn't us. They were destroying everything. Faye was gone, this time for good.

Nico, respond. What happened down there?

I don't know, I said, and cut the connection.

Cal scowled as a gust of wind blew. She looked down at me.

"Hey, what do we do now?" she asked again.

"We wait."

"Wait," she snorted.

"Quietly," I said, and that's how it ended.

Well, more or less.

13

Dawn

Zoe Ott—Pleasantview Apartments, Apartment 613

"Hey, you okay?"

I caught myself staring into space again. I'd been doing that a lot. After everything was over and I finally got back, nothing felt the same. I guess I hadn't really been gone very long, but it felt like forever.

I tipped my glass back, smelling the licorice and letting the fire fill my mouth, then my throat and belly. Karen watched me do it, but even though I don't think she approved, she still smiled. I think she didn't expect to ever see me again. I know I didn't expect to see her again.

"I'm okay," I said. "Thanks again for letting me stay with you. My place is kind of a crime scene."

They had held me for a while and asked a lot of questions. I wanted to see Nico, but they wouldn't let me. I was brought to another room where they tried to stick me with a needle, but I made them let me go. When the cab dropped me off, there were some cops still in my apartment and yellow police tape was all across the front door. The place was totally trashed, and no one would tell me anything. There were markers on the floor around a giant bloodstain, and kind of in the middle of it was the outline of a body in white tape. I found out later that it was my next-door neighbor. The revivor that took me killed him right there in my living room.

They asked me if I had anywhere else to stay while they finished their investigation, and when I said I didn't, they said I should get a hotel for a few days. I was too afraid to ask what happened to Karen. I was looking around, afraid to find another outline, when she showed up in the hallway. She got me something to eat, and better still, something to drink. It was like she was waiting for me.

"Did they tell you anything?" she asked. I shook my head.

"Me neither," she said. "Did they find out who it was?"

"No."

"Well, you can stay here as long as you need."

"What about what's-his-face?" I asked. I didn't see the oaf in the tank top anywhere around.

"He doesn't live here; he just stays here," she said. "He's going to stay at his place for a while."

Her eyes got kind of teary, and she wiped at the big, nasty double shiner she got when she ran in and tried to rescue me.

"Sorry you got hurt," I said. She smiled, but she didn't even remember how it happened. She never mentioned the revivor that broke in and attacked me, because she didn't remember it. When I wiped her memory, it was like for her that part never happened. She knew only what she'd been told afterward. "What about your friend, the agent?" she asked.

"Nico's going to check in later."

"You'll get to see him again, then."

"Yeah."

I didn't know how I felt about that. He didn't just say he'd check in; he wanted to use me as a consultant, on the department payroll. He wanted to keep it very quiet, though. I thought that would make me happy, but it didn't.

Mostly that was because he changed. At some point between the time I left him in the storage unit and the time he held me in his lap outside the factory, he'd changed. Not his personality, even though his face had changed a little and his left eyelid had gotten a little droopy. He still acted the same, and he still talked the same, but he was different.

"I can't change him anymore," I said into my glass.

"What?"

"Nico," I said. "I can't change him anymore. I can't—"

I almost said "control him," but I stopped myself. When I looked, I could see the colors around him. I could see the pain and the confusion and all the rest of it, but when I pushed, the colors didn't change.

"It's not the end of the world," Karen said. She didn't get it. She couldn't.

"How am I supposed to know what he's thinking?"

"You're not supposed to know," she said, smiling a little.

"Then what do I do?"

"Get to know him."

Get to know him. That was easy for her to say.

My drink was gone, and without asking she poured me another one, but a small one.

"Oh, by the way, I found this slipped under the front

door," she said, fishing in her pocket. She pulled out a blank business card with some writing on it. "It doesn't mean anything to me. Is it for you? From your friend Nico, maybe?"

I took the card and turned it over. There was handwriting in small print on the back of it.

You did it. Your place is with us. My stomach dropped a little.

"It's not from Nico," I said.

"Do you know what it means?"

I crumpled up the card in my hand, then dropped it in the trash.

"No," I said. "If it's okay, I think my place is with you."

Calliope Flax—Bullrich Heights

A couple days after the whole thing went down, I stood out in the cold to wait for the bus, and it was goddamn gray out. The sky, what you could see, was gray; the buildings looked gray; everything was gray. The wind howled down the street, kicking up the dusting we got. It was cold. I heard that where I was going they had the opposite problem, but it couldn't be much worse.

When the bus finally showed, it looked like it was going to blow by, but he saw me there and pumped the brakes. It rolled to a stop, front tire half in a puddle of slush when the door squealed open.

I hoisted my bag up on one shoulder and got on. It was warm in there and all the glass was fogged except the front. The driver looked like he came with the bus, and he'd get buried with it too.

"Pass," he said.

I took out the little yellow chit they gave me when

I signed up to serve. The driver gave it a look and I dropped it in the slot. It landed in the box with a few others.

"Just you?" he asked.

"Yeah."

"Have a seat," he said. "It's a long trip."

There were three other guys in the back. Two looked like they were passed out, and the last one looked like he wished he was. I sat down as far from them as I could and put my bag in the seat next to me. I wiped the fog off the window and watched with my head against the cold glass as we pulled out of Bullrich Heights.

I'm not sure what made me do it. Part of it was the G-man and something he said. He said he thought I was worth more than the arena. He said I impressed him down in that hellhole. He didn't say "Go sign up"—that part was my idea—but I think I believed him.

That was part of it. The big thing, though, was that once it was all over, nothing felt right anymore. When I got back to my place, it was like it didn't even look the same. As soon as I was through the door, I knew I'd leave. Anyplace had to be better than there, even the grinder.

The guys made some noise and we all went out for a big bash my last night, and I drank until I puked. I passed out facedown and said good-bye to my life, for what it was worth.

As the bus took me out of there, I thought about the G-Man, Nico. The training and the skills were just the start. The implant, the wiring, the strength, and the power . . . it could all be mine. I held his card in my hand as the bus took me where I was going, reading his message and his number.

For better or worse, things were going to change.

Nico Wachalowski—FBI Home Office

The first thing I saw when I finally woke up was the last of the diagnostic messages scrolling past the darkness behind my eyelids. The second thing I saw was the communication-pending message from Noakes marked URGENT.

Opening my eyes, I saw Sean sitting at the monitor on the bench in front of me as I lay in the maintenance chair. The rice paper underneath me crinkled as I cracked my back, and he glanced over, thin lips grinning. The dark shadow still floated in front of my eyes.

"Welcome back," he said.

"How long was I down?"

"A long time."

He got up, and I saw he hadn't shaved. He looked tired as he stepped over to the chair and looked down at me, holding the scanner up to my right eye.

"How am I doing?"

"All things considered, pretty well," he said. "I had to call in some help on this one. Your sternum was split, so it had to be replaced with an artificial one, and that plate you had behind it got dimpled, so it had to come out."

"What about the rest of me?"

"You suffered a severe myocardial infarction and a lot of blood loss," he said. "The chemicals released by the JZI kept you alive, but they take their own toll. It took almost a total transfusion to get you right, but you'll be back on your feet."

"I've got a blind spot in front of my right eye."

"You had some oxygen starvation even despite the implant; you were down for a long time. I won't lie; you had some pinprick necrosis in a section of your brain, but you got lucky."

Wachalowski, it's Noakes.

"Hang on," I told Sean.

What do you want?

I want your report, Wachalowski.

I'll file one when I get out of here.

Where is the revivor?

The last time I saw Faye, she was with one of the black-market revivors Fawkes had brought in. While I waited with Zoe and Calliope outside for the EMT to arrive, I'd searched for her signature, but I never picked it up again.

She—I mean it—was still down in the factory last I saw. No one found it?

Whoever was behind this rigged the place to do a very slow, very hot burn. Experts are saying the lower levels could smolder for months. Nothing past the parking garage can even be accessed by firefighters right now.

I thought the soldiers burned the place. Weren't those their orders?

I don't know what their orders were and neither do you, Wachalowski. The people responsible for this burned the place, along with the prisoners they were keeping there, to cover their tracks. End of story.

My memory of what happened down in the factory was a little fuzzy, but that didn't sit with what I had seen. Still, I knew when something was a done deal. If I was going to pursue this further, it wasn't going to be in front of Noakes.

So, we stopped them.

The ring of smuggled revivors and weapons was traced to a terrorist cell that was using the old factory as a base of operations, from which they organized a series of kidnappings, murders, and terror strikes. We've broken up the smuggling ring, found those responsible for the at-

tacks, and, with the aid of the military, taken out them and their headquarters. Yes, we stopped them.

Noakes, this is Sean.

What is it?

I'm sorry, sir, but I need to finish the reinitialization of the JZI, and that will include the communications array. Can this wait until I'm finished?

Fine. Agent Wachalowski, good work. The governor is happy. The mayor is happy. I'm happy.

Yes, sir.

You are too, Wachalowski.

Yes, sir.

The communication broke; then the array went offline, thanks to some internal tweak from Sean.

"Thanks."

"No problem."

"What happened to Zoe and Calliope?"

"They interviewed them, of course. Ott insisted she was unconscious the whole time and didn't remember anything about her capture or her abductor."

"They believed that?"

"I can't explain it, but they just let her go."

Maybe he couldn't explain it, but I could.

"What about the other one?"

"Flax backed up the story you gave when you were brought in. They held her for a couple days, then cut her loose."

"So that's that?"

"Yeah."

"No one cares about Cross, or the breach at Heinlein, or what was really going on down in that factory?"

Sean smiled faintly, then sat down next to the maintenance chair. He leaned in a little closer, putting his face near mine, like he was going to whisper something to me.

Instead, his stare became fixed, and a second later I watched as his pupils dilated almost all the way open. I felt a little wave of dizziness, but then it passed.

"Mark one three one," he said. I was about to ask him what he was talking about when he spoke again, this time in a different tone of voice.

"Stop pursing the specifics of what was going on down in the factory," he said, his voice authoritative and calm. "Any and all links to Heinlein Industries were opportunistic, to make use of their resources in order to maintain their smuggled revivor soldiers. There was no link between the murders investigated by Detective Dasalia and the events leading up to the strike on the factory. You never found the prisoners being kept in the underground facility, and as far as you know, they were burned along with everything else. Do you understand?"

His stare and his statements took me by such surprise that I thought I almost said something before I realized what was happening. As I watched him from the other side of that dark spot swimming in front of my eyes, I realized he was staring at me the same way Zoe had that time, the way I'd seen her stare at others when she was controlling them.

He was one of them.

Sean was looking at me, pupils still wide, waiting for an answer. Except for some reason his little trick wasn't working, and he hadn't realized that. Not yet. His eyes narrowed.

I'd had pinprick necrosis in a section of my brain. Whatever had happened to me, it seemed to have left me immune to their influence.

I let my mind go blank. I stopped thinking about anything else except what he'd said.

"I understand," I said. His face relaxed.

"This was a win across the board," he continued. "Whatever you saw or heard down there, forget it. Do you understand?"

"Yes."

Sean's eyes stayed the same, but his face relaxed a little and his tone of voice changed when he spoke again.

"This is for your own good, Nico. Stay out of this."

I had known Sean for years. Our relationship had always been the same, and I trusted him with my life. Seeing him then, it was like he had pulled off a mask.

"Just tell me one thing," he said, leaning closer, "then forget everything to my statement 'mark one three one.' I need to know one thing."

"Okay."

"Where is Samuel Fawkes? Did he get out of the facility?"

I knew there was a lot riding on my answer. This was important to him, very important. I had never seen him so serious about anything before in my life. Fawkes had been telling the truth. The group he described, they did exist. They had infiltrated even the FBI, and they knew about him.

"No," I said.

"No?"

I could have told him I didn't know or I could have told him the truth, but something told me to play that information close to the vest.

"Samuel Fawkes is dead."

"You're sure?"

"He's dead," I said.

What the hell. It wasn't a lie.

ABOUT THE AUTHOR

James Knapp grew up in New England and currently lives in Massachusetts with his wife, Kim.

THE DRESDEN FILES

The #1 *New York Times* bestselling series by Jim Butcher

"Think *Buffy the Vampire Slayer* starring Philip Marlowe." —*Entertainment Weekly*

The Bestselling
DEATHSTALKER Saga
by Simon R. Green

Owen Deathstalker, a reluctant hero destined for greatness, guards the secret of his identity from the corrupt powers that run the Empire—an Empire he hopes to protect by leading a rebellion against it!

Praise for the DEATHSTALKER Saga:
"[Simon R.] Green invokes some powerful mythologies."
—*Publishers Weekly*

"A huge novel of sweeping scope, told with a strong sense of legend."
—*Locus*

DEATHSTALKER

DEATHSTALKER REBELLION

DEATHSTALKER WAR

DEATHSTALKER HONOR

DEATHSTALKER DESTINY

DEATHSTALKER RETURN

DEATHSTALKER LEGACY

DEATHSTALKER CODA

Available wherever books are sold or at penguin.com